WHISPERS
BETWEEN
THE SHEETS

CONTENTS

WHISPERS BETWEEN THE SHEETS

Victor McGlothin
Earl Sewell
Phillip Thomas Duck

sepia

BET BOOKS

BET Publications, LLC

SEPIA BOOKS are published by

BET Publications, LLC.
c/o BET BOOKS
One BET Plaza
1900 W Place NE
Washington, DC 20018-1211

ISBN 0-7394-5730-6

Printed in the United States of America

A Player's Paradise

Victor McGlothin

1

Thrill of the Hunt

Kenton Reese slowly eased off his silk necktie after a long day at the office. A preoccupied valet attendant waved him forward after ogling a fetching entourage of high-spirited females who had exited the luxury sedan just idling behind him. The waiting list for a dinner table at Café Bleu, a trendy eatery known for its legendary happy hour consortium, began to swell and it was only seven o'clock. By nine, a younger and quite a bit more anxious multitude was sure to be spilling out into the cobblestoned courtyard, replacing the easygoing upscale corporate crowd that fit Kenton like an Armani suit. At age thirty-five, wealth and fine women inspired him, both equally so and not necessarily in that order. A dollar was a dollar every day of the week, but having his choice of beautiful women wrapped in chic designer fashions made Friday nights at the Café a holiday every time.

A brilliant smile lit up Kenton's flawless, clean-shaven, Harlem-brown complexion after the valet booth attendant caught the car keys he'd tossed with one hand and held the other one out for a gratuitous tip to ensure that his European trophy would be parked up front and raring to go the moment he was. All eyes landed on Kenton as soon as he stepped away from the sandstone-hued, chrome-wheeled S-series Mercedes he'd purchased on a whim a few months ago but had already grown tired of. Fancy cars weren't the only trophies that bored him after he'd gotten accustomed to taming their powerful motors while pleasuring himself with all the accompanying overpriced accessories. He also changed women like he changed his clothes, and on a good night he changed his clothes two or three times before the sun came up. Kenton Reese was not like most men, he was what most men aspired to be—a dyed-in-the-wool, true to the game player with all the right moves and aptly trained to use every single one of them.

Oozing confidence, adrenaline coursed through Kenton's veins as he entered the bustling hot spot. He tossed a cordial wink and nod to an attractive woman loitering just inside the restaurant. She seemed out of place standing there for no apparent reason. But her full heart-shaped lips and high cheekbones, framed with thick, black, shoulder-length hair, warranted additional attention. The woman's business suit, a stylish charcoal gray number, had sustained its firm creases late into the evening. Kenton always did recognize quality, in women and wardrobe alike.

The loiterer, in the smartly tailored suit, had accepted Kenton's silken salutation as gracefully as the valet attendant had one-handed his car keys, but her stock dropped dramatically when she couldn't muster the strength to turn away from Kenton's haunting gaze. She was hypnotized and too curious to downplay her obvious and immediate interest. She couldn't help the fact that tall, dark, handsome, and fine caused her to stare longer than what proved to be prudent. Kenton shouldn't have held it against her, but he did. As he glided past her, the loiterer sighed deeply, offered a promising smile and an innocent compliment. "Blue looks good on you," she said casually. "Regal."

It wasn't until he'd found himself in the midst of other women vying for his attention that the woman's words sunk in. He circled back to thank her for the favorable opinion regarding his swanky three-button Kenneth Cole suit—an opinion he also shared—but she was gone.

Back to the hunt.

Poised to order a drink at the atrium bar, Kenton's eyes drifted up to rest on a black satiny size-eight cocktail dress clinging tightly to a size-ten behind. His mouth watered when the lady wearing the short dress turned in his direction to retrieve her small leather handbag from atop a nearby bar stool. Her skin tone was in the semblance of a hot buttered biscuit and was just as tempting. With her hair swept away from her face, she reminded Kenton of a wonderfully overgrown Halle Berry, a hot buttered biscuit with extra syrup, and he could see nothing past a fun-filled night of biscuit sopping and lip smacking.

When it was apparent that she was seeing the same vision as Kenton, it occurred to him that she had been hooked after having been lured too easily. The woman appeared to be healthy and able-bodied enough to keep up with his high-wired sexual acrobatics, but he was on the prowl for something rare. With a bit of luck, he'd catch something wild and exotic in his snare, not someone so easily lured. The excitement was, after all, in the hunt. If worse came to worse, easily lured served him just as well if she happened to be double-jointed, ultrakinky, or knew how to get her kicks while enjoying the ride. Otherwise, Kenton Reese wasn't in the mood to spend his time giving easily lured what she'd undoubtedly be recounting, stroke-for-stroke, with her girlfriends later.

Undoubtedly.

See, Kenton prided himself on two things: an unrivaled bedroom aptitude worth paying for and an overwhelming desire of becoming the ultimate catch—without ever getting caught. An ever-increasing trail of satisfied but stranded sistas with hapless hopes, dreams deferred, and broken hearts continually affirmed that he had achieved both goals simultaneously.

All accolades aside, the woman's eyes quickly intercepted his transfixed leer, anchored on her wiggle box. Busted! Kenton chuckled awkwardly. "Oh, excuse me. You saw that?"

"Some things are hard to miss," she answered, smiling back at him. "Very hard," she added in a sultry voice just this side of seduction.

"Who you tellin'," Kenton joked, noting her sculptured features. "By the way, I'm Kenton. Kenton Reese." When he extended his hand to complete the formal introduction, the bling didn't go unnoticed.

"Nice to meet you. I'm Kim Gallagher." She accepted his hand, appraised the diamond-studded Rolex and gold monogrammed cuff links. She smiled again, this time brighter than before, considering he not only had good taste, but also the money to go with it.

"Can I order something for you to—" he paused to repeat the introduction. "Did you say your name was Kim?"

"Uh-huh. Why, did you have a thing go bad with some other Kim? Or something else you'd rather forget?"

Suddenly, Kenton's smile dissipated into a faint distant memory. "What a shame." Kenton reeled off a twenty from his money clip and laid it on the bar top as if it didn't belong to him. "It seems that I've overcommitted myself. Please have a drink on me. You're a beautiful woman, but I'll have to move around." The lady wrinkled her nose, wondering what had just happened to a previously promising meet and mate. "Sorry" was the word that trailed off into the noisy barroom chatter as he made his getaway.

Kenton contemplated an entertaining buttered-biscuit booty bounce, but there was no way he'd get involved with another Kim while already having two of them on speed dial at the time. And, as much as he wanted to add a third, it didn't conform to the Reese Rules of Romance, prohibiting him from delving into potentially unfavorable situations that he couldn't readily control. Once, his housekeeper took the liberty to return a call from Kim 1, thinking she was Kim 2, to inform her about having found the electronic organizer she'd lost the night before. Kim 1 was quick to argue that she'd never owned an electronic organizer and then began to argue on general principle that she was out of town on business the night before. Luckily, Kenton overheard the conversation, told Kim 1 that the housekeeper had a drinking problem, promptly ended the call, explained to the housekeeper his fondness for both Kims, then immediately put her in check to ensure that it never happened again. Kim 3 was not a practical option. Not then, not now, not ever.

Conflicted feelings zigzagged through Kenton as he walked away from the atrium bar and a possible disastrous situation with Kim 3. He glanced down at his extravagant timepiece then at the sprawling swarm of mingling men and women flirting with the chance of meeting someone new, someone nice. Through the valley of dolls and dudes, he caught sight of the fellas, his partners in crime, Ran Sanders and Ellis Robinson, posted up at the island bar on the opposite side of the restaurant. Glimmers of recognition spread across his face when it occurred to him that the fellas were looking to get in way over their heads, if they were lucky.

Maneuvering through a winding path of commingling cologne and casual courting, Kenton literally bumped into someone he used to know, Challis Fields-Rea. She was fairer than what generally struck his fancy and still thin for her age. Although barely one hundred and twenty pounds at five-seven, her lengthy study of karma sutra techniques more than made up for what she lacked in the back. It had been nearly a year since he'd laid eyes on her, and hands, too, for that matter. However, by the way she looked him over, twice, it appeared that his fingerprints had made an indelible impression. There was no denying it, she was still up for grabs, regardless of how long it had been since Kenton had her speaking in tongues, screaming his name and loving every minute of it.

"Heyyyy Keeenton." Challis giggled while balancing her third cosmopolitan with all ten fingers. "Been a long time."

"Yeah, it's been a minute, Challis." Searching for a wedding band that was nowhere to be found, Kenton leaned in for a pleasant embrace. After pecking her cheek softly, he figured it might be worth investigating what was with the absentee platinum that ushered her right off the market once she realized that Kenton wasn't interested in anything more serious than what they'd shared for months on end, playtime. "So, Tolliver Rea still taking good care of things? I saw his last game. The brotha's got mad handles on the court."

"Well, we'll just have to see how his skills match up in divorce court," she answered, staring deeply into Kenton's dark brown eyes. "Seems that he couldn't handle this too well." Challis took Kenton's wrist, turned it to her waist, then ran his open palm across her narrow white linen slacks. "At least, not like someone else I know." The seductive manner in which she offered sex on a platter spoke of a hunger that needed to be fed, and Challis had the type of appetite that Kenton treasured above all others. Unfortunately, the Reese Rules of Romance also prohibited explicit physical contact with married women, legal separations included.

"Sorry to hear about the breakup," he replied eventually. "You never know, maybe he'll come around and—"

"Kenton Reese, don't play with me," she interrupted, while turning to face him. "I'm not trying to hear about my soon-to-be ex-husband coming around or coming anywhere else. I want what I used to have on the regular, the only man who knows how to push all . . . the buttons . . . in my cockpit. I'm a big girl now, and I'm ready to accept a however limited role in your life. I knew about all the other women, and I'm sorry but I just got greedy." She made no bones about her desire to get back into his life, even at the bottom of the rotation. "I'll be good and I'll behave, just the way you like. I still remember how to do those things you taught me; you know, with that tiny box of mirrors. What do you say to every other Monday night?"

"Challis, look, I would love to pick up where we left off. What we had was cool and all, but I don't get into married women's business, and I don't let my business get into married women." He removed his hand from her waist finally and winked his good-byes. "Holla at me after you've dropped the hyphen and the brotha's last name you're trying to shake. We'll talk then."

"This ain't right, Kenton," she pouted as he backed away. "We can talk right now. Kenton! Kenton!" She was still calling his name when he approached the fellas, who were nursing bottles of light beer. Neither of whom could manage to take their eyes off a round table stacked with luscious ladies on a girls-night-out excursion.

Ran Sanders, all five feet eight inches of him, was the darkest shade of reddish brown imaginable. His idea of a good woman was any woman on her back, and by the way he was licking his chops, he thought he'd found at least five potential good women to choose from. If it were up to him, two good women would do just fine. Even though the one time he did convince two good women to show up at his place at the same time, they were so intrigued with the notion that all he got to do was watch. Ellis Robinson was something different all together. He was an eternal optimist, if whatever he was being optimistic about didn't require too much work. A slender build that never did fill out accentuated a Soul Curl kit that never would take. His beige complexion gave him constant hope that the once irrepressible predilection for light-skinned black men would someday make a smashing comeback. He just didn't think it would take so long.

"What's up, Ran? Ellis?" When Kenton's hellos went unanswered, his head swiveled to get a look at what had his closest friends entranced. "Oh I see, quite a talented bunch, if I do say so myself."

"Uh-huh, that's why we're on lock," Ellis agreed, his voice muted in an overtly secretive tone. "This is the best spot in the joint."

Kenton counted five sistas sophisticate, but there was a vacant spot at the table. There was a telltale half-full wineglass and an empty chair. He shrugged off observations, then offered halfhearted congratulations to Ran and Ellis. "Yes, very nice. You boys have done a great job of locating the talent. Now what?"

"Oh. What up, Kenton?" Ellis muttered, his eyes locked on the ladies. "When'd you get here? I thought I heard somebody calling your name."

Although the fellas had more than their fair share of playmates, neither of them had consumed the necessary amount of liquid courage to attack such an impressive pack of lionesses, where the risk of rejection was astronomical.

"Now what?" Ran repeated. "I 'on't rightly know . . . but I was thinking . . . about waiting it out until a few of them leave, then slip in and ambush the stragglers. Yeah, just chill in the cut, let 'em get good and liquored up, then hit 'em up when they're drunk and stumbling."

"Drunk is good. That's one way to go about it," Kenton asserted. "But, if you let that many women get good and lifted, they're bound to start discussing how men ain't nothing but dogs. You know, cussing, crying, and more cussing. It won't be pretty."

Ran broke the gaze he'd previously held on the talent to reflect on Kenton's timely analysis. "As usual, you got a point. I'm feeling you; it could get out of hand."

"Well, what is we gone do now, boss?" Ellis asked with his best antebellum slave impression.

Kenton slid his right hand down inside his front pocket and came out with his money clip. "Bartender! I need a couple of shots, Quervo Gold. Straight, no chaser. Much obliged." The plot thickened now that he had the fellas' full attention. "All right, listen up, 'cause I'm only going to run through this once. So try to keep up. Now then, starting from left to right. Those first two, they're married and more than likely with children. The one in the middle, sucking on the mixing straw, she's married but flexible—that explains why she's advertising. And the other two, Nikki and Rasha, well . . . let's just say they're both known to be very accommodating."

"Accommodating?" echoed Ran with a raised brow. "Very accommodating, as in super-sneaky-super-freaky accommodating?"

"I can personally vouch for 'em, and I was you, I'd head on over there to get my swerve on before they order another round. I swear you'll be spanking 'em and thanking 'em by midnight."

"Hold on a minute. Kenton, you can personally vouch for 'em. Both of 'em? You sayin' they been to the Pleasure Palace?" Ran squealed anxiously. "Palace Playettes?"

"Guest appearances, once or twice." Kenton confirmed, now searching the crowd for something he might have overlooked.

"Ahhh, hell yeah," Ellis howled. Overflowing with enthusiasm, his voice boomed louder than he anticipated. He held one finger up to his tightly pressed lips in an effort to apologize for the outburst while trying to calm the emotions triggered by the thought of getting the kind of action that went on at Kenton's extravagant lakefront home. "Whewww, all right, all right. Okay, I'm back. I'm back."

When the bartender delivered two identical shot glasses, brimming with tequila, Kenton grinned and paid the man. "Don't say I ain't never gave y'all nothing. And y'all better represent 'cause you know how sista's talk." Yeah, obviously brothas do, too. Kenton slapped off equaled doses of dap, then prepared to make new acquaintances of his own.

"Man, where you going?" Ellis asked nervously from the other side of questionable intentions.

"Get at me later. I got to check some traps," Kenton told him. "Oh, by the way, whoever ends up with Rasha, put a pillow under her ass; she likes it like that."

The hunt continues.

Subsequent to offering impressive insight, overwhelming endorsements, and after sponsoring two liquor shots of golden nerve, Kenton's job was done. No sooner had he stepped away from the island bar, his eyes landed on something caught in his net. She was nicely packaged in a tangerine-tinted two-piece skirt and sleeveless blouse ensemble with perfectly matching Gucci slingbacks. The way she wore her hair pinned up came across as well-defined elegance, although she appeared bored and alone, two things definitely worth considering. There was something vaguely familiar about her, but Kenton would have certainly remembered had he known her intimately. Or so he'd like to believe. Ran and Ellis watched intently as Kenton stalked his unsuspecting prey; he crossed directly in front of her, close enough to be noticed, then immediately doubled back to tighten the cinch. With his eyes trained on hers, he eased beside her and whispered softly into her ear. The woman giggled, nodded her head assuredly, giggled a bit more, grabbed her things, then proceeded to exit the restaurant with her handsome escort. After seeing the master work his magic, the fellas wasted little time tossing back their drinks before making a beeline to heed Kenton's advice regarding Nikki and Rasha, the Palace

Playettes, and braving the pack before the men-bashing symposium began.

Kenton's hunt was over, and although this one didn't seem to put up much of a fight, he couldn't pass up another bird in the hand, regardless of how easily she'd be coaxed out of the bush in the end.

2

Catch of the Day

Just outside Café Bleu, Kenton sent two valet attendants dashing off to retrieve their automobiles. He realized their swift departure wouldn't have allowed for the traditional getting-to-know-you discourse with the woman he'd selected to spend the evening with, so he settled for the necessary greeting ritual that involved learning the woman's name.

"Now that we're alone, I should probably introduce myself," Kenton offered.

"Perhaps you should," she agreed. "Generally, I am accustomed to getting at least a brief introduction before being whisked away by a handsome man's honest intentions, no matter how smooth his delivery."

"Ahh, you liked that?" Kenton blushed, unintentionally. As usual, he was having his way, an avenue he knew all too well.

"I'm out here, aren't I?" she answered softly. "But don't get too carried away with yourself. Let's just say that I'm interested."

"Interested? That's interesting," he thought aloud. "Nice to meet you, Interested. I'm Kenton Reese."

"That's clever, but actually, my given name is Delta. Delta Niles."

Before they knew it, a young valet was climbing out of Kenton's Benz with a grin stretched across his face. The skinny kid waited patiently while taking the opportunity to appreciate the automobile's flawless features. Likewise, Kenton stood there actively appreciating Delta's in the same manner until her SUV arrived. The second driver didn't happen to share the other one's mild temperament as he tooted the horn to summon Delta along.

"Looks like we've overstayed our welcome," was Kenton's pathetic attempt at justifying a potential rendezvous. "Why don't you write my number down and call me for directions. Unless you'd rather follow me."

"I have another suggestion," Delta offered plainly. While digging around in her purse, the charming smile she'd worn with ease had begun to require slightly more effort to maintain. She was clearly not feeling him on the idea of being led around by the nose. "Since I am not a follower by nature, I would rather you hit me with an intersection, cross street, or an address instead and I'll meet you there." When Kenton's eyes narrowed, she sensed his concern. "Don't worry, Kenton Reese. I said I was interested and I meant it. I'll show." With reservations, he jotted down his home address on the back of a business card that she provided.

"Good. I'll find it," she insisted while buckling into a shiny black Lincoln Navigator. Her graceful smile materialized again as the power windows raised. Without hesitation, she skillfully maneuvered around Kenton's sedan, leaving him to speculate whether the fish had just cleverly jumped off the hook and swam away downstream or if she was the self-assured independent type who he loved turning into jello, just for the sake of the challenge.

In no mood to be discouraged, Kenton hurried home. He was actually anxious to see what the night held in store. Whether he'd get the opportunity to cut wide swaths through Delta's Independence-Day routine or whether he'd end up taking a walk through his trusty rolodex if she happened to stand him up, Kenton had both bases covered. However, he couldn't shake the persistent thought of having met her once before. And there was something else about Delta that was all too familiar, something intriguingly familiar.

As soon as Kenton turned onto Atlantis Park Drive, his eyes narrowed with the same concern as before. There wasn't any shiny black SUV idling by the curb or any signs that one would mysteriously appear any time soon. But one thing was certain. Kenton sure could pick them, women. He rarely erred in judgment concerning a woman's wants and needs. Studying women had become an art form. And as players went, he was a Picasso. He knew right off why Delta had shown up at a second-tier social gathering overdressed. He also knew that she'd planned on getting undressed. What he didn't know was how many other men's addresses she'd written down before his. That was troubling.

Suddenly, a car horn sounded just as his garage door lowered.

Someone had blown the horn again before the garage door motor had the chance to reverse its forward motion. When Kenton ducked underneath the elevating door, all of his uncertainties vanished, along with any doubts that his visitor was going to fit in rather nicely with all his various current playmates—once he'd had the chance to put his stamp on her, that is.

Idling in the driveway, Delta's expression was relaxed, playful. "Hey, Slick," she announced behind a sexy smirk. "Told you I'd show."

"You said you'd find it, didn't you?"

"Navigators navigate," she responded, speaking of the automobile's satellite system. "It's just one of those things I never leave home without."

So far, Delta was a woman of her word but how long would that last? Kenton found himself pondering. Probably until everything was over but the crying, he surmised, just like all the times before. Guessing that she wouldn't be any different, he'd resigned himself to saddling up, riding it out, and making the best of the situation until it bucked him off. Just like all the times before.

Standing behind Kenton and pointing at the spacious three-car garage, Delta dove into a pool of shameless flirtation. "So, do you have room for me in there or should I park up front? I'd hate to get you into trouble."

"Where you park it is on you, but just so you know, trouble and me . . . we've never been on speaking terms. You can put that thing wherever you feel comfortable."

"Oh my, isn't that hospitable of you," Delta replied, blushing over his innuendo. "Maybe I'll have the chance to offer you the same advice later tonight."

Surprisingly, Kenton was entertained by Delta's somewhat lofty level of self-assurance and obvious quick wit. It reminded him of someone he admired immensely—himself. And, since her body was slamming, he was chomping at the bit to help her obtain what he knew she wanted to get—naked. Always thinking two steps ahead, Kenton purposely triggered the handheld remote, closing the garage door quickly just in case Delta had decided to store her ride for the night. He didn't want to be awakened, afterward, when she gathered her clothes off the floor to leave. Funny thing is, Delta was thinking the same thing. Except that she was leaving herself a back door in the event that Kenton couldn't stand up to his reputation.

The reputation that sent her to Café Bleu looking for him. It seems that Kenton was right about her being on the prowl with lewd intentions of her own, all of which involved him. Good thing he took the bait, hook, line, and sinker.

After Delta eased down from the front seat, Kenton closed the car door he'd held open for her. She thanked him with a gracious smile while sauntering toward his magnificently ostentatious home with her overnight bag in tow. Kenton was caught between his inclination toward chivalry and his second mind to ignore her hell-yeah-I'm-sleeping-over kit. Make no mistake about it, she recognized the dreadful expression that he fought to suppress when he first laid eyes on her luggage.

"Nice neighborhood. How'd you get in?" Delta joked to ease the tension that Kenton was unsuccessful at masking.

"I told 'em over the phone I was white," he answered. "By the time they found out, it was too late. I'd already moved in." Kenton's sly insinuation that he didn't want her to get the same idea was received loud and clear.

"Humph, I'm sure you're a nice man and probably real cool, but maybe this wasn't such a good idea after all. You seem to be a bit guarded. Is there something I ought to know?"

Immediately caught off guard, Kenton held his tongue as he unlocked the massive manor-style front door for Delta to enter. "Delta. It was Delta, right?" he asked, to be sure. "I'm sorry, please come on in." Once inside, Kenton treated himself to a more thorough once-over than he had earlier at the restaurant. "There is something I've been wanting to ask you but instead I kept pushing it out of my mind."

"Maybe you should get whatever it is off your chest because I'm beginning to think that I left that smooth carefree brotha who invited me over back at the Café. All this looking-over-your-shoulder posturing, afraid that a sista is thinking to change her address, is killing my groove. That would be such a pity, too, before we've had the chance to let a few obscene sexual encounters come between us . . . like normal folk."

"That's exactly what I was talking about. If I didn't know better, I'd think we were fighting."

"Ease up, Slick. You just lost me." Delta couldn't keep up with Kenton's indirectness. "Maybe you should get to the point."

"What I'm trying to say is . . . do I know you? It might sound crazy because I know we just met, but do I *know* you?" He flashed her a suggestive leering eye to accentuate his point when she still didn't appear to catch on. "Have you and I gotten . . . biblical before?"

More embarrassed than she had ever imagined on a first date, if you could call it that, Delta burst out laughing in Kenton's face when she realized that he had no idea just how much she had heard about him and from whom. Admittedly, an explanation was in order, but she'd have to stop laughing first. "Us, getting biblical? That's cute," she added, with a smidge of harmless sarcasm. "I'll try not to think about that when I'm saying my prayers. It seems that I might owe somebody an apology because I assumed you knew who I was when you stopped me at the restaurant."

Kenton was more confused than ever and somewhat at a loss for words. "No, I didn't know you then and I still don't."

"I think I'm going to need a drink," Delta heard herself say, when her earlier assumptions went awry. "Are you telling me that you routinely meet women whom you've never met, knock them over the head with that tired, played-out, Teddy Pendergrass game you ran on me, then drag them back to the Pleasure Palace to get *butt-naked biblical?*"

"Not since you put it like that," he responded, a tad bit defensive. "Well, except for the back-to-the-Pleasure-Palace-to-get-butt-naked part."

"Oh boy," Delta huffed, exasperated. "Now I know I could use a drink."

"Whoa! Hold up! Nobody's drinking anything until I find out what's really going on." Too intrigued to ask Delta to leave, Kenton's suspicions had gotten the best on him. "Ran and Ellis put you up to this? Huh? You ain't no dude, are you?" Kenton asked, praying that she wasn't an exceptionally accomplished female impersonator paid to pull his chain. "Please tell me you ain't no dude 'cause that's how people get hurt."

"No, silly!" Delta declared, attempting to regain her composure. "Well I'll be. Don't worry, I'm all woman and then some!"

"See, it's that 'and then some' that I'm worried about." Kenton pointed below Delta's waist, where her "and then some" might have been hanging. "You could be one of those gender benders that—"

"Okay, enough already. Let me set the record straight."

"Yeah, straighten the record. Straight works for me 'cause I'm standing here like, who in the hell have I let in my house?"

"A grown woman, that's who. Look, Rasha Blevins is my second cousin. I thought that she ran into you and told you about me."

"Freaky Rasha Blevins?"

"Freaky? From what I've heard, that sounds like the pot calling the kettle black. That's the same thing she said about you."

"Now you're talking," Kenton confessed. "What else did she say?"

"Anywayyy, I am not trying to talk about your and my cousin's sexploits. I've already gotten a play-by-play from when y'all hooked up back in the day. She told me about you and some of your areas of expertise. I'm sure she wouldn't have told all your business had she known I'd up and move down here from KC, then bump into you. Then, lo and behold, while having a few drinks with a few girlfriends tonight, guess who fell into the spot? I was waiting for my roommate to drop off an outfit when you came in. I didn't know who you were until after I had innocently complimented how nice you looked in blue before hitting the ladies' room to change into this little orange number."

"You complimented me tonight?" Kenton began replaying all the discussions he had with women, from the end of the day to the beginning, when the lightbulb came on. "The loiterer! That was you?"

"The what?"

"Never mind that. You're the charcoal gray business suit that I went back to thank for your astute observation of me in blue, but she, you, were gone."

"When Rasha spotted you walking away from some drunk chick, yelling your name all out like you owed her back child support, I excused myself from the hen party."

"Ahhh, the empty seat at the table," Kenton concluded.

"Could you blame me? After all the things I'd heard about you, my horns were showing and Rasha called me on it. I figured it was probably a good idea that we met, so . . . here I am."

"That's got to be one of the craziest stories I've ever heard, but that still doesn't explain why you came at me all off center before you realized I didn't know who you were."

"Because, I assumed that Rasha had hipped you to her lil' cousin, who happens to have one hell of a crush on a certain someone. I called myself giving you a hard time for trying to run through the family. My bad for assuming anything."

Kenton lowered his head, chuckled over the absurdity of the situation, and rubbed his chin before putting the discussion to bed. "Nah, don't sweat it." Kenton moved to open the door and escort Delta back to her vehicle. "Just tell that big-mouthed cousin of yours that I owe her a good talking to."

"And why would I do that?" Delta asked, genuinely confused by his request. Now it was her turn at being perplexed. "I was serious when I said how interested I am in hanging with you. I've been here a couple of months and haven't had the chance to really kick it yet. Been too busy busting my behind on the job I transferred down here to do."

Kenton surmised that he had almost unwittingly overcomplicated matters to his detriment. There was a very attractive woman standing in his foyer who had planned on sticking around for the magic show. Not to mention that she was also the second cousin to one of his past flavors of the month. Kicking it with Delta was a win-win, any way Kenton looked at it. Furthermore, coming up on some coochie-by-referral, that was even better.

"Now, can a sista get a drink?"

3

The Commitment Trap

Delta kicked off her shoes while Kenton busied himself by whipping up a batch of frozen cocktail smoothies and something quick to nibble on. With two aching feet cheering her decision to set their soles free, Delta took it upon herself to get a lay of the land. Kenton's elaborate home was tastefully outfitted in contemporary Mediterranean. The broad and striking architectural design, buff-colored stucco, and private courtyard walled in by giant tinted panels of beveled glass put Delta in the mind of ostentatious ocean-front mansions that drug dealers inhabited on the gulf coast. It definitely had the whole *Miami Vice* theme working to perfection. A single man with access to five bedrooms, a complete workout facility, a master bath with a sunken Jacuzzi, a wall-screened media room, marbled foyers, and granite countertops was usually single-minded and wanted to stay that way. Delta had seen it all before, from wealthy entertainers whose paths she'd crossed momentarily to all-star athletes who wanted momentary satisfaction. Young men, with mountains of things, generally did not appreciate half of those things or the mountains erected because of them. Playthings and playtime was their usual order of the day, and Delta understood the hedonistic attitude. Actually, she embraced it. So much so that she adopted the same self-indulgent mind-set. Oddly enough, it absolutely drove men crazy when a tail refused to chase the dog.

In the process of protecting her most valued asset, her heart, Delta unwittingly stumbled onto four nuggets of gold that men have kept secret from the beginning of time: (1) Men want what they can't have. (2) Men most desire what someone else appears to be enjoying more than them. (3) When a man decides to settle down, no one can stop him. (4) Conversely, if a man has it in his head not to get involved with affairs of the heart, no one can make him. Those four golden nuggets, which Delta had picked up along the way, kept her safe. They kept her sane. She knew better than to get all caught up by falling in love with a man who hadn't fallen for her first. She knew better.

Climbing the back staircase to the second floor, Kenton figured that his houseguest had plenty of time to become thoroughly impressed. He was well aware that abundant success often doubled as a fast-acting aphrodisiac. Besides, he never forced the issue when it came to getting what he wanted from women. They generally served it up, nice and hot, like sex on a platter. On the other hand, getting those very same women to comply with his prescribed rules of engagement, afterward, required quite a bit of courting and coercion. Some things are not always so easily explained.

"Hey, there she is," Kenton proclaimed, peeking into the library. "Sorry you didn't get the dollar tour, but I trust you had the chance to look around nonetheless. Here, I think you'll like this." He handed Delta a tall, eight-ounce goblet filled with a frozen wine concoction.

"Ooh, this is a big one," she said playfully, batting her eyes. "Just kidding. Thanks, Slick."

"It's a sangria sling, but don't let the smooth taste fool you or I'll end up baby-sitting instead of misbehaving."

"Uh-uh, I can handle my own." She took the straw with her thin fingers and guided it in between her perfectly shaped lips.

Kenton swallowed hard, wishing he were that straw. "Yeah, I bet you can at that."

Swaying her hips to a natural beat from deep within, Delta continued sipping from the frosty mixture. "This is sooo good," she moaned.

"See, all that cooing is going to get you into some grown-folk trouble."

"Humph, is that right?"

"It's kinda hard for me to say what's right, when all I want to do is wrong."

Noticing that Delta's cocktail glass was half empty, Kenton thought it wise to look out for her best interest as well as his own.

"Come on downstairs. I think I'd better put something on that stomach. There's a Greek salad with your name on it, and I just put a chicken enchilada casserole in the oven. You good for about forty-five minutes?"

"Oh, I'll make it," Delta answered, pleasantly surprised. She was much more impressed by his gestures of generosity than by his luxurious furnishings. "Kenton, you didn't have to go through all the trouble of cooking dinner for me. But thank you."

"Who said that you were having dinner? Nah, you only get the salad," he replied, with a sly wink. "And don't mention it."

Considering how it wasn't every day that a man prepared dinner for Delta, especially without having been cornered into it, she felt celebrated, although it died a quick death when she started to wonder how often Kenton went out of his way to accommodate his visitors. Suddenly, Delta was reminded not to take the private time she spent with him so seriously, knowing that he wouldn't. Instead, she decided at that very moment to work the program to fit her specifications, not his.

After clearing away the flatware, Kenton began unbuttoning his long-sleeve work shirt down the middle. With a firm head nod, he motioned toward the master bedroom. His bedroom was the only carpeted room on the first level, which was otherwise covered with earth-toned ceramic tile and imported stone.

"I hope you don't mind, I'm running your bath," Kenton told her, not waiting for a response. "C'mon. I've got both gels and powder."

"Gel," Delta whispered quickly. Actually too quick to pretend that she hadn't already agreed to the whole bathing, gelling, getting naked thing the very instant it was presented. "I . . . I prefer bath gel," she repeated for no apparent reason other than perhaps to be sure she was still breathing. She'd also heard about the super-sized sunken Jacuzzi, in detail. But it was her turn now. Her turn to receive the attention she'd swooned over after listening in on a first-hand personal account from cousin Rasha, freaky cousin Rasha.

Sufficiently tipsy, Delta cradled her second cocktail glass as she accompanied Kenton down a long corridor until it ended at the mouth of a formal sitting room, separating the hallway from the master suite. When she stopped near the beige-colored mole-hair sofa,

Kenton presumed that she wanted to get undressed there. "There's plenty of room in the back for you to change," he informed her, offering his hand to escort her there.

"No, it's not that." Delta took a deep breath, then flashed an anxious, crooked smile. She tried her hand at reading Kenton's expression, which appeared to be stuck somewhere between apprehension and loss. "You've already proven to be a big-time sweetie, and I'm sure that you treat every woman you bring here the same, special . . . for the time being. Every sista deserves to know how good that feels, even if it's only temporary. But before I go any further, I feel we need to talk about what to expect after . . . the afterglow."

Kenton shook his head, cleared his throat, then smacked Delta with a solemn poker face. "I see. You want to discuss expectations? That's an easy one. With me, don't have any."

"Uh-huh, just as I suspected," Delta thought aloud, tossing back the same deadpan gaze that he'd given her. "So, you and I will do whatever it is that we'll do, without a net . . . meaning no strings attached?"

"Absolutely no attachments."

Delta grinned uncomfortably, then looked down toward the floor to shrug off any double-crossing second thoughts. Then, she lifted her head and fixed her eyes on Kenton in a peculiar way that trapped him in her sights. "No attachment. That's an understanding I can live with, but I'm not so sure you can."

"Dayyyum. Is it like that?"

"And sometimes, it gets even worse," was her affirmation. "Oh yeah, I'm talking restraining orders, call block, stalking, all in the name of brothas trying to renegotiate their terms."

"I'll try to keep that in mind, Delta, and I admire your confidence, but let me hip you to something." Kenton approached her much in the same way he had at the restaurant, from the front then from behind. He wrapped his arms around her waist, breathing in her scent. "I never, under any circumstances, renegotiate."

After feeling the warmth from Kenton's soft whispers, the hair on the back of Delta's neck stood on end. Almost positive that he could hear her heart beating louder, she sought to move away from him, but her feet didn't cooperate. "Good, then we agree on the terms—or the lack thereof?"

"Agreed."

No sooner had they agreed on their lack of terms, Kenton carried Delta through the master suite and into the candle-lit bathroom. After he lowered her into the depths of a warm, scented pool, he bathed her, caressed her, and cherished her. She was ushered into another place, far from anything she'd imagined as he surveyed her soft skin with legions of passionate kisses that trailed along her inner thighs and beyond. She was semihexed in semidarkness when she heard her own shameless screams reverberating off the ceiling and floor, in breathless exclamation. Using every limb, Delta held Kenton's powerful frame close each time the fire burning from deep inside drove her senseless; she welcomed those shameless cries of ecstasy again.

Delta wanted to believe she was different from all the others who allowed their screams of passion to ring throughout the walls of Kenton's bedroom as he took the time to massage every inch of their bodies while tracing his fox-trotting fingertips with kisses hot enough to singe the soul. Eventually, she gave up thinking of what ifs and idle agreements to concentrate on the moment, their moment in time. It was obvious that Kenton had his hands full and his own agenda, giving Delta more than she'd hope for and exactly what she needed.

As the rain fell, night melted into morning. Around five or so, Delta eased out of Kenton's arms. He stirred slightly but didn't wake. If he had, he might have been alarmed at the sight of Delta's hair, stretched out in every direction like deformed fingers on a withered hand. Feeling less than perfect, she promised herself to keep it in perspective as best she could. What they did and shared during the night was only an exercise in futility, regardless of how many times she'd called his name in the shadow of darkness and cursed him silently for taking her past the threshold of pleasure and pain. Common sense warned her to grab hold of her wits when Kenton started talking in his sleep, mumbling several other women's names. She was sure then that their moment in time was gone. Having been with him, too, though only for one night, she fully understood why so many other women allowed themselves to get caught up with his loveless loving and dangerously endearing ways. He was so damned enjoyable, for goodness sake, but mostly for Kenton's sake. And although Delta's entire body had continued tingling long after he'd fallen asleep, she couldn't allow herself to feel that it was anything more than the result of a mesmerizing, long, slow screw. She wanted to believe that it was something more, a lot more. But she knew better.

Kenton was surprised when he rolled over in bed but didn't find Delta lying next to him, shaken and stirred and utterly satisfied. On the contrary, she'd spent the remainder of the night on the sofa in the sitting room, just outside his. When he found her sitting there just after eight, fully dressed in a coral-colored nylon sweat suit and hair pulled back in a long ponytail, words didn't come easy for him.

"Good . . . morning," he offered, voice slightly graveled like a tired stretch of bad road. "Delta, did I say or do something wrong last night?" What he really wanted to ask was why she'd declined to share his bed after having freely shared everything else, but he didn't want to come across as if he actually cared.

"Good morning yourself, Slick," she answered finally. "No, last night was great and so was this morning . . . both times. I thought I'd camp out here and wait on the rain to stop."

"Couldn't you have done that in there with me?"

"No, I don't think it's a good idea to get too comfortable where I don't belong." Standing up from the sofa, Delta collected her overnight bag and started out of the side door when Kenton tugged at her sleeve.

"Why don't you stay until it lets up? It's still storming out. I'm not trying to tell you what to do, but big girls get into car accidents, too, you know. Stick around. I could fix breakfast, maybe we could hang out today and—"

"And what, Kenton? What? Play house? I'm afraid I'll have to pass. Thanks for dinner, though, and dessert."

"You're more than welcome." Kenton nearly smiled when he realized that she'd actually called him by his name. Not Slick, Baby, Daddy, or any of the things she'd labeled him in the thirteen hours since they met. Standing in the doorway in silk sleeping pants and leather slippers, he folded his arms when the wind kicked up. "Stay," he insisted one last time.

"Call me," was her reply. "I left my number on your bathroom mirror. Write it down before you have it removed."

Kenton almost appeared vulnerable, wondering why Delta refused to accept his offer, knowing that she wanted to. Delta took a mental snapshot of him huddling up to stay warm and wanting something he couldn't have, when he wanted it. She considered his sexy eyes, his muscular body, and the notion that she might not have been just like all the others; then reality snatched her down off that cloud. It was just a thought, but she knew better. She knew better.

4

Cold Day in Hell

Feeling hunger more than any other emotion, Kenton watched Delta as she backed her Navigator out of his long driveway. What a pity that such an all-too-familiar scene came with the territory. Another thoroughly dazed and confused female, backing away, licking her wounds, and sulking off with him heavy on her mind. Him. The bona fide, soul-stirring, earth-shaking, no terms, no exceptions, heartbreaker. Kenton's world generally consisted of eating good, good times, times eventually changing, and changing women. Women who hung around long enough grew to respect his relaxed revolving door policy that offered bilateral booty-call benefits. Of course, most of the beneficiaries overestimated their capacity to change him before realizing their futile efforts had been trumped by his capacity to remain the same. That typically heralded the beginning of their ending.

However, despite all of his shortcomings, his sometimes suspect courting practices, and his questionable morals, the one undeniable character trait that vaulted Kenton Reese above all the other players with similarly obvious designer flaws, was truth. He knew what he was and didn't deny it. Never. Lying was too easy, and he couldn't in good conscience enjoy life to the fullest with all the complications that follow lies like the night follows day. Truth he preserved at all cost. The truth according to Kenton.

Truth is what he found himself trying to cover up so that he wouldn't be explaining it when his next date arrived. Crystal, the flight attendant, was a coochie referral who called earlier to remind him that she was due in at two o'clock for a five-hour layover. That presented him with more than enough time to tidy up after his wild tryst with Delta, in the event that she might have planted incriminating evidence or strategically placed strands of hair for the next woman to find. Kenton had seen it all and had foiled the best of the best. Scheming, marking territory, and various other passive-aggressive behaviors kept him alert and on his toes. Operation Clean Sweep is what Kenton called desensualizing his surroundings, which included changing the linen, hand vacuuming every stitch of furniture, and discarding all proof that he'd been up to sexual mischief. A full canister of ginger-peach was his fragrance of choice to equalize any willful remnants that still lingered in the air. Remnants that only a woman's keen sense of smell could detect.

After Kenton felt secure that his place had been sufficiently decontaminated, he collapsed on an oversized sofa in the living room in a tired stupor until a ringing telephone snapped him out of it. Crystal was calling from the airport shuttle to explain how much time she had and exactly how she didn't want to waste any of it. After five minutes of saucy speak and heavy breathing, it was clear that all the conversation she'd planned on having had just taken place because she then yelled at the shuttle driver to step on it; then she immediately ended the call. As anticipated, Crystal came and went, mostly came, and in less than four hours after the fact, Kenton was alone and enacting Operation Clean Sweep again. It was a vicious cycle; one that he liked to ride.

A lot.

When Sunday rolled around, Kenton had to battle against the rolling tide of sleep deprivation in order to pull himself out of bed. Lunch with the fellas was mandatory, at least once a month, and it happened to fall on a day that he wished was another eight hours of sleep away.

"Hey, Ellis, look at what the cat dragged in," Ran scoffed jokingly when Kenton arrived. The well-built hostess, who escorted him to the table, flirted as best she could, but she was no match for a steaming hot cup of coffee. Ran, on the other hand, was wide awake and willing to skip dessert for a decent shot at seeing what she looked like hosting with her clothes off. Preferably at his house if it was up to him.

"Late as usual, too," Ellis hummed from the other side of the sports page. "And I'd have it no other way. Last man standing buys lunch."

"One day, I'm gonna surprise both of y'all and be the first one here," Kenton replied flatly.

"Since that hasn't happened in all the years we've known you, we'll take our chances on getting free lunch until our kids graduate college. Ain't that right, Ran?"

"Yep," Ran quickly agreed. "That's a good bet and neither of us have kids."

"You brothas are cold blooded, kicking a man when he's down," Kenton added.

"Ain't that the best time to kick him?" Ellis suggested between flipping pages.

"Uh-huh. You can get in some good ones then," echoed Ran.

"And if I didn't know better, I'd have to guess that Kenton got his self into a slight sticky situation since we saw him last," Ellis said, awaiting an answer.

"There's nothing slight about Crystal, although I do feel you on the sticky part."

"Crystal blew through town?" Ran asked as an afterthought.

"Yeah, and she wasn't in a talkative mood either," Kenton replied.

Ellis was looking up at the ceiling as if he could see the lady's face up there had he stared hard enough. "Crystal? Is she that nurse, who—"

"Nah, that's Chris. Crystal is a stewardess who I get with from time to time."

"They call 'em flight attendants now," Ran corrected him. "And Crystal is top-of-the-line, too. What does she go, Kenton, about six-one, one-fifty?"

"At least that," Kenton boasted with his chest stuck out. "She's getting thicker, too."

Ellis snapped his fingers when he finally remembered who the others were talking about. "Oh yeah. Long, tall Crystal with the green eyes and the carpet burns."

"That's the one, but she rolls with knee pads now." Kenton nodded, then shook his head to bridge both comments. "Carpet burns don't heal like they used to."

"Wait a minute. I thought she went gay," Ran asked to no one in particular.

"She did, but she came back," Kenton assured him with utmost certainty. "Ahh yeah, she damn sure came back."

"I see why you're broke down then. A six-foot switch-hitter

sound like a handful," Ellis surmised. He lowered his voice and leaned in closer to Kenton. "I know you walked the dog, dawg."

"I walked the dog up and down the block until she was begging the dog to stop," Kenton bragged. "Man, Crystal's the reason I had steps put in the shower."

Hearing about Kenton's newest amenity caused Ran to choke on an ice cube from his water glass. "You can't be serious. Please tell me you didn't get no steps in your shower?"

"Four of 'em," Kenton's said while holding up corresponding fingers.

"See, now you got to let me and Ellis come through and bring some honeys to check that out."

"That's cool, but you can't trust females like that. Take the wrong kind too far out of her element and you run a risk of having her doubling back by the house without you, to kick it with ole Kenny-Ken." Kenton winked at Ellis, who was brooding. "Tell him about it, Ellis." Ellis took a deep breath while trying to play off the fact that he still hadn't forgiven Kenton for sleeping with his date after having been introduced. "That's how I met Sundae Germane." Kenton chuckled, thinking back.

When Ellis heard that name, he slapped Kenton on the back before laughing out loud. "Whew, I'd forgotten how that actually turned out in my favor. Thanks, Kenton, I owe you for that one. Every time I think about it, I start laughing all over again." Kenton smirked his displeasure with the manner in which he and Sundae had parted ways. "Yeahhh, yeah. Sundae every-day-is-fun day Germane. Tell him what went down. Tell him about it, Kenton."

Ran's ears perked up when it seemed as if a female situation had actually gotten the best of their pal Kenton. "So, is somebody going to tell me what went down or y'all going to leave me hanging?"

"All right, it happened to me, so I'll tell it. Ellis introduced me to a stewardess."

"Flight attendant," Ran corrected him.

"Ran, are you going to let me tell this story or not?" Kenton barked. "You're the only one who doesn't know it, so you might want to stop ya yapping. All right then, that's more like it. Admittedly, Sundae was one of the finest sistas I've ever been with. No doubt, but because she was so fine, I let her drive the bus on occasion. You know what I mean, take charge in the bedroom. Or should I say, at the airport."

"At the airport, dawg?" Ran began licking his lips.

"C'mon, Kenton, you're stalling," Ellis prodded. "I knew you were gonna do this."

"Hold on, Ellis. Ran, listen to me. Terminal A, Ran. Terminal A!" Kenton paused to get his mind off what went down at terminal A. "Man, the places this girl liked to get busy would blow your mind, but check it out. You remember that white Escalade I used to drive? Yeah, the company car. Well, I'd just had it detailed. It was so fresh and so clean until I swooped Sundae from the airport. She had this car fetish for slapping skins in high-dollar whips."

"Whuuut?" Ran was seriously intrigued at this point. "Kenton, I saw that on the spank-tro-vision. *Backseat Booty Babes*, number seventeen."

"Can I finish the story? Can I finish?"

"G'on ahead and finish then. I'm just saying that a lot of women are into that sorta thing."

"Good, because I'm just about to wrap it up. Uh-huh, the last time she came up to see a brotha, it got real cold after it had been raining all day." Kenton shot a stinging glare at Ellis, who was laughing so hard that he could barely stay in his chair. "It ain't that damned funny, Ellis."

"But it's about to be. Go on, tell him."

"All right, it was wet and cold. So while I was tattooing it, and believe me, I was stamping it good, too, I had to leave the windows up. Somehow the moisture jammed up the electricity so the windows got stuck."

Hanging on to the edge of his seat, Ran waited impatiently. "And?"

"And she called her boyfriend on the cell phone while we were steady in the mix," Kenton revealed. "Man, it was too weird for me. I couldn't get with it, so she had to finish the job herself."

"Dayyyum, that's uh . . . that's kinda sexy when you really think about it," Ran said aloud. "I'd have represented 'cause I'm a soldier like that. That's raw dawg thug passion right there."

Kenton flinched when the waitress appeared out of nowhere to deliver food he hadn't ordered. A fluffy two-egg, Tex-Mex omelet with a side of crispy hash browns and cheese grits was close enough to his idea of a balanced meal, so he gladly accepted it. Someone was going to be upset, but that wasn't his concern. Ellis folded the newspaper in half, then peered over it after noticing Kenton was ready to get his eat on.

"Hey, Ran, Kenton's not getting in either. They're gonna shut the pearly gates on him for stealing somebody else's food. Although it does look kinda good." Ellis craned his skinny neck toward Kenton's plate. "Smells good, too. But speaking of heaven, who was that angel you tipped off with from that Friday night happy hour?"

"Who, Delta? She's just a little something I got. I told you I was heading off to check my traps. Every now and then, something nice and succulent gets caught in the snare."

Ran began eyeing Kenton's plate as well. "Hey, I meant to ask if you knew her before y'all bounced together?"

"Nope, but you might say that we spent all night getting acquainted. And stop looking over here like you're going to jack my grits."

"Kenton, you've got to tell us how you do it." That was Ellis really wanting to know.

"Do what?"

"How do you lie so good that sistas drop everything, including us, and leave with you?"

"You want the truth?" he managed to say between fork bites of omelet. "The whole truth?"

"Yeah, I can handle the truth."

Kenton sipped from his glass before dropping the number one rule from Reese's Rules of Romance. "Most sistas can't handle it. The truth, I mean. I never lie to women. The truth confuses the hell out of them just fine until they realize it's more important to me than any one of them."

"That's it? You tell the truth?" Ran asked in disbelief.

"Well, yeah. I'm truthful about what I want from women, then I ask for the business. If I make it that far without getting shut out, I have a better chance at closing the deal. Ran, pass me that Tabasco sauce from other there."

"No problem, but what if that doesn't work? Then what?"

"Rookies, it's a wonder that y'all get any play at all." Kenton was annoyed by the fellas' lack of understanding regarding the fairer sex. "It's also important to remember that women are stronger than men but more delicate than flowers. They're also nurturers and lonely by nature, right?"

"Huh?" Ellis muttered, obviously clueless. "Oh yeah, right."

"Women need a man to make them feel whole, complete. Ever since Adam gave up that rib, sistas have been craving the bone."

"Drop that science, boy," Ran signified.

"Here's the kicker. I let a sista think she's doing me a favor by trying to tame an incorrigible bad boy while I'm providing the time, effort, and energy required to smack that ass to personal specification." The fellas agreed silently as Kenton made himself comfortable atop his soapbox. "Take the one I met the other night. Y'all saw her. She's a dime piece, and there's no arguing that, but where opinions vary is how to approach the upper echelon of fine sistadom."

"Hell yeah, if a brotha comes at a dime from the wrong angle, it'll be a long night." Ran caught himself admitting that he'd made the mistake before, then began to backpedal. "One false move and she'll be hollering for security. Well, that's . . . that's what I heard."

"Everybody's done it," Kenton confessed. "Made a slight miscalculation, then spent more time than you planned and more conversation than you ever wanted. It happens to the best of us, but when you nail it, they'll be trying to meet your momma. Know what I'm saying?"

"So, what truth did you spill on Friday night?" Ellis asked in an insistent tone. "Because that had to be your quickest snatch and grab."

"I saw her trying real hard to look bored and uninterested. That's when it was obvious to me that she wanted to be swept off her feet, without too much mingling. I complimented her taste in clothing, which always gets a woman to feel better about herself. The blushing starts, the guard's down, and then I say something suave and easy like, 'We don't have to go to your place, and we don't have to go to my place, but I've got a sneaky feeling that you'd like to get out of this place.' Now, that's how you ask for the business." The fellas were looking at Kenton as if he'd made up some preposterous story that didn't seem plausible until they both remembered seeing how well it had panned out for him.

"Ooh, that's a page straight out of the player's handbook!" Ellis declared as if he'd know a real player move if he saw one.

"Uh-huh, old-school Teddy P. with a dash of the O'Jays," Ran agreed.

"I keep telling y'all everything you ever needed to know to keep your game tight, they already put on eight tracks. I got one off the garage."

After falling out over Kenton's joke, Ellis had a premonition when he saw someone he recognized. "That dime piece from the other night, how long you think she'll swing on it before she's hooked on the crook?"

Kenton shrugged, took a napkin, and wiped his mouth before answering. "Don't matter none 'cause once I get 'em, I got 'em. You feel me? Yeah, tried to play hard but she's a pushover powder puff." He had really begun to feel himself, even if no one else had. "I'll put this on all I love that it'll be a cold day in hell before she lets another brotha get next to that ass."

"Then the devil must be pissed 'cause they done just turned off his heat," Ellis whispered behind alerting glances.

Kenton's heart skipped a beat after he turned toward the front door and discovered his pushover powder puff strutting into the restaurant with another man. Hell must have experienced its first freeze that day. It was the same day that Kenton's world stood still. His embarrassment compounded the moment he realized that Delta happened to be with his company's biggest client. "I'll be damned, that is her and she's with Martin Burke, owner of the Smile Bright Grocery chain. I thought I knew that dude."

"Looks like she knows him, too," Ran said, thinking aloud. "Uh-huh, she's probably been spending her nights getting acquainted with both of y'all."

"Don't trip," said Kenton, mapping out his next move to save face. "Watch, she'll be falling all over herself when she sees me. Check it, here they come."

As Delta and her lunch date neared their table, Kenton couldn't help himself. Suddenly, he popped up from his chair. "Martin Burke, I thought that was you."

"Kenton? It's good to see you. I called you last week, as a matter of fact, but I'm sure you'll get back to me . . . at your earliest convenience." When Delta's date considered introducing himself to Ran and Ellis, they stalled the idea by mean mugging him while ogling over Delta's tight behind wrapped inside a pastel printed sleeveless dress.

Plagued by the nagging thought that perhaps he'd misread Delta, who was now avoiding eye contact, Kenton figured he'd make an attempt to get even. "Well, didn't mean to keep you and this beautiful lady from your lunch. I recommend you try the *Greek* salad. It's delicious," he suggested peculiarly. With his eyes parked on Delta's, he stepped over the line. "Yeah, it's delicious. I've had it."

Martin picked up on something that smelled suspicious. "Oh, I'm sorry. Have you two . . . met?"

"No," Delta answered flatly. "And perhaps another time, Martin. Right now, I need something much more substantial than a salad. I'm simply famished and need to get a satisfying meal before I begin to pout."

"We can't have that, now, can we?" Martin said convincingly.

"Nah, uh-uh," Ran agreed.

"Oh no, we can't allow that," was Ellis's two cents worth of nothing.

Martin placed his hand on Delta's back to initiate a departure. "Good seeing you, Kenton. Gentlemen."

"All right then, Martin," said Kenton, before they continued on to another section of the restaurant. "I'll return your call first thing Monday morning."

As the fellas watched Delta's hips sway effortlessly to and fro, they found it hard to restrain their comments. "Yo, Kenton. That Martin dude must have some steps in his shower, too," Ran suggested.

Ellis nodded assuredly. "Now I know the devil is pissed. What is he gone do when it starts snowing?"

Unsettled, Kenton found himself in an unfamiliar place, a place he couldn't identify. It was a place he didn't like. He wanted to leave that place, and the only way out of it was through the same channel that had him feeling less than perfect in the first place.

5

Pimpin' Ain't Easy

After paying for lunch, as usual, Kenton pretended to listen to Ellis and Ran's account of how they messed up a can't miss opportunity with Kenton's ex-playmates. Somehow, something went wrong with a flawless plan when Kenton's name came up. As it turned out, Nikki and Rasha worked at the same insurance company, but neither of them knew about the other's fondness for the Pleasure Palace and what they experienced there. Nikki said something about getting busy on the glassed-in courtyard, then Rasha topped her with a story about christening the rooftop on a cool summer's night. Once Rasha realized she'd been one-upped, Kenton's name was dirt. Consequently, every man with a Kenton Reese affiliation was dirt, too, as far as she was concerned. For the fellas, the rest of the night barreled downhill from there.

Kenton clearly explained how they played themselves by bringing him up to break the ice and how using another man's name to score points with a female he'd been with usually resulted as a deal breaker instead. Without any further explanation, he said his casual good-byes, leaving them to ponder just how badly they'd lost out, considering that women generally refused to sleep with close friends, barring exceptions. Unfortunately for the fellas, there were not enough exceptions to go around.

While the fellas were still kicking themselves for making an inexcusable mistake, Kenton raced home. Breathing fire all the way, he second-guessed himself for letting Delta get away when she thought it best to turn tail and run. He knew what was happening at the time but erred in judgment, believing what he'd put on her two nights before was enough to cement his place in her desires for good. Now that the fellas had witnessed his player pedestal wobble, Kenton had to make up for an ill-timed moment of compassion. One that he wished he had a second chance to manipulate differently. And that's just what he decided to do, manipulate the situation to get Delta back on the hook and save face.

Remembering that Delta's phone number had been wiped away during a clean sweep with her name on it, Kenton rolled up his sleeves and tore through the plastic trash receptacle outside his garage. The napkin that he'd transferred her digits to had been thrown out mistakenly, but he had to find it—although rummaging in trash while wearing linen had to transgress at least one of Reese's Rules. It was probably the rule prohibiting him from wading elbow-deep in refuge, like a starving dog. Yeah, that's the one.

"Is that . . . is that it?" Kenton said aloud, flicking cold damp noodles off a three-by-five size fragment of paper with the name Delta scribbled on it. Six out of the seven numbers were legible, but the last one was soiled by marinara sauce. "That ought to be good enough to get me back where I belong," he hailed, shoving the paper into his shirt pocket. "Back into the player's pit."

In a mad dash to prove how tight his game was, Kenton neglected to clean up the pile of mess he'd left. On the floor in his laundry room, he collapsed against the wall to revere his sought-after trophy. With a cordless phone as his ally and an unquenchable taste for vindication to root him on, Kenton was prepared to stoop to the second level of shameless desperation. Trashcan tipping was the first.

By using deceit to readminister what he thought had been sufficiently sextacular in the first outing, he straddled the line while treasuring a shot at flipping the script in his favor. Honesty and truth were not always mutually exclusive, but Kenton was willing to turn them against each other if it suited his purpose. "Two-one-four, five-five-five, six-three-one," he called out while dialing each number. When he couldn't make out the last digit aided by indoor lighting any better than he could outside, he resorted to deductive reasoning. "I'll start at the top and work my way down." Kenton grimaced at the sight of thick red sauce smudging against everything it touched, so he smeared the rest of it against his pants to be rid of it.

"Hello? Hey, is this Delta?" he asked awkwardly when someone answered on the other end. Kenton wasn't embarrassed that he'd forgotten the woman's last name after tripping the night's fantastic with her. He was simply annoyed that he couldn't remember it. "Oh, this isn't? Sorry to bother you." He'd dialed the same sequence of numbers with an alternate ending until he reached the right one. "Good ole number seven," he cheered. "Luck, be a lady tonight."

Loud knocks coming from the front door summoned him to vacate his foxhole. Initially, he let the knocks go unanswered but they grew more insistent. "What!" he shouted in protest to the constant pounding. "Hello? Delta? Oh, it's voice mail." He heard her recorded greeting asking callers to leave their name and callback number. "Hold on. I'm coming!" he yelled toward the front door. I'm coming!"

Holding the phone up to his ear, Kenton whipped the door open. "Yeah, what is it and why you looking at me like that? Told you I was coming." The neighbor, Todd O'Brien, was a middle-aged uptight stockbroker who shared his home with two dogs and a very homely wife. Todd was not at all amused with Kenton's attitude or the fact that his driveway was disheveled and littered with beer bottles, paper napkins, and other more repulsive waste. When his miniature poodle returned home coughing up disposable items she'd found next door, it was time to hold Kenton accountable.

"Delta, I'll call you back." He meant to press the end button on the phone receiver but inadvertently recorded the conversation with his grumpy neighbor. "Hey, it's not cool to be running over here, huffing and puffing like you're gonna do something." The neighbor took a good look at Kenton's stained clothing and assumed the marinara sauce was dried blood. He retreated a few feet before standing firm.

"My Lady, bless her heart, came stumbling home reeking of beer and choking on pizza crust and used condoms," the neighbor spat back. "Well, this had better be the last time something like this happens or I'm calling the cops!"

"Used condoms, damn. My bad. Sorry to hear that, man. I see why you're buggin'. My bad. It'll never happen again, and I promise to clean up behind myself from now on. But a word of advice. Take that funky attitude with you when you get off my yard." Neighbor Todd was still gawking when the door slammed in his face.

Kenton was typically more cordial, but that Delta incident had his nerves exposed. He made his way around to the side of his house, picked up the scattered debris, and reminded himself to get the neighbor's dog a miniature chew toy in efforts to make amends for the secondhand-condoms incident. In the meantime, he called Delta's number a few more times, until he got the feeling that she wouldn't return his calls until she got good and ready.

He tossed and turned during the night, mostly from being upset with himself and wondering what Martin might have done to keep Delta from a telephone. "At least she could take a breather and call a brotha," he said, trying to reason with his renegade thoughts. "That would be the sensible thing to do, although sensibility is easily overlooked when somebody's got you naked with your face pressed against the headboard." Kenton flopped over on his stomach, then back over again, staring at the ceiling. "Martin ain't got nothing on me. What he's putting down can't be that good. I bet it ain't that good. What if it is that good?"

When morning crept in, Kenton dragged himself out of bed and puttered into his office. Three messages awaited his arrival, none of which meant anything to him because Delta didn't have his office number. Meaning, none could have been from her. Her. Delta whatever her last name was. She had him slipping and didn't know it. However, the seven messages he'd left her should have been a fair indication.

His assistant, Tonja Carson, was forty-one, thick around the middle, divorced, and as tough as she was smart, but no amount of business savvy could have saved Kenton from his own actions and she knew that. After two years of baby-sitting the playmates he'd left in his dust while in the pursuit of new ones, Ms. Carson figured that whatever it was that had Kenton closed in his office happened by his own doing. So she spent the next thirty minutes filing her press-on nails, drawing her eyebrows exactly where she wanted them to be, then challenged herself to returning all the e-mails she'd received from her friends and family. When Kenton found the need to buzz her, he would. On the other hand, if he hadn't summoned her by eleven, she'd take it upon herself to strike out on a spiritual-enrichment lunch. A shopping excursion that would begin just after eleven and end some time after one, with her praying all the way back to the job that she wouldn't get reprimanded or perhaps even fired. The pitiful way Kenton moped around the building led her to thinking about heading out to the mall for the remainder of the day.

Before Ms. Carson forwarded all of her lines to eternal voice mail, her buzzer sounded. "Yesss," she answered, with second thoughts about her carefree afternoon.

"Ms. Carson, could you please come into my office for a minute?"

"I'll be right there, Mr. Reese," she replied, getting up from her desk. "Shoot, and Macy's has a shoe sale."

With steno pad in hand, she turned the corner and entered Kenton's self-inflicted realm of misery at her own risk. Surprised at what she'd stumbled on, she dropped her pad on the floor. Kenton had stripped off his shirt and necktie in order for her to get a thorough look at what Delta wasn't addicted to yet.

"Ms. Carson, please close the door," he ordered, while tracing his chest with his fingertips.

"Uh . . . I'm not so sure that's in compliance with company policy." Her mouth was saying what it should have, but her body acted in accordance to its own nature. Refusing to fan herself until Kenton turned away to view his muscular back in the closet mirror, Ms. Carson envisioned tracing his dark, rich, chocolate skin with her own roving fingers.

"Ms. Carson, c'mon now. If you want to remain the envy of every executive assistant at Dream Creams, with damned near unlimited perks, then you ought to close that door." Of course she complied. All things considered, she had it going on and then some.

"Good. Now tell me, am I getting pudgy?"

"Pudgy? No, sir, Mr. Reese."

"So, you would consider me the example of virile masculinity?"

"I want some. I mean . . . yes! Yes, I would say that a woman would be happy to . . . know you in that way." Now, beads of perspiration were mounting on her forehead and her legs began to tremble.

"Are you sure? I think there's an outside chance that I may have lost my edge." Kenton flexed his bulging biceps and compared one to the other. "The left one looks a little soft to me. Why don't I come over there and you tell me what you think?" As Kenton made one step in her direction, Ms. Carson stumbled back against the closed door.

"Oh, hell naw!" she declined, reaching down on the floor for her notepad without taking her eyes off Kenton's statuesque physique. "How would you expect me to work for you after pressing my hands up against all that? Uh-uh. See, I'm not one of these young bunnies you fool around with, Mr. Reese. If I touch it, I gots to have it, and I don't think this office could hush me once I got to getting loud. With all due respect, you'll have to ask someone else what it feels like because I ain't gonna be able to do it." Almost out the door, she ducked her head back inside to get one last eyeful of what had gotten her so nervous.

Kenton's day stretched out like the silk necktie hanging over his chair. Regardless of how hard he worked at promoting positive energy, he'd continued to get stuck on reasoning why Delta hadn't tried to reach him. Eventually, returning Martin Burke's call from the Friday before seemed to be a feasible way to gather information, even if his feelings happened to get trampled in the process.

As it turned out, no news was bad news, Kenton assuming the worst. Martin's secretary informed him that he'd taken a personal day and wouldn't be in until the following morning. "All right, thanks. Please tell him that I tried to reach him." Shut out in the first round, Kenton was running out of ideas. If he couldn't get Delta to respond to his calls, perhaps he could find out where she lived. Suddenly, he stopped everything and sat down. "That's exactly what she said—brothas blowing up her phone and stalking her, but I'm not going out like that. I'm Kenton Reese!" he declared loudly.

"Good. Then you're just the man I'm looking for," Mr. Tearny announced, fingering a feeble comb-over. He was standing there, business-like, in the doorway that Ms. Carson fled through. Donald Tearny III, all five foot four inches and one hundred eighty round pounds of him, inherited the Dream Creams snacks giant from his father, who had almost gambled away the family's fortune until a heart attack stopped him in his tracks. Now that Donald Tearny was at the helm, he relished every bean and stem. He was thrilled that Kenton had joined the management team because his business savvy helped raise the stock, brand awareness, and profits to an all-time high.

"Reese, I've called and left word with your helper," he said, pointing over his shoulder. "By the way, where is she?"

"She's out to lunch," Kenton replied quickly. "A little spiritual-enrichment thing. Don't worry. It works."

"Not a bad idea, Reese. We could all stand to be a bit closer to the carpenter's son, I always say."

"I believe *Jesus* was the carpenter, Mr. Tearny."

"Who?"

"Never mind, sir. I'm just thinking aloud."

"Well, the reason I stopped by was my anxiety over the slippage in our sales numbers for the quarter. If it continues, we may have to make some drastic moves. And I, for one, would hate to be forced to initiate difficult career decisions for members of our management staff. Perhaps you should call a meeting and look into our recent losses. Get back to me when you've come up with something concrete. The bleeding has got to stop."

"I'll get right on that, Mr. Tearny," Kenton answered, while overlooking the graveness in the owner's tone. "I'll fix it."

Hours later, Nikki apologized for running her mouth to Rasha. And Kenton welcomed her back into the fold. "Oh yeah. Oh hell yeah," Kenton panted eagerly. "You've got to learn behave."

"Git it, Daddy," she wailed, her heels stretching toward the ceiling fan. "I'll be good from now on. I'll be good. Ooh! Git it, git it."

"Uhh-huh, uhh-huh," he groaned. "Ain't nobody . . . like . . . yo body, baby." From the nightstand next to the bed, the phone rang. Without missing a stroke, Kenton peeked to see if it wsa Delta calling, finally getting back to him. His caller ID read UNKNOWN CALLER.

"Ooh no. Don't stop, Kenton. Don't stop," Nikki pleaded. "You're gonna make me . . . make me." Kenton tried to pull away, but she'd fastened her arms tightly around his neck. "Ahhhhhhhowww! Oohhhhm!" she howled, while her thighs trembled. Eventually, Nikki released the headlock she'd administered to assure that he couldn't quit until the job was finished.

The phone continued its annoying battery of rings. Not wanting to risk it, Kenton tossed the bedsheet over Nikki's head, then leapt across the bed to answer the phone. "Yeah, this is Kenton." Making sure that his current in-house entertainment remembered her place, he shook his head deliberately to combat her evil glare. "Ellis? Where? Ah, hell. Jail? Dude, which jail? Airport security is taking you where?" Kenton scratched his head, yawned, and then took down the information as Ellis blabbed to him. It wasn't until he'd shown up at the city's night court to influence the female prosecutor into letting Ellis off easy that he learned the full extent of the charges.

It all began several hours earlier, when Ellis deplaned at the airport fresh off a short business junket to Houston. He couldn't believe his luck when Sundae, the flight attendant who'd been with

Kenton, exited at the next gate. A few drinks and several lies later ushered Ellis into the terminal C "book of shame." Ellis literally welled up when he recounted his story to a very alluring lady assistant DA, with Kenton listening in. As soon as his pants slid down around his ankles, he explained, airport security started receiving calls of strange activity in a Chevy Blazer, rocking like it was about to blow. Overzealous security officers arrived in full SWAT assault gear, ready to secure the homeland, if not merely that one terminal. They were surprised to find Ellis's full moon jammed against the back passenger window. Although hardly a terrorist threat, it was a case of public indecency nonetheless. The judge ordered Ellis to pay a two-hundred-dollar-fine, twice the amount of an airport hotel room, and to promise that it would never happen again. Sundae didn't get hauled in because she pulled her shirt down when the cops came storming into the parking garage.

Ellis owed Kenton a debt of gratitude for paying his court fees. Kenton owed it to himself to finagle a hot date with the cute lawyer chick. And the entire airport security force benefited by getting to watch the tape that captured Ellis's fifteen minutes of shame.

6

Naked

The first thing Kenton did after he exited the city court building was to locate his car in the covered parking lot and transfer the lawyer chick's personal information into his black book. Rosalind Hughes was the name he entered. Her navy blue blazer and legalese barked all business, but her curvaceous hips, swaying in a tight-fitting skirt when she walked, whispered something else. It was the something else that he wanted to hear more about. Ellis's unfortunate embarrassment led Kenton to the shores of another ocean of opportunity. He'd never once considered what it might have been like to deliberate the finer points of the law before that night, but suddenly he could see himself discussing everything from what really goes on in the judge's chambers to debating plea bargains for suspected murderers. He had manipulated more than enough lies to know that there was more than one way to spin circumstantial evidence in order to arrive at what could be construed as the truth. However, his intentions had nothing to do with the law, deliberation, or the truth; it had everything to do with what lay underneath the lawyer chick's tight skirt, and he was hell-bent on getting to the bottom of it.

The early morning sun, peeking over the Dallas skyline, may have just as well been snickering at Kenton because of what it foresaw, later in the day, and in plain view. Kenton's cell phone vibrated as he wheeled closer to his ritzy subdivision. Initially he balked at the thought of answering it until he remembered that he'd call-forwarded his home number. Who could be calling him this early? ran through his mind when the incoming number didn't register.

"This is Kenton," he said, not sure if there was cause to be alarmed, due to the odd hour.

"Good morning," a soft voice answered back. "This is Delta."

The magnitude of shock that surged through Kenton nearly knocked the pocket phone out of his hand, but he adequately regained his composure before making a further fool of himself. As if leaving a ton of messages didn't sufficiently do the trick. "Delta," he said, with more sarcasm than surprise. "You're a hard woman to pin down."

"Not when I want to get pinned."

"I see," he replied, rather humbled by her smug comment.

"No, I don't think you do or you wouldn't have blown up my voice message service." After a long pause, Delta sensed that Kenton's ego was a bit more bruised than he was accustomed, but the need still persisted to have a sit-down and clarify the small print on their agreement. "Look, Kenton, I didn't call this morning to ruin your day, but I thought it better to discuss a few things before I run the risk of letting you ruin mine."

Not sure how to respond, Kenton gazed out of the window. There was that damned sneaky sunrise again, opening its eyes wide to see how this would play out, and it was probably snickering, too. "Well, it seems that I have overstepped my bounds," he said finally.

"I'm glad that we agree, but I don't want you to take any of this the wrong way; that's why I think it best to meet in person today, so that there won't be any further misunderstandings."

"Okay, then. How's your lunch schedule?"

"No, this is much too personal to discuss in public. Your place is on my way to the office. Why don't I stop by for a minute? If you don't mind."

"No. That's cool. I'm in the car, but I should be there in about ten minutes," he said, hoping that she assumed he was out on an all-night booty call. "I'll leave the front door unlocked. After the night I had, I need a long hot shower." He had no way of knowing if his subtle insinuation served his purpose of leveling the playing field, but he felt compelled to remind Delta that he was Kenton Reese, a ladies' man, and that his reputation wasn't to be taken lightly. If she failed to recognize that, she'd be the one missing out. That's what he kept telling himself, but he wasn't so sure that it was entirely true.

When he arrived home to an empty house much too large for

one man, the crisp coolness from the air conditioner met him at the door. For the first time in his life, something oddly peculiar stood out amidst the four thousand square feet of copiously furnished grandeur. What stood out was emptiness, a whole houseful of it, in fact. It would take several days for him to realize that he desperately needed to redecorate. The outdated emptiness had to go.

Too weary to facilitate a proper by-the-book clean sweep from the jaunt down memory lane he had taken with Nikki just hours before, Kenton decided that his room would simply be off-limits when Delta stopped over to, as he later joked, "set him straight." He hopped into the shower, then threw on some comfortable sweats, overlooking something in his bedroom that he should have noticed.

Delta was different. He'd eventually come around to admitting that to himself, but a few more days in the pleasure den would take some of the starch out of her attitude and reduce her overblown self-importance to a level that suited his needs. Kenton didn't want to break her spirit, although taming it was necessary, he'd reasoned. Wearing down her defenses and stripping her naked, he'd concluded by the time she rang the bell, was the most appropriate course of action. Beneath her manufactured tough-girl exterior, she was merely a woman. If he played his cards right, Delta would likely drop her guards and have no other choice but to submit to his powers and fall in line. Kenton would go out of his way to give the fellas a ringside seat, up close and personal, when she did. That was the plan.

"Good morning again," Delta said, uncomfortably, as she stepped past him into the foyer.

Kenton neglected to fasten the last two buttons on his silk nightshirt, while he watched her venture, step by step, into the living room. She wore a smartly tailored pantsuit, black trimmed in pink. She had confidence on her side, a swagger that she'd maintain as long as possible. Instead of taking offense, Kenton was really turned on by it. Intriguing, he thought. Here was this woman who had only been a visitor in his home once, yet she sauntered around in it as if she had the run of the house. As far as he was concerned, Delta was going to get everything she deserved, and it would be his pleasure giving it to her—thoroughly administered and one wonderful stroke at a time.

The route Kenton took led through the kitchen. When he appeared in the living room with a glass of milk in one hand a chocolate-covered, cream-filled cupcake in the other, Delta seemed perturbed. "I'm sorry, did I interrupt your breakfast?"

"Not really, not yet," he said. "Just refortifying. You hungry? Got milk. And I'm sure I can rustle up a Ding-Ding for you."

"A Ding-Ding?"

Ding-Dings were the top seller of all Dream Creams' snack products. Kenton knew that sex sells, and if positioned right, a catchy one-liner could prove very beneficial to the Dream Creams marketing strategy. "If you don't have a Ding-Ding, you could probably use one." The cheesy campaign proved sound as housewives traded in Bon Bons and other favorite brands by the millions for Ding-Dings. Since it was Kenton's baby, he enjoyed all the benefits of hitting a major marketing home run.

"Yeah, I've heard the jingle," Delta informed him, "but I didn't come here to talk about snack cake."

Kenton nodded, then rested his glass of milk and breakfast on the thick rectangular glass coffee table. He took a seat next to her, allowing his "All right, let's hear exactly why you did come here." He appeared annoyed by her audacity, but it was a ploy to keep her off balance, considering how he had played himself by blowing up her phone like a lovesick teenager.

"First of all, Kenton, I think that it was just plain wrong for you to sleep with your neighbor's wife, then clown him when he came over to confront you about it. And another thing," she began to say, before her reprimand registered with Kenton.

"Hold on! Back up! Pump your brakes. What are you talking about, me and my neighbor's wife? You obviously haven't seen my neighbor's wife or you would understand how ridiculous it is for you to think that. Looks like she's had way too many Ding-Dings in her life already."

"Well, I guess one more didn't matter to you because I saved the message you must have recorded by mistake, with you and your neighbor arguing over his wife. Remember, her stumbling home and the stupid chick still had the used condom?"

"Whuuut?" Kenton yelled, leaping off the sofa. He paced back and forth while scanning his mind for something he might have forgotten, although the last neighbor's-wife incident occurred when he was a junior in college. The woman had a full-time job and extra cash, Kenton was struggling to make the rent, but that's another story.

"Don't whut me," she told him, following his steps with her eyes, "and don't try to lie because you're not that good at it. Anyway, the neighbor's wife sounds like a stank ho, if you ask me."

Kenton continued pacing and processing what Delta had started his day off with until his head hurt. "Let me get this straight. You're saying that I mistakenly left you a message, arguing over me banging another man's wife?" He threw his hands up after coming up blank. "You're tripping."

"And you're lying."

"That wasn't me," he offered with a flippant shoulder shrug.

" 'That wasn't me,' " she mocked, mimicking his high-pitched denial. "That's your defense? That wasn't me. How original."

"I don't need no defense, I'm single."

"That you are, Mr. Reese, but don't insult my intelligence by lying about what you're lying about. I specifically heard the man say that his lady got into something over here and came home stumbling."

"Lady!" Kenton belted out. "My neighbor's Lady is a dog."

"Funny, I bet you weren't saying that when you were tapping it." Delta didn't know what to make of Kenton's seemingly cavalier attitude about defiling a married woman, regardless of whether or not he thought she was ugly. "Delta, is that what all this is about? What you thought you heard over the phone? Lady is the name of my neighbor's dog. The dog got hold of some things that she shouldn't have, and that's why the man was so upset. Hell, you almost had me thinking I'd tapped somebody's wife."

"Well, maybe I didn't hear what I thought I heard, but that's only thing one to jump out the box. Thing two is the six subsequent voice mails, all of which ended with you demanding that I call you as soon as my date with Martin concluded. Are you on drugs? Kenton, we talked about this very thing. No ties, no terms, no commitments, no issues."

"And I'm cool with that," Kenton said out of nowhere.

"No, you're not or you wouldn't have seen me with Martin and assumed that he and I were more than friends. I do have men in my life who are special to me, but Martin is not one of them."

"Okay, I did cross the line, but I had no idea that I was really digging you until I saw you with ole dude."

"Humph. Don't you mean not until your boys saw me with ole dude?" she countered. "The looks on their faces gave it away. If you hadn't been telling your business, they wouldn't have even known about me and you." Before Kenton was confronted with the thought of lying, Delta gave him an out. "Just as I suspected. Got yourself stuck behind that male ego, didn't you?"

"Delta, they saw me tipping out with you at the Café. I'm sure they assumed right off that we left to get cozy and commingle."

"Commingle? Is they what they're calling it now when a man and woman spend time getting to know each other?"

"No, that's what I call it, but . . . I 'ont have to front for them," Kenton declared, voice raising two octaves. "I just thought maybe you felt a little something extra when you were here."

"Oh, I get it. Just because you sex a woman down real good, she's supposed to put her life on hold and sit around hoping you'll someday get around to falling in love with her?"

"Well," he answered quickly, before thinking.

"Not this woman. Not now, now tomorrow, not ever. I would have to be insane, which I am not, to let myself fall into the spell that so many other sistas do and get caught up wondering if some man is going to call me like he said he would or if he'll waste some of the best years of my life while he tries to figure out if there might be a chance he can do better than me. That game is way past tired. I have too many things to accomplish in life to allow a casual freak session, or its consequential emotional attachment, wreck my flow. I'm a runaway train, determined on reaching my destination on time, with or without a man. So, you need to get on board with my program or get the hell off the track before you get run smooth over in the process." After hearing Delta's tirade, Kenton wasn't so eager to speak. "If you haven't heard one word I've said, hear this. I won't compromise my principles. I can't afford to. I can't."

"Can you afford to overlook one transgression of our strict no-terms policy on my part? I'll admit, I slipped." Kenton raised his hands in surrendering fashion. "There, I said it."

"Kenton, I'd like to work with you, but I can't have you acting all needy and compulsive. Six voice mails. That's a bit much, don't you think?" Delta was giving him a hard time because she knew he was up to something but she didn't know what. In the meantime, she'd let him stew in his own juices.

"Look. I said I slipped, but you can't keep holding that over my head for eternity," he said, pausing to rectify his mistake. "Besides, you know you ought to let a brotha make it up to you. You know, real nice and slow."

"What if a sista wants it real hard and fast?" she cooed seductively.

"I can handle that, too." Kenton reached for her hand, casting his eyes toward the bedroom. "Yeah, I can manage that." When it appeared that Delta was inclined to participate in some early morning mischief, it suddenly dawned on Kenton that his bedroom was filled with naughty remnants of Nikki. "Oh, oh, oh! I almost forgot. I have a million things to do this morning. Ellis needs to pick up his car after it got impounded. His head ain't right after what he went through. That's why I'm just getting home."

"So you spent the night with Ellis?" she teased playfully, although she'd been dying to know what Kenton had actually done during the darkest hours.

"No, I didn't spend the night with Ellis. He got himself in a jam, so to speak." Kenton shared a laugh over Ellis's touchy SWAT situation, then jotted down Delta's cell number and private office line, just in case he needed to reach her during business hours. Delta was wise enough to beware of possible ulterior motives for Kenton going out of his way to stick so closely to her. If he wasn't totally on the level, and there was room for skepticism, it would show itself in due time. Delta realized that the corporate time clock was ticking on without her, so she prepared to head for the office. Before she left, she pulled a business card from a stack in a shiny metal case. Although Kenton had only recently mended fences, he was still above pretending that he cared what she did for a living, so he refused it. As far as he was concerned, he had all the contact information he'd ever need. That little faux pas would later come back to haunt him and flip his world upside down.

As soon as Kenton ushered Delta to the driveway to say his good-byes, a troubling thought resurfaced. Finding it difficult to keep a straight face, he insisted that it was time for him to get going with his day as well. When Delta backed out of the driveway and turned the corner, Kenton sprinted through the front door so fast that his feet barely touched the ground. What he feared had become a reality. There was Nikki, staggering toward the kitchen, wrapped in bed linen toga-style, her hair uncombed and sticking up every which way. Eventually she caught a glimpse of Kenton, enjoyed her long stretch and yawn, then offered an innocent crooked smile.

"Hey, man, I'm hungry. Please tell me that you still keep some of those Ding-Dings stocked in the pantry. I don't have a Ding-Ding and I do want one," she joked, singing an altered version of the popular cupcake jingle.

Closing his eyes to block out visions of the catastrophe that could have been, he sighed deeply. It slipped Kenton's mind that Nikki was still asleep when he'd climbed out of bed to assist Ellis; that major oversight wouldn't have happened before he became hyperfocused on hooking up again with Delta. What if Nikki had awakened and pulled the hungry-houseguest routine five minutes sooner? The fact that he did care how Delta might have reacted should have clued him in that he was digging her more than he thought. Fortunately, he dodged the bullet virtually unscathed. Virtually.

"By the way," Nikki shouted from the kitchen, "next time you want to fight with your lil' girlfriend in the A.M., try to keep it down. I need my beauty sleep."

"Okay," he answered softly. "Wheww, I'm getting too old for this."

7

Dirty Deeds

After sleeping a couple of hours, Kenton called in to apprise his trusty executive assistant that he'd be working from home because of important research he needed to complete. Rosalind Hughes, the sexy lawyer chick, had called earlier to see when he'd be available to get together for a bite, and perhaps dessert. Kenton returned the call, explained that he'd taken the day off, and agreed to lunch. Subsequently, he wouldn't have to wait long before realizing that he had ordered one too many desserts already.

They decided to meet at a small outdoor sandwich shop just north of the downtown district. When she exited a high-rise apartment building directly across the street from the quaint restaurant patio, his eyes lit up, although it was impossible to tell hidden behind dark designer sunshades. The hours since meeting Rosalind hadn't allowed for much rest, and his eyes were retaliating because of it.

In the natural light of day, Rosalind was even more alluring than Kenton remembered. The faded fluorescent courthouse lighting didn't adequately represent her delightful cinnamon complexion and almond-shaped face. With her hair free-flowing instead of pinned up in the tight bun style she reserved for the courtroom, Rosalind definitely deserved his full attention. The girl had potential. A shortened sea-green sundress revealed that her legs were toned and tanned, two things that Kenton wanted to investigate immediately. Matching two-inch slingbacks clicked against the concrete as she made her way over. The slingbacks he'd insist she keep on during and after stripping her of that wonderfully green dress.

"Hey, you." Kenton saluted, standing from the small wrought-iron table to welcome her into his world again. "Wow, green never looked so good. You dress down very well."

"Hello, Kenton." Rosalind smiled on tiptoes and craned her neck to accept a casual peck on her cheek.

"Thank you. That was sweet enough to cause cavities." As Rosalind took the seat next to Kenton, he removed his shades to get an uninhibited eyeful. "I'm sorry for staring, but I'm just trying to get used to seeing you like this."

"What, in my street clothes?"

"That's a nice way to put it, yes."

Kenton had gotten that old feeling again—the one that always led to some woman's panties hitting the floor. He loved the sequence of making a new acquaintance, the infatuation phase that proceeded, and every splendidly intimate episode that was sure to follow. The "delicious cycle" is what he called it, and once he'd had a taste, he'd continue dipping his spoon as long as it benefited him. Looking at Rosalind the way that he was failed to conceal his plans of eating the apple, all the way down to the core. He had already begun mapping out a timely regime involving trading in frequent lunch hours for butt-naked nooners with a certain lawyer chick.

Rosalind blushed, noticing that Kenton's tongue was all but wagging. "You okay?"

"Yeah, why wouldn't I be? I'm torn away from a warm bed to rescue my friends from ruthless assistant district attorneys all the time. Why, just last week it happened twice."

"You are so full of it," she said, slowly brushing a couple of wayward strands of hair away from her face. "Are you always this witty?"

"Of course." Kenton chuckled behind an arrogant smirk. "I got mad jokes."

"Yes, I'm sure you do, but I'm interested in learning what else Kenton Reese has to offer. What makes him more than a man with mad jokes?"

"Without compassion, thoughtfulness, and generosity, what kind of man would I be?"

"Typical," was her simple reply.

"That word isn't in my vocabulary and definitely not one used to describe you, I'm sure."

"And charming as well." Rosalind blushed, allowing her eyes to drift away from his until she couldn't resist any longer. "A complicated man. I don't usually get the privilege of meeting a brotha with so much in his arsenal."

"I get by," he replied, trying to sound modest.

Kenton continued laying it on during several bouts of exchanging glances and shameless flirting over ham and cheese croissants, salami on sourdough, and potato chips. After refills of peach-flavored ice tea and lingering small talk, Rosalind took it upon herself to take their acquaintance to the next level. It seemed that she had her own afternoon delight in mind. "So, are we going to sit here all afternoon making eyes at each other or can we continue this conversation in cozier confines?" She glanced toward the apartment building that she'd strutted out of before the flirting started. "I'm renting a condo there, third floor."

"Do I need to stop by the store to pick up anything?" When his brow raised a full half-inch, she understood what he meant.

"No, sweetheart. I have condoms, if we let things get that far." Her expression was as business-like as her courtroom demeanor. She proved capable of sliding right into mission mode and so did Kenton.

If we let things get that far, he thought. Not if. When.

Once inside her modest two-bedroom flat, Kenton was impressed with the decor. Caramels and creams dominated with hints of turquoise and rust. The theme smacked of the Southwest, bold but not overstated. When he walked through the front door, he guessed that she hadn't been there long. Boxes marked BATHROOM and ATTIC were pushed into the corner, probably holdovers from a larger place.

"This is nice, very nice," Kenton complimented, taking a seat on her sofa.

"Wine? Merlot or Chardonnay?" she called out from the kitchenette.

Kenton ventured into the same area. He found himself salivating when he discovered her bent over at the waist, examining wine labels from a slender rack. "Excuse me? I didn't catch that."

"Wine, red or white?" she repeated in the event that he wasn't as well heeled as she'd suspected.

"Oh, a dry Chablis. If you have it."

"I was right about you; a fine man who enjoys fine things. This should be fun."

After helping Rosalind manipulate an ornery corkscrew from

the mouth of the bottle, Kenton poured a stout glass of wine for her, then as much for himself. Rosalind cued up a smooth jazz number from her CD collection. Unfortunately, Kenton wouldn't be around long enough to thoroughly enjoy it.

After sipping from a conservative selection of Kendall Jackson, Rosalind wanted to slow dance, stating that she couldn't remember the last time she'd done so. Kenton, considered to have great moves, accepted her offer like he'd accepted everything else since they'd met. He took her hand and pulled her close to him, holding her gently. The chemistry between them was magnetic. He wanted to show her what he could do to a woman's body. She wanted to see it, too. "C'mon," Rosalind whispered, heading to another room in the rear of the apartment with Kenton in tow. She led him into her bedroom, drew the shades, then turned on a table lamp beside an early modern fashioned bed. "I want to watch," she said, kissing his neck. "Can I watch?"

"Anything you want," he answered, returning her heat with a good measure of his own. When Rosalind slid her hand down Kenton's pants, he moaned. "Ahhh, Delta. You really got me going, girl."

Rosalind hesitated briefly, then pulled back on the controls. "What was that, Kenton?"

"I was just saying . . . how . . . I really want you," he replied, easing her panties down past her thighs. "Damn, you're sweet all over." Kenton feverishly unbuttoned his short-sleeve shirt with one hand and tickled Rosalind's hot pocket with the other. He'd remember to kick himself later for neglecting to wear an easy-to-shed pullover.

"You think it's sweet, huh? You don't know that yet."

"I'm about to."

"Hold on, wait." Rosalind scooted onto the edge of the bed. After she closed her legs and pulled down her sundress, she blew a long stream of anxiety into the air. "Kenton, who's Delta?"

"Who?"

"Do you love her?"

"Huh?"

Kenton didn't love Delta, he was sure of that, but the question blindsided him when all he could think of was capitalizing on the fact that Victoria's Secrets were already off and on the floor.

"What's so special about this Delta that you can't shake her from your mind?"

"What are talking about?" He was extremely confused and ridiculously horny. Thinking straight resulted in a difficult task when the majority of his blood had headed south after having been requisitioned to sustain a massive and impressive erection. "Who said anything about Delta?"

"You did," she informed him, before getting up to retrieve her underwear. "You said that Delta really had you going. Unfortunately, my momma named me Rosalind."

Kenton was at a loss, his heart pumping and blood racing. When he didn't have the words to right the situation he'd royally vexed, knowing that anything that proceeded from his mouth would have come out sounding like a lie, Rosalind put the booty on lockdown. "Kenton, I meet hundreds of men every week, some good, some bad. I've pegged you as potentially exceptional or you wouldn't be here. The thing is, I'm not one to eat from another woman's plate, even when her man's willing to eat from mine."

"Huh?" he said again, still panting and oblivious that his erection was about to give up on him, too. "Rosalind, don't do this. Please. Delta is just some sista I know. She's real cool but it's nothing serious, a little something to kick it with, nothing else."

"I'm sorry, Kenton, but in the court of Rosalind Hughes, a man is guilty until proven otherwise. I'm afraid that I'm going to have to ask you to leave. Let the judge and jury know when you figure out who this Delta is and exactly what she means to you. I'm very much the hopeless romantic who isn't accustomed to sharing another woman's man, whether he admits it or not. You have the number; lock the door on your way out."

While taking his time to stuff his penis back in his boxers, he leered at Rosalind as if she were a woman who'd just sentenced him to solitary confinement when he had ideas of breaking her back with hours of hard labor. "This is cruel and damn sure unusual punishment," he said, drawing a measured breath. "I'll go, but I'm innocent."

"Uh-huh. The door, lock it. Thank you."

Kenton's tail was hardly the only thing dragging between his legs as he walked two blocks, until it dawned on him that he'd parked his car behind the tiny sandwich shop across from Rosalind's apartment. He couldn't resist glaring up at her bedroom window as he pulled away from the curb. "I'm innocent," he repeated when the realization that a prime cut had been dangled in his face only to be snatched away before he had the chance to sample a single piece of it. All he wanted was a piece.

Crossing over the Trinity River Bridge and away from the Hughes Hell House, Kenton couldn't believe he'd been so stupid. Sure he'd called the wrong woman's name before while in a compromising position, but he'd done it to purposely compromise a flailing relationship. It had proven to be the quickest way to get a woman to leave him and feel that she was the one calling it quits. And it worked like a charm. However, he never imagined it working in reverse. Trying to nail Delta had him acting out of character. It must have been her fault, he reasoned. Digging through garbage was one thing, but now she'd gone and done it. Somehow, she'd caused him to get tossed out of a naughty noon rendezvous.

It was war, he'd decided by the time he arrived at the grocery store. Not a war of the hearts but of an ego uprising. He needed a fail-safe strategy to strip Delta of her overblown self-assuredness. Since putting the mack down didn't appear to scratch the surface, he'd have to turn up the heat to full blast then ration the water. All of a sudden, Kenton began to hum up and down the grocery aisles, tossing items in his shopping cart to get the fires going. "Whip cream," he whispered, barely audible. "Yeah, strawberries, chocolate syrup, and caramel, too. A fresh fruit tray during the halftime show might come in handy. Better make that two fruit trays. Massage oil, massage cream, or massage butter," he read aloud, contemplating which of them might provide an edge over the others. "Hell, I'll take all three. Where's the Natural Glide lubricant? There it is. I'd better get the economy size with the power pump. And what's this?" he said when something caught his eye. "Can't ever have too many tubes of Sassy's hair-removal gel." As he wheeled down the vitamin and health supplements aisle, he smiled sheepishly. "Don't sleep on the ginseng tabs. I need to make her ears pop while I'm banging dents in that uterus." On his way to the checkout stand, he picked out two boxes of assorted condoms.

His pushcart, full of bad-boy goodies, drew the attention of several housewives who'd taken an interest in the handsome man who was apparently ready, willing, and able to use the equipment he'd selected. The cashier was a lady in her thirties, thin and brunette.

She had a peculiar habit of smacking on a wad of gum as she rang up each item, which forced Kenton to pay her more attention than he wanted to. Eventually, the woman's curiosity begged to be acknowledged. "Looks like somebody's planning one heck of a bachelor party," she suggested.

"No, actually I've got a hot date."

"Oh my." She giggled, blushing over the thought of being the object of all that intended affection. "I wish my man thought enough of me to go through all this trouble."

Kenton flipped out his wallet to present a debit card when he assumed the cashier's appetite for sticking her nose into other folks' business had been adequately satisfied. "Not that it matters, but she's not my woman."

"Humph, after you're done using all this, she'll wish she was."

Several of the female shoppers watched him until he exited the store. "Honey, I wouldn't let a man like that come around me unless he knows CPR," an older customer hollered from two registers over.

"A man like that," the cashier said under her breath, "I know I'd rather pass out before I'd let him quit. Oh my."

8

Tickling and Tumbling

On Tuesday evening, Delta acquiesced to Kenton's bidding to bring an additional business outfit for the following workday. He planned on taking his time setting her on fire. Removing obstacles that could potentially interfere with those plans necessitated a certain degree of foresight. Since Kenton had the next four dates orchestrated from beginning to end, there wasn't any room for error. He'd promised himself that by Saturday, Delta would be old news because Rosalind was next in line to get served, and he wasn't accustomed to being refused by any woman.

"Welcome," Kenton said when he opened the door to find his date standing on the other side. "Come on in." He lifted her plaid-patterned designer overnight bag from the welcome mat after offering a cordial embrace. "I've been thinking about you."

"Have you?" Delta asked. Her many thoughts of him bled through the transparently contrived coy act she'd rehearsed on the ride over. She rested herself on the first in a row of swivel bar stools and stepped out of her business pumps.

"Delta, hopefully you won't take this the wrong way, but I've actually kept my fingers crossed kinda hoping you've had a pretty rough day."

Her eyes narrowed but there was a smile behind them. "Yeah, you're gonna have to explain that one."

"How could I kiss it and make it better if it doesn't hurt?"

"Oh, after the trying day I've had, there are a few places that need some attention. I could number them if you'd like to play connect the dots or something more creative."

"Later," Kenton suggested with a sly wink. "There're a few things waiting for you in the bedroom."

Although Delta was immediately stricken with excited anticipation, she composed herself and held her enthusiasm in check while entering the long hallway that led from the living area to Kenton's bedroom. The moment she recognized the fragranced scent of American Beauties, a trail of scattered rose petals ushered her into the master suite. Lying on the bed were several negligees, in various styles and colors. They ran the gamut from very tasteful to downright tawdry. The hot-pink getup that unsnapped in the seat held Delta's gaze. She almost giggled out loud when she stole a quick glance at the collection of price tags. Right off, what she saw confirmed two things. One, that Kenton had been a very busy boy because none of them were purchased at the same store. The second thing sent chills up her spine. Every single piece of lingerie was just her size, which meant Kenton thought enough of her to take notes during her first visit. Before she knew it, she had begun feeling all "better than his other women" again.

"See something that suits you?" a soothing voice asked from the doorway. "Just decide what you like and it's yours."

"This is all very impressive. Thank you for going through the trouble of shopping on my behalf," she said, smiling uncomfortably. With her back still facing him, she frowned. "Question."

"Ask away."

"What if I see something that I really like but it's not on display?"

"Unfortunately, you're looking at all I have to offer," he answered. His words were carefully selected, like a newly elected politician.

"That's kind of what I thought. Just checking I guess."

Kenton liked what he was hearing. Delta had apparently been considering more than their casual agreement, he assumed, but he remained convicted to staying on the course he'd charted. His dubious plan was in the early stages but shaping up nicely. Good thing Kenton had decided against picking up little keepsake trinkets to present after their date. He'd hate to see Delta buckle so easily under pressure of the all-enticing bling bling.

"Here," Kenton said, handing Delta a tall mixed fruity cocktail. "I hope you like mango."

"Ooh, well done. Looks tropical." She sipped from the glass, nodded her approval, then hummed her delight. "This is very good. Do I taste Jamaican rum?"

"Yeah. It's nice, huh? I figured you'd like it. Oh, before the oil gets too hot, your presence is required upstairs."

"Jamaican rum and oil, huh? That certainly sounds interesting." Very interesting, Delta thought. "I'll be right up."

Kenton had climbed the entire staircase before realizing that he'd been shooed away. He couldn't come up with an answer why, but she'd sent him off for sure. Delta wanted privacy while getting undressed. Kenton wondered if she was being guarded due to his compulsive bevy of phone calls, which was simply an overreaction, never to happen again. He shrugged it off and entered the game room, where the billiards table had been removed and replaced by a special-ordered monogrammed massage table. Since Kenton always kept the wet bar stocked with half-pints of liquor, fruit juices, and popular drink mixers, he wouldn't have to travel downstairs again until business had been thoroughly completed on the second floor. His event-facilitation skills were top drawer. His proficiency in other more sensual areas was damned near legendary.

Having heard numerous pulsating tales praising Kenton's sexual appetite from her cousin Rasha, Delta would have been foolish to expect anything other than an infrequent appetizing affair that had no future of blossoming into something substantial. With that in mind, she approached the upstairs landing prepared to carpe diem. Seizing the day was a much more palatable alternative to becoming subdued by it. Having Kenton Reese make a fuss over her, as if he actually cared, was simply a tasty bonus.

"What's with all this?" Delta asked while basking in the serene ambience that Kenton had created just for her. Soft music serenading a legion of scented candles transformed the spacious entertainment area into a veritable perfumed paradise. Even if the spectacle of sight and sound served no obvious purpose other than pure enjoyment, Delta vowed to record it for prosperity's sake. The man she'd claim for her own someday would undoubtedly need to possess a similar passion for spoiling her, because Kenton had a knack for stroking a woman's ego in the best way and she liked his style.

"I told you I'd been thinking about you," he said with a smile that sparkled in the candlelight. "Why don't you lose that towel and make yourself comfortable on the table. I'll be ready to get started in a minute."

Delta blushed. She happily followed directions to the letter, allowing the large beach towel to cascade to the floor. Her giddy expression caused Kenton to fight off a slight chuckle. He roamed her body with his eyes, licked his lips, and swallowed hard, then he slowly covered her with white linen from the neck on down.

With hesitant whispers, Delta called out to him. "Kenton, what are you going to do to me?"

"Apologize."

Kenton spent the next two hours apologizing. He apologized between her thighs with fiery kisses. He apologized with a regime of intense deep-tissue hot-oil caresses. He apologized until she exploded with seven splendidly spectacular deep-as-the-ocean orgasms. When he felt that Delta had been thoroughly apologized to, he carried her wilted frame downstairs to the master bath to wash away any doubts that he was sorry for acting out of character. After topping off the apology with a satisfying shampoo, Kenton kneeled next to the bed with a silver-plated dinner tray.

Delta's eyelids fluttered momentarily before opening. "Hmmm, I thought I was dreaming that I smelled something."

"And they say dreams don't come true," he joked, removing the domed cover. "I figured you'd get hungry after your catnap, so I sent out for a Hawaiian pizza. Roast duck and pineapple was all they had." He climbed into bed along with Delta, nibbling here and there, then nibbling on a slice of pizza when he thought his guest had drifted off to sleep.

"Before I forget," she whispered, barely audible, "apology accepted."

I know it is, Kenton thought to himself. *I know it is*.

By the time morning came, Delta had pulled her second disappearing act. Kenton threw his legs over the side of the bed instead of hitting the snooze button for the third consecutive time. Awaking to a new day with a renewed resolve had him feeling crisp as a new dollar bill. On the way out the door, he passed through the kitchen and reached into the frig for a quart of bottled water. A warm sensation came over him when he saw the envelope Delta left for him to find. It was strategically placed against the empty sliced-pineapple can Kenton used to make dinner the night before. A genuine smile traced his lips while opening the white letter-size envelope. *Hey, Slick. Thanks for a wonderful evening.* The note was signed *D.T. Niles,* but the unfamiliar name did not register with Kenton.

For three days running, Delta received an early morning phone call after leaving Kenton's place minutes before dawn. Four dates in four days was the diagram he'd drawn up earlier in the week. The Apology Session took place on Tuesday. On Wednesday, they enjoyed dinner on the lake, prepared by a gourmet chef. A private concert for two was performed in the park by a smooth saxophonist on Thursday. And when Friday afternoon came and went, Kenton double-checked the necessary arrangements he'd made for what he intended to be the date to get Delta out of his system before tossing her aside like he'd done weekly to so many other unsuspecting beautiful playmates.

"That's right, Ellis," Kenton said into the telephone. "Make sure you and Ran come through around eight. Yeah, see you then." After he hung up, he gazed past the stack of sales reports that he neglected to go over during the week. Disregarding his boss's request, Kenton continued to shirk his primary responsibilities. His priorities had wandered off and had gotten lost in the midst of the Delta shuffle, in more ways than one.

Byron Myers, Kenton's top sales producer, was a thin, pale thirty-three-year old supporting a wife and four kids. He was wired so tight that he often appeared ready to jump off a ledge at the slightest sign of failure. When Byron slinked by Kenton's office at quitting time, he expected to be terminated after losing two very important accounts to their detested competitor, Tasty Treats. Byron was relieved that no dismissal papers decorated his sales manager's desk. "Mr. Reese, 'mind if I visit with you a minute?"

"Of course not. Are the girls all right? Sarah isn't sick, is she?"

"No, it's nothing like that. The kids are fine. Sarah's fine."

Kenton casually passed a football back and forth from hand to hand, much like he was passing the time until moving on to Rosalind Hughes lawyer chick or whoever came after Delta—literally. His focus was so far off the charts that he'd forgotten Byron stopped by until the man cleared his throat, trying to work up the nerve to inquire about the decline in sales and subsequent client orders.

"Uh, Mr. Reese, I must admit that I'm surprised you haven't called a meeting to talk about . . . the new numbers." Byron glanced at the perfectly arranged and undisturbed tower of monthly reports, neatly stacked atop Kenton's desk. A quick glance toward the overflowing in-tray affirmed what Byron had finally concluded. The sales and marketing manager had no idea what he was talking about. When Kenton displayed a puzzled expression, Byron tempered his skepticism while standing to make a fast getaway. His head was destined to end up on the chopping block soon enough, and there was no sense in hastening his fate. If there was ever a time to savor the weekend, Byron decided there was no time like the present. "Sorry to bother you, Mr. Reese. I can see that you have other things on your mind."

"You sure?" Kenton asked, now spinning the football on his fingertips. "I wouldn't be too worried about the production numbers. Mr. Tearny gets a little bent out of shape from time to time, but as long as our biggest accounts are safe, there's nothing to get worked up over. Kiss the wife for me and have a good weekend."

As Kenton mentally dismissed him and prepared to hit the streets, Byron backed out of the office slowly, just as the executive assistant did when she thought Kenton had lost his marbles. Only this time, Kenton's behavior bordered on corporate management insanity. After Byron walked past the office window, he took a suspicious peek, expecting to see Kenton doing handstands on the desk or some other exhibition just as peculiar.

But there would always be Monday.

9

Trouble in Paradise

The doorbell rang at seven-thirty; Kenton looked out the bay window. Delta's Navigator was parked close to the garage door, just like he'd trained her to do. She was catching on fast. If he had the time and energy to shape her into the kind of playmate he wouldn't mind seeing once a week, he may have considered it. But seeing how she had required too much of his time already, her status was about to change.

"Let me give you a hand with those," he said, removing two bags from her arms. "You bought groceries?"

"Thanks, Kenton. No, it's more like I *brought* groceries, from my house. You know, that place where I used to sleep. Between practically living at the office and spending so much time here lately, I'm not sure where to pick up my mail." Once they had retrieved the remaining bags from the SUV, Delta emptied all of them onto the kitchen counter. "Now, I had grown very tired of eating alone and then I met you. In honor of that, I would like to spring for dinner and a movie."

"You're gonna cook?" He looked at her peculiarly, wondering if she could boil water much less put together an entrée. Kenton's mother had worked two jobs when he was growing up. It was often left up to him to prepare meals for his younger siblings, so the sauce-and-simmer thing was second nature to him by the time he was on his own. He couldn't say the same for Delta, though. Come to think of it, Kenton didn't know that much about her life or how she lived it outside of her moments with him.

"And I packed one of my favorite DVDs. Want to guess?"

"What do I get if I'm right?"

"You get . . . to apologize again," she answered suggestively.

"Okay, okay," he agreed, laughing at her flawed reasoning. "And what if I'm not right?"

"You mean, if you're wrong?" she asked, making a definitive point of semantics.

"No. I'm never wrong," Kenton responded, smirking playfully. "I might not always be right, but I'm never wrong."

"You know what? It really doesn't matter 'cause I'm going to put these seafood nachos on you, check out Jamie Foxx and that crazy fool Mike Epps in the movie, *Bait*; then if you're still up for it, I can practice *apologizing* to you." Delta blushed after coming off the cuff with a shameless innuendo.

"Oh, you can do that now. Let's skip the prelims and go straight to the finals. I bet you're ready to go for the high score anyway. Hold on, let me get my stopwatch."

"See, there you go. I don't know about you." She looked him over, shaking her head leisurely. "I just don't know."

"Thanks for clearing that up."

Kenton had trouble remembering why he'd reasoned it clever, on Tuesday, to get the last laugh on Delta and for all his fellas to be in on the private joke. He wasn't sure what happened while gawking at Delta's behind as she wheeled around the kitchen in peach-colored cotton shorts. She felt comfortable with its snug fit, which exposed exactly what Kenton had grown fond of, more than he ever imagined he would.

When the doorbell sounded, Kenton stuck out his chest and hastened to let the fellas in. "She naked?" Ran asked, pushing his way through Kenton's doorway.

"Hell, no, she ain't naked," Kenton barked. "Ain't nobody said nothing about her being naked."

"What's the haps, Kenton, and where is our serving wench?" Ellis added, sniffing around in the air. "I smell Mexican food. You hiding a Mexican up in here?" Ellis stopped dead in his tracks when he stumbled on Delta leaning over the stove, shaking seasonings on sautéed shrimp, chicken, and sweet onions. "Nah, her great-grandmomma was sho nuff tribal. Probably related to Kunta'nem. Look at that Watussi booty."

"Here, Delta, put this on," Kenton advised, handing her a pair of navy blue yoga workout tights. "It might get mildly inappropriate, if you know what I mean."

"No, I don't know what you mean." Delta leaned against the bar with a bit of butt cheek still visible. "If you didn't want your friends to get excited about *my ancestry*, you shouldn't have invited them in knowing that it was hanging out."

Kenton was astounded. He'd just been scolded in his own home. "Un-un, she did not just loud talk me."

"Uh-huh." Ellis nodded.

"Yes, she did," Ran seconded. "I heard her, too."

"What in the hell is going on? All I wanted was a quiet evening, maybe some homies rolling through."

Delta lowered the heat on the stove but refused to conceal what the fellas were salivating over. "So, which is it?" she demanded to know from Kenton. "You want a quiet evening or some homies rolling through? It's plain to see that you can't always get what you want."

"I like this one, Kenton. Yeah, man, she's got spunk," Ran proclaimed as if she were a sporty new automobile. "Like my daddy used to say, she's built up like a Buick."

"Ran has got a point. She is fine. So fine it's got to be a crime," added Ellis.

"It's downright unlawful," Ran quipped.

Ellis grinned at Delta, although she tried to ignore him. "You can get a murder charge for packing all that without a permit."

"Ellis, what you know about that?" Kenton spat halfheartedly. "The last time I saw you next to a tight body, she was unhooking your shackles."

Ran's eyes widened when Kenton crossed the line in mixed company. Delta wasn't supposed to have the four-one-one of Ellis' unfortunate detainment. "Oops, we'd better be going. It's about to pop off up in here."

"Hold on, hold on," Ellis insisted, stalling to get another eyeful of Delta's ancestry. "Kenton, you'd better be glad we're second cousins on my daddy's side 'cause if we wasn't . . ."

"You'd do what, Ellis?" Kenton challenged.

"It don't matter because we are. You just better be glad that I'm still claiming my kinfolk after you went and put my business out there like that."

As Kenton worked at ushering the fellas out the door, both of them gave Delta high marks all around, then thanked him for the bottles of beer and wine he let them appropriate on the way out.

"Later, fellas. I'll get at y'all tomorrow."

When Kenton returned to the scene of the crime, Delta's nachos steamed almost as much as she did. "That was quite a show, Kenton." she hissed.

"All they were doing was showing off in the presence of a booty-ful woman."

"And you were you showing off, too?"

"Huh?"

"You. Why all the posturing, like you were marking territory? You may as well have raised your leg."

"Well if that's the thanks I get for trying to protect your honor," he objected, fighting back the urge to bust out laughing.

"Go on and laugh. You know you want to." Delta watched his quiet snicker evolve into Kenton doubling over. "I knew it. All three of y'all put together ain't worth two dead flies. And wash your hands, it's time to eat."

Dinner was delicious, as was the Jiffy Pop popcorn that Kenton labored over while Delta continued to hurry him from the comforts of the media room. Dinner and a movie never felt so good. That's the thought that followed Delta out the driveway and down the street when it came time to leave. Once again she'd left before dawn, thinking that might somehow spare her undue heartache in the end. It was just a thought.

Kenton's thoughts were altogether different. He felt relieved and vindicated. It took some doing, but solidifying himself again as the player supreme in the fellas' eyes was well worth the effort. What a man's friends think of him is often more gratifying than what he thinks of himself. This was Kenton's foremost predicament, accompanied by many others he'd soon come face-to-face with. His impending dilemma would be one for the ages—preserve the image he always enjoyed or exchange it for the reality he never considered. To commit or not to commit, that was the question begging to be answered.

While reveling in his renewed superinflated ego, Kenton carefully maneuvered his 'Benz through a busy full-service car wash. After ordering the platinum package, which included the works and then some, he strolled inside the adjoining building to relax while the staff feverishly buffed his chrome to a sparkling shine. What happened next was totally unforeseen and equally devastating.

Before Kenton knew what he was up against, he'd been struck

by the previously inconceivable revelation that Delta was not entirely seduced by his wondrously wicked ways. But there she was, merely hours after stealing away from his back door, cuddled up beside one of the biggest biceps he'd ever seen. The colossal mound of muscle appeared quite comfortable sharing his gargantuan stature with interested onlookers as well as with Delta. Her escort was big enough to be a ride at an amusement park, Kenton nearly said aloud. That's when his teetering bravado shrank down to just about nothing, allowing the opportunity for irrational behavior to make another preposterous appearance.

Kenton ducked behind a tire-treatment display before being detected by Delta and her dinosaur. Other patrons noticed Kenton's awkward conduct and cautiously moved away from him. Seething with jealousy he didn't know existed, Kenton refused to wait until he got home before confronting his demons. Unlike the time before, when Delta appeared out of nowhere inside the restaurant, he felt compelled to strike while the iron was red hot. Delta's cell number was the last entry on his recent-call list. "Let's see what you've got to say about this," he said, loud enough to draw the attention of a young man perusing the display that Kenton used as an obstruction. "Mind your business," Kenton growled through clenched teeth. The man squinted his eyes, visibly annoyed.

"Excuse me?" he hissed, clutching a man purse tightly against his bony frame.

"G'on now. I said beat it," Kenton warned him after his initial attempt at bullying failed.

"You've got your nerve, freak!"

"And you'll never be the man your momma was, so I guess that makes us even."

After the nuisance stormed off in a tizzy, Kenton selected Delta's number, then pressed SEND. He watched to see how she would react when receiving a call from him while she was in the company of another man, a ridiculously enormous man. The plot thickened as Delta opened her handbag to search for the ringing flip phone. She located it, pulled it out, identified the caller, and then turned it off before sliding it back into her purse. Kenton was beside himself. That reminded him of the sort of stunt he might have pulled. How could she be so much like him, he wondered.

It took every ounce of his being not to call again and force her hand, but there was no way in hell he was foolish enough to make a scene and have to deal with Muscle Mania. Furthermore, that would have landed him right back in the very place he had spent a week climbing out of—a frustrating life-sucking ditch called desperation. He'd made up his mind that he wasn't going back there willingly, not for Delta, not even for any woman. To be or not to be free. Free from the many games; free from separating wins and losses and keeping score. Whether to turn his back on all that he previously deemed sacred, Kenton would have to decide to exercise his freedom or travel the avenues of the world he created, alone. Unfortunately, that decision would be postponed until after he'd had the chance to properly muddle through an appropriate amount of personal loathing.

For the remainder of the weekend, Kenton fought against his better judgment to track down Delta and demand satisfaction for being dismissed when his call went unanswered. He also fought a gang of self-pity, doubting his ability to finesse every woman into gleeful submission. Sure he had, without hesitation, shared his bed with Nikki and Crystal since Delta dropped in on his world, then immediately dropped a bomb on it. Past visions of grandeur floated through his mind, when his game was tight and scoring at will was par for the course. Then the taxing visions of Delta ignoring his number, flashing on her call screen, swept those grand visions away. His self-esteem barreled downward until it knocked him flat on his high-minded behind.

Moping on his living room sofa for hours, Kenton was oblivious to the onslaught of typical Saturday booty-call invitations he received while wallowing in his own misery. He drowned his sorrows with endless glasses of Moet. He passed on Crystal's seductive enticement to spend her long layover with him, whereby she'd requested to spend most of it on top. Either Kim I or Kim II offered to swing by for a quick romp after her sister's wedding had concluded, although Kenton couldn't for the life of him figure out which one of the Kims was doing the offering. Nikki called several times asking for a weekend tune-up, and Challis left a sensual message informing him that she'd signed divorce settlement papers and couldn't wait to celebrate the three-million-dollar gold mine she referred to as an unfulfilled marriage. Kenton would later give thought to hopping a plane to Las Vegas and painting the town red with some of Challis's newfound money but couldn't muster the energy to pack an overnight bag. What a strong hold pity had on him. A late-evening buzz from Rosalind, calling for an update on his status, didn't even make a dent. He had it bad but didn't know what to do about it. So, he popped another bottle of champagne, hoping to drift closer to a resolution without feeling compelled to uncork another one after that.

After he plopped down on the loveseat, Kenton smirked displeasure over the way his brief concert ended. "Another good man down, but I ain't going out like that. It ain't over. It ain't even close to being over." By the time his head bobbled forward, his chin resting against his chest, it was all over. The pity party had been shut down; what hadn't ended was his angst for settling up with Delta.

10

A Player's Predicament

Sunday morning ushered in more of the same awkward sentiment that tucked him in the night before. It took Kenton over twelve hours to sleep off one hell of a drinking binge and another two additional hours to wash the stale taste of expensive champagne from his mouth. He eventually broke down and called Delta twice during the day and once more before calling it a night. He had no earthly idea that his life was about to change, a change that took a full forty hours to run its course.

On the following Monday, Black Monday as it would be referred to around the Dream Creams camp, Kenton was caught in the cross fire when Delta got around to returning his calls at the exact time that his severe managerial neglect forced a come-to-Jesus meeting with the boss.

Kenton's eyes scanned the floor in front of him as he headed off the elevator and down the hall to his corner office. Had he been more aware, he would have surely noticed that the company flag outside had been lowered to half-mast, indicating that something important had died. Mr. Tearny thought is served as a fair representation of the outpour of money the company had lost over the past month. He would have also sensed that all was not well at the Dream Creams corporate office.

"It's Kenton," he said, carefully holding the cell phone to his ear as he jiggled a key to unlock his office door. Ms. Carson stood at attention when he passed. She attempted to get his attention, but he quietly shushed her into the shadows. "This is important; I'll be with you in a second," he whispered. "Oh, not you, Delta. I was speaking to my assistant."

"So, how was your weekend?" she asked routinely.

"Not as good as yours was, if I had to guess."

"What does that mean?"

"That simply means that I'm betting you've been getting your kicks since I've seen you last." Kenton eased off his suit coat, then hung it on a wooden rack resting by the door. Ms. Carson implored him with her eyes to surrender a minute of his time, suggesting that something was urgent. Again, he waved her off.

"No, I'm asking what that subtle sarcasm in your voice means." Delta's deep sigh was followed by a long pause. "Kenton, if there's something you want to say, you should just come on out with it. These guessing games have to stop."

"Guessing games," he repeated, irritated. "You're calling me for the consecutive Monday morning after not returning my calls for the consecutive weekend and you're accusing me of running game. Delta, I saw you with Goliath at the car wash on Saturday."

"Car wash?" She paused to think back. "But you called my cell while I was there with Titan."

"So that's his name? You're real cool about it, too. As cool as the other side of the pillow."

"Titan is my personal trainer, and that's as far as it will ever go. He's not my type of hype, and he already has more women than he has good sense. Reminds me of someone else I know, but I don't get down like that."

Kenton tried to flip the script and shove accusations in the other direction. "Are you telling me that you aren't sleeping with him or Martin Burke?"

"I'm not trying to tell you who I'm sleeping with because it's not your business. You've made that resoundingly clear from jump, so don't take it there. Anyway, that's beside the point. If you saw me at the car wash, why didn't you speak?" Instantly she recognized that something familiar was happening "Wait a minute. Don't tell me you're getting all weird on me again? Aren't you the one who had it all figured out as long as it suited you?"

"I'm just now figuring out what truly suits me, and it suited me a lot better before you came along, pulling a Houdini every weekend."

"What? Oh, I get it. Sounds like somebody wants a bigger better deal. I don't believe this. You're trying to renegotiate?"

"Nah, nothing like that," he replied. "Actually, it's a bit more simple. I've decided to terminate our agreement. I'm not feeling it, and I'm not feeling us." Suddenly there was a hard knock on his office window. While the pounding sounded off behind him, Kenton waved his hand frantically at the window, threatening the knocker to cease and desist before he became really annoyed with their interruptions.

"Fine, Kenton," Delta agreed, although reluctantly. "That's fine with me, but don't you go fooling yourself into thinking there was ever any us. There was only enough room for you." Delta hung up the phone before Kenton had a chance to respond to her parting comment. Simultaneously, that pesky knocking at the window kicked up again, only this time it was accompanied by beeps from Ms. Carson's intercom.

"What!" he yelled, planning to tear whoever was causing the racket a new one. He turned to find Mr. Tearny so steamed that he was shaking.

"That's a very good question, Kenton. What has gotten into you?" his boss asked behind a reddened face and veins popping out of his head.

"Mr. Tearny, I'm sorry," was all he could say. He didn't have too long to wonder if his simple apology was enough to pacify the company's owner.

"Sorry just about sums up how you've been running the sales and marketing group lately." The boss came inside the office, closing the door behind him. Half of the employees on the floor had overheard Mr. Tearny's assessment of Kenton's recent performance. "Son, look. You've done an exceptional job since day one, and I don't mean to get overly sensitive about our rapidly declining market share, but lately we have not been getting a decent return on investment and I'm afraid that includes you. I specifically asked you to look into why there's a hole in my pocket. You assured me that you would do just that." By the bewildered look on Kenton's face, he could tell right off that Kenton didn't have the answers he'd asked for. What he didn't know was why not, and he didn't really care. What he did care about was the stream of money flowing from his company's coffers.

"You'll have an answer by the end of business today," Kenton promised him.

"I hope so, or I'll have to dig it out myself, and if that's the case, I wouldn't have much use for you. Would I?" Mr. Tearny lowered his head, patted Kenton on his back softly, then turned to leave.

"No, sir. No, you wouldn't," Kenton answered before his mentor exited his office. Then Kenton's eyes landed on Ms. Carson's, which were flooded with tears. She had heard the owner's rants before but never tied to ultimatums. This was serious. Kenton's personal life had spilled over into and had infected his professional life. He'd worked too hard building a top-notch sales force and a marketing department that should have taken two men to assemble. He owed it to himself to discover which variables had changed in the marketplace and map out a strategy for rolling with those changing times. Now furious that his obsession with scheming on Delta almost cost him a six-figure position and all of his self-respect, Kenton buckled down and got busy securing both of them.

Kenton pressed the intercom to alert his assistant of his immediate needs. "Ms. Carson, please hold all of my calls unless informed otherwise."

"Yes, sir."

"I'll also need you to pull last year's sales reports for the third quarter."

"I'll take care of that, sir."

"Then, see if you can pull last month's premise-visits log. Oh, and one other thing."

"Sir?"

"Schedule an emergency sales meeting for noon, everyone's dining in today."

"I'll get right on that, sir."

"Thank you, Ms. Carson."

"You're very welcome, Mr. Reese," she said, smiling from ear to ear. After turning off the intercom, she began to chase the orders that Kenton had barked without hesitation. With a song in her heart, Ms. Carson floated off to the copy room with documents in hand. "He's baaack, and there's gonna be trouble."

For the first time in his career, Kenton was in trouble. He was determined to make that trouble go away, even if that meant having to deliver the burden to someone else's doorstep. After Ms. Carson provided the records that Kenton had requested, he closed himself in the confines of his office and slashed through them with a skillful pen and microscope. He was on a mission and left no stones un-turned. Three hours later, he hit the intercom button again. "Ms. Carson."

"Sir?"

"Please locate Byron Myers and have him report directly to my office, asap."

"Yes, sir. Is that all, Mr. Reese?"

"Dream Creams is at war, Ms. Carson."

"I know, sir."

Kenton spent the next twenty-seven minutes pacing in his office and cursing for getting blown so far off course that his livelihood and business reputation were at stake. He shook his head, cursed the night he met Delta, and tried to convince himself that he was better off now that she was a painful but fleeting memory. Memories he'd soon forget, or so he thought.

"Yes, Mr. Reese?" announced Byron Myers, standing in Kenton's office like a timid animal. "You sent for me?"

"Yes, I did, Byron, but why don't you call me Kenton?" He walked over to his best sales rep and casually threw his right arm around Byron's neck, offering a friendly gesture while closing the door with his free hand. Before Byron had the chance to see the next pitch, it had already zoomed by him. "You might be asking yourself why I think it's a good idea that you call me by my first name after all these years of keeping it professional? Well, it's be-cause I will no longer allow you to defile my family name!" he shouted.

"But, Mr. Reese!"

"Kenton!"

"No, Mr. Reese, I can't. I'm sorry, but I don't want to insult you."

"If you didn't want to insult me, Byron, you should have come to me when your major chain-store orders dipped twenty-five per-cent."

"Please forgive me," Byron whined, misting up around the eyes. "You've put so much time into training me, and I didn't want to let you down. It was like a bad magic trick that went terribly wrong. At first I couldn't pull the rabbit out of the hat; then I couldn't pull anything out of it. It was like a bad dream, especially losing some of my top accounts to the Tasty Treats' hired gun."

"Tasty Treats? They brought in a ringer?"

"Uh-huh, this D.T. Niles is supposed to be a real heavy hitter from Kansas City."

So vehemently frustrated that the competition had imported a big shot to steal the accounts he'd personally landed before passing them off to sales associates, the closer's name slipped past him. "But this is my town," Kenton proclaimed, reminiscing on yesterday gone by. "It wasn't long ago that I blew in from Philly and pulled the same jack move on some sleeping dogs that had gotten too fat to get off the porch to hustle for business. There's one thing I had to learn the hard way, though—sometimes it's best to let sleeping dogs lie, because they just might get the notion to bite that ass. Isn't that right, Byron?"

"Ass biting is good, sir. I highly recommend that we hop off the porch and get to biting that ass. Sir."

"That's the killer instinct we need around here. Meet me in the conference room with the others and we'll discuss how to send this Niles dude back to KC with his drawse on fire." Kenton declared war on their newest rival, Tasty Treats and their new hired gun, assuming he was up against the powers of a man.

With five of his top sales reps on hand, Kenton scolded them for letting another company take food from off their tables, and he admitted that he was also guilty of sleeping at the wheel. After he dispensed with the blame, there was the business of sharing the sales analysis he put together. "Listen up and hear me well, because our futures hinge on what happens over the next week," Kenton warned them. "Dream Creams has been attacked. Our sales force has been attacked. And most of all, your reputation as crackerjack closers has been attacked. Maybe that's acceptable to you, but I'm not having it. On a whole, our sales numbers are down for the first time in three years, and there is no one to blame but us. This is what we'll do to win back the accounts we've lost and increase orders from the clients who've placed us on the bottom rack." Kenton ordered each of his top producers to hit the stores they've done business with and compare the availability of shelf space against Tasty Treats products. Next, they were told to contact their buyers by phone, then send a small token of appreciation in the way of a thanks-for-your-business gift, and follow those up by a surprise "I care" visit to see how their kids are doing in school and if they're still on the diets they started last year. Kenton had pulled all of those tricks and countless others to build rapport with a potential decision maker and with store managers who needed a little encouragement to increase their orders from time to time.

Kenton also knew that his larger clientele, especially those with female buyers, were accustomed to getting his personal attention at least once a month. But because his client list grew exponentially, there was no way for him to continue spreading himself around and manage his team at the same time. So far, junior associates had adequately picked up the slack and learned the business one sale at a time, although the absence of Kenton's signature touch still left much to be desired. Clients with male buyers had standing gentlemen's agreements to sustain their orders and contact him personally if they planned on decreasing them significantly. Since he had received only one such call from Martin Burke, there were a few gentlemen on his list who had some explaining to do.

After adjourning the meeting, Kenton sent them off to do as he instructed. Byron stood around awaiting instructions from his immediate manager. "What about me, Mr. Reese?"

"Glad you asked. Grab your presentation bag and meet me down in the parking garage."

"Where are we going?"

"To see some old friends."

11

Tasty Treats

Byron chauffeured while Kenton plotted dual sales calls throughout the day. The first stop was the Big Elf Vending dealership. Jack McGinty ran a growing business, a business near ruin until Kenton suggested the owner sell franchises to interested buyers with whom he had long-term relationships. Within a year, Jack had purchased two thousand new machines and had sold hundreds of out-of-town franchise packages. He was rolling in the dough, but his purchases from Dream Creams had all but come to a screeching halt. Byron got nothing short of the runaround when he did call to inquire why, but Kenton knew how to cut to the chase and spread it on real thick.

Byron sat anxiously in a vinyl-covered chair in the reception area, with his presentation bag resting on his lap. Kenton never could sit still when money was on the table, so he paced back and forth until Jack McGinty sent for them to enter his office. Byron stared peculiarly at the small man dressed in a black apron, busy shining a huge pair of lizard-skin boots just outside Jack's office. Upon entering the owner's office, Kenton remembered how much of a stereotypical Southerner he was. The office was decorated from wall to wall with ranch-hand keepsakes and football memorabilia. The crowning piece was an actual Texas longhorn head, stuffed and mounted above an antique writing desk, hand carved from solid oak.

"There's the man I want to see," Kenton said with arms opened wide. "How's my favorite Texan these days? You old rattlesnake." He could talk the talk as well as walk the walk. Byron cowered back in the corner because Jack's girth, brashness, and glass eye scared the life out of him.

Mr. McGinty, all six foot five and three hundred pounds of him, stood from that ridiculously Western tree stump of a desk and clomped over to greet Kenton with only athletic tube socks covering his enormous feet. "Well, if it ain't Kenton Reese. Come on over here and give her a shake. It's been a month of Sundays since you brought your skinny butt around these parts." He brushed his broad forehead with the back of his thick paw after he began to sweat. "Things will be a heap easier to swallow when the Cowboys get their quarterback situation straight. Another game like the last one, and I'm gonna have a talk with that interception machine they just signed from Bal-ti-more."

"And the grandkids?" Kenton asked, knowing that would really get him going.

Jack gusted with pride over the mere mention of them. "Hell, they're all growing taller than Mississippi swamp grass, but my wife done went and put 'em in some sadiddy private school."

"Private school?" Kenton shouted, playing the game. "Whudda y'all trying to do, ruin 'em? That'll make 'em soft'n bathroom paper."

"That's what I told my Rose, but she went and got the idea that the grandkids ought to be more cultured."

"And what's that cost of the culture you can't wash off after that snotty school gets done with them?"

Jack's smile grew until it rolled into a hearty chuckle. "That's why I've taken a shine to you, Kenton. You take the time to be neighborly."

"Who're you kidding, Jack? You've taken a shine to me because I figured out a way to put money in your pockets after you'd taken a bath on those crappy snacks you couldn't give away." Kenton's expression hardened when it was time to get down to the reason he stopped by. "Now, I need something from you. I've heard a rumor that you're doing most of your business with another outfit called Tasty Treats. That makes me look bad to my people, Jack. Private schools and football aside, how's business?"

"You know, I can't complain." He glared at Byron, who was afraid to look him in the eye, the dead eye. "But that scrawny little pip over yonder, he comes around wasting my time and tripping all over his words. I can't stand a man who can't look you in the face when he's trying to sell you something."

"Humph, is that why you've stopped trading with us, 'cause you don't approve of my associate?" When Jack shook his meaty head, Kenton knew there was more to it than that. He placed his hand on the giant teddy bear's shoulder. "There was a time when I could count on you, Jack, and you could count on me. Well, you can still count on me. Can I say the same?"

Jack McGinty's barrel chest heaved out as he took a deep breath. He nodded, his good eye locked on Kenton's. "Yep, Big Elf Vending is up and running today because I took your advice when you didn't know me from a bastard calf."

"I told you those newfangled Fudgitos were a big mistake. Nobody likes chocolate poured over salsa chips. But you know what everybody does like?"

"Dream Creams snacks?"

"Yep," Kenton answered, "Dream Creams snacks."

Kenton waved Byron over, who'd been told to have an order form ready for Jack to sign. He'd seen Kenton work his magic before, but this performance was breathtaking. It took all he had not to start bawling and get the contract all soaking wet. As Jack agreed to double his previous orders, he choked back on a tear or two.

"I hope this fixes things between us, Kenton. I owe you big, and I should have let you know the first time that pretty girl showed up here pushing discounts for her product line."

While looking over the order form, Kenton wanted to make sure that his ears still worked as well as his charm. "Jack, did you say a pretty girl is the one who almost busted up our friendship?"

"Yep, but she was real pretty and offered a hefty discount."

Byron wanted to disappear when Kenton turned his head with a stinging leer to burn him down where he stood. "Nobody told me that I was losing business to a female," he huffed, flashing his male-chauvinism card. "Byron, you're getting beat out by a girl."

Jack actually giggled when he heard Kenton berate his associate. "She could run circles around him and kick his scary ass up and down the block. And she's real pretty."

"So you've told me; but since when did you start letting a woman bulldoze you?"

Jack stroked his chin before answering. "Well, let's see. I got married back in seventy-two. You want me to go back further than that?" It was hopeless. It seemed that everywhere Kenton looked, men were being persuaded, dissuaded, and deflated by a woman, him included. "Kenton, you might know this one. She's your sister."

"What do you mean? I don't have a sister."

"She's a colored girl," Jack answered, as if that made all the sense in the world. "I thought all you brothers called your women sisters."

"Oh you mean sistas."

"That's what I said, sisters."

"Jack, you're not making it any better. And are you suggesting that every brotha knows every sista?"

"Well, yeah. This'n was a smooth talker like you, and real pretty," he added again, behind a wide smile.

Funny thing was, Kenton did know her. He just didn't know it. He looked at Byron then back at Jack, who was still smiling after getting his favorite salesman's goat. "Both of y'all better be glad I like white people." Kenton smirked with a raised brow. "Come on, Byron, we've got to make tracks. Oh, and Jack, I want a pair of those lizards sent to my office, size twelve."

"No problem, Kenton," he yelled as his visitors departed on good terms. "You should probably look that sister up. She was real pretty."

As soon as they made it to the car, Kenton began looking at the day planner for the next appointment. Byron wasn't sure whether to offer congratulations or further excuses after that potential train wreck. "Mr. Reese, what went on back there was the best close I'd ever seen. Pure genius. I'm so sorry it came to this. You doing my work, I mean."

"Don't mention it, but I hope you won't forget it, either. That's what a good relationship can do for you when it's time to knock one over the fence in a pinch. Every closer should build relationships that mean something to all of the parties involved. You'll do fine if you remember that instead of trying to get people to buy something they don't need. But everyone can use a good working relationship."

"A new contract from Jack McGinty and a pair of boots all in ten minutes," Byron marveled.

"I'm glad you're impressed. He's billing my boots to you."

As Byron reflected on how easily his boss had worked over his toughest client, he knew the rest of the appointments were guaranteed successes. After seeing Kenton sweet-talk two blushing Wal-Mart buyers before lunch, his assumptions for success were on the money. Kenton was back in action and a force to be dealt with. In fact, the entire week followed suit. Byron had the majority of his clients back, and dozens of orders for prepackaged desserts flooded Mr. Tearny's office.

By Friday, Kenton's swagger had returned and his confidence was restored. A note met him at the door after he danced his way down the hallway leading to his office. "Morning, Ms. Carson," he sang.

"Morning, sir," she said, reading him like a sales advertisement. Seconds later, she stood from her desk and sambaed her way over to the filing cabinet. "Whatever he caught is contagious."

Kenton's week had gone by so fast that he didn't have time to think about Delta. From the moment he made the decision to push her out of his life, it had been all gravy. He loved gravy. He also loved the idea of getting back to the way things used to be. Welcoming a hopping Friday night with the fellas at the Café happy hour and catching up on some old business, or two or three, felt good down to his toes. He was still buzzing with those good vibrations when he read the note that was taped to his door. "Mr. Reese, Byron called in sick," he read aloud. "Has urgent meeting with Shine Bright Grocers at nine." Kenton glanced at his watch. "It's already eight thirty-five. I'd better get another pair of boots out of this."

He grabbed the tablet filled with the research he'd requisitioned earlier in the week and asked Ms. Carson to page him at precisely 9:30. He'd be in the middle of making a stellar presentation by then, and an emergency page always makes the buyer think the closer is in high demand. It's an old salesman's trick that's still as effective as it was the first time someone thought to try it out.

Shine Bright Grocers' corporate office was an eight-story brown-brick golden opportunity for a man with bright ideas and the determination to keep them afloat as long as necessary to capture the brass ring. Kenton was that man. He'd placed the brass ring in a trophy case, and now someone was trying to take it from him. The Shine Bright account had always been the crown jewel, one that he wouldn't give up without a fight; but he never anticipated being pitted against his newest nemesis, D.T. Niles. That was a match for the ages. One of epic proportions, and the audience would not be disappointed.

Martin Burke thought it best to invite sales representatives from his two leading snack food manufacturers to make their sales pitches to his leadership team, which was comprised of local store managers. The only problem was, no one warned Kenton. He was caught off guard when he learned the rules of engagement, although it paled in comparison to what he discovered as being fair in love and war.

The discovery portion of the lesson began the moment Kenton stepped off the elevator on the eighth floor. Delta had already checked in and had taken a seat outside the conference room. She was wrapping up a business call, or so it appeared when Kenton informed the new receptionist who he was and that he had arrived to meet with Martin Burke at nine o'clock. The Barbie doll look-alike smiled at him longer than Delta deemed appropriate, so she snapped the flip phone shut, making a loud noise to signal her disapproval. Only it was Kenton she was signaling to. Her tactic worked, too well for the young receptionist's taste. Barbie turned up her nose as she called to alert Martin that both competing companies were duly represented.

Somewhat pleasantly surprised to find Delta lounging in the visitor's area, he assumed she was there on a personal call to see Martin. "Hey, Delta, I wouldn't have expected to see you here, but I guess it makes sense; although you might have to wait before you get to visit with Martin. He and I have a few business concerns to discuss."

"And so do you and I," she said, neglecting to say hello. "But I thought that some Byron somebody was making the pitch for your company this morning." When Kenton flashed a blank look back at her, she shook her head. "Something tells me that you still don't have a clue why I'm here. And you can rule out me hooking up with Martin, 'cause it's strictly business between us."

"Frankly, I don't care what's between y'all. I'm just passing through to make some magic happen, then bounce."

"I heard about the magic act you ran on Big Elf Vending," she hissed, with her arms folded. "I could have sold Jack McGinty the Brooklyn Bridge, but no, you had to go getting all up in his head and confusing matters. I worked hard to gain his confidence when in the beginning all he could see was a pretty young thing in a tight skirt."

For a total of five seconds, Kenton replayed every interaction that tied his business to Delta, including Jack going overboard about how pretty the smooth-talking sister was. He rethought the discussion he'd had with Byron when he first heard of a big-shot closer brought in from Kansas City, which happened to be Delta's home town; then he flashed all the way back to the morning she left a cute little thank-you note on his kitchen counter, signed D.T. Niles. Five seconds later, reality smacked him upside the head.

"You!" he shouted. "You're D.T. Niles."

"Delta Tonise Niles," she announced proudly. "Yes, but I go by D.T. from nine to five because there are too many chauvinistic cavemen who wouldn't let me in the door if they knew I was a woman before they booked appointments."

Kenton, still shocked, held his mouth open while she spoke. "You're the ringer from KC?" He began to laugh hysterically. "If that don't beat all. You've been pumping me, for what, information? Company secrets?"

"No, I've just been pumping you," she answered, then rolled her eyes up toward the ceiling.

"Uh-uh-uh, Delta is Tasty's big hitter." Kenton was determined to make the situation worse. When a man decides to make a fool of himself, no one can stop him. Delta was about to learn that firsthand.

"Before you go too far left to get it right, I was going to tell you about my job that night we met, then one thing led to another. You started in with all that noncommittal stuff and I thought I'd never see you again. Besides, Kenton, during all that noncommitting and apologizing we've been up to, you've not once asked me what I liked, how I made a living, or even where I live. You don't know anything about me because what matters to me wasn't important. With you, it's got to be about Kenton, all about Kenton, and nothing but the Kenton, so help you God."

"Is that your best shot?" he asked, unimpressed and apparently unmoved.

"Not hardly," Delta answered plainly. "But now that I've said my piece, I'm prepared to march into Martin's team meeting with your selfish ass and show you what my best is. You'll know you've been in a fight when I'm done."

"Good, so you've had a chance to catch up," Martin teased when he stumbled on the nasty spat between former acquaintances. "Before we begin the presentations for Shine Bright's business, does anyone need more time to prepare? No? Then let's get the show on the road."

12

Old Player's Retirement Home

Seven of Shine Bright's eager team leaders relaxed around a mahogany conference table. When Kenton got a sense of how this concocted competition was going down, he asked Barbie to make nine copies of three different reports before he took his seat. Barbie dashed away and Martin stood to introduce the representatives from both companies.

"As you all know, we've asked our top two snack manufacturers to visit with us this morning and present their cases for our limited shelf space. I've had dealings with them both, and I'm sure that they'll be brief, to the point, and civil." Martin smiled nervously at Delta and Kenton, remembering the tone he heard just moments before. His associates passed confused expressions among themselves, regarding their guests' civility. This was a business meeting after all. "Since I am a Southern boy at heart, I'll allow D.T. Niles of Tasty Treats to proceed first." He glanced at Kenton, who was staring out the window as if his mind had traveled several miles away. "I hope you don't object to that, Kenton?"

"Ladies first, I always say." Sure he wanted her to go first, so he could stare her down and rattle her confidence.

Delta stood, handed out prepackaged pamphlets, which were produced by her marketing department, then she jumped right into the ring. "Good morning, everyone. As Mr. Burke said, I am D.T. Niles, the lead sales rep for Tasty Treats. What you have before you is a thorough product breakdown of our extensive line, one that has been awarded the FDA Crown of Consciousness, recognizing the company making the biggest strides toward a healthier America. And also might I add that our signature line of Mini-Munchables are low carb and sugar-free." The associates began looking through the handout, nodding as they followed along, until Kenton began thinking aloud.

"Mini-Munchables aren't the only thing that's sugar-free."

Martin's eyes rose from the notes he'd jotted down. He held his breath and looked at Delta for signs of trepidation, but there were none. She shook her head ever so faintly, winked at him, and poised herself to continue.

"On page three, you'll see that the latest health study proves that Americans are moving in a positive direction that can be summed up in the following fitness and low-fat diets. It's no news that Americans have steadily packed on the pounds over the last five decades, and unfortunately, we've not put our past behind us but are rather putting up with bigger behinds because of our past." The witty joke drew slight chuckles from both men and women seated around the table. "The climate is changing in the snack food industry, and Tasty Treats is leading the way." Delta stood near Kenton to make her next point, while getting back at his snide remark. "We are committed to helping those who want to stop gorging themselves on reconstituted, overvalued, chocolate-covered, nonnutritional desserts. Americans deserve better and we've positioned ourselves to offer delicious, fulfilling products. A company would have to be too self-absorbed with tired, self-indulgent, self-destructive behavior, in the business sense of course, to pass on such an outstanding proposition as ours." She looked down on Kenton's head, smacked her lips, then moved along to continue. Martin had to cover his mouth with his hand to keep from laughing out loud. Score another one for Delta. A few team leaders had certainly caught on that something was simmering beneath the surface. Others sat at attention when they got the feeling that the meeting was sure to get even more spirited. Their wishes came true when Kenton scratched his cheek and tore the wrapper off a can of wait-until-they-get-a-load-of-me.

"Is that it?" Kenton asked with a bored expression.

"I don't think you'd know what "it" was if it was to sit down right next to you," Delta suggested as she smirked and took the seat beside him. This time Martin let a chuckle slip out before he could stop it, but he tried to cover it with a loud cough. Now everyone around the table had suspicions that Delta and Kenton's relationship was more than business related.

Barbie returned with a stack of copies for Kenton and placed them on the credenza. She threw Kenton a subtle smile before she sashayed away. Martin missed it because he was fixated on how things were getting out of hand. He swallowed hard and exhaled even harder. "Perhaps this meeting should be rescheduled for a more appropriate time," he recommended, figuring that things could get worse, a lot worse, if allowed to continue. When Kenton stood to insist that he be given the opportunity to defend his company's honor, every associate looking on breathed a sigh of relief. After years of lackluster presentations, this was shaping up to be a snipe-fest extravaganza.

"If you don't mind, Martin, I believe the show must go on." Kenton straightened his designer necktie. He eyed the stack of well-documented trends and sales reports he'd brought along but thought better of issuing them. It was time for some good old-fashioned grandstanding. Martin acquiesced and sat down. Now that Kenton had the floor, he relished the chance to wipe it with Delta. "Good morning. I'm Kenton Reese, for those of you I haven't had the pleasure of meeting personally. At Dream Creams, my responsibilities include managing a topflight sales team and assuring that venders, as well as store managers, understand exactly what it is that we offer to our consumers." The tall redhead sitting at the far end of the table looked as if she wanted to become a consumer on the spot. "True, it's no secret that Americans have generally passed on sodium-free, taste-free, albeit healthy, snacks utilizing sugar substitutes in order to avail themselves of fluffy, cream-filled, chocolaty goodness. We all want what's good for us, but not all the time. Take Ding-Dings for instance, our marquee item. There's something about taking a shot at being sinfully satisfied that upstages the thought of wasting time with mini-munchies. That's why Dream Creams' products continually outsell the competition, whose offerings tend to leave one wanting." All eyes averted from Kenton to Delta, eager for a tasty comeback.

"Just so that I understand what my company is up against, are we to believe that Dream Creams considers itself a top-shelf snack maker while manufacturing the likes of low-end ghetto cupcakes and marketing them as a Ring Ding knockoff?"

"That's cute, but our consumers just can't get enough of our *Ding-Dings* exploding in their mouths."

"Hold on a minute," Martin protested. "I'm not sure if we're still talking about dessert snacks or not, but if I don't stop this now, I'll need a cigarette." He read his wristwatch, then the faces of his anticipating associates. "Why don't you two step out in the reception area and let us discuss a few impending matters. We'll send for you when we've made a decision."

Delta grabbed her purse and stomped out the door with Kenton on her heels. "You're a trip," he spat as they spilled out into the waiting area. "Self-absorbed? Self-indulgent? You're the cover girl for Freak-of-the-Weekday magazine."

Delta huffed, then snapped at Barbie, who was pretending to be fast at work but who obviously had both ears open and tuned in. "Is there some other place you could be right now? I think you've showed your tail enough already." The receptionist removed her headset and took her sweet time collecting her belongings before she made herself scarce, stating that it was almost time for her morning break anyway.

"Okay then!" Delta backed Kenton up against the wall by poking her index finger against his chest. "I've had about all I can stand from you, too. Let's put aside all the snide comments and bravado and speak plain English. I never meant to conceal my job, but you wanted to keep our thing casual to the point of keeping everything non-Kenton out of our conversations. I allowed it. That was my mistake, but our agreement is the reason why I had to keep you at arm's length or jeopardize getting my feelings hurt."

"What about my feelings?" Kenton said, trying to melt Delta's defenses.

"What about them? As far as I'm concerned, you don't have any."

"Oh, that's cold. Just because I don't wear them on my sleeve doesn't mean I'm less than human. I have feelings like everyone else."

"If you don't show them, Kenton, how do you know they exist?" Kenton's befuddled expressions proved Delta's point. "Just as I thought. That's the problem with men who have it all but refuse to share it with anyone. You're going to turn into the kind of man who everybody laughs at behind his back, a perverted rusty-dusty sugar daddy chasing after young tail and living in an old player's retirement home. Take a good look at yourself, Kenton Reese, because that's the future of a man who grows old trying to keep his options open at all costs. That's the cost, a disgusting Viagra-popping senior citizen, paying for what you're getting free today. Enjoy it while it lasts. Time has a way of fixing selfish brothas in the end. You'll see, when you're old, crusty, and alone."

Martin ducked his head out the door to invite them into the room, but Kenton's icy glare sent him back to where he came from. "If I didn't know better, I'd think you really cared. That's cute, the way you're all hot, bothered, and pissed off. All at the same time, too."

"Whatever man," she responded, visibly exasperated.

"It's okay if you care about me. Actually, I think I like it. It kinda tickles." At nine-thirty on the nose, Kenton's pager went off. Ms. Carson was on the job.

"I guess that's one of your playmates trying to holler?"

"Nah, that's my executive assistant paging me like I asked her to. I told her that I would be in the middle of something and may need a distraction, leverage."

"Are you going to utilize the distraction, considering how you've passed on the leverage option by being straight with me?"

"I could have said that it was a sista trying to get at me, but why would I want to mess up what I'm working on here. Especially when she cares about me and she's so pretty."

"That's the first real compliment I've gotten from you." Delta blushed, melting where she stood. "You know what else? It kinda tickles, too."

"I think that's my first time pulling it off without actually touching a woman."

"Silly man, you touched me all right, where it counts the most. You should do that more often. If you want to get real good, it'll take some practice, but I'm willing to work with you."

"Oh, you're willing to work with me? That's good. I'm looking to schedule all the practice I can get." Kenton felt around in his pockets in dramatic fashion, as if he was looking for something. "Where'd I put my Platinum Player Card? Looks like I'll have to cancel my account, probably got too many frequent-hoochie miles on it anyway."

"You gonna stand there and play with me? Because I'd be more than happy to call downtown and have your player privileges revoked," Delta played along.

"On the serious tip. I do need you to know that my life has been different in the short time you've graced it with your presence. I've missed meals and lost sleep because of you, which told me what I needed to know. That's why I'm telling you I don't want to be a player no more, and I sure as hell don't want to grow old and crusty all by myself." Kenton was as serious as the atmosphere allowed. He had fallen hard for Delta and had confessed it to her after finally admitting it to himself.

Martin opened the door, wider than the first time. "Uh, excuse me, but we're running out of jokes to pass the time, so could you please?"

Delta had to resist the urge to hold Kenton's hand as they returned to the meeting room. Funny thing was, he was fighting the same urge. The associates watched them attentively, noting that the tone had changed dramatically. Although the show was over, they imagined what the sequel might have held in store.

"Even though we'd all like to know what was behind the pensive sparring session, I'm sure it's not any of our affair," Martin told his guests. "On another note, regarding the other reason we assembled today, I've heard enough from both of you to know how important it is to offer Shine Bright's customers the option to be both good and bad, when either mood hits them. That's why we have decided to retain both distributors and sign a multiyear contract. At Shine Bright, we value passionate individuals and good relationships. Hopefully, the both of you will, too. Congratulations."

Kenton followed Delta down the hall, to the elevator, and out to the visitor's parking lot. She smiled the entire way, thankful that she played her cards right. Now she was looking forward to a real shot at love. Whether she knew it or not, she hooked him by refusing to lay her head where she didn't belong and by refusing to sacrifice her peace of mind for the sake of preserving his. And to think she almost caved in against her better judgment. Good thing she knew better.

Kenton's brand-new smile was caused by other reasons altogether. He was contemplating all the benefits of becoming a one-woman man and building memories instead of trying to keep them straight for fear of getting busted if he didn't. For him, there would be no more half-truths and no more clean sweeps. The more he thought about it, the more he wondered why he hadn't given this love thing a shot long before then. A love deferred was always there, just waiting in the wings, as it has for every man. Fortunately for Delta, Kenton didn't know better, until he met her.

At Your Service

Earl Sewell

1

Franklin

Franklin plopped a stack of papers down on his desk, slouched down in his chair, and inhaled deeply to calm his nerves. He'd just scampered from his boss's office where he'd been criticized, yet again, about the quality and production levels of his work. Franklin and his golden-haired, overweight, and bloated boss Chris seemed to be going through some sort of respect slump. Being Chris's subordinate was becoming increasingly difficult. Chris seemed to have an issue with the notion that Franklin couldn't flip open his skull and read his mind or think exactly like him. The thought of Chris made Franklin pinch his eyebrows into an angry expression. He contemplated marching back into Chris's office to bark at him like a maniac, just to get some things off of his chest, but at that moment his phone rang. He glared at the phone as if it was a foreign object. He focused on the caller ID display and saw that it was Chris phoning him.

"What the hell do you want now?" Franklin hissed through clenched teeth before answering the phone. He knew that when Chris wanted to, he could be as cold as January in Chicago.

"Yes, Chris?" Franklin attempted to sound pleasant, but it was difficult because contempt for Chris was in his heart at that moment.

"Did you finish registering all of the traders who had disciplinary actions against them? It was a priority, remember?"

"No, I haven't. You gave me another priority last week that took up all of my time." He listened as Chris grumbled with dissatisfaction into the phone.

"I just don't understand why you couldn't get the registrations completed," Chris expressed his irritation.

I just told your ass why, thought Franklin.

"I would have made that a priority over the other priority."

There goes Chris again with the I-would-have philosophy. What, am I supposed to be able to read your jacked-up brain? Franklin thought. Franklin wanted to snarl at him and tell him that he hadn't taken Mind Reading 101 and didn't appreciate him trying to use the fucking Jedi Mind Trick on him.

"You need to get the rest of those traders registered; it's a priority."

"What about the assignment you just gave me a moment ago? You said it was a priority that needed to get completed before lunch. Which one do you want me to work on first?" There was a long pause, and Franklin knew Chris's lard ass didn't know what he wanted completed first.

"Umm, you should work on the registrations first. No, wait, finish up the New York accounts first, and then let me see what you've done. No"—he was about to change his mind, yet again—"the auditors are coming and those traders would be accused of illegal activity if the auditors discovered they weren't registered. Register the traders first."

"I'm on it," said Franklin, and placed the receiver on its cradle. Franklin leaned back in his seat and stared mindlessly up at the light fixture, unconcerned with Chris and his recent order. Franklin began to think about how their professional relationship had gone sour. He believed it began when he decided he wanted to take the Series 63 test and become a licensed stockbroker. The more Franklin worked with stockbrokers, the more he realized where the big money was. Working with successful brokers who could produce one million dollars a year excited and encouraged him to blaze his own path in the world of finance. Chris, on more than one occasion, attempted to discourage him from studying for the exam. However, company policy stated it would pay for any employee who wanted to take the exam. The hook was, if an employee passed the exam, they would agree to stay with the company for at least two years. Franklin believed Chris had an issue with him wanting to be a trader rather than stay in the restricted position where he had authority over him. *He'd probably have a heart attack if I passed the exam*, Franklin reasoned, because he knew Chris had taken the exam twice and had failed both times.

Franklin only planned to stay in the financial industry until he earned enough money to achieve his dream of owning a sports club. He began to organize the entrepreneurial thoughts that were cluttering his mind. Ever since he was seduced into bodybuilding as a young teen, he'd yearned to be the owner of a fitness complex. Over the years, Franklin had developed the concept of an all-inclusive state-of-the art facility. His facility would offer guidance on nutrition, injury prevention and recovery, along with training programs for athletes of all levels and backgrounds. His vision included offering programs for people who only wanted to walk to stay fit to athletes who wanted to compete at fitness expos, bodybuilding competitions, or do something extreme like bicycling across the country. He would have professional massage therapists on staff and would offer programs for people who didn't know their way around a gym. He'd offer everything from proper weight-lifting techniques to selecting the proper shoes for the walking club members. He even had a name for his visionary facility. It would be called "Body Shaping."

"What's up, playboy?" Darzel, Franklin's burly friend from the Information Technology Department, sauntered into his office.

"My shit is all funky today, man," answered Franklin. "People around here are tripping out."

"Calm down, player. Don't let them see you sweat. You know everyone catches an attitude when the auditors come."

"Sometimes it's hard to keep your cool when your heart isn't in it," Franklin admitted. At that moment, Franklin's phone rang yet again.

"Damn," he hissed without looking at the caller display.

"Look here, don't go postal up in here; keep your cool, all right? I don't want you to end up tossing some dude's salad in prison." Darzel slapped the top of Franklin's wooden desk twice with the palm of his hand and then excused himself. The phone rang three times before Franklin finally picked it up.

"Franklin, I need you to handle this call." It was Chris. "I have a stock broker on the line who is trying to put a big trade through in California, but they won't let him because he has no registration paperwork on file."

"All right, transfer the call," said Franklin, relieved that Chris wasn't calling with more disparagement.

After Franklin ended his call and took care of the traders' needs, he got up from his desk and headed for the break room to fill his container with ice water. By the time he returned to his desk, his phone was once again ringing.

"This is Franklin," he answered without glancing at the caller ID.

"Hey there," greeted the voice at the other end. "How are you doing today?"

"Mom?" Franklin was making certain it was his mother on the line. She only called him at work when some type of drama had happened or was on the horizon.

"Yeah, it's me." She sighed depressingly.

"What's up?" Franklin sat down to prepare himself.

"What time will you be home tonight?" she asked.

"Why? What's going on?"

"I need to talk to you about something, in private. I don't want that nasty girlfriend of yours around when I drop by. You know I don't like her eyes. She looks shifty. Whenever she talks to me she can't look me in the eyes. I don't like people like that. She must be dynamite in other areas, because she can't get by on her looks. And the next time I call your house and she smacks her lips on the phone at me, I'm going to pop her in the mouth. She needs to respect me as your mother."

"Mom, you know what, I really don't have time for this. I'm already stressed out. I've got work that needs to get finished." Franklin grabbed the pile of registration papers from his work-in-progress basket.

"And that woman's attitude needs to be tightened up." His mother, Lois, ignored Franklin and continued expressing her disdain for his live-in girlfriend. "Never in my life have I ever met a woman who always has her panties in a knot."

"Mom," Franklin decided it was time to end their conversation. "I'll call you on my lunch break, all right?"

"Why? Don't you have time for me anymore?" Lois was offended by her son's lack of interest in what she had to say about his relationship.

"I don't have time right now." Franklin began pulling file folders from his desk drawer.

"Well, I'm going to drop by your apartment tonight. I need to borrow some money from you." That got Franklin's attention.

"Money? What for this time?"

"What do mean, what for this time? You act as if I call you every day asking for money."

"It feels that way. And just so you know, I don't have anything extra to give you."

"It's that nappy-headed girlfriend of yours, isn't it? Ever since you got a bank account with her, your money hasn't been right. Are you just handing her your paycheck like some damn fool? I've taught you better than that. What you need to do is open up an account with me. I'm your mother, and you'd never have any cash-flow problems if I was handling things for you."

"Mom, I'm going to get off the phone now. You have a nice day."

"Don't you hang up on me, boy!" Lois barked at Franklin. "I need a loan from you."

"For what?" Franklin asked again.

"The city has put a boot on my car and towed it away."

"Damn, Mom. I've told you a million times not to park that car illegally. How much do you need?" Franklin asked, wanting to avoid conflict and a long drawn-out argument with her.

"One thousand dollars."

"A thousand dollars!" Franklin raised his voice louder than he intended to.

"You say it like I asked for one million dollars." Lois had a defiant tone in her voice.

"A thousand dollars is a lot of money, Mom."

"And?" Lois said with an edgy tone. A moment of silence hung in the air before Lois broke it. "You can get the money, right?"

Franklin exhaled aggravated wisps of air. "Do you really need the money?"

"I wouldn't ask for it if I didn't need it, honey. You know how much I depend on you. We're a team. Whenever one of us gets in a jam, we're there for each other. You know that. It's always been that way. You're a big man with a college degree, making big money. I know you can spare a little for your mother who helped put you through college." Lois tossed in a reminder to refresh his memory about the scheming she had to do in order to help pay for his education.

"Yeah, I know. Let me talk with Cassandra about it and see what she says."

"Cassandra!" Lois got angry. "She doesn't need to know my damn business. I'm your mother. Cassandra doesn't have a damn thing to do with what transpires between you and me. You're treating her like she's your wife or something. You need to get your priorities in order, son."

"Cassandra and I are talking about marriage; you know that. We've been saving money for it."

"I don't have long in this world. I've got one foot on the ground and the other one in the grave. I ask for a little help from you and you want to bring me a conversation about Cassandra. You're picking her over me. That's cold-blooded, Franklin. You might as well push me in the grave and toss dirt on me." Franklin's head began pounding as if someone was inside his skull hitting it with a sledgehammer.

"Mom, you know that's not true. I'm not trying to put you in your grave."

"Yes, you are," Lois disputed his claim.

"Damn! Fine!" Franklin had had enough of the cat-and-mouse game with his mother. "I'll have the money for you." Franklin gave in, just as Lois knew he would.

"Excuse me." Franklin glanced up and saw Chris standing in the doorway with a dissatisfied expression on his face. He wasn't sure how long he'd been there eavesdropping on his conversation.

"Just come by my house tonight, all right? I'll give it to you then."

"Good, because you know I wouldn't ask for it unless I needed it," Lois continued.

"Yeah, okay, good-bye. I'll see you tonight," said Franklin, rushing her off of the phone. Before Lois could start again, Franklin hung up.

"Have you completed the registrations yet? The auditors are here."

"No, let me do it now," Franklin said, and began working at a blistering pace, feeling like a solider who'd been caught defying a direct order.

"Ugh," Chris expressed his dissatisfaction yet again as he marched away. Franklin knew he'd be hearing about this at some point. This incident would most certainly resurface during his annual performance review.

Franklin worked diligently all morning and even worked through his lunch to try and complete the registrations. At two o'clock in the afternoon, he took a break. He brought the stack of registrations he was working on with him to the lunchroom.

"The last thing I need is for one of the auditors to see this stack of paperwork and inquire about the traders who just got placed into the system today. Chris would have a fit if that happened," Franklin said aloud. He had seen Chris buzzing around the office like a fly at a picnic, gathering information the auditors were requesting.

When he entered the break room, he sat the registration papers down at an empty table while he went over to the vending machine to pay for a snack. As he was contemplating his choices, Darzel entered the break room.

"Are things going any better?" asked Darzel.

"A little," answered Franklin. "It would be even better if my mother would stay out of my pocket."

"So, you have problems with your moms on top of everything else. That's jacked up." Darzel chuckled. "I'm so glad my family doesn't bother me the way your mother and sister hound you," admitted Darzel, who had listened to Franklin on more than one occasion vent about coming to the rescue of his mother and sister. "I mean, I get hassled from time to time, but nothing like how you get harassed."

"She wants me to give her one thousand dollars," Franklin informed Darzel.

"Damn! What the hell for?"

"Her car has been impounded by the City of Chicago." Franklin made his selection and waited for the healthy snack to fall to the belly of the machine.

"Well, you can't turn your back on your moms, man."

"Yeah, I know." Franklin sighed wearily.

"Look, partner, you're not alone. My mother will call me up for some money in a heartbeat and think nothing of it. Get used to it. We're single men, and until men like us select a woman who becomes our priority, our mothers believe they're the queen of our heart."

"I have a girlfriend," Franklin challenged Darzel's logic.

"Frank, girlfriends come and go. Mothers don't give a rat's ass about a girlfriend. When you start talking about turning a girlfriend into your woman or wife, then Mom may develop an issue.

Especially if the girlfriend isn't a strong enough woman to deal with an overbearing mother."

"Darzel, we're getting off the point. I don't care about the mother versus girlfriend thing. I need to come up with something justifiable to tell Cassandra when she finds out the account is off by one thousand dollars."

"You're not going to tell Cassandra you're taking the money?" Darzel groaned.

"No, I'm just going to take it and give it to my mother. That way, it will be a done deal, and we can argue about it afterward." Franklin was rationalizing his unsavory plan.

"Frank, doing something like that to your girlfriend is going to backfire. The trust in your relationship is going to be damaged. Cassandra isn't going to take something like that lying down. Do you have a backup plan?"

"Backup plan?" Franklin chuckled.

"Frank, that's the type of move that will get your ass tossed out of the house."

"Man, please. I wish Cassandra would try some stunt like that. I'm not worried about her trying to put me out of my own condo. She lives with me, remember?"

"Well, shit, she may leave you." Darzel offered another scenario for Franklin to consider.

"Cassandra doesn't have any place to go," Franklin declared, brushing the idea off as if it lacked merit. "Besides, she'd never leave me. I'm her world. She'll be mad for a moment, then she'll get over it."

"So, you have Cassandra wrapped around your finger like that?" questioned Darzel, who didn't believe for one moment that Franklin had that type of power.

"Look, Cassandra is hooked on me like heat on fire. She'd be a fool to leave all of this." Franklin struck a pose to bring attention to his physique, which he spent countless hours at the gymnasium sculpting.

"Then why are you so worried about coming up with a justifiable answer? You're contradicting yourself, pimp daddy. You should be able to just tell her what you did, and that should be enough."

"That's right." Franklin got cocky. "I am a pimp, and what I say goes." Franklin wanted to sound convincing, but there were traces of uncertainty in his voice.

"All right, pimp daddy. If you're the king of your castle, you shouldn't have an issue." Darzel tapped Franklin on the shoulder and made to exit the break room.

Franklin was about to make a wise remark when he saw something that suddenly upset him. "Oh, shit!" Franklin whispered loudly.

"What?" Darzel asked, startled.

"One of the fucking auditors just picked up the stack of papers I left over on the table and walked out."

"What papers did you leave over there?"

"A list of newly registered traders who were trading illegally in states they're not supposed to be doing business in. Fuck, this day couldn't possibly get any worse."

"Hell, man, go catch him and get your shit back."

"That's only going to make it all the worse because then he'll make an issue out of it. They're supposed to see everything, but that was something we didn't want them to see. Damn!" Franklin's heart was pumping so hard he could feel it in his throat.

2

Lois

After Lois got off the phone with Franklin, she went into her kitchen, turned on the faucet, pulled her black cast-iron skillet from the cupboard, and washed it out. After drying the excess water out of the skillet, she turned the dial on her gas stove and placed the skillet on top of the left burner. Lois poured cooking oil into the iron skillet, eyeballing the proper amount of oil needed. As the oil warmed up, Lois scooped out some white cooking flour from its container and dumped it into a small brown bag. She opened up her refrigerator and pulled out the pork chops she had marinating in a glass bowl. She placed two pork chops in her brown bag and shook the bag. Once the oil in the skillet was hot and the pork chops were floured, she carefully placed the meat inside the skillet and watched as they sizzled. Lois then sat down in a chair at the kitchen table, crossed one leg over the other, and began to think. She couldn't stand Franklin's girlfriend Cassandra. "Cassandra makes my asshole hurt," Lois grumbled. Cassandra had access to her son's wallet, and she took issue with that.

"I've told that boy a million times that a woman should never know how much money he has. Franklin hooked up with that girl and got stupid. Cassandra is trying to undo all of the things I taught him. She's trying to change his way of thinking and cloud his judgment as to who has priority in his life," Lois grumbled aloud. She took issue with Franklin considering Cassandra's feelings above hers. No one knew or understood her Frankie the way she did. Frankie would always love her and would never leave her behind. If she wanted to, she had the power to convince Franklin of most anything. She'd instilled in him at a young age to never turn his back on her or ever challenge any of her seedy and unpardonable money-making scams. If she wanted to, Lois could convince Franklin that he could make a million dollars selling fake time-share vacation packages.

"I'm not ready for Franklin to be his own man yet. He doesn't need to rush into settling down with that nappy-headed heifer. Can't he see that she's trying to take him away from me?" Lois murmured as she continued to mull over her feelings.

"Whenever I'm in a jam, I know I can count on Franklin to bail me out. That sneaky girl is up to no good. I can feel it." Lois knew Cassandra was sneaky when she swayed Franklin into combining their bank accounts. "Then the scheming heifer turned around and moved into Franklin's condo with him," Lois continued venting. As she was examining her thoughts, Latoya, her twenty-three-year-old daughter, came bouncing into the kitchen with her music headphones on.

"Those pork chops are smelling good." Latoya spoke louder than she needed to. "What else are you cooking with them?"

"Get away from the damn stove before you scald yourself," Lois barked at her daughter, who stood in front of the skillet that was full of hot bubbling grease. "Take those damn headphones off." Latoya was a chocolate woman with beautiful black hair and raven-black eyebrows that gave her a more unique appearance. Latoya was wearing an oversized Outkast concert T-shirt, baggy blue jeans, and white tennis shoes.

"You should make some mashed potatoes to go with this," Latoya suggested as she removed her headphones and checked the status of the pork chops.

"Start peeling some potatoes if that's what you want," said Lois.

"Why? Are you headed somewhere?" Latoya asked.

"Franklin's house," Lois answered.

"Are you taking the bus or getting a cab?" Latoya asked.

"The bus." Lois sighed. "Why? Do you have money for a cab?"

"I'll pay for your cab ride over there and hook up the rest of this food if you can convince Franklin to loan me two hundred dollars."

"Two hundred dollars, for what?" Latoya's bold request irritated Lois.

"I borrowed money from my friend Vanessa. She's been hounding me for it, but I just don't have it right now. Anyway, she's got her thongs all in a knot about her money and has even hinted around at attempting to kick my behind if I don't pay her. Before I make her talk to the hand and wave to my fingers, I want to give her back the chump change she loaned me."

"Hand me the cab money." Lois held out her hand. Latoya stuffed her hand into her right pocket and pulled twenty dollars out. "I'll see what I can do, but I can't make any promises," Lois said, now that she had her fare in her hand. "Make some gravy and onions to go with the pork chops," Lois said. "I'll be back. Just leave me a plate on top of the stove. I'll heat it up when I come back," said Lois as she stood up to run her errand to Franklin's house.

Lois curled her wrist to glance at her wristwatch as she shuffled up the steps of Franklin's building later that evening.

"Franklin had better not be here yet," Lois muttered as she noticed a peculiar and scruffy-looking white man exiting the building. To her surprise, the stranger displayed good manners by holding the door open for her.

"Thank you," she spoke just above a whisper as she eased past him. She turned right, walked over to the elevator, and pressed the silver up button. She stared up at the orange elevator light, which was paused on the fourth floor. She sighed impatiently as she turned around to glance out of the window behind her. She noticed Cassandra's black sedan parked on the street but didn't see Franklin's car.

"Good." Lois sighed. "I'm glad I got here before Franklin." Lois was about to get foul with Cassandra by letting her know she was the only queen in Franklin's life.

"There isn't room for two queens," Lois grumbled.

When the elevator arrived, Lois stepped inside and pressed the third-floor button. When she got off, she turned right and walked down the hallway to Franklin's door. She curled her fingers into a fist and knocked hard with her knuckles. The echo of her knuckles drumming against the wooden door made her cringe. A short moment later, Cassandra answered the door.

"Who is it?" her voice squeaked from the other side.

"I can see your eyeball in the damn peephole. You know it's me standing out here." Lois immediately set the tone.

"Miss Harris." Cassandra opened the door. "I wasn't sure who it was or how they'd gotten into the building without ringing the buzzer. Sorry, I wasn't expecting you. Franklin hasn't made it home yet. I'm not sure when he'll be here." Lois studied Cassandra's phony smile. Cassandra was a petite caramel woman with a high-pitched voice that annoyed Lois.

"So what do you want me to do? Stand out in the hallway all evening until he arrives?" Lois had a load of snakebite in her voice. "He gave me a spare house key so you can't lock me out, even if you wanted to."

"Oh, no, I wasn't suggesting not letting you in." Cassandra's voice reached an annoying pitch. Lois frowned as she attempted to laugh off her rudeness. "Please, come on in and have a seat."

"Miss Thing, I don't know where your manners are. Franklin can do so much better for himself. I don't know why he has such a soft spot for strays like you."

"Excuse me?" Lois knew she had Cassandra's attention by the way her face wrinkled into an ugly expression as if she was sniffing a foul odor. Lois smirked at her. She was about to give Cassandra a complex, and she was going to enjoy doing it because she knew Cassandra was full of insecurities. She knew of her flaws, because Franklin had told her what they were. Lois didn't give a damn about the catty glint in Cassandra's eyes because she was about to trample all over her self-esteem.

When Franklin arrived home, he could hear through the door Lois criticizing Cassandra about the condition of the kitchen.

"It's not like you and Franklin have a bunch of children rushing around here pulling down a new glass every five minutes. I just don't understand how an educated woman like yourself can be so filthy."

"This kitchen is not filthy, Miss Harris," Franklin heard Cassandra's squeaky voice retort back at Lois.

"Damn!" Franklin hissed, realizing he was about to walk into a war he wanted no part of.

"Look at how nasty this stove is. Yellow grease stains are caked up on the damn thing. When was the last time you cleaned it? No wonder Franklin likes to come back home to eat. You're cooking his food on grime!"

"Damn," Franklin said to himself as he began pacing back and forth in the hallway. He wasn't prepared to deal with this kind of drama tonight. Especially after the stressful day he'd had.

"Miss Harris, would you please have a seat in the living room?" Franklin sensed the tightness in Cassandra's voice. He could feel the tension hovering in the air.

"I guess so. It seems to be the only clean spot around here," Franklin heard Lois remark. After a short moment of silence, the clatter of dishes banging around the sink was confirmation that Cassandra was pissed off. Franklin took a few deep breaths, approached the door, and opened it.

"Hey, baby," Franklin greeted Cassandra.

"We need to talk." She had daggers in her eyes.

"Little Miss Squeaky, please, your little attitude isn't putting fear in anyone," remarked Lois as she walked over to greet Franklin. "How is my baby boy feeling? You look a little pale. Are you trying to poison my son, Cassandra?" Lois continued her verbal assault.

"Franklin, I'll be waiting in the bedroom to speak with you."

"If you keep the bedroom the way you keep the kitchen, I wouldn't rush up in there. Franklin, haven't I taught you that everything that glitters isn't gold and—"

"Mom," Franklin cut her off midsentence before she made the situation worse. Cassandra marched into the bedroom and slammed the door so hard that one of the pictures hanging in a glass frame on the wall fell to the floor and shattered.

"How long will it take for you to clean that up? A month?" Lois hollered behind Cassandra as she rolled her eyes in contempt at the bedroom door.

"Franklin, I'm telling you, you need to get rid of that trifling girl. I haven't been here a good hour and that girl has got my blood pressure sky-high." Lois pointed her finger at the bedroom door. "This is your condo; she moved in with you. I personally think she's trying to set you up. It just seems mighty strange the minute you purchased your condo she suddenly had trouble keeping a home of her own. Ever since she moved into your place, she has kept it like a pigpen. The girl may have education, but she doesn't know shit about running a house. Don't screw up and have a baby with her. She wouldn't know what to do. I can see it now." Lois was purposely speaking loud enough for Cassandra to hear every word she spoke. "If you have a baby girl, she wouldn't know the first thing about tending to the child's hair. She'd be the type of heifer who would take a newborn to the hair salon."

"Mom, calm down, please. I'm the one who has to sleep here tonight, not you."

"You can always come back home to me, Franklin. My place may not be much, but at least it's clean. From what I can see, Cassandra has turned your cozy bachelor pad into her personal slop jar. Look at this place; she has dirty laundry all over the sofa. What's up with that?"

"Look, here is your money." Franklin handed Lois an envelope. "Let me walk you down to my car so I can drive you home." Franklin realized that he'd better get his mother out of his house before Cassandra came out swinging her fists in fury. Franklin told Cassandra he'd return shortly and then left.

Franklin grumbled at the notion of driving all the way across town to take Lois back home. He knew he'd have to listen to her belittle Cassandra the entire drive. He didn't dare defend Cassandra or disagree with his mother's low opinion of her, especially in her current mood. Franklin was flawed like that. When they got situated in the car, Franklin started it up and began driving. He didn't say much because his thoughts were focused on his screwup at the office.

"What's wrong with you? What's on your mind?" inquired Lois. "I see the stress in your eyes," Lois spoke softly.

"Nothing, I'm cool," Franklin answered.

"Who are you trying to fool? You can trick some of the people some of the time and a few people all of the time, but you can't fool your mother at any time. I wouldn't worry myself over that pitiful excuse of a woman you're with. Trust me, Frankie, she's not good enough for you."

"It's not Cassandra I'm worried about. I had a bad day at work. Today I registered a bunch of traders in states that they had been trading in illegally. Anyway, the auditors were there, and they found out about it. I wasn't supposed to let them find out, but I did."

"Don't worry about it. You should stop beating yourself up over it. It was a mistake."

"That's easy for you to say," Franklin said, finding minimal comfort from her words.

"Listen to me, Franklin. You're in there busting your ass forty hours a week. You're a good worker who made an error. They'll get over it. You work your ass off for that company. I think you work too hard. Sometimes I worry because I think you're going to let that job worry you to death."

"They may not get over this one so easily. Damn, I need my job, Mom. I can't afford to lose it." Franklin was stressing out all over again.

"Listen to this, Franklin. I was reading in the paper the other day that a man died at his office from a heart attack, but no one noticed he'd died for three damn days. It wasn't until the weekend cleaning lady asked him if he was okay did anyone realize the man had passed away. When the police investigated his death, all of his coworkers talked about how dedicated he was to his work and how he always wanted to do a good job. But in the end, those dirty dogs didn't give a damn about him. The man allowed his employer to work him to death. Now, where is the glory in that?"

"You have a point there, but still. I've got bills to pay."

"Franklin, don't you know that on the day you die, you're going to have a bill that needs to be paid?"

"All right already, I see your point." Franklin had grown weary of listening to Lois and her twisted philosophy.

"You need to come on back and get into the scam business with your sister and me. Snatching yourself some quick and easy money is the name of the game in this country."

"I don't do that anymore; you know that. I have a college degree in fine arts. No, thank you, I'm not trying to go to jail."

"I'm your mother and I'd never let anyone put you in jail." Lois spoke as if she'd be the judge presiding over his trial. "Well, have it your way, but your sister Latoya is making herself some quick cash by sending out spam e-mails over the Internet. I'm not sure how it works, but I do know she's being paid for it."

"Oh, Lord, don't tell me she's one of those people who sends a crapload of junk e-mail." Franklin shook his head disapprovingly. "How much money is she pulling in from the scam?"

"You know Latoya never tells me how much she's getting. She just gives me a little something to keep me happy. But I do know she's been getting some good pops with her work-at-home e-mail scam." Lois laughed. "For some reason, people seem to believe that everything they read on the Internet is true. She has a work-at-home e-mail scam that tells people they can make a ridiculous amount of money by working at home over a short period of time. However, they can't get all of the details until they call what they think is a toll-free number. And then—"

"Stop. Just stop," Franklin cut his mother off. "It's wrong, Mom. You shouldn't encourage her to rip people off."

"Wrong!" Lois almost screamed the word. "Let me clear up the fog in your head right quick. Today you were at your job plugging up a loophole for traders who were spending their client's money illegally. But because you're working for a company, it's not a scam, right?"

"It's not like that, Mom."

"Oh, really, then what is it like? It sounds like a damn scam to me. The brokers gain the confidence of their client, take their money, and run off with the promise of a big payday. If they lose the client's money, oh well, sorry. That's the way it goes. What makes what we're doing on the street so different from what you're doing in an office?"

"Nothing, when you put it like that." Franklin finally reached his mother's apartment building. He pulled into a parking space and was about to turn off his car and escort Lois safely inside.

"No, you get back home. I can see myself inside," said Lois.

"Are you sure?"

"I'm positive. I'll make it from here. Thanks for the money." Lois was suddenly abrupt, and Franklin thought that he'd irritated her.

"Well, when are you going to pick up your car?" Franklin asked as she slammed his car door shut. He hit the power window button.

"What about your car? When are you going to pick it up?" Franklin yelled out as Lois picked up her pace.

"Tomorrow. I'll talk to you later." Franklin got suspicious because Lois wasn't sharing any details with him. He began to wonder if Lois had fabricated a story just to extort money from him.

"She's not beyond such a thing. Then again, I'm her son, and she'd never do anything like that to me," Franklin told himself. At that moment his cellular phone rang.

"Hello?"

"Yeah, motherfucker, it's me." Cassandra's high-pitched voice shrieked in his ear.

"Baby, calm down. I know my mother being at the house upset you. You shouldn't pay any attention to what she said."

"Franklin, I don't give a rat's ass about your ghetto fabulous momma. What you need to do is explain where one thousand dollars of my money is at." Franklin panicked.

"Baby, I'll explain everything when I get home. Do you want me to stop and pick you up something?"

"Franklin? Where is my damn money?"

"Baby, something important came up and—" Franklin heard a few quick beeps on his cellular phone and then looked at the display, which read LOW BATTERY. "Shit," Franklin hissed. He searched for the plug but couldn't find it.

"This has been one jacked-up ass day," He said out loud as he sped off.

Franklin walked in the door with a set of carnation flowers from the neighborhood grocery store. He was hoping to use them as a peace offering. Franklin noticed several packed suitcases sitting at the door. Cassandra was sitting on the sofa with her arms folded across her chest with her eyes narrowed to slits of contempt.

"What's up with the packed bags?"

"Where is my money, Franklin?" Cassandra asked yet again.

"Baby, part of the money belonged to me."

"Franklin, you deposited one hundred damn dollars to open the account. The rest belonged to me. Now where is my money?"

"Come on now. Why do you have to be all angry?"

"You gave my money to your damn momma, didn't you?" Franklin's nerves were on edge because Cassandra had figured out what he'd done.

"Baby, I'm going to get your money back, okay? It's no big deal. My mother needed cash for an emergency."

"You gave my money to that fucking psycho bitch? After she came up in here ripping me to sheds like she was Jack the fucking Ripper!" Cassandra was furious. "On top of that, you didn't say one word in my damn defense! You're a piss-poor fucking excuse for a man, Franklin."

"Cassandra, she needed money badly, okay? You understand don't you? I had to help my mother."

"I don't care if she needed a damn kidney transplant to save her miserable life. You took my money without asking me. You stole from me, Franklin."

"Come on, chocolate doll. I'm going to replace the money. How is that stealing?"

"You took it without asking, Franklin. That's called stealing in my book. And you're damn right! I'm going to get my damn money back from your ass." Cassandra stood up, grabbed her coat, and walked over to the door, pushing Franklin out of her path.

"Where are you going?"

"I'm leaving!"

"Cassandra, don't you think you're being overdramatic here?"

"Franklin, let me tell you something. Your momma and your retarded-ass sister are pimping you like a five-dollar whore. What you need to do is grow some fucking balls and become a stronger man."

"I am a strong man." Franklin wasn't about to allow her to insult him in that manner.

"Oh, really, you could have fooled me." Cassandra intruded upon his personal space. "It's over!" she concluded bitterly. "I don't want to marry a man who doesn't have my interests as his priority." Franklin saw an angry tear rush down Cassandra's cheek.

"Come on, chocolate doll, it is not that bad." Franklin tried to embrace her.

"No! Get away from me!" she shouted as if she was being battered.

"I'll be back to get the rest of my things later." Cassandra picked up her suitcases, turned her back, and walked out the door.

"Shit." Franklin slumped down on his sofa and covered his face with the palms of his hands.

3

Savannah

Savannah's rented limousine driver brought the car to a halt in front of the George Hotel in Washington, DC. The driver put the limousine in park, got out, and rushed around to her side of the vehicle to hold the door open for her. Savannah stepped out of the limousine, and the doorman of the hotel held a large umbrella over her so she wouldn't get soaked from the downpour of rain.

"Welcome back, miss," the doorman said politely as he escorted Savannah up the steps of the hotel and into the lobby. *What a day*, thought Savannah. She'd been on her feet most of the day and was eager to slip out of her clothes. She was wearing a navy blue Jones of New York business skirt suit, which was called "A Walk In Rome." The suit gave her an image of influence, which was the perception she always displayed. Savannah was in Washington, DC, managing damage control for a client who had been receiving negative press for a recall of one of its products. Savannah had been in town for a few days coaching the president of the organization on how to handle difficult questions during an interview. The extra coaching was a precaution to ensure that the client didn't say something that could be misinterpreted and cause greater damage to the organization's reputation. Savannah coached the client by conducting several on-camera rehearsals before the journalists arrived. Although the interview had its intense moments, her client handled the stress of the negative exposure excellently.

Savannah caught a glimpse of herself in a mirror in the hotel's lobby. Her shoulder-length hair was styled with a roller set and complemented her oval-shaped face. She approached the mirror and studied her eyes for a moment, searching for age lines. Thankfully, she didn't find any. Savannah headed toward the elevator that would take her to her suite but was distracted by a roar of voices filled with merriment emanating from the hotel's restaurant, the Bistro Bis. She decided to investigate who was dining there with the hope of perhaps meeting a senator, congressman, or a celebrity who had come to dine. She walked into the restaurant and surveyed the room, noticing it was filled with middle-aged businessmen drinking perhaps more than they should. One businessman in particular caught her attention because of an exceptionally attractive woman lounging on his lap. Savannah found it peculiar that such a woman would be interested in the company of a dumpy middle-aged man.

"Will your date be arriving soon, miss?" The intrusion of the hostess's voice caught Savannah off guard.

"No," answered Savannah. "I am alone. Is a date required?" Savannah had taken offense to her comment. Not because she'd asked the question, but because it reminded her that she wasn't in a relationship. It reinforced the fact that she had chosen her company and career over marriage and a white picket fence. Although she had wealth and respect, from time to time, when she was alone, she questioned if she'd selected the right path. At forty-one and in the fall of her years, being a single woman frightened her.

"No," replied the hostess, noticing the tension in Savannah's eyes. "I just wanted to make sure that I seated you properly. I have a nice table near the window. If you'll follow me, I'll seat you."

"Um, no." Savannah stopped the woman in her tracks. "I'm sorry." Savannah changed her mind. "I think I'll order room service tonight."

"Are you sure?" asked the hostess.

"Yes, I'm sure." Savannah smiled slightly.

"Okay, perhaps you'll join us tomorrow evening for dinner. Besides," the hostess relaxed her professionalism and whispered, "I know you don't want anyone from that rowdy bunch approaching your table."

"No, I don't," Savannah agreed as she excused herself to retire to her suite. Once inside, without further ado, she exhaled as she slipped out of her heels.

"Oh, that feels so much better," she said out loud as the soles of her feet enjoyed the soft feel of the carpeting. She entered the bathroom and was pleased with the maid for organizing her cosmetics. Savannah turned on the shower and began disrobing. The pressure of the shower felt magnificent against her skin and was relaxing the tension in her muscles. Savannah lingered in the shower longer than usual to fully enjoy the escape it offered. She exited the shower, dried herself, and wrapped another large towel around her. She sat down at the desk where her laptop computer was and booted it up. Savannah got on-line and began checking her e-mails and following up with her staff to see if they had completed the tasks she'd assigned. Being the chief executive officer of her public relations company was constant work. Savannah was closely involved in the strategic planning for all her clients and in her organization's day-to-day operational activities. Her job was never ending, and the work was constant. Once she was finished replying to company e-mails and leaving voice mails for her staff, she checked her personal e-mail account. As she scrolled through numerous spam e-mails about working from home and earning large sums of tax-free money, she noticed she'd received an e-mail from her former boyfriend. The subject line read, "It's been a long time." Savannah hesitated before she opened the e-mail from David. It had been two years since their official parting of ways, yet some tenderness related to their separation still lingered in her heart. She'd broken David's heart. She didn't want to break it, but there was just no other way. She was honest with herself and her feelings. David was a good man and was everything a woman in her position could want. He was handsome, well educated, financially stable, and in love with her. She and David dated for two years and during their courtship, David proposed to her. She accepted his proposal. At the time, both she and David were already what most would have considered to be blessed. David, who was an engineer, began bringing up children and family shortly after her acceptance of his marriage proposal. Savannah determined long before she'd ever met David that she didn't want children. She considered David's request but in the end, refused to comply with what he wanted. Savannah had to be honest with herself. At the time, she knew that being a stay-at-home mother would eat away at her. She broke off the engagement and bruised David's heart with her decision.

As Savannah glared at the computer screen, she began thinking about the intimacy she and David once shared. David wasn't a creative or exciting lover. He was a simple type of lover who preferred it a particular way all the time. This was an area in which Savannah tried to coach him but little improvement was achieved. However, since it had been a lengthy amount of time since Savannah had invited a man to her bed, the prospect of seeing David for a little servicing appealed to her. The last time they'd communicated, he mentioned that he was involved with someone, but she didn't care as long as he wasn't married to her. Savannah could live with herself if she and David shared an intimate time together for old time's sake. She opened up his e-mail.

Hello, Savannah, I hope you're doing well. A bit of time has come to pass since we last spoke. I believe it has been a year now. For the moment, I will blame it on our busy lifestyles. The other day I was standing at a newspaper stand and saw a magazine called *African American Women In Business*. Your photo was on the cover! That blew me away. I purchased the magazine and read about how you risked everything and purchased a mediocre public relations company and turned it into a moneymaking empire. I'm proud of you. You're doing exactly what you've always wanted to do. I hope that you've found happiness. I still work long hours for the government but somehow found the time to get married. My wife is a professor at Howard University. We've been married for a few months. I know you don't want to hear the details of my relationship, so I'll get to the reason why I'm e-mailing. My wife, Lisa, is responsible for co-ordinating career day at the university. She was wondering if you'd be interested in being the keynote speaker at the event's luncheon. We both know you're a very busy woman, but if you could find the time to do this, Lisa says the university will cover your travel expenses. You can either e-mail me back or call me. My number is still the same. I hope to hear from you soon, David.

"Oh, you've got to be kidding me, David," Savannah exhaled with disappointment. "You didn't even send me an invitation to your wedding, and now you want me to do you a favor?" Savannah rolled her eyes. "Men," she hissed. Savannah deleted the e-mail, feeling foolish for holding out hope that David was available and still had a romantic interest in her.

"I hate being alone all the damn time," she admitted to the empty room.

Later in the evening, Savannah couldn't fall asleep no matter how comfortable she attempted to get. Sleeping in an unfamiliar environment was always difficult for her. She turned on the television and mindlessly channel surfed, but she wasn't finding anything that was holding her interest. She thought about getting on-line and entering a game room to free her thoughts from the depressing condition of her romantic life but ditched the idea when she became interested in an erotic story from the program *Red Shoe Diaries*. Savannah viewed the program, hoping that there was a man out there who could stir her passion, romance her in exciting ways, and make her feel desired. The men who knew her only saw the strict professional side of her and not the sensual or passionate side. In business, it was necessary to project a certain image to command the respect she wanted. However, on the inside, Savannah was longing to be involved in a love affair that drove her to the edge of passion. There was a large void in that part of her life. She often had fantasies of relinquishing her power and being tamed by a bad boy who would whisk her away on some exotic and risqué adventure, where she'd dance with wild abandon and make love in ways she'd only heard people whisper about.

Savannah wiped away a bit of sweat from her forehead as she sat with bated breath and viewed the steamy love scene from the program.

"Savannah, girl, a little dick would do wonders for you right about now." After the program ended, Savannah was not only restless, but also horny. She closed her eyes and allowed her hands to gently glide over her stomach, down to her hip and inner thighs, and back up again. She closed her eyes, continued to caress herself, and fantasized about a lover who knew every inch of her body the way her soft hands did. She fantasized about how her perfect man would arouse her entire body with what he said to her and how he moved on top of her. Her lover would have to adore her small sensitive breasts. He'd understand that with the proper amount of foreplay, she could have an orgasm through sucking, kissing, and caressing them. Savannah cupped her breasts and rotated the palms of her hands around her nipples. A delightful rush of pleasure danced through her body as she bowed her back and rolled onto her stomach. She slid her fingers between her thighs and awakened her goddess by applying perfect amounts of pressure exactly where she wanted it. She imagined the weight of her lover on her backside. She imagined the firmness of his manhood between the cheeks of her derriere.

"Oh, how I love the feel of a man's erection against my ass," she whispered. She imagined him placing moist, sweet kisses on her neck and back. The thought of her imaginary lover's kisses gave her goose bumps and brought forth the sensation she'd been stirring up. Once she got her release, she drifted off to sleep.

The following morning, Savannah was awakened by the sound of her cellular phone ringing. She opened her eyes, found the phone, and answered it.

"So how did things go?" asked the voice on the other end.

"Leatha? Is that you?" Savannah asked, wanting to confirm that it was her girlfriend.

"Yes, it's me. Were you expecting someone else to call?"

"No," answered Savannah.

"So did things go well?" Leatha asked once again.

"Yes, they went well," answered Savannah, who wanted to drift off to sleep again.

"So, did you spend any time exploring the city? Did you go to dinner? Meet a man and get some much needed romance?"

"Leatha, it's too damn early to be talking about sex."

"Shit, it has been too long for your ass. You can't even recall what a hard dick first thing in the morning feels like."

"Leatha"—Savannah wasn't in the mood to talk about sex at that moment—"let me call you back."

"Well hurry up, because I want to talk to you about coming to a sex toy party with me."

"Sex toy party." Savannah rolled her eyes. "Yeah, right."

"Don't knock it, honey. A woman in your situation could use a good vibrator."

"Whatever, I'll call you back," Savannah said as she disconnected her call.

4

Franklin

The following day at work, Franklin was edgy because he was anticipating another confrontation with Chris first thing in the morning regarding the documents the auditor confiscated the day before. Franklin worked through the morning without his boss mentioning the documents found by the auditor. *Perhaps the auditor didn't see a need to bring it to Chris's attention*, Franklin rationalized.

While sitting in his office, he began to think about Cassandra. He decided he'd make a peace offering by suggesting they have dinner at the Capital Grille Restaurant. In his mind, a nice dinner would aid in smoothing things over so that she would come back to him. Franklin picked up the phone and dialed Cassandra at work. When he discovered she'd taken the day off, he contacted her through her cellular phone.

"Hey, baby," greeted Franklin when she answered her phone. "Can we talk now?"

"There is nothing to talk about," answered Cassandra. "I've moved on."

"Moved on?" Franklin didn't give her comment much weight. "No, you haven't. Look, let's have dinner tonight. I'll make all of this up to you." Franklin was confident that Cassandra would give in and leap at his offer.

"Franklin, it's over! The sooner you get that through your thick head, the better," Cassandra snapped at him with a tone of voice Franklin had never heard.

"Why are you acting like this? I mean, damn, I'll return the fucking money. What's the big damn problem?"

"You just don't get it, do you, Franklin. You need to learn how to treat a woman. You have to put your woman first, not your mother. Listen to fucking Jaheim, he can tell you all about it."

"I treated you just fine. I even let you move in with me. And can we leave my mother out of this?" Franklin sneered back.

"You know what, Franklin, you're confused." Franklin could hear her voice quaking.

"What do you mean, I'm confused?"

"I don't have time to explain what I mean to you, Franklin. When you grow the hell up, you'll understand where I'm coming from. By the way, I'm at your condo right now with two movers, getting the rest of my belongings."

"Now wait one damn minute. Hold up, Cassandra. You just can't come— hello? Hello?" Franklin looked down at his phone and saw that he'd been disconnected.

"I know she didn't just hang up on me," Franklin said out loud. He immediately phoned Cassandra back, but this time he got only her voice mail, which meant that she'd actually hung up on him and turned off her phone.

"Son of a bitch!" Franklin hissed as he glanced at the clock. It was only two o' clock and Franklin wanted to leave, but he thought better of it, especially since he and his boss weren't seeing eye to eye. Franklin stood up to go step outside of the building for a moment to get some fresh air. As soon as he stood up, Chris phoned him.

"Hello, Franklin, do you have minute?" Before Franklin could answer, Chris said, "Come into my office." Franklin didn't like his tone but wasn't about to assume anything. He grabbed a pad and a pen walked down the hall to his office. When he stepped into Chris's office, Jan, the director of human resources was sitting at the small table in Chris's office with a gray envelope marked CONFIDENTIAL. Franklin gently closed the office door.

"Have a seat." Chris instructed him to take a seat next to Jan.

"I think it would be best for both of us to sever our business relationship." Chris just came right out and said it. There was no beating around the bush, no saying, "I'm sorry about this." Just a clear-cut statement saying, "You're fired." Franklin had a feeling this was going to happen. On the one hand, he was upset that he was being terminated, but on the other, he was glad that he didn't have to deal with Chris's bullshit any longer.

"What are you offering as a severance package?" Franklin asked without blinking an eye.

Franklin rushed through the train station to catch the last express train out of downtown Chicago. Once he got on the train, he had to walk through several train cars before he finally found an empty seat. He tilted his head back, closed his eyes, and tried not to stress out over how he'd screwed up with the auditors and got fired. He refused to allow Chris to lower his self-worth, even though at that particular moment, he wasn't feeling confident or self-assured. *Sometimes, when one door closes, it opens up another one that leads to a brighter future*, Franklin thought to himself as he tried not to relive the final moments of his employment with the brokerage firm. He made a mental note to phone his buddy Darzel at some point so they could keep in touch.

The train came to a stop and more passengers boarded. Two female passengers sat down in front of Franklin and continued a conversation that was carried over from the train platform. Franklin wasn't trying to eavesdrop, but the women were speaking in a soft whisper, as if they had the juiciest secret in the world. From what he could piece together, one woman was recommending an escort to her friend. She was sharing the experience of how good he was. Franklin smiled, finding amusement with their conversation. Franklin thought about his cousin Curtis, who worked as an escort and wondered if the woman in front of him was a client of his. He continued to eavesdrop a bit more as the women shared their hot secret. The woman who'd had the date raved about how wonderful her escort made her feel and his exceptional dance skills.

"I felt desirable with him, but not in a perverted way. It was like he noticed everything about me, from the style of my hair to the color of my toenail polish," Franklin heard the woman whisper. When the train arrived at his stop, he wanted to get a look at the woman who ordered the escort but didn't want to stare at her like he was some weirdo. Franklin made a mental note to himself to hook up with Curtis and ask if he'd taken a woman out dancing lately.

When Franklin arrived home, he caught Cassandra just as she was about to pull away in her car.

"Cassandra," he shouted out in order to get her to halt as he jogged down the street to catch her.

"Where are you going?" Franklin rested his hand on the door frame of the car.

"I'm not about to tell you where I'm going." Cassandra pinched her eyebrows into an ugly expression.

"Baby, stay. I need you. I lost my job today," Franklin pleaded.

"Franklin, don't lie in order to get me to stay." Cassandra didn't believe Franklin for one moment.

"No, baby. I'm serious. I got fired today and—"

"Oh, well," Cassandra snapped at him without any sympathy. "Maybe your almighty momma and sister can come to your rescue for a change. The way they bamboozle you is too ridiculous for words, Franklin. Every time one of them needs a Band-Aid, you seem to be the only one who can buy it for them. Never in my life have I seen such an absurd codependent family."

"Don't talk about my mother and sister like that, Cassandra." Franklin felt his irritation swelling up.

"I don't have to, I just did." Cassandra pulled away, leaving him standing in the center of the street. Cassandra drove a few meters, then tossed her set of his condo keys out the car window. Franklin walked down the center of the street and scooped up the keys.

"Damn, player," he whispered to himself, "your shit is all fucked up." Franklin decided to go to the gym instead of going inside to sulk about the latest turn of events in his life.

Once Franklin changed clothes in the locker room, he went directly to the weight room. He put four forty-five-pound plates on the bench press, two plates on each side. He lay flat down, hoisted the weight, and pumped out twelve reps. Franklin did four more sets before he decided to do some incline dumbbell presses with the sixty-pound weights.

"What's up, dawg?" Franklin recognized his cousin Curtis's voice immediately. Curtis was two years older than Franklin and was a handsome, well-built caramel man with a bald head and an earring stud in his right ear.

"Hey, man." Franklin stood up and greeted Curtis.

"What are you working on tonight? Chest and shoulder muscles?"

"Yes," answered Franklin dryly.

"Damn, Frank, you sound all depressed. What's going on?"

"Drama at the job. I got let go today," Franklin confided in

Curtis. "Then when I went home, Cassandra cut out on me. I'm in here blowing off steam big time before I hurt someone."

"Sorry to hear that, Franklin. But, hey, if it is of any worth to you, sometimes when stuff like that happens, better things come along," Curtis tried to comfort Franklin.

"I know," grumbled Franklin. "How are things going down at the Queen of Clubs? You still own the place, don't you?" asked Franklin.

"Franklin, you know damn well I still own the club. Stop tripping, man. If you need a job to hold you over until you get on your feet, you know I got your back. In fact, what would you say if I told you I could hook you up on a job where you could make as much as one thousand dollars a day."

"Doing what?" Franklin looked at Curtis suspiciously.

"Look, come take a quick walk with me. I don't want everyone to hear what I'm about to tell you." Franklin followed Curtis into another section of the weight room, which was a bit more private. Franklin sat down on the abs machine, and Curtis sat down on the leg press machine.

"Frank, you're a nice-looking brother. You have the looks and the body for this type of work. You have a college degree and you know about finances. You're still into the arts, right?"

"Yeah, that was one of the things Cassandra liked about me. Or so she said."

"Franklin, all you need is some polishing. Let me share the secrets of the trade with you. You can make some big money."

"Doing what, Curtis? You still haven't told me what I'd be doing."

"Well, you know I do the escorting thing on the side. At certain times of the year, the crowd at the club is rather light, so in order to balance things out, I offer my services as an escort."

"Are you really pulling down that type of money being an escort?" Franklin asked, recalling the conversation he'd heard two ladies having earlier that day.

"Frank, have you ever known me to fall on hard times or be without money?"

"No, but man, you're talking about turning me into a sex worker. You're talking about having sex with hideous overweight women, wrinkled up old ladies and chicks with gruesome afflictions. I can't sleep with just anyone."

Curtis began laughing. "It's nothing like that, Franklin. Most of the women who are clients of Jaguar Services are from thirty at the young end and sixty at the high end. There are a few exceptions, but they're primarily looking for someone to talk to."

"Curtis, your ass is setting me up, I know it."

"Look, I'm your boy, I'm family. I'm not going to get you into some fucked-up shit. Jade, the owner of Jaguar Services, only deals with top-notch female clients. You'd be surprised at who some of her clients are. Jade doesn't play. She's like an agent, and she has a solid reputation. She doesn't deal with the dark side of business. No drugs are ever involved, and sex doesn't always take place. Mistress Jade only hires her men through referral. Trust me, Frank, clients would pay handsomely to spend time with a man like yourself."

"Seriously, man, how much are you getting paid? All bullshit aside." Franklin connected with his cousin's eyes.

"It depends on what the client is looking for. If I stay a full night, we negotiate the price."

"How much does Jade get?"

"It's a fifty-fifty split."

Franklin paused in thought as he considered the pros and cons of becoming an escort. "Let me think about it."

"What is there to think about? If you allow me to mentor you, I'll have you up to speed in no time at all."

"Curtis, I have bills to pay. I have a mortgage."

"And I'm telling you that by doing this, you can get paid, and quickly I might add."

"Why are you so gung ho about getting me into this business?"

"Because Jade has an opening, but she will not take you on unless you're polished. You can leave the polishing to me."

"Dude, let me think about it and get back to you. Seriously, let me think it over," Franklin said.

5

Lois

Lois never did care for Valentine's Day and couldn't understand why people made such a big fuss about it. "It's just another way for retailers to rip people off with a smile," she declared to herself. She'd decided she'd spend the lover's holiday doing laundry at the twenty-four-hour Laundromat. Lois began stuffing unclean laundry into one of the jumbo washtubs, careful not to allow her clothing to fall on the grimy floor. Once the washtub was filled, she poured in the proper amount of detergent, placed quarters into the slots, and started the machines. Lois had a sweet tooth that needed to be satisfied, so she moseyed toward the rear of the Laundromat where the vending machines and restrooms were located. She stood facing the snack machine and read a sign that was posted on the window of the machine. PAY AT YOUR OWN RISK. MANAGEMENT IS NOT RESPONSIBLE FOR ANY MACHINE MALFUNCTION. Lois chuckled and wondered how much the owner of the machine was making off of that con.

"Over the course of a month or two, I'll bet he or she can pull in at least a few hundred dollars," Lois said, and then determined that she would not fall prey to the con game and lose her hard-earned money. She'd just suffer with her sweet tooth until she returned home. Lois moseyed to another part of the Laundromat and took a seat to patiently wait for her loads to complete their cycle. She picked up a newspaper someone had left sitting on the seat next to her. She began reading a local news story about a respected school-teacher who had kicked her nineteen-year-old son out of her home because he was selling narcotics. Once he was gone, she found one hundred thousand dollars in illegal cash stashed away in his room.

"Damn!" Lois uttered as she continued to read the news story.

The schoolteacher took the money and spread it out over several bank accounts.

"Smart move," Lois whispered out loud. She concurred with the schoolteacher's course of action.

"I would have done something similar, just so that all my eggs were not in one basket," Lois reasoned. Eventually, the owner of the money, who wasn't her son, came to collect it. At that point, Lois stopped reading the story because she could read between the lines as to what happened to the schoolteacher. *When you find money like that*—Lois's keen hustling mind began formulating a master plan in case she stumbled across a large sum of unclaimed cash—*you have to pack your shit and start over. You have to move to a different city where no one knows you. Poor woman*, Lois thought. *She was in over her head.*

Lois stepped outside of the Laundromat to catch some fresh air. As she watched people and listened to the noise of the city, her thoughts began to focus on how happy she was now that she'd gotten rid of Franklin's intolerable girlfriend. Franklin was not going to marry the likes of her as long as she was living.

"Shit," Lois hissed to herself. It was bad enough when Franklin moved out of the house to be his own man. "I kept telling him that he could stay at home as long as he wanted to. But, no, he wanted to be a man who could be in control of his life." Lois scowled at her memories. "He was already a man. He was my man, and I guided his actions," Lois uttered. "I'm not about to let some scrawny little woman take him and his income away from me. Not after what I went through to make sure he stayed in school. It's bad enough that after all these years the factory closed and I'm out here without a steady source of income. At least when Franklin was living at home and working, he was able to take care of the bills." Lois stopped talking to herself and headed back inside the Laundromat. She checked the machines and noticed the wash cycles had completed. She removed her clothes, placed them in a dryer, and started them. Once the clothes stopped drying, Lois took them out and began folding them. As she was doing this, she came across Franklin's old college sweatshirt. She held the red cotton jersey in front her before she began folding it.

"He'll probably want this back," Lois said as she wondered how the sweatshirt found its way to her laundry basket. Then she thought, *Latoya had probably borrowed it and never returned it to*

Franklin. Lois recalled the last time she saw Franklin wearing the sweatshirt. She and Franklin were arguing about his future and how she wanted him to participate in a real-estate swindle that she and a few accomplices worked out. All he had to do was drive around the city and write down the addresses of properties that appeared to be neglected. He would get one hundred dollars for every property he found. Lois would then go down to the city's recorder of deeds office and order a copy of the property deed from a friend there. A forgery of the deed would be made and taken to a crooked notary public who would approve the authenticity of one of Lois's aliases on the forged deed. Then she'd head back to the recorder of deed's office to file the claim, and presto, she would have a stolen home she could sell for an unbelievably low price.

Lois's argument with Franklin was a bad one. She felt as if college had turned her baby against her.

"I will not do something illegal like that with you, Mom," Franklin had said.

"What?" Lois sharpened her emotional blades so that she could attack his self-esteem. "Have you forgotten what I had to do so that you could finish college? Huh? Have you?"

"Mom, you're twisting things around. I'm not discounting the sacrifices you made in order to put me through college. All I'm saying is I don't want to run con games anymore. I want to earn my money legitimately. Who knows, perhaps one day I'll own my own business."

"Own your own business? Are you still holding on to that silly boyhood dream of owning a sports club? You can't be serious, Franklin."

"Mom, I can do it. I just need to plan it out." Franklin tried to stand his ground, but Lois wasn't going to let him.

"Don't you know that a dream like that will never come true for you? Don't you realize that? I'm going to sign the death certificate on that dream right now, Franklin. So just drop it. Chasing dreams is not worth your energy, chasing money is. You need to listen to me and do what I say. I have your best interest in mind all the time, Franklin. Don't you know that? Don't you know me by now?"

Lois put the sweatshirt in a bag because it was bringing back too many unpleasant memories. She didn't like having to cut her baby's dream at the throat, but she had to. She was dependent upon him, and losing her control over him just wasn't a possibility. Not then and certainly not now. Lois knew Franklin was only trying to be an honorable man. Hell, that was his largest flaw in her book, trying to be honorable in a world that was full of dishonesty.

Lois parked her white sedan in front of Franklin's condo. She grabbed Franklin's college sweatshirt from the passenger seat and walked up the steps to the outside door. She pulled out her set of his house keys and opened the door. As she approached the elevator, she saw Franklin standing with his black gym bag in his hand, waiting for it to come.

"Franklin," she called to him as she approached.

"Hey," Franklin answered dryly. "What are you doing here?"

"Can't a mother come and visit her only son?" Lois ignored Franklin's indifference about seeing her again.

"I don't know if I'm still mad at you for causing Cassandra to run away from me." Franklin's attitude was sour. The elevator chimed, signaling its arrival. The doors opened and both Franklin and Lois stepped inside.

"Look, there is no need to walk around being angry at me."

Franklin rolled his eyes and harrumphed.

"Did I catch you at a bad time?" asked Lois sarcastically. "That girl has been gone from your life for almost a month, and you're still dawdling around as if it happened ten minutes ago."

Franklin lassoed his feelings of grudge for the moment and responded, "What brings you by?"

"This," Lois said, showing him his college sweatshirt as the elevator door opened on his floor. "Oh, thanks," Franklin answered, disappointed because he was hoping that Lois was actually going to return the thousand dollars she'd hustled out of him. Franklin opened the door to his condo, and they both went inside. He walked into his bedroom and placed his gym bag there.

"Now this is how your home should look at all times," Lois spoke out loud, noticing how clean his home was. Lois went into the kitchen and noticed that it was spotless. She smiled and took the cleanliness of the kitchen as a small sign that Franklin was moving on from his relationship with that intolerable woman. Lois tugged open the refrigerator door and began searching for something to drink.

"Why don't you have anything in here to eat or drink?" Lois moved a few items around on the shelf.

"Hello, I did lose my job," Franklin answered as he walked into the kitchen. "Or have you forgotten?" Franklin said quickly and sarcastically. "Watch yourself," Franklin said to Lois as she moved out of his way. He removed his protein shake from the top shelf of the refrigerator.

"There is no need to get smart with me," Lois snapped back. Franklin took his liquid food into the living room and plopped down on his sofa.

"Something will come up, Franklin. Just give me a little time. I'll think of something good. Something that will produce some quick income for us."

"Mom, please, not another one of your schemes. I'm not in the mood to hear about it. I'm not even open to it." Franklin picked up his television remote and clicked on the television and DVD machine but had to quickly turn it off when he realized that he'd left one of his sexual instruction DVDs in the player.

"What in the hell was that I just saw?" Lois asked with a scolding glare. The last thing Franklin wanted his mother to know was that he was watching an instructional sex video.

"It's nothing," Franklin said with embarrassment. Lois's eyes began searching around the apartment and stopped when she saw the spine of a book on his bookshelf that read, *Drive Her Wild in Bed*.

"Was the breakup with Cassandra that bad?" asked Lois, who was suddenly concerned about him.

"Don't you mention her name to me, all right! You're the reason we broke up," barked Franklin. "On top of that, she snatched my credit card and charged up—" Franklin stopped midsentence because he didn't want Lois to know what Cassandra had done. Thankfully, Lois wasn't listening to what he was saying very closely.

"Boy, please," Lois said, discounting Franklin's tone with her. His little irritation was meaningless to her. Lois stood up, walked over to the bookshelf, and pulled the book down. "That haughty little girl wasn't worth your time. I'll bet this book is something her prissy little ass gave you. She seemed like the type who would have made something as natural as making love complex. But since you're all sensitive about your pompous ex-girlfriend, I'll drop her name out of our conversation." Lois opened up the book and began reading one of the passages.

"For your information"—Franklin suddenly wanted her to leave

but didn't have the courage to kick his mother out of his house—
"she didn't give me the book, Curtis gave it to me."

"Curtis?" Lois questioned suspiciously, because she'd heard
through Latoya that Curtis had gotten into the escort business.

"He has this crazy idea that I would be able to make good
money as a male escort."

"Really?" Lois's mind began clicking and working rapidly. A
grand scheme was formulating in her consciousness. "Did he say
anything about the type of clients he services?"

Franklin picked up the remote to the stereo and clicked the ON
button. One of his relaxation CDs began playing. Franklin loved
his relaxation CDs because the music calmed his nerves and helped
him focus. Right now, Lois's presence was making his blood pressure rise, and he needed the assistance of the music to level off his
annoyance.

"According to him, the service he escorts for only caters to
wealthy clients. It's a high-society operation, and the clients like to
have a discreet evening, free of complications."

"Really?" Lois repeated herself because her mind was moving
faster than she could speak. "How wealthy are these people? I
mean, how much money can you make?" Lois asked, not wanting
to let Franklin in on the fact she was devising a way to get a cut of
the percentage Franklin would take in.

"It depends," Franklin answered, surprised that Lois was even
remotely interested in how the business worked. "According to
Curtis, one night he pulled in three thousand dollars. But on a more
typical night he pulls in around one thousand dollars."

"Are you thinking about doing this?" The green eye of greed
washed over her as she awaited his answer.

"No. I need a damn job making at least as much as I was if not
more. I'm up a damn creek without a paddle right now."

"You should listen to Curtis, Franklin. You're better looking
than he is and have a much better physique."

"Yeah, right." Franklin laughed it off. He glared at Lois,
strangely trying to decode the look in her eyes.

"Franklin," Lois was more direct. "Listen to Curtis and get your
foot in the damn door."

"You're serious, aren't you?"

"Of course I am. You'll probably get to travel nationally and inter-
nationally. You'll meet influential people with money, and who knows,

you might even meet an investor who is willing to help you open up your business. That's how rich people do those kinds of things." Lois was making an assumption based on some grand fantasy she was creating in her mind.

"You may have a point there." Franklin pondered the feasibility of meeting a client with enough money to make an investment in his dream. *If they have money to blow on a gigolo, then money is probably not an issue for them*, Franklin reasoned. He'd even heard a rumor that a popular television host uses an escort service whenever she needs to attend award galas.

"Of course I have a point, baby." Lois gloated on the fact she was persuading Franklin. In a dark closet of her mind, she was thinking that there was no way she was going to allow Curtis to pimp her son, especially without getting her slice of the percentage. Lois had a plan; a hidden agenda that was going to place desperately needed money in her pocket.

6

Savannah

Savannah walked through a corridor of the elegant Ritz Carlton Hotel, which was located in the heart of Chicago's Gold Coast community. Everyone from actors to professional teams stayed at the hotel when they were in town. Savannah was at the hotel attending a black-tie gala for minority women who were successful business owners. She'd paid a handsome price for her ticket but felt it was well worth it because she wanted to hear the keynote speech being delivered by a well-known and respected female entrepreneur.

Savannah was feeling edgy and awkward because she wasn't able to bring a date along with her. The friend she'd invited received word at the eleventh hour that his sister was gravely ill, and he needed to rush to her side.

"Just my luck," Savannah murmured.

Savannah stopped at the coat check, gave the attendant her coat for safekeeping, and then continued down the carpeted corridor to the reception area, which was overflowing with elegantly dressed attendees. There was a consistent hum of voices from the multiple conversations taking place at the same time. Savannah noticed the doors to the ballroom had not yet been opened, so attendees were spending time drinking cocktails and networking. As Savannah surveyed the room, she noticed most of the women in attendance had a gentleman they could loop an arm around. Even though Savannah had both beauty and wealth, being there alone somehow made her feel inadequate. She sauntered over to the bartender to order a drink to help her feel more relaxed.

"Good evening, madam," greeted the bartender. "What can I make for you?" Savannah mulled over her thoughts for a moment before she decided. A glass of wine would have been nice, but for some strange reason she had a taste for something else.

"Can you make a piña colada?" asked Savannah.

"One piña colada coming right up," he said, then began preparing her drink. Savannah turned her attention away from the bartender and searched for a familiar face. She was praying that perhaps she'd see one of her clients who she could have a conversation with. However, to her disappointment, she didn't come across a familiar face.

"Here is your drink, madam." The bartender set her drink on the countertop. Savannah carefully picked it up and took a light sip.

"Umm," she cooed. "This is very good," she complimented the bartender.

"I'm glad you like it, miss," replied the bartender as he took the order of another person who walked up to the bar.

Savannah milled around the crowd and eventually made her way over to the handsome piano player, who was dressed in a black tuxedo and was playing a tune that was familiar. When the piano player finished the tune, Savannah asked what the name of it was.

"You don't want to try to guess first?" asked the piano player.

"I'm very bad at guessing games," Savannah conceded.

"Come on, give it a try just for fun," encouraged the piano player, unwilling to accept her concession. "Here is the tune again." He began to play.

"Hmm," Savannah pondered as she leaned on the piano and met his alluring gaze. "It's something by Beethoven, right?"

"Yes," the piano player said as he continued to strike the keys more firmly.

"I got it," Savannah announced with excitement. "Für Elise, right?"

"See there, and you thought you were bad at guessing games," declared the piano player as he began to play with more passion and enthusiasm. Savannah noticed that he never took his eyes off of her. She felt as if she was the only woman in the room and this handsome man was playing only for her.

"Do you like that?" asked the piano player.

"Yes, it's very nice," Savannah answered.

"Okay, see if you can catch this one." The handsome man began playing a very familiar song. Savannah set her drink on a nearby coaster and hugged herself as the vibrations of the music swept through her and caused her nerves to tingle.

"You're versatile as well, I see. That one is "Superstar" by Luther Vandross.""

"Very good," said the piano player as he continued playing. Just as he was finishing the melody, a strikingly beautiful woman came to his side. The woman's features were exceptionally unique. Her skin was cinnamon brown like Savannah's own, but her eyes and hair were unquestionably Asian.

"Are you done showing off?" said the woman with what sounded like a British accent.

"I wasn't showing off. I was only adding a bit of ambience to the room," the piano player said lightheartedly.

"You're not being paid to add ambience at this event." The woman tried to utter the words underneath her breath, but Savannah caught everything she whispered to him. At that moment Savannah realized the man wasn't hired to play. He took it upon himself to sit at the piano and display his talent just for the joy of it. The woman gave Savannah a quizzical stare as her man escorted her into the ballroom, which had just opened up. *The woman probably thinks I was trying to lure him away from her or something*, Savannah thought as she analyzed the woman's quizzical gaze. She waited for the mass of attendees to enter the ballroom for dinner before she did the same.

"May I see your ticket, madam?" asked the maître d' who stood at the door. Savannah presented her ticket.

"You're seated at table number twenty-five, madam. It is straight ahead and to your left." The man snapped his fingers twice to summon another maître d' to escort her to her seat.

"Escort Ms. Styles to her table," ordered the first maître d'.

"Thank you," Savannah replied as she placed her ticket back inside her small egg-shaped purse. She looped her arm around the maître d' and allowed him to show her to her seat. Savannah felt as if someone had tossed a pail of ice water on her when she saw that she was being escorted to the same table the piano player and his girlfriend were sitting at. Savannah huffed a bit, hoping the woman wouldn't be the type to launch daggers with her eyes all evening.

"Here you are, madam." The maître d' pulled out her chair for her.

"Thank you," said Savannah as she took her seat like a civilized lady of wealth. Once the maître d' left her side, it was clear that everyone at her table was a couple. Savannah immediately felt awkward, and she disliked the position she was in.

"Hello," greeted a woman who appeared to be in her late thirties; her man held her seat out for her.

"Hello." Savannah returned the greeting as pleasantly as she could.

Once all four couples were seated at the table, it was as clear as day to the other women that Savannah was unaccompanied.

"My name is Jade," said the strikingly beautiful woman who had pulled the piano player away from her earlier. "Are you here alone this evening?" Savannah was all set to catch an attitude for the woman's intrusion into her situation. She allowed her face to go stone as she glared at woman. She'd paid for her ticket just like everyone else had, and whether or not she came unaccompanied should have been of no concern to the woman. However, this woman Jade was not unnerved in the least by Savannah's prudish glare.

"I'm not after him, if that's what you're implying." Savannah wasn't about to let a stranger ruin her evening.

"No, I'm not implying that at all, my dear." The woman's British accent was very thick and seemed to be filled with unjustified judgment.

"Excuse me," Savannah said as she stood up to head to the ladies' room just to step away from the situation for a moment. As she walked toward the bathroom, she heard someone call out her name.

"Excuse me, Ms. Styles." Savannah spun around and was flabbergasted to see Jade pursuing her. "May I have a word with you?"

Savannah was so taken aback by the woman that she didn't know how to respond.

"I'll take your silence to mean yes." Jade smiled at her. "You and I got off on the wrong foot a moment ago, and I want to correct that, Ms. Styles."

"How do you know my name?" Savannah asked.

"Come," said Jade. "Let's have a seat over there where two ladies can speak privately."

Savannah reluctantly followed Jade to a sofa, away from the buzzing noise of the ballroom.

"You're Savannah Styles, owner of Styles, Inc., your own public relations firm, correct?"

"Yes, how did you know that?" Savannah questioned.

"It's my job to know these things, dear. Servicing wealthy and powerful women is my business. Those ladies sitting at our table are my clients."

Savannah was confused and didn't know what to make of this woman or what she was saying. It was obvious she was a woman of power in her own right. Savannah could see that, but she didn't have a clue as to what the woman's business was.

"Do you know any of the women you're dining with tonight?" asked Jade.

"No," answered Savannah.

"My clients like to be discreet when it comes to the pleasures of life."

Savannah stared at the woman, even more confused.

"Hear me out, it will all make sense in a moment," said Jade. "One client is a senator from another state. Another one owns a cosmetics company, and the third one runs the largest video production company in the Midwest. And I am the owner and founder of Jaguar Services International. All of the gentlemen sitting with us this evening work for me."

Savannah was now curious as hell, and it showed by the expression on her face.

"They work for me, dear," answered Jade, trying to clear up her confusion.

"I'm sorry, am I missing something here? They're just your staff, right?" asked Savannah.

"You're a powerful, wealthy, and busy woman, Ms. Styles," Jade continued with an elite air. "Let me know if I'm off the mark. Either your date cancelled on you at the last minute or you couldn't locate a date who met your high standards to bring to this event."

Savannah was awed by Jade's intuition.

"I would imagine that your line of work requires you to take lengthy business trips, where after a hard day's work, you retire to your hotel suite alone. Perhaps you find yourself playing solitaire on your computer or continuing to work on other projects. Perhaps at times you think something is wrong with you because you haven't settled down yet. However, my dear, that is far from the truth. There is nothing wrong with you. Your schedule and commitments just don't allow you the time to nurture a meaningful relationship. However, invariably, in your line of work, social obligations such as this one arise. Engagements such as this would be more fully enjoyed and notably less awkward, like you feel now, were you to be accompanied by a gentleman. Let me be frank for a moment. Even though women in our society have great successes, we still need the accompaniment of a man to attend certain functions. It just looks better. Do you know what I mean?"

"Yes, I'm following you," answered Savannah.

"That's where I come in. All of those handsome gentlemen back at our table work for me. They're escorts. All well educated, handsome, and talented—as was displayed by Gerald's piano playing. Gerald has a master's degree in fine arts and writes commercial jingles. Austin is a journalist, and Henry is a practitioner. So, Ms. Styles, what I'm saying is perhaps I can be of service to you in the future." Jade handed Savannah a business card. "Everything is confidential and the services my organization provide are top-notch. No client has ever been disappointed with my service."

Savannah took the card but didn't know what to say. She digested what she heard for a moment and then spoke.

"What other services do you offer, besides, um"—Savannah paused midsentence—"escorts?" Savannah asked, completely fascinated by Jade and her business. Jade presented Savannah with a mannish smile, and then moved closer to her so that her voice wouldn't carry her words too far. "My dear girl, all of my men are well trained and will have you calling for their services again and again." Jade's words held a double meaning. "Women like you and I demand perfection in every part of our lives, correct?"

"Yes," Savannah answered, feeling as if she was sharing a very naughty secret. "A well-trained gigolo can do wonders for a woman's disposition, wouldn't you agree?" Both Jade and Savannah laughed together. Savannah realized she'd misjudged Jade and knew that one day she may be daring enough to contact her for her service.

"May I ask you a question?" asked Savannah.

"Usually, when a person asks permission to ask a question, they're looking to find the answer to something personal," responded Jade. "If it's a personal question you want to ask, you can ask it, but if I feel that it's too personal, I will not answer it."

"Okay, that seems fair enough," Savannah stated.

"Culturally, what is your background?" asked Savannah, feeling as if that question would not offend Jade. Jade smiled.

"You're curious about my brown skin, Asian eyes, and accent."

"Yes." Savannah laughed because she'd never met anyone as unique as Jade.

"I'm a mixture of Polynesian and African American. My mother is Polynesian and my father is black. He is a military man. We traveled a lot when I was a baby girl but eventually settled down in Australia. My accent comes from the land down under."

"That is so interesting," Savannah said, wanting to know all about Jade but thought better of asking her too many questions about her life and how she got into her business. Savannah glanced down at the card Jade gave her once again and read it more thoroughly this time.

"Jaguar Services," Savannah mumbled. "Your pleasure is our business."

"Call anytime, day or evening," encouraged Jade.

The next morning, Savannah was at her home in Beverly Shores, Indiana, sitting at her kitchen table, which overlooked Lake Michigan. She read the newspaper while she sipped on her morning cup of coffee and listened to the soothing sound of the cold water washing ashore. She was casually reading a story in the *Chicago Tribune* about how the fraud unit of the Chicago Police Department had shut down a lucrative credit card operation run by high-tech criminals. The article stated that once the criminals obtained the credit card number of a victim, they'd use computers to create dummy credit cards that could then be used for purchases without the victim ever knowing it until they received a credit card statement. Right then Savannah made a mental note to have fraud protection placed on all her major credit cards. Just as the story was getting interesting, she was interrupted by the chime of the doorbell. She got up from her seat and walked through the kitchen to the front door. She looked through the peephole and saw it was her girlfriend Leatha.

"Are you just going to gawk at me through the peephole or are you going to open the door?" Leatha scolded. Savannah laughed as she opened the door.

"I should leave your trifling behind standing out there, especially since you didn't return my phone calls while I was in Washington."

"I did return your calls. I just didn't feel like leaving a voice mail message. I hate voice mail. Besides, when I called you so early in the morning, you didn't seem like you were too happy."

"You woke me up," Savannah reminded her. "I'm going to find me a new best friend if you don't start leaving voice mails," Savannah said playfully.

"Girl, please. No one is going to be bothered with your trifling behind like me." Leatha continued babbling on before Savannah could respond to her wisecrack. "How did it go last night?" Leatha asked as she walked toward the kitchen. Savannah shut her front door and joined her shortly thereafter.

Leatha opened Savannah's refrigerator door, took out the gallon of orange juice, and poured herself a glass. "Girl, I've been working my ass off trying to make sure the Black Women in Law conference goes off without a hitch," Leatha said as she picked up one of Savannah's sweet rolls. "Come on, tell me," Leatha spoke with her mouth full as she took a seat. "In fact, just skip the conference and tell me how your date went."

"Troy cancelled on me at the last minute because of a family emergency," Savannah answered Leatha's question. "I thought you were him knocking on the door."

"Oh, wow. What happened?" asked Leatha, concerned about how Savannah must have felt.

"He said his sister was pretty ill, and he needed to be with her. I didn't argue with him even though I wanted him to say he'd come to the event rather than go be by her side. I know it was wrong of me to think that, but I don't like being put on the back burner. Even if the situation is a grave one. But enough of that; Troy and I weren't exactly dating anyway." Savannah sat down. "Hell, I'm not sure what we were doing besides talking to each other about our careers."

"Well, I hope everything turns out okay for him."

"I do too. He'll call eventually and tell me what the deal is. He'll probably try to make it up to me in some way. But knowing Troy, his dull ass will just want to have dinner. The man has absolutely no adventure about him. Hell, a lot of men lack creativity in the romance department."

"Savannah, you sound as if you've given up on men. Lighten up, girl."

"I haven't given up on men, Leatha." Savannah leaned forward in her seat and massaged the back of her neck. "I'm just bored with them. None of the men I meet are exciting. Actress Mae West said it best: 'It's not the men in my life, it's the life in my men.'" Savannah and Leatha laughed at Mae West's intuition.

"Well, one thing is for sure—you and I could certainly use more adventurous men in our lives," Leatha concluded. "Are you coming to the sex toy party this weekend?"

"Yeah, I'll be there. Speaking of sex and the sex toy party. Something interesting happened at the event last night." Savannah's voice switched from monotone to upbeat.

"How interesting?" Leatha raised her eyebrow, noticing the change in Savannah's voice inflection.

"You'll like this; it's freaky and right up your alley. You won't believe this, but I met a woman who owns an escort service," Savannah said.

"Escort service?" Leatha blurted out as Savannah anticipated her next series of questions.

"The woman's name is Jade. I was sitting at her table last night. She noticed that I was alone and feeling awkward because each woman at our table had a man, with the exception of me. Anyway, to make a long story short, we had a discreet and interesting conversation about the services her organization offers."

"So you met a high-class madam." Leatha's ears were buzzing in search of more information. "Are you going to use the service? No, wait a minute, girl. We could have a man come to our sex toy party and blow his damn mind with all types of freakishness."

"Girl, calm your hot ass down," Savannah said. "I don't know. I've never done anything like that in my life. Here is her card." Savannah reached into her purse, which was on the table, and pulled it out.

"Let me see it," Leatha said, snatching the card."

"Why? Are you going to call her up and rent at date?" Savannah laughed sarcastically.

"Yes, I am," Leatha responded defiantly. "Shit, I've been a good girl all of my life. I stayed in school, got my education, and ignored boys. Now that I'm a fully grown woman, I'm looking to make up for lost time. I'm ready to get my fucking freak on." Leatha laughed. "Look, Jade has a Web site. Have you checked it out yet?"

"No." Savannah's tone switched yet again. "Wait a minute, I thought you and Phil were hitting it off well."

"Oh, I haven't talked to you in a while, have I?" Leatha said.

"Come on, out with it," Savannah said, a little hurt that Leatha hadn't updated her.

"There is really not much to tell. He's confused as to what he wants. Men can be so damn flaky sometimes. He presented me with an ignorant conversation about not wanting to be tied down. I told him that I didn't have any damn ropes and then asked what the real problem was. He danced around the issue for a minute and finally came out and said he had met someone new."

"Why didn't you tell me? You know I would have offered my support."

"Savannah, this all happened while you were in DC. You had enough to deal with and didn't need my drama clouding your judgment. Besides, I knew it was over long before we decided to admit it." There was a short moment of silence as Leatha once again glanced down at the business card.

"Let's log on to the Jaguar Services Web site and see what's posted on it." Leatha was full of youthful energy, and Savannah had a hard time understanding how she could be so upbeat after a breakup. The ladies went into Savannah's home office, got on-line, and entered the Web site address. They waited a moment for the welcome page to fully load.

"Okay, what do we have here," said Leatha as she sat poised and ready to click on a link. The Web site had a picture of a very attractive businesswoman on the phone, staring out of a corporate office window. There was a gentlemen gallery that listed the cultures of the types of men that were available.

"Look at this," Leatha said, full of astonishment. "You can order an Asian, Latin, Caucasian, or African American man."

"Click on the link for black men," Savannah directed as she peered over Leatha's shoulder.

"Damn!" Leatha shouted. "Now see, that's the shit I'm talking about." There were publicity shots of several men on the page. The information listed next to their photograph had their name, height, weight, and body type. "That's the guy who played the piano last night." Savannah pointed to Gerald's photo. "Click on his photo right here." Savannah pointed to the screen.

"Gerald," Leatha said his name as she clicked. Gerald's publicity photos downloaded. There was a photo of him dressed casually, one of him in a business suit, and one of him in a tuxedo. Below the photos was a description of him that Savannah started reading out loud.

"Gerald, has a kind and gentle manner. He has the capability to make those around him feel eminently comfortable and truly at ease. His friendly, effusive smile and enchanting charm further contribute to the pleasant air enjoyed while in his presence. Gerald is a well-traveled man, having been to London, Germany, Rio, and Asia. Gerald holds a master's degree in fine arts and is fond of literature, theater, and music. Gerald is also a most captivating pianist. Being accompanied by Gerald to any event will always be an intriguing and illuminating experience. To reserve your time with Gerald, contact Jade at Jaguar Services."

"Damn, he sounds too fucking good to be true!" Leatha said.

"No, it is true," Savannah confirmed. "He is everything that his profile says he is."

"Are you for real, Savannah?"

"Why would I lie?"

"See, now that's the kind of man I need. Well dressed, educated, and fine as hell. Does Gerald look as good in person as he does in his photos?" Leatha asked.

"Honey, that man had me the moment he looked at me. I'm not going to even front. If Jade had not come to get him, I wouldn't have left without getting a kiss and a phone number. The brother was just that damn charming."

"Let me click on another man," Leatha said as she selected a more athletic man. There was a shirtless publicity shot of the next man. He had a physique that made both Leatha and Savannah gasp.

"Was this man there last night?" asked Leatha.

"No," Savannah said. "Look, he works out of the Caribbean."

"Shit," Leatha said as she studied the tall chocolate man. "I need to take a trip just to see him. He'd probably have my ass crawling up the damn wall. You know, I've heard that the men in the Caribbean hang around the resorts just to hook up with American women. I'll bet he's one of those sweet chocolate island men who'll turn a woman completely out."

Savannah laughed. "Stop being so bad. Read what it says at the bottom of the screen, Miss Hot Between the Legs."

"Jaguar Services doesn't condone any illegal activities by its associates or clients," Leatha read the statement. "Savannah, please. What goes on in a room between a man and me stays in that room," Leatha declared with just the right amount of justification and self-righteousness. "Let me click on the Latin men," Leatha said as she moved the mouse over and clicked the link. Several photos of handsome men downloaded.

"Oh, shit." The words left Savannah's mouth before she had a chance to stop them. "Look at Emilio, girl."

"I'm looking," Leatha said, studying the photo. "He reminds me of Enrique Iglesias. You know I have a thing for Spanish men. Hell, he can be my hero anytime he wants to." Both women broke out in laughter.

"What does it say about Emilio?" asked Savannah.

"Um, it says that he is originally from Mexico but now lives in Chicago." Leatha quickly scanned his description. "It says that in addition to his entrancing accent, this debonair man is fluent in three languages and is a compassionate listener." Leatha leaned back in her seat and studied his photo. After a brief moment, she went back to the home page, copied the link, and began sending herself an e-mail with the link to the site.

"What are you doing?" Savannah asked.

"I have an idea. I need a date for the Black Women in Law convention next month. I'm going to take my time, look at this site, and order me a man."

"You can't be serious," Savannah commented.

"Hell, yes, I'm serious." Leatha answered Savannah, full of conviction.

"Don't you think it's dangerous?" Savannah asked, concerned about Leatha's safety.

"What's so dangerous about it? We'll probably talk on the phone before we meet."

Savannah frowned with concern.

"Look, the conference I'm working on has an awards gala. I don't have a man and don't want to go alone or with another woman. If people can rent a nerd, clown, stripper, or DJ for a party, then why can't I rent a gentleman to escort me to one? All I want him to do is behave like a gentleman and not some ghetto-fabulous clown who doesn't have a clue. I want him to be able to hold an intelligent conversation, treat me nice, and take me to the gala. I don't want to do his damn laundry, clean his house, shop for his clothes, or have his babies. I like the way this Jade woman operates. She's taken the complication out of everything for busy professional women like us. Right now, we don't have the time to go through the cat-and-mouse game of trying to start a relationship."

"That's the same thing she said." Savannah started chuckling.

"Wow, look at him," Leatha said as another man caught her eye.

"Are you sure you need to go home to do your on-line man shopping?" Savannah teased. "Because you've just taken over my computer."

"Girl, you're not using it right now. I'm only going to be a minute."

Savannah rolled her eyes playfully at Leatha, then went to the closet to retrieve her briefcase.

One month later, during the middle of March, Savannah and Leatha entered Honey Child Salon and Spa on North LaSalle Street. Savannah studied the windows for a moment, which were swathed with honey-colored drapery. The soothing sound of New Age music, along with the delicious scent of honey wafting through the air, was putting Savannah in a mellow state of mind.

"Good afternoon, Ms. Styles," greeted the young blond receptionist. "It's good to see you again. I have you down for one thirty P.M. pedicure and a two P.M. massage. And Ms. Meadows," said the receptionist as she acknowledged Leatha, "I have you down for the same thing. If you two will follow me upstairs, I'll get you all set up." Leatha and Savannah were escorted to the second floor where they removed their shoes and stored them away in a guest closet. They were then seated next to each other at the pedicure stand. They placed their feet in a warm tub of water that had smooth stones at the bottom, which felt heavenly on the soles of their feet.

"So, how did the conference go?" Savannah inquired as she curled her toes with delight in the tub of water.

"Girl." Leatha leaned toward Savannah to whisper. "I have something to tell you," Leatha confessed.

"What is it?" Savannah whispered, knowing Leatha was about to share some scandalous detail.

"I had my first orgasm," Leatha said with absolute certainty.

"What?" Savannah wrinkled up her face. Hearing about Leatha's orgasm wasn't what she'd anticipated.

"I'm serious. I slept with my escort Emilio."

"You did what?" Savannah almost shouted.

"Shhhh, damn, Savannah. Keep your voice down," Leatha scolded her. "Savannah, I'm telling you, all of my sexual experiences combined don't compare to what Emilio did to me. Girl, he was so good and my orgasm was so intense, I blacked out for a moment."

Savannah stared at Leatha as if she didn't fully comprehend what she was saying. How could an orgasm be so intense that she blacked out?

"Don't look at me like that. I'm not crazy, and I wasn't drinking that night," Leatha defended her claim. "Savannah, it was incredible. The feeling that washed over me made every nerve in my body quiver. Emilio made me feel as if . . . shit, I can't explain it. All I know is that my body came alive in a way I never knew it could. Emilio was well worth the money I spent."

"Okay, back up," Savannah ordered, "and start from the beginning. I want to know details. I can't believe you slept with him." At that moment, two pedicurists interrupted their private conversation.

"Let's go to that Brazilian restaurant, Fogo de Chao, for dinner," Leatha suggested. "I'll tell you everything that happened over a glass of wine and dinner."

7

Franklin

Three months had come to pass and Franklin was still unable to secure full-time employment. He ditched the concept of hustling knock-off merchandise on street corners and beauty salons, which Lois suggested he try. Instead of being swindled into another one of his mother's get-rich-quick schemes, Franklin exercised good judgment by contacting a number of temporary employment agencies, as well as headhunters. He was able to find work, although it was at irregular intervals. He did temporary work for several companies and submitted his resume to the human resources department, hoping that once he got his foot in the door he'd be in a better position to interview. However, none of the companies were knocking on his door to request an interview. Franklin's predicament compelled him to take Curtis up on his suggestion of becoming an escort. Franklin reasoned that he would only do it until he got back on solid footing.

On a Thursday evening, Franklin visited Curtis at his downtown condo to discuss his decision to give the escorting business a try.

"Come on in," Curtis welcomed Franklin to his home. "I figured that it would only be a matter of time before you came to your senses," Curtis said, walking into his kitchen, which was illuminated by several candles, romantic scoop lights, and the glow of night lights from the city skyscrapers that entered through his enormous kitchen windows. Curtis stood at his sink and began running himself a glass of ice water. Franklin took a seat on one of the wineglass-shaped chairs. Curtis took a sip of his water and then joined Franklin, who focused on the kitchen window and the spectacular evening view.

"You're not expecting company, are you?" Franklin thought he'd better ask in case he was inadvertently interrupting Curtis's evening plans.

"No," Curtis answered as he leaned back in his seat and crossed one knee over the other.

"Have you had a chance to read through the materials I gave you?"

"Yes, I read through it and watched the videos," Franklin confirmed. "That was good material you gave me. There were a lot of things I've never thought about. I mean, I probably thought about them at one point or another but never practiced it."

"I want you to do well in this business. It's not as easy as one might think. There are demands and pressures just like any other business. And every client isn't easy to please." Curtis paused in thought. "Franklin, women request an escort for a variety of reasons. Some clients only want a date for the evening; others are looking for some type of adventure they can't get at home; others are seeking lost youth, or sometimes they just want a really good fuck. Women request an escort to fill their particular need. It is your job to fill whatever void they have. No matter how outrageous their demands are. Sometimes a woman is looking to express herself sexually in ways that she can't do at home. A woman may have a husband who has abandoned her emotionally, has erection problems, or is too busy working to pay attention to her. By the way, some clients who request the service of an escort may be married women who are looking for a discreet date. Do you have a particular problem with that?"

"No," answered Franklin. "But what if her husband shows up or follows us. What do I do then?"

"Don't be so damn green, Franklin. You're a bodybuilder. No overworked and out-of-shape husband is going to risk getting knocked on his ass by the likes of you. I've been doing this for a while and that situation has never presented itself. Married women who require my service are extremely careful and take precautions to ensure they're not exposed. The last thing they want is to destroy their marriage over a lover-for-hire. However, if you ever need to make a quick exit, always be prepared by making sure you do the following: One, never take your ID inside the hotel room or inside their home. Two, purchase a small magnet key box and place a spare car key inside of it. Stick the magnet key box to the under-carriage of your car. This way, you'll always be able to leave without searching for your keys. Three, keep a spare set of house keys in your car under the spare tire. Finally, always keep a spare set of clothes in the trunk."

"Okay, I'll take care of those things," said Franklin. "But what if her driver has taken me to some hotel and I'm unable to leave my belongings behind?"

"Franklin, if you get into a situation where you feel threatened, call the police. I highly doubt that will happen, but calling the authorities is always best in a situation that gets out of hand."

"Okay," Franklin answered as he continued to learn from Curtis.

"Another thing," Curtis went back to the topic of conversation, "never keep the lady waiting. Always be on time." Curtis was passionate about this issue. "For the amount of money they're paying, they don't want to hear excuses about being tied up in traffic or some other holdup."

"Don't worry, my watch isn't set on Colored People's Time," Franklin joked.

"Just make sure you're always prompt, Franklin. You'll also need to keep your wardrobe in impeccable shape. Never show up to take a lady out with unpolished and run-down shoes. Also, don't carry loose change in your pocket. No woman wants to walk with a man who has jingling coins. Mark Twain once said, 'Clothes make the man.' What you wear defines who you are, whether you like it or not. Your clothes also define how other people perceive you. Clothes can make you look successful or like a hobo."

"Curtis, I already know this, man. Why are you giving me an old-school fashion lecture?"

"Because it is critical to what you'll be doing, Franklin. Just hear me out," Curtis demanded.

"All right, my bad. I'm all ears." Franklin chuckled as he got up to run himself a glass of water as well.

"Ninety percent of your body is covered with clothing. Upon that all-important first meeting with your client, her eyes are going to be filled with your image. Ninety percent of which is what?"

"My clothing," Franklin finished Curtis's sentence as he allowed the faucet water to fill his glass.

"Exactly. Remember this, Franklin. Women go gaga over a sharp-dressed man way more than they do for the guy with natural looks, understand?"

"Yeah, I understand." Franklin comprehended where Curtis was coming from. "I need to dress like a chocolate James Bond," Franklin joked as he took his seat again.

"Yes." Curtis popped his fingers. "That's it, man. I couldn't have said it better myself. You're the ultimate gentleman, but when the need arises, you can transform into the most confident, daring, and erotic man your client has ever known. Also, your sexual techniques must be impeccable, Franklin. Every man has an off night, and if it happens when you're with a client, you'd better be able to get creative. I have some more videos for you to watch. They're from the Alexander Institute."

"Alexander Institute? Who are they?" inquired Franklin.

"Sexual psychologists. They've done extensive research on human sexuality," Curtis said as he exited the kitchen to retrieve the DVDs. When he returned, he handed them to Franklin, who read the cover titles.

"*What Women Want* and *More of What Women Want*." Franklin read the titles out loud.

"It has interviews of women who share what they find attractive in a man. It's good stuff. Oh, you'll need to purchase a tuxedo," Curtis said as an afterthought as he walked over to the sink and placed his empty glass in it.

"Dude." Franklin chuckled. "My cash is real tight right now. I don't have money to purchase a tuxedo."

"Yeah, I figured that." Curtis leaned his behind against the sink and folded his arms. He paused in thought. "Franklin, I need to know that you're serious about doing this, man."

"Curtis, I'm serious. I need to fucking survive. And right now, jobs aren't exactly knocking down my door. On top of that, I'll be learning sexual techniques that I never even heard of. That in itself is worth giving this business a try, for a while at least."

"Franklin, most men learn about sex through trial and error. In fact, the first time men have sex is usually in some tight-ass car or dark room where they can't see what the fuck they're doing. It's like they're hunting with a fucking blindfold on. It's no surprise that so many women are unsatisfied. Grown men are out there screwing the same way they did as a teenager. Men primarily discuss sex in terms of dick size. It's rarely about techniques they used to drive a woman wild. Dick size doesn't mean shit if you don't know what the fuck you're doing. I can't even begin to tell you how many big-dick motherfuckers can't please a woman." Curtis chuckled to himself. "All right, enough of that. When I'm done with you, you're going to be able to make a woman wet with desire just by talking to her. I must warn you though. Once you enter into this business, you'll find it difficult to return to a regular nine to five. The money and the variety of women are unimaginably seductive."

"Curtis, if this works out, I plan to use the money and open up my own gym. I really don't want to go back to working a nine to five. I want to be a business owner."

"Good. That's a good way to be thinking," Curtis responded. "I'm going to loan you some money to get you started. I can't have you taking a lady to the opera wearing one of those corporate-boring suits you're fond of wearing." Both Curtis and Franklin chuckled.

"There is nothing wrong with my suits," Franklin disagreed with Curtis.

"Your suits are corporate boring, Franklin. They're nice but lack a certain style. I'm going to send you to my tailor. In fact, hang on a second." Curtis left the room. He returned with a pad of paper and a pen. He began writing. "When you get home tonight, check out this Web site. This is where I shop. Any man who wants to look good shops there. My tailor will create a stylish look for you that is second to none. I want you to go by there this week and get fitted for four suits and a tuxedo. I'll handle the rest."

"Dude, that's going to cost an arm and a leg."

"Franklin, trust me on this one. It is well worth the investment. Besides, we're not only family, we're best friends. Shit, if it wasn't for you stopping me for getting in a car with a drunk driver, I'd be dead right now. I can afford to give the loan. The money I'm pulling in from the nightclub and escorting has me living comfortably. Not that I'm fucking rich or anything, but life is going well right now."

"All right, big baller," Franklin teased.

"Hey, don't joke. People will have the same perception of you once I'm done mentoring you." Curtis smiled. "I have a hunch you're going to do very well in this business."

8

Savannah

Savannah was continually amazed at how swiftly time moved. Although another year was nearing its conclusion, Savannah was thankful that the crisp fall air wasn't too chilly for her to enjoy a quiet evening of peeping at the stars and the moon while listening to Alicia Keys bellowing on about falling in and out of love. She adjusted her high-powered telescope so that she could gaze at the full moon through it.

Savannah wrapped her shawl around her neck and shoulders to keep warm. She dreaded going through the upcoming Thanksgiving holiday alone. She had planned to fly back to her hometown to visit with her parents, but they had made plans and would be traveling to Europe for the holidays. Leatha was also going to be out of town, taking a cruise with her new lover she'd met through Jaguar Services.

"Girl, I'm going to work on Emilio," Leatha had said to Savannah before she left.

"Damn, Savannah," she spoke to herself. "Is this what all of your hard work has boiled down to? You've become a woman with respect and wealth, yet you come home to an empty house. There is no romance, excitement, or passion in your life. The last time you had decent sex was so long ago you can't remember it. Your company has become your lover," she admitted to herself as she studied the moon. She recalled a romance book she once read when she was a budding teenager. The heroine in the story stood out on her balcony, gazed at the moon, and made a wish for Mr. Right to present himself. Just as the heroine made her wish, she saw a shooting star. Savannah laughed at the girlish memory, but somewhere deep within her she made the same wish before she wheeled the telescope back inside.

Savannah curled up on her sectional sofa and picked up a book she'd been reading by Mary B. Morrison called *He's Just a Friend'* When she picked up the book to read, she noticed that a stray envelope was stuck to the back of the book. She removed the envelope, opened it up, and saw that it was an invitation to a fund-raiser for public television. There was to be a soul music concert featuring popular performers. The full list of entertainers was an impressive one. Savannah continued to read and saw that the concert would be taking place over the holiday weekend.

"How did I miss this envelope?" Savannah asked herself. She read on about how money raised from the concert would go toward programming for public television. The event would take place at the Borgata Hotel Casino & Spa. Tickets to the fund-raiser were still available because the deadline date had yet to pass. Savannah decided right then to fly to Atlantic City, New Jersey, that upcoming weekend to attend the event. She would make a weekend of it. She could go to the fund-raiser, hit the spa, and do some shopping. She got up from her sofa to grab her purse from the countertop near the kitchen. When she returned to the sofa, she picked up her telephone and began dialing the number to order her ticket. As soon as she got a connection, she hung up.

"Damn," Savannah hissed. "I hate going everywhere alone. Once again I'll be in a strange city all by myself. Not that being by myself or traveling is anything new." She sat for a moment staring at the invitation, trying to decide if she wanted to do something so nice alone.

"Damn, Leatha, why do you have to be out of town next weekend?" Savannah complained because she didn't have anyone else she wanted to drag along with her. Savannah was about to give up when a crazy idea came to her. *Order an escort*, she thought to herself, then laughed at the silliness of the idea.

"What the hell, Savannah," she convinced herself. "Why the hell not. You only live once. Splurge a little. You could be missing out on the adventurous time you've been longing for. You can order the escort, cover his expenses, go to the fund-raiser, have a great time, and come back home." Savannah walked into her home office and found the business card Jade had given her. She logged on to her computer, went to the Jaguar Services Web site, and began man shopping. She narrowed her selection down to two men named Curtis and Franklin. She was having a difficult time selecting one, so she pulled out a coin from her desk drawer.

"Okay, heads for Franklin and tails for Curtis." Savannah flipped the coin in the air, caught it, and then slapped it down on her desk. "Heads," she said, and looked at Curtis once more. "Sorry, Curtis, but I'm going to select Franklin. His eyes seem honest and yours seem mischievous." Savannah took the business card and walked back into the living room where her phone was. She picked it up, called the service, and ordered Franklin.

The following day, Savannah returned to her office from a meeting with her executive staff. Her cellular phone was beeping, indicating that she had a new voice mail message. She listened to her voice mail message and for the first time heard the charming voice of her escort, Franklin.

"Hello, Savannah. I wanted to take a moment of your time to say hello and that I'm looking forward to our upcoming date. Please feel free to contact me at any time if you'd like to have dinner or just talk in advance of our date. I find that having a chance to at least speak to each other beforehand makes for a perfect evening free of awkward moments. I look forward to speaking with you soon." The voice mail concluded and Savannah quickly saved it. She immediately called her assistant.

"Beverly," Savannah spoke.

"Yes, Ms. Styles," she answered back.

"I'm going to shut my door, and I want you to hold all of my phones calls."

"Okay, just forward your phone to my line," said Beverly.

Savannah rushed over to her door and shut it. She took a deep breath and slowly released a nervous sigh.

"I can't believe I'm this nervous about calling him back," Savannah uttered. "Come on, girl, get yourself together."

She gathered her thoughts before walking back to her desk. She swallowed hard, picked up her cellular phone, and dialed Franklin back.

"Hello," a male voice answered the phone. Savannah immediately lost her courage and didn't know why.

"Hello?" the voice asked again. Savannah wanted to speak but she was too nervous.

"Well, I know I'm not crazy because I did hear the phone ring. And I do hear someone breathing on the other end. So I'm going to assume you're too nervous or shy to speak." Savannah still couldn't utter a word but felt embarrassed by the fact that he could hear her breathing like some perverted prank caller. "I'll tell you what. Why don't we play a little game. I'll ask a question and you can answer by saying yes or no."

"Is this the first time you've ever done something like this?" asked Franklin.

"Yes," Savannah answered.

"Do you want to keep our meeting and conversations a secret?" asked Franklin.

"I don't know."

"Well, I'm going to have to dock you a point for that answer. You're only supposed to answer with a yes or no." Franklin chuckled. He could here a change in Savannah's breathing and knew that she was smiling.

"So, will I ever get a chance to see how pretty that smile of yours is?"

"How do you know I'm smiling?" Savannah asked.

"I can hear it," answered Franklin.

"That's impossible. No one can hear a smile."

"Are you smiling now?" Franklin asked.

"Yes." Savannah laughed.

"See there, I'm psychic, too," Franklin joked, which made Savannah feel more at ease. "I'll bet you have questions, don't you?"

"Yes," answered Savannah.

"Well ask, I'm very open. Ask anything."

"Is it really you?" Savannah asked.

"I think so. Let me check. Franklin, is that you?" he said out loud. "Yup, it's me." He heard her laugh again.

"No, I mean, do you really look like your photo."

"Yes. I have a Webcam if you want to do a video conference via a computer."

"No. That's okay." Savannah paused in thought. "Oh, God," Savannah didn't mean to say what she was thinking, but she couldn't stop the words. In the back of her mind she was thinking about what crash diet plan she'd go on to lose a little weight.

"No, I'm Franklin. I shouldn't be confused with God," he joked again.

"You're a quick one, aren't you?" Savannah's voice quivered before she could steady it.

"Only in the humor department," Franklin teased.

"Do you see a lot of women?" Savannah asked curiously.

"In my line of work, yes, I have escorted a fair amount of women."

"Are you married? And have you ever been in love?" asked Savannah.

"No, I've never been married. I thought I was in love, but things didn't work out. What about you? Are you married?"

"Who, me?" Savannah laughed. "No. But do you see married women?"

"Sometimes," Franklin answered honestly, but then he heard silence as if there was some type of calculation in progress.

"My girlfriend ordered an escort," Savannah offered as information. "I don't understand why she did it. Do you? I mean, why would my girlfriend, or even a married woman for that matter, want to go out with a guy like yourself?"

"I don't know exactly why your friend decided to do it, but I can tell you some answers I've heard," Franklin said. "The reasons vary from person to person. Perhaps your friend wanted some adventure, a change, or excitement in her life. Perhaps she was bored or neglected by her husband." Franklin heard her laugh and figured he'd nailed the reason for her girlfriend's call.

"Are you available later tonight?" Savannah asked.

"What do you have in mind?" Franklin asked.

"I just want to talk to you again, on the phone."

"Okay, what's your name?" Franklin asked.

"Oh, I'm so sorry. That's so rude of me." Savannah swallowed hard.

"Sss . . . Savannah," she stuttered her words like a drunk.

"Hello, Savannah," Franklin greeted her formally. "When would you like to call me?"

"Tonight, after I get home, around eight o'clock. Is that okay?"

"That will be fine. We'll talk more then."

"Okay," Savannah said, and hung up the phone. That was a large leap for her. Never in her life had she ever stepped outside of her comfort zone. Never in her life had she ever done something so outrageous. She sat at her desk, feeling the nervous energy pulsate through her. For the first time in a long time she felt herself come alive. In one breath, it was exciting to her, but in another one, she was afraid of losing herself in undiscovered territory.

Over the next several days, Savannah went on a crash diet to try to lose a bit of weight she'd picked up. She was overly concerned about her appearance because of Franklin's physique.

"The last thing I need is for him to be disappointed by my appearance," Savannah said to her reflection in the mirror as she turned to the side to see if her stomach was protruding too much. Although she and Franklin talked at length and he assured her that her appearance would not be an issue, she refused to take any chances.

"Savannah Styles, you know damn well you can't pull off a weight-loss miracle in four days, so why are you even bothering?" she asked herself as she pinched what she considered to be un-wanted body fat around her behind. "If somebody came out with an instant weight-loss pill, I'd buy several bottles. I'm carting around way too much ass. You should just cancel this entire thing," she told herself. "You're acting crazy, and your nerves are so bad right now that your stomach is feeling torn up." Savannah got frus-trated with her indecisiveness. Finally, after accepting that she couldn't drop twenty pounds in four days without ending up in the emergency room, Savannah concluded that she might as well go and make the best of it. She shifted her thoughts to what she was going to wear. She had four days to find something before meeting up with Franklin in Atlantic City, New Jersey.

Savannah was driving herself crazy looking at herself in different mirrors around her hotel suite. Although the curls in her hair from the roller set were holding and in perfect condition, she still fiddled with her hair, trying to make sure that not even a strand was out of place. She kept studying her strapless black dress, which had shimmy fringes around the bust area and hemline. When she walked, the stringy fringes sashayed. She had a matching scarf that looped around her neck and down her backside. The black dress was formfitting, and Savannah was concerned about the way it pulled across her hips.

"Ooh, sometimes I hate having so much hips and ass." Savannah had also, for some reason, become concerned about her small breasts.

"Damn, I should have gotten those implants," she criticized her-self. Although the dress accentuated her beauty, she was still concerned about how Franklin would perceive her. The straps of her black heels snaked around her legs and were covered with gemstones. The heels highlighted her drumstick-shaped calf muscles. She looked at her legs again in search of dry skin, unsightly veins, and unnoticed bruises.

Franklin had already phoned her room earlier to let her know that he'd arrived in Atlantic City safely. They would meet for the first time in the lobby of the Borgata Hotel. From there, they would head over to the concert.

When Savannah finally came down to the lobby, she spotted Franklin right away. He was much taller than she'd imagined and much more handsome. He had gorgeous even brown skin, a strong jaw line, and a fresh tapered haircut. He looked handsome in his black tuxedo. Not only did he look well groomed, but he also looked as if he owned the hotel. She watched him as he sat down on one of the lobby sofas and crossed one leg over the other one. Savannah decided to study him for a moment before she introduced herself.

Franklin glanced down at his watch and then decided to walk over to the water fountain for a drink. As he walked across the lobby through the heavy traffic of people, he commanded enough attention to make the heads of other women turn and notice him. Savannah decided to introduce herself before some strange woman got bold with her date. Savannah positioned herself directly in Franklin's path.

Franklin saw a goddess dressed in a black dress looking directly at him. He knew right away it was Savannah, and for the first time since he'd become an escort, he was thunderstruck by how beautiful she was. His mouth was agape, and he was at a loss for words.

"Hello, Franklin," Savannah greeted him with a smile. "I'm Savannah Styles." Franklin extended his hand for a handshake, but Savannah was more interested in seeing what it felt like to be within his arms. She nervously stepped into his social space and hugged him. Franklin embraced her snuggly.

"Damn, you feel good," Savannah whispered. "You're not what I expected," Savannah admitted.

"Really," Franklin said with a bit of worry. "Would you like for me to change clothes?"

"No," Savannah said. "It's not a bad thing. You're just much more handsome in person."

"And you're the most stunning woman I've ever had the pleasure of spending an evening with," Franklin complimented her. "Look at you." He studied her beautiful eyes, hair, and wardrobe.

"I'll bet you say that to all of your clients."

"Well, if you placed that bet, you'd lose a large sum of money." Franklin smiled at her. "You look lovely tonight. I'm going to have to fight someone if they look at you in a way that I don't like."

"And what way would that be?" Savannah laughed.

"No man had better look at you with desire in his eyes unless he wants to deal with me."

"Oh, stop it, Franklin, you're making me feel self-conscious." Savannah smiled, loving every minute of the attention Franklin was giving her.

"Okay, but I'm telling you I'm going to be handing out some evil glares at men who try to flirt with you with their eyes." Franklin smiled and Savannah noticed his beautiful white teeth.

"Shall we head over to the fund-raiser?" Franklin asked.

"Yes," Savannah answered, feeling as if the evening was going to be one she'd always remember.

Savannah and Franklin walked into the theater and took their seats that were located in the front row. Savannah paid extra for the seats, but she felt it would be well worth the extra expense. Before the stage curtain rose up toward the ceiling, she and Franklin saw the members of the orchestra get into position.

"Ladies and gentlemen," the announcer's voice thundered over the crowd. "Please welcome Miss Patti LaBelle." Patti came out onto the stage in classic Patti fashion and began singing "Lady Marmalade." The audience came alive, stood in front of their seats, and began grooving and clapping to the music.

As the show wore on, the performers took both Savannah and Franklin back in time with classic love songs. They found themselves caught up in the rapture of the evening. The rhythm and blues group that came onto the stage was After 7. The four men were dressed in identical black suits with matching silk yellow shirts and ties. They began to sing their classic song "Baby I'm for Real." Their harmony and timing were flawless. Franklin surprised Savannah by guiding her to some open space in the aisle and began slow dancing with her. She put her arms around his waist, and he placed his arms around her shoulders. Savannah was nervous because she hadn't slow danced in ages. Franklin found the perfect rock-and-groove motion and Savannah followed his lead.

"You feel so good," Franklin whispered. Savannah embraced him more tightly and nestled her head on his chest. She inhaled the masculine scent of his cologne, closed her eyes, and lost herself. Savannah allowed herself to be whisked away on the melody of the music.

Savannah, girl, she thought to herself. *One date with this man is not going to be enough, and you know it.*

9

Franklin

After the concert, Franklin suggested that they go to the hotel's restaurant for casual conversation and a late dinner.

"I would have thought a man like yourself would have suggested we order room service, especially after listening to so much romantic music." Savannah was on fire with passion. Her pussy was buzzing, and she felt like taking him up to her suite to fuck him just like Leatha had done with her escort.

"Do you prefer to eat in your room?" Franklin asked, wanting to be sure she received whatever her heart desired.

Savannah smiled and gazed at Franklin with unmistakable desire. However, before she went too far, she lassoed her lust.

"No," Savannah answered lightheartedly. "To be honest with you, Franklin, I only wanted to come to the concert and listen to some good music. But you danced with me. That was so"—Savannah paused in thought—"unexpected. You just took me into the aisle and danced with me, and you didn't care if it was improper or if people stared at us. You have no idea of how long it has been since I've danced with someone," Savannah confessed. "Having dinner with you would most certainly be a nice touch to this evening," Savannah said, buzzing with energy. It had been such a long time since she felt excited about being with someone. Even though Franklin was being paid for his services, Savannah felt as if his actions were genuine.

If Franklin wasn't an escort, Savannah thought, *I'd make the time to date him seriously.*

* * *

Franklin was now inside his hotel room undressing. He felt grand and giddy as he sat down on the edge of the bed. In the closet mirror he glimpsed at the red lipstick on his cheek from the good-night kiss Savannah had given him. After dinner he and Savannah had gone to the casino and gambled a little just for fun. They behaved like teenagers who'd discovered love for the first time.

"I connected with her," Franklin mumbled to himself. "I haven't had nearly as much fun with any of my clients as I had with Savannah tonight. And hell, we didn't even have sex." Franklin chuckled as the image of her alluring eyes flashed in his memory.

"Damn, Savannah," Franklin mumbled. "How do I get a woman like you to take me seriously?" Franklin wondered as he sat on the edge of the bed and continued to study his attraction to her.

"She treated me like a person and actually encouraged me to pursue my dream of becoming a business owner," Franklin said out loud as the answers to his own questions began to present themselves. "She's nothing like the ridiculously wealthy, spoiled, self-centered, and rude women who have been requesting my services. On top of that, during our dinner conversation, she inquired about how I got into the business and what I wanted to do with my life. Somehow she deduced that I only planned to be in this business for a limited time; that has to mean something," Franklin reasoned.

Over the course of the year, Franklin had been ill treated and humiliated by elite women who could afford to order an escort. Curtis glamorized the business by giving him the impression that the lure of sex and a variety of women would make him feel like a black James Bond.

"Humph," Franklin huffed. "That's a laugh," he uttered as he took off his shoes. Nothing was further from the truth. Most of the clients who'd been ordering his services were too difficult to please. A lot of his clients graduated with honors from the Hilary Banks University of snobbery and superiority. They were phony, wound-up, wicked women who had nothing better to do than carelessly spend their wealth and attempt to outdo each other at their exclusive social events. To them, Franklin was nothing more than a boy toy to be used however they saw fit, as long as they were paying him. Franklin thought about Susan, a client who trampled all over his feelings in front of her girlfriends while at a political fund-raiser when he attempted to join in on a conversation about personal trainers.

"My personal trainer is best at everything. And I do mean every-thing, ladies," Susan said to her circle of snobby clansmen, who all laughed at the hidden meaning behind her comment.

"I'm a certified trainer," Franklin shared with them. "I plan to open up a state-of-the-art fitness center one of these days."

"Like, was anyone talking to him?" one of the ladies said with a prissy Valley girl tone.

"I'm totally sorry, ladies. You'll have to excuse him. He's all brawn with no brain." Susan rolled her eyes at Franklin. "My reg-ular gigolo wasn't available, so I'm slumming it with this cheap one who doesn't know his place. I'll handle him, ladies. Excuse me."

Franklin was speechless and couldn't believe Susan had actually said all of that about him. At that moment he wanted to knock the hell out of her but didn't because he needed the cash.

"Look, Tae Bo, let's get one thing straight," Susan scolded him as if he were a child.

"Franklin, my name is Franklin, not Tae Bo," Franklin corrected her.

"Excuse me!" Susan had a very dissatisfied expression on her face. "I can call you anything I damn well please with the amount of money I'm paying for you. Now, one more peep out of you and there will be no tip, plus I'll write a letter to Jade expressing how disappointed I was with your service. Now, your job is to be my cute little dog for the afternoon. You should only speak when spo-ken to. Is that clear?"

Franklin cringed at the memory. Susan made him feel discounted and inadequate.

Then there was Ethel, who he believed was a sweet, wealthy widowed client who enjoyed having dinner with him on Tuesday evenings. After their fourth dinner, she offered to pay him a tip of fifteen hundred dollars if he could make her have an orgasm with-out penetration.

"Come on now, don't look like that. I'm positive that a stud of a man like yourself is constantly providing extra services for widows like me. My pussy is still good."

Franklin didn't know how to respond because he'd never been paid for sex before. This was the first time he'd been propositioned.

"Two thousand dollars, in cash. That's my final offer." Franklin couldn't believe that Ethel, an elegant elderly woman, was willing to pay two thousand dollars for an orgasm.

"Well, Franklin? What's it going to be?" She glared at him without blinking. "You'll be getting paid for doing something everyone else does for free. You do need the money, don't you?" Ethel coaxed him into agreement.

"Yes," Franklin admitted, suddenly feeling manipulated.

"I thought so." Ethel grinned like the damn devil.

"Stick out your tongue and make it touch the tip of your nose," she said, and Franklin complied.

"Oh, yes," Ethel chirped. "You have a very nice, long tongue."

Franklin performed well and gave Ethel several orgasms with his tongue, lips, and fingers. Franklin later learned that Ethel was part of an exclusive circle of wealthy widowed women who ordered gigolos constantly for their sexual pleasure. Ethel circulated Franklin's name to her elite circle of friends. They lured him in with the promise of handsome tips for his service. However, none of them appreciated Franklin for his marvelous skills. Once they got several good releases, they paid him and put him out without even saying thank you for a job well done. He had become a sex toy to be used and discarded at will.

Franklin tried to push the vile memories out of his head, but they wouldn't stop flashing in his mind. During this time of ill treatment, Franklin focused on the money he was getting and how to best put it to use for opening up his fitness center. Equipment, rental space, insurance, and payroll for employees were serious business. Franklin spent a fair amount of his spare time touring other facilities to gain ideas. All of his treadmills, and stair machines would have to have television monitors with cable television. He'd have to have Internet access station with computers so that members could check their e-mail account or surf the Web. He also attended fitness seminars to make sure he was still current with what the industry was offering. He also worked diligently on his business plan. The plan that he was creating would be the road map of his success for his departure from Corporate America and the escort service. During this time of business planning and ill treatment, Lois was constantly riding Franklin into submission to be a dishonorable man.

"Why do you spread paper out all over the table like this?" Lois asked as she sat down at his circular glass kitchen table.

"I'm working on my business plan," Franklin answered. "Right now I'm trying to determine what my membership rate will be.

Then after that I have to create guidelines for recruitment and retention of members."

"That's too much damn work, Franklin." Lois placed a sour expression on her face. Her unhappy frown reminded him of a client.

"When it's your passion, it doesn't feel like work," Franklin responded back to her. "I could say the same about all the mess you go through to find a good con."

"That may be true, but scheming pays much quicker. You've been planning this place for some time now and haven't made a single dime with all of your planning."

Franklin ignored Lois's comment and continued on with the business of pressing buttons on his calculator.

"I'm going to need an attorney to draw up a fitness agreement for me," Franklin mumbled to himself as he wrote down more notes and tried to ignore Lois. "I'll contact Emilio from Jaguar Services," he whispered. "He's an attorney."

"So how is the escort business going?" asked Lois, purposely interrupting his concentration level so that he'd stop and pay her some attention.

"It's okay. Some of the clients are hard to please and are downright mean." Franklin stopped working and glanced up at Lois. He was about to tell her the bare-naked truth. "With some of them, I feel as if I'm their slave. At least that's the way they make me feel. There is no emotional connection with anything that I do for them. One client said that I was cheap at one thousand dollars a day. She said some other things that made me want to knock the shit out of her, but I didn't because I needed the money." The only thing that Lois focused on was how much money Franklin said he was getting.

"One thousand dollars a day?" Lois repeated. "Those women have it like that?"

"Yeah, they have it like that," Franklin said, not paying attention to Lois and the calculating glint in her eyes. He also ignored the fact that he broke his rule about informing Lois of how much he made.

"Franklin." Lois reached across the table and grabbed his arm at the wrist. "I want you to hear me out. If those women are that wealthy and treat you so poorly, I say let's make the snobby bitches pay extra for making you feel that way. I would imagine any other man would knock those bitches on their asses."

"You got that right." For once Franklin agreed with Lois. She grinned because she knew that she'd struck the right chord with him.

"Franklin, clients who make you feel discounted need to pay extra for that." Lois twisted the situation around and was reshaping an otherwise bad experience into a justifiable and profitable one. "Get their credit card number and security codes, Franklin. And leave the rest to me. If you can provide me with that information, I can make sure you have the best designer clothing good credit can buy."

"Mom." Franklin didn't want to hear it, but Lois cut him off.

"No, listen, baby. I'm trying to teach you how to turn a negative experience into a profitable one. Listen, your fitness center is going to have a shower and locker room, right?"

"Of course."

"You'll need supplies for those areas. Fresh towels, soap, skin moisturizers, and cleaning supplies. If you do what I ask, I'll make sure your future supply room stays stocked. I can see it, Franklin; it'll be so easy. All you have to do is get the numbers."

Franklin laughed off his mother's ridiculous idea and had absolutely no intention of defrauding his clients. He elected to be honest and ethical with everything he did. However, as he continued to work as an elite escort for women of wealth, privilege, and power, he soon accepted that certain privileged women wanted him only for sexual fulfillment.

"I'm like a fucking poodle with a hard-on to these ladies," Franklin admitted to himself.

Franklin developed a reputation around the exclusive circles of women as a dynamite gigolo with a tongue of gold and a diamond dick with incredible staying power. Women paid him well for a fabulous time and explosive orgasms. Once they were gratified, it was time for him to go. None of the clients gave a rat's ass about giving him pleasure or satisfying his physical needs, and that didn't sit well with him.

Franklin thought he'd caught the break he'd been searching for when he began sleeping with Gina on Sundays. Her husband was a professional basketball coach, and Gina had an obsession with having sex during basketball games.

"I like watching him on television while you fuck me until I'm tender. It turns me on to be looking directly at him as if he's watching me."

Franklin participated in Gina's obsession because he was in search of an investor for his fitness center. He brought up the idea of Gina introducing him to her husband one afternoon after he'd gone the extra distance to please her by wearing her husband's suit while he screwed her.

"Introduce you to my husband!" Gina spoke loudly, and then sat up in the bed and glared at Franklin. Her expression was stone at first, but then she started laughing uncontrollably. "I'm not going to introduce my famous husband to some prostitute." Gina kept laughing at Franklin. However, Franklin didn't find anything funny.

"That's a good one, Franklin. I can see it now: 'Honey, this is the male prostitute I've been screwing while you've been out of town.' Get real, Franklin. I'd never introduce you to my husband." She laughed at him some more. "You should do stand-up comedy. Now, be a good little cocker spaniel and go fetch my purse so that I can tip you and put you out for the night." The more Gina thought about what Franklin suggested, the harder she laughed. She was cold and heartless, and Franklin suddenly wanted to silence her. He got up and went into the other room where her purse was sitting on the credenza. He didn't notice that the purse zipper was unzipped. When he picked up the purse, all of its contents spilled out onto the floor. The first thing Franklin focused on was the gold MasterCard. He could still hear Gina cackling at him like a witch riding a broom. At that moment, he thought about his mother, Lois.

Honey, if they're going to discount and humiliate you, make them pay for it. You're at their service. You're there for their pleasure. If that sort of thing pleases them, they should pay for it. Franklin located the justification to do what he didn't think he'd ever do. There was a pad and pen on the credenza. He grabbed a sheet and took down her credit card information and the information on her driver's license.

"You're too damn funny, Franklin." Gina continued to cackle at him. "I can't wait to tell the girls about this one. You looked like you really thought I would introduce you to him." Gina searched her purse and then pulled out a white envelope. "Here you go," she said as she looked into his eyes. "Just let yourself out."

* * *

Franklin emptied the contents of his slacks and came across a hotel napkin that he'd written Savannah's credit card number on. He had gotten so accustomed to obtaining that type of information that when the opportunity presented itself, he did it out of habit. As he stared at the napkin, he thought about how he'd gotten it.

"I'll pick up dinner," Franklin had told Savannah when the waiter presented the bill.

"No, please," Savannah insisted. "Let me pick up the expense." Savannah gave her credit card to the waiter and he rushed off. "Will you excuse me for a moment? I'm going to run to the ladies' room," said Savannah.

"Sure," Franklin said. The waiter returned and placed the receipt and credit card on the table before Savannah returned. Franklin quickly jotted down the numbers on a napkin and stuffed it in his slacks.

Franklin crumbled up the napkin and was about to flush it away. He wasn't about to allow Lois to screw up Savannah's good name.

"She doesn't deserve that," he said. Just as he was about to flush it away, the sound of the ringing phone distracted him. He placed the napkin back in his trousers and answered the phone.

"Hello."

"Hello, Franklin, I just wanted to say Happy Thanksgiving and to tell you again how much I enjoyed myself."

Franklin got comfortable on his hotel bed.

"Happy Thanksgiving to you too," Franklin murmured, feeling valued for the first time.

10

Lois

Lois and Latoya had just finished stuffing themselves with the Thanksgiving dinner that Lois prepared. Lois sat down at her small dinette table, reared back, and unsnapped the button on her blue jeans so that her stomach wouldn't feel so restricted.

"You have that affliction now, don't you?" Latoya joked about black folks getting lazy and sleepy after eating a heavy meal.

"Yeah," Lois confirmed, "I'll be taking a nap in a minute to let my food settle down."

"Well, you go ahead and relax. I'm going to take a plate over to my guy's house and hang out with him for a while," Latoya said, getting up from the table.

"What are you guys going to do?" inquired Lois.

"He's probably watching the football game. I'll probably end up falling asleep on his shoulder while he's watching his team," Latoya responded.

"All right then." Lois stood up, walked to her bedroom, and settled down on her bed. "Wash those dishes before you leave, Latoya," Lois shouted out.

"Okay," Latoya hollered back.

Lois had what she wanted. All summer long she'd been using the credit card information Franklin was providing her with to run her mobile retail business. Once she got a card number, she placed her orders through various pay phones around the city so she couldn't be tracked. Lois took pride in maxing out a credit card in a short period of time. Lois had the financing to purchase counterfeit designer merchandise, such as handbags, by the caseloads.

"You're such a clever old fox," Lois said to herself as the

thought of her brilliant scheme comforted her. Instead of having the merchandise delivered to her home, she had it delivered to numerous post office boxes set up with fictitious identities, like Eddie May Wiley, which was one of her favorites. Once Lois retrieved her merchandise, she'd sell it out of the trunk of her car at beauty salons and neighborhood festivals. Lois got so bold with her con that she even hung around the church parking lots on Sunday afternoons to sell her illegally obtained merchandise to the sanctified women of the church. Lois grinned at the absurd amount of money she earned from church sales.

"You should sell some of this stuff on the Internet," Latoya suggested to her one afternoon after she'd come back in the house with several boxes of merchandise.

"Why?" Lois asked.

"We can sell this stuff on-line to the highest bidder," Latoya informed her.

"Naw, that's okay. I like to do my business cash-on-the-barrel style. You know what I mean?"

"Yeah, but the advantage of the Internet is that people can shop anytime, day or night. Plus, you wouldn't have to keep hauling all of the stuff back and forth to your car."

"Really?" Lois asked, intrigued.

Latoya convinced Lois to let her handle some of the merchandise, and she set up shop on an Internet site. Latoya was correct; she sold a respectable amount of merchandise.

"When you come back in here tonight," Lois shouted out to Latoya again, "I want you to check that site thing and see about my orders. Tomorrow is going to be the big day for retail salespeople like myself," Lois spoke with a tone of truth. "It's the busiest shopping day of the year."

"I will," Latoya once again hollered back her response.

The more clients Franklin serviced, the more merchandise she was able to buy, and before long, Lois had a ton of it piling up in her living room.

"How in the hell am I going to move all of this shit?" she mumbled to herself one afternoon as she sat on her sofa. Then an idea came to her.

"The flea market," she said out loud. "I could move this stuff much more quickly if I purchased booth space at the flea market."

After that realization, Lois paid the fee for her space and hit pay dirt. It was easy for her to pull in as much as fifteen hundred dollars in cold hard cash over the two-day weekend. After that, various flea markets around the city became the Promised Land to Lois. Between what Latoya was pulling in off of the Internet and what she was pulling in from flea market sales, things were looking good in her world.

As promised, Lois looked out for Franklin and made sure that he had expensive designer clothing and jewelry so he'd look appealing to all of his clients.

"No one is going to pimp my baby except for me," she said when she stopped by Franklin's house the night before he left for Atlantic City to pick up her supply of card numbers.

"What do you mean, pimp?" Franklin took offense to the comment.

"Just what I said. No one is going to pimp you except for me. I'm going to make sure that you look extra good so that your ridiculously wealthy clients keep recommending you to their friends."

Franklin released a deep sigh and leaned against a wall. Even though he had plenty of clients who humiliated him, he still felt uneasy about stealing.

"I'm thinking about getting out of the business," Franklin whispered. Lois laughed because she was certain that he was toying with her.

"What are you talking about?" Lois coughed to clear her throat. "We've got a smooth operation going here. How can you turn your back on all of the women and the sex? You have every man's dream job. You're at their service."

"There is no emotional connection with these women, Lois. They're just using me. I feel like shit."

"And you're using them back. So the shit is even. What's the damn problem, Franklin?" Lois got irritated and concerned about the possibility of her hustle coming to a rather abrupt end. Franklin studied the exasperation etched in her facial expression.

"You don't understand. You're not dealing with them like I am. They don't respect me. I'm like a slave who's been bought and paid for. When I'm no longer amusing to them, they put their foot in my back. I have goals and dreams just like the next man. I have education. I'm not some street-corner whore."

"Listen, Franklin." Lois placed her hands on his shoulders.

"You're allowing your heart to get in the way of making money. Don't allow that to happen. Do you understand where I'm coming from?" Lois asked.

"No, Mom, I don't. Not all of the clients are bad, but there are certainly enough of them who are, and I only take from the ones who are mean-spirited. Even though they tip me well, I just can't do it anymore. I think that when I return from New Jersey, I'm going to call it quits."

Lois got angry with him and raised her voice. "Do you want to see me and your sister living out on the street? Stop thinking about yourself so much and consider what would happen to us." Lois glared at Franklin with a stone face. "Everything is not about you, Franklin. We've got a good thing going here. Don't screw it up. Don't piss me off," Lois said as more of threat than a warning. She then took her credit card numbers and walked over to the door. Before she left, she turned and looked at Franklin.

"Don't do it, Franklin. It would ruin my life if you did," Lois said, placing a heavy burden squarely on his shoulders before she left.

"She just said the wrong thing to me," Franklin mumbled with resentment.

11

Savannah

Savannah walked through the lobby of her office building to the escalator, which would carry her to the first floor and out the door to her driver. Christmas was only a few days away, and once again Savannah was feeling the sting of being alone for the holiday. She'd phoned Jaguar Services earlier that day to order Franklin again, but when she picked up the telephone she lost her courage.

"He's just a playboy, after foolish rich women," Savannah reasoned. "Don't be so silly, Savannah, you're much smarter than that," she told herself. Although Savannah willed her reasoning into the truth, she missed Franklin in a way she didn't think she would.

When she got to the front door of her office building, she glanced out onto the street and noticed snow was cascading down at a steady rate. She bundled herself up a little more snugly in her full-length mink coat before she stepped out into the chilly evening air. Christmas carolers and last-minute shoppers were buzzing around on the streets. Savannah walked toward her driver, who was dressed in his usual black suit with the exception of a red and white Santa Clause cap. Savannah took her eyes off of him for a moment and focused on a gentleman approaching her on the street. He was wearing a long gray coat, a gray fedora hat, and matching gray gloves. She couldn't see his face because of the way his hat was tilted.

"Well there is a jauntily dressed man," she whispered to herself as he walked toward her.

"Would you like to attend a cocktail party this evening?"

Franklin asked as he stopped, turned around, and lifted his head up so Savannah could see his face.

"Franklin," Savannah responded, suddenly feeling vivacious. "What are you doing out here?"

"Trying to find you," Franklin answered as he noticed the large snowflakes billowing down all around them.

"What if I don't want to be found?" Savannah said.

"Then if that is the case, I've made a mistake." Franklin was all set to chalk up all of his hard detective work as one big blunder. He turned to leave.

"You give up too easily." Savannah grabbed his arm and stopped him. "You shouldn't give up so quickly." She studied his affectionate eyes.

"Tell your driver to take the night off. I'll make sure you get home safely," said Franklin.

"Is there a charge for your services?" asked Savannah. "I thought for sure a man such as yourself would be off gallivanting around Rio with one of your clients for the holiday."

"You assume too much," Franklin countered. "I'm no longer in the escort business, I gave it up."

"Is that so?" Savannah raised her eyebrow with intrigue. "So what does an out-of-work escort do for a living?"

"Have dinner and a cocktail with me and I'll tell you," Franklin said, stepping closer to Savannah and brushing away the snow that had landed down on her shoulders.

"All right," Savannah agreed. "Where do you want to go? I'll have my driver take us."

"Does your driver take you everywhere?" Franklin asked seriously. "I do have a car, you know."

Savannah, smiled shyly. "I'm sorry, I'll give him the night off as you suggest." Savannah walked over to her driver and relieved him of his evening duties. She rejoined Franklin and they began to stroll down the Magnificent Mile on Michigan Avenue.

"My car is very old," Franklin said. "When I start it up, gas fumes come in through the vents, and when I make a left turn you have to hold your door shut or else it will fly open." Franklin watched with amusement as Savannah stopped in her tracks.

"Let me call my driver back. I'll have him take us." Savannah quickly searched her purse for her cellular phone.

"Savannah, I'm just joking." Franklin laughed. "Where is your sense of humor?"

Savannah put her cellular phone away.

"Come on, smile."

Savannah gave him a half smile.

"Your car is in good condition, isn't it?" Savannah was suddenly leery.

"Would you relax? I have a very nice sedan that is very clean and rides very smoothly. The car thing was part of a bad-blind date story I once heard."

Savannah finally loosened up and allowed herself to laugh.

"That must have been some date," she said as they continued on.

Savannah and Franklin made their way over to Bandera's Restaurant. Once they were situated, Savannah began to speak.

"So, tell me why you quit the business."

"Let's just say that it really wasn't for me," Franklin spoke truthfully. "I wasn't getting any respect. I started my own business. I earned enough money and got the rest by putting my home up as collateral," Franklin said. "In fact, I've already purchased a moderate-sized sports facility. Right now it is undergoing some remodeling."

"You're not kidding, are you?" Savannah asked, impressed that Franklin wasn't wasting time reaching his business goals.

"No, I'm not," he said. "When we were in New Jersey, you put the spark I needed under my ass. How did you put it? You said, 'Franklin, you have a great idea, but you need fire under your ass to get you to pursue your dream.' I've always wanted to be a business owner, and well, now I am. And with a bit of luck I hope to be successful enough to open up several more facilities."

"So you took the leap of faith like I suggested?" Savannah now had newfound respect for Franklin.

"Yes, I did. It was time," Franklin said. "I've been planning to do it for years. I'd love to show you the place once the remodeling has been completed."

"And I'd love to see it," Savannah said. "What is the name of the facility?"

"Body Shaping," Franklin answered.

"That's a catchy name," Savannah said.

"May I ask you a personal question?" asked Franklin.

"Sure."

"I want to know if you're seeing anyone special."

"I'm seeing you. And I think you're pretty special," answered Savannah.

Franklin chuckled. "Okay, do you have a current boyfriend?" Franklin asked.

"No," answered Savannah. "I'm so busy with my career that it has become difficult to nurture a healthy relationship." Savannah paused. "Let me correct my statement." Savannah decided to stop hiding from how she truly felt. "I would like someone special in my life," she admitted. "And to be perfectly frank, I'm hopeful that the special man I've been searching for is with me right now. I have a good feeling about you."

Franklin smiled and placed one of his hands on top of Savannah's. "Savannah, I'm not a wealthy man, but I'm not poor either. If you'd give me a chance, I'd like to prove to you that I am a man worthy of taking care of your heart. I will not break it, lose it, bruise it, or abuse it."

Savannah's eyes started batting rapidly as Franklin's words went straight to her heart. She didn't know how to respond to him. It had been so long since she'd let a man near her heart. She was also trying to understand how Franklin got under her skin so quickly.

"Are you saying that you want to date me?" asked Savannah, who wanted to be absolutely clear.

"Yes, I want to date you and be proud of the fact that you're my woman."

"Your woman." Savannah let the words wrap around her feelings but then became afraid. "You don't know me, Franklin. I'm not an easy woman to deal with. I get stressed and I'm cranky. I like perfection and I'm a neat freak. I work a lot of hours, and I don't know how to cook. I'd probably bore you in bed because you're such an experienced man and—"

"Whoa, where did all of that come from? Let down your defenses, Savannah. I don't care about all of those things. I care about the way I feel when I'm with you. I like the way you treat me, and never think you're a boring woman in the bedroom."

"I'm just saying I'm not as worldly in that department as you are. I've been a good girl all of my life. I'll probably disappoint you in the bedroom."

"You're not a virgin, are you?"

"No." Savannah laughed.

"I'll show you exactly how to please me," Franklin said. "A woman who has been a good girl all of her life is just dying to let the bad girl within her come out and play. Wouldn't you agree?"

"Yes," Savannah said, surrendering to Franklin's reasoning.

Franklin studied Savannah for a moment and then smiled at her. "You're perfect. Do you know that?" he whispered to her.

"No," replied Savannah.

"Well, now you do."

Savannah wanted to shout out with joy but contained herself out of fear of appearing idiotic.

"Can I trust you, Franklin?" she asked.

"Savannah, I'll never give you a reason not to trust me."

"If you hurt me . . ." Savannah clenched her jaws tightly.

"I will not hurt your heart, Savannah," Franklin repeated, but this time Savannah looked into his eyes and believed him.

"I have a question I must know the answer to."

"What?"

"Safe sex. Did you practice safe sex?"

"Savannah, my body was my business and I made damn sure I didn't abuse it. Yes, I practiced safe sex. Hell, I was so paranoid that I got tested every few weeks just to be certain. What about you? When was the last time you were tested?"

"I've never been tested. But if it will ease your fears, I will."

"I think it would ease both of our fears. We could get it done together," Franklin said.

"One more thing," said Savannah. "I don't share. If we are going to nurture something special, I don't want to have fears about you sneaking off with a former client of yours."

"Savannah, trust me when I say I have no intention of ever seeing any of my former clients."

"Even if they pay you?" Savannah raised her eyebrow suspiciously.

"No amount of money is worth my pride and self-respect. That's one of life's lessons that I'll never ignore again."

12

Lois

On the third day of the new year, Lois dropped by Franklin's house in the afternoon to see if he had gotten her some more credit card numbers. She walked into his living room and plopped down on his sofa. Franklin positioned himself directly in front of her to lay the heavy news on her.

"You're not going to like this, but I don't have any new card numbers for you," Franklin said. "I've quit my job as an escort."

"What the hell do you mean you quit?" Lois howled at him.

"I had to get out, Mom," Franklin barked back.

"What do you mean you had to? The only things you have to do in this world are stay black and die." Lois was fuming about her free ride coming to an abrupt end.

"Jade called all of her gigolos into a meeting," Franklin explained. "She said that she's been getting complaints from clients about credit card fraud and that she was being accused of being the ring leader of a theft empire. She was pissed off and swore that if she ever discovered that any of us were behind the thefts, we'd meet the bitch within her."

"What's wrong with you?" Lois glared at him with a perplexed expression. "I don't give a damn about her. She's never going to find me or ever know who I am. And if by chance she does happen to roll upon me, I've got something for her."

"You're not listening." Franklin was completely aggravated with Lois.

"Jade's threat wasn't the only reason I left. After Jade's speech, Curtis talked to me once we were away from the office. Curtis suspected that it was me stealing those numbers."

"How did he know? Did you tell him my business?"

"It wasn't hard for him to figure out, Mom. Curtis is family, and everyone in the family is familiar with your work. He knows how you operate. He didn't directly come out and say it, but he suggested that I get the hell out of Jade's path because if she discovered that it was me, she'd have me removed from the face of this earth. Those were his exact words."

"Now, Frankie, you know that I'd never let her do that to my baby." Lois tried a softer approach, hoping to get him to change his mind. Lois and her inability to see anything other than profit for herself disgusted Franklin. Trying to talk sense into her was at times like talking to a wall.

"What am I supposed to do when I run out of stock?" Lois was now trying the pathetic approach. "Am I supposed to live on the street? Is that what you want? You want your mother and sister to be locked out. Hustling is the only thing I know, Franklin. That's the only way I know how to survive."

"Right now, I don't have time for this. I have plans for the evening," Franklin said, and walked into the other room. Lois felt as if Franklin had hit her with a hammer. His decision had knocked the wind out of her.

"What are you going to do now, Lois?" she mumbled to herself.

"Franklin, listen to me. I want you to get back into the business. Consider going to another service. We had the perfect setup," Lois hollered out. She was unyielding about using Franklin for her survival.

"It's time for you to go," Franklin said as he walked back into the room. "I'm not going to discuss this with you anymore."

"It's not right, Franklin," Lois said as she stood up and gathered her purse. "It's not right to put your own mother out like this."

"You have it twisted around, Mom. It's not right for you to manipulate me the way that you do. Happy New Year," Franklin said, wanting them to part on civilized terms.

It was now June, and Lois had sold everything and had squandered all of the money she'd made. She was once again in desperate need of cash. Franklin had been avoiding her and wouldn't return her phone calls, even when she left word on his answering machine that it was urgent he returned her call. She knew that he'd finally opened up a fitness center, but he wouldn't tell her the name or the location of it. Lois didn't care because she couldn't see any way to make a quick profit from a health club. She didn't even want to work for him. What she wanted was for Franklin to get back into the escorting business and start supplying her with what she needed. Lois was surprised by how well Franklin could suddenly pull away from her. Whenever she popped up at his home unannounced, he wasn't there; his home was neat and clean and appeared untouched, as if he hadn't been there in weeks. All of his expensive suits hung neatly in the closet and looked as if he hadn't worn them in some time.

"Franklin, where are you?" Lois mumbled as she stood in the center of his kitchen floor one evening when she'd yet again let herself into his condo. Lois opened up the refrigerator in search of something cold to drink. She found an unopened can of soda and began to drink it. She finished off the soda and then left his house. Lois got into her car and began driving home. On the way there she began to think hard. It was so unlike Franklin to just disappear without saying anything to anyone. Then it dawned on her who Franklin was talking to.

"Latoya," Lois said out loud. "Latoya probably knows where he is." When Lois got home, she found her daughter sitting on the sofa eating a bag of pork skins soaked in Louisiana hot sauce and watching a rented video.

"What are you watching?" she asked as she studied what appeared to be a silly movie.

"*Deuce Bigalow: Male Gigolo.* This shit is funny as hell. I wonder if Franklin had to deal with odd women like the ones in this movie."

"Speaking of Franklin, Latoya, where is he?" Lois asked, taking a seat next to her.

"Where is who?" Latoya replied as if Lois was speaking a foreign language.

"Franklin. I know that you've been talking to him. He's avoiding me, and I have a feeling you know where I can find him."

"Mom, leave him alone. Franklin doesn't want to be bothered right now."

"Excuse me." Lois caught an attitude. "I'm his mother."

Latoya tried to ignore Lois by just staring at her video. Lois decided to take away the distraction by turning the television off.

"Dang. Why did you do that?" Latoya tossed a quick tantrum.

"I want some answers!" Lois bullied her daughter.

"Well you won't get anything from me talking to me like that," Latoya snapped back.

"Okay, is he all right?" asked Lois.

"He's doing fine. He has a new woman. He's crazy about her."

"A new woman. So that's it," Lois said, louder than she intended to. She curled her lips as she thought about how she would dispose of his latest girlfriend.

"Why didn't he tell me he was seeing someone?"

"He knows how you are. He didn't want you sabotaging it before it got started."

"Bullshit," Lois discounted Latoya's statement. "I don't care who he dates," Lois lied. "So where is he?" Lois asked once again.

Latoya ignored her and picked up a sports clothing catalog for men from the coffee table. Lois watched her as she began flipping through it.

"Wait a minute, hold up. Let me see that fashion book."

Latoya handed her the book and Lois studied the cover of the catalog.

"What the hell. That's Franklin on the cover. When did Franklin start modeling men's sportswear?"

"He was looking to make a little extra money, so his girlfriend suggested he give modeling a try. She knew some people who owed her a favor and got him hooked up. He looks good, doesn't he?"

Lois grumbled. She began to suspect that Franklin no longer wanted to help her out. She feared this new woman in his life would try to change him, and she couldn't risk having that happen.

Lois began thinking about how much things have changed over the last six months. Latoya had admitted to her that Franklin convinced her to stop scamming people and take a real job. He even helped her put together her resume, which landed her a decent-paying job as an assistant at St. Joseph's Hospital. The money she brought home covered the bills, but that didn't matter to Lois. She was accustomed to having her own money, and when she didn't have it, she wanted it from Franklin. She couldn't imagine herself breaking the cycle of dependency. But as she analyzed her situation, she concluded that Franklin was attempting to break away from her.

"Latoya, I'm going to ask you this one more time. Where is Franklin at?"

"You can't reach him right now, Mom. He took his girlfriend on a romantic vacation to Jamaica."

"He what!" Lois couldn't believe that Franklin had gotten that serious about this new woman.

"He's in Jamaica. He's in love, Mom. His new woman inspires him, or so he told me. You know how it is when you first meet someone and you can't stand to be apart from them," exclaimed Latoya.

Lois began to think. She needed to find out where Franklin's health club was. It became painfully clear to her that he was making money and wasn't telling her about it at all.

"What street is his health club on, Latoya?"

"I can't tell you that."

"Why?"

"He made me promise not to tell you where it is."

"Oh, so it's like that now, right? You guys are ganging up on me."

"Mom, give him a break." Latoya was clearly siding with Franklin, and Lois didn't like it one bit. "I like my job down at the hospital. I'm making decent money right now, and the bills are getting paid. Franklin has shown me the way to earn an honest living. I like working. I feel better about myself because I'm not ripping people off. The hospital has an educational reimbursement program. I'm thinking about going to night school."

"Well, whoop-de-fucking-do for you." Lois felt as if her children would abandon her and place her in an old-folks' home. Her worst fear was becoming a reality. "I'll be back," Lois said bitterly.

She went back to Franklin's place and began snooping around for information about his fitness center. As she was snooping in his closet, she ran across a napkin that must have fallen out of the pocket of one of his slacks. It was from the Borgata Hotel in Atlantic City, New Jersey. She wouldn't have paid it much attention if it weren't for the numbers scribbled on it. Lois looked at the numbers.

"Savannah Styles, Visa number." Lois smiled. "Looks like Franklin forgot to give me one," she said as she took the napkin and placed it in her pocket. Lois went through his file cabinet and located the address to Body Shaping.

"I found it," she said aloud as she wrote it down on some scrap paper she'd located. "Now, Ms. Styles, let's see how strong your credit is." Lois shut the file drawer and left Franklin's house.

13

Savannah

"Wake up, baby," Savannah whispered as she rubbed her index finger across Franklin's smooth brown lips. "The plane is about to land." Franklin came to life and stretched his legs out before him.

"Put your seat back in the upright position," Savannah directed him, because she'd just overheard the flight attendant tell the same thing to another passenger.

"I can't believe that I actually got a good nap in." Franklin felt refreshed as he opened his window shade.

"I can't believe we're in Jamaica." Savannah leaned over to peer out of the window. "Look at that beautiful coastline," Savannah pointed to the paradise beneath them. "Ocho Rios, here we come," Savannah could barely contain her enthusiasm.

Savannah and Franklin were impatient and wanted to check into their suite at the Hot House Resort for Couples. However, before they could begin their weeklong escape from the reality they'd left behind, they had to wait their turn in the customs line, which snaked around several corners. It was unbearably hot standing in line, but the stifling heat wasn't going to dampen their spirits. Once they made it through customs, they grabbed their luggage, went outside, and boarded an air-conditioned resort shuttle, which was awaiting their arrival.

"Welcome to Jamaica, man," greeted the driver, who seemed sincerely happy to be at their service. Franklin and Savannah got situated and cozy.

"I can't believe you've whisked me off to Jamaica, Franklin."

Savannah was bursting with happiness as she gazed out the window. "We're actually here."

"It is hard to believe, isn't it?" said Franklin as he put his arm around her shoulder and leaned her in closer to him. Their shuttle bus soon filled up with other vacationers. Once the shuttle was filled to its capacity, the driver got in the driver's seat.

"Yeah, man," said the driver with a thick Jamaican accent. "My name is Eugene, and I will be your driver for the next two hours. The drive will be very comfortable, and you'll get to see the real Jamaica. First of all, raise your hand if this is your first time in Jamaica." Savannah and Franklin raised their hand along with another African American couple.

"In Jamaica we always say hello by saying, 'yeah, man.' And if you agree with something, we say, 'yeah, man.' Secondly, in Jamaica we never have a problem, we only have a situation." Everyone on the bus laughed as the driver began to pull away from the airport. "I want to thank you for selecting the Hot House Resort for Couples," the driver said. "It is a resort owned and operated by people of color, just like you and me," said Eugene. "We work very hard to make sure that your stay here in Jamaica is enjoyable and free of situations. Many African American people from the States are interested in the history of Jamaica. So as we drive through the towns I will be telling you a bit of our history. But first, since it will be a two-hour drive, I am going to stop at the store and get everyone something to drink. Is that cool with everyone?"

"Yes," responded everyone on the shuttle.

"No, you're supposed to say, 'yeah, man.' "

"Yeah, man," everyone corrected themselves.

Eugene drove to a nearby quick mart, took everyone's order, and then rushed inside to get what they'd requested. He returned with everyone's order. Once he was sure that everyone was satisfied, he began driving again.

"Normally, my bus is filled with white vacationers and I am forced to play the Bob Marley for the entire drive. That's the only Jamaican singer they've heard of," Eugene boldly stated. "But since we are all people of color, I'm going to play some updated reggae music. Don't get me wrong, I love Bob Marley, but I also love Shabba Ranks, Maxi Priest, Shaggy, and Sean Paul. Is it okay if I play Maxi Priest?" asked Eugene.

"Yeah, man," everyone answered in agreement. Now that he had everyone's approval, Eugene hit the PLAY button.

As they drove across the Jamaican countryside, Franklin kept whispering in Savannah's ear.

"I can't wait to get you in the suite," he whispered. "I'm going to have you crawling up the wall," Franklin mumbled. His words tickled Savannah in such a way that it gave her goose bumps.

"Stop it." She slapped his thigh.

"You don't want me to stop," he said, nibbling on her ear. Savannah wasn't expecting him to do that, and a sudden rush of passion caught her by surprise and caused her to squeal louder than necessary.

"Are you okay?" asked Eugene, gazing up into his rearview mirror.

"Yeah, man." Savannah giggled her answer, feeling embarrassed by how loud she was.

"If you don't stop, I'm going to grab your dick and twist it," Savannah whispered through her clenched teeth. A woman who was with an older gentleman sitting across from Savannah heard what she said, raised her eyebrow, and snickered. Savannah turned her stare toward the woman.

"Get him, girl," she said in a friendly sister-girlfriend manner. Savannah winked at her.

"Don't worry, I'm going to handle his ass," said Savannah, full of cockiness.

"We'll see who handles who," said Franklin.

"There is a clock tower in the center of each town," Eugene said as they approached a small town. "Also, if you look to your right, you will see a church that was built in the 1700s by slaves. The church is still in use to this very day."

"Oh, wow," said both Franklin and Savannah. Everyone studied the church as they drove past a slice of world history they could not ignore. A short while later, they came upon a small Jamaican town called St. Ann's Bay. "We will be at the resort in about ten minutes," announced Eugene.

Once they arrived at the Hot House Resort for Couples, Franklin went to the reservation counter to check in while Savannah waited to tip Eugene for unloading their luggage from the bottom of the shuttle bus.

"Thanks, Eugene," Savannah smiled as she gave him a twenty-dollar tip.

"Yeah, man," Eugene responded. "You're a beautiful woman."

Savannah was surprised that Eugene had the nerve to try and hit on her. But then again, Savannah was flattered by it because over the past six months, she'd lost fifteen pounds and had toned up her legs, stomach, arms, and behind, thanks to Franklin's one-on-one training. She'd dropped two sizes and was down to a sexy size eight. She felt so good about herself and her accomplishment.

"Watch out there now, Eugene," Savannah gave him a playful warning.

"Yeah, man." Eugene understood her message. "Say, do you need anything to smoke?" asked Eugene, who was offering more of his special service in case Savannah needed some Jamaican marijuana.

"No, thank you," Savannah answered. "But if I decide that I want some, I'll have the front desk contact you."

Eugene smiled at Savannah, tipped his straw hat, and said, "Have a good time." He then got in the driver's seat and drove off.

Savannah walked up behind Franklin, slipped her arms around his waist, and rested her head on his back, feeling happy to be his woman.

"Come on, baby, let's take a look around. The receptionist said to give her a few minutes to get everyone checked in. Once she's done that, she'll come and give us a brief orientation."

Savannah looped her arm around Franklin's waist and headed toward the patio, which led to the beach and the ocean. The breeze swirling off the ocean felt divine as it whirled around and gave their skin goose bumps.

"Look at how beautiful the ocean is." Savannah gasped as she moved toward the concrete rail to take in the view completely. "Oh, this is so wonderful, Franklin," Savannah whispered as she listened to the light melody of reggae music drifting through the air. Franklin was focused on an island that was about a half mile from the shore.

"You know what that island is out there, don't you?" Franklin pointed to the island and kissed her on the cheek. Savannah glanced at the island with a frisky smile.

"Don't even think about asking me to go out there to the Au Naturel Island."

"What? Why not?"

"No," Savannah answered, trying to present him with a stern glare. She couldn't hold the evil stare because she started laughing. "I'm not getting naked in front of strangers."

"I see. We'll see about what you will and will not do," Franklin said, challenging her to be a bit more daring.

"I'm not going out there," Savannah restated. "I'm a good girl, and good girls don't do that sort of thing."

"If you say so," Franklin shot back, not believing her excuse of being a good girl. *Savannah, baby, that good girl is going to graduate and become a woman down here in Jamaica.* Franklin smiled at the thought of his wicked intentions.

"Would you care for a glass of wine?" A resort employee was serving wine to all of the guests who'd just arrived.

"Yes," said Savannah, and took two glasses of white wine from the tray. Savannah and Franklin took their drinks back inside the lobby sat on one of the bright yellow sofas.

"Okay, may I have your attention please." The young thin receptionist stood in the center of the lobby. "Welcome to Jamaica," she said, then proceeded to tell everyone important information they'd need to know, including a big pool party where guests were encouraged to come out for a night of fun and festivities. After the information was conveyed, everyone was given their room key and told that their luggage would be delivered to their room shortly.

Savannah and Franklin went to their fourth-floor suite, and once inside, Savannah drew back the drapes and unveiled a breathtaking view of the ocean.

"Franklin, this is so beautiful," said Savannah, glowing as she stepped out onto the balcony. Franklin approached her from behind and began kissing the back of her neck.

"Stop, we can't get started yet. The bellman will be here with our luggage soon," Savannah said, all jittery with excitement.

"I'll just tell him to leave it outside the door. Come on and get in the bed with me." Franklin ached for her at that moment. Savannah was tingling from his kisses and was about to escort him to the bed, push him down on it, and ride him. However, the moment she decided to do it, there was a knock at the door.

"See, I told you," said Savannah.

"Wait here," Franklin whispered, "I'll handle it."

While Franklin dealt with getting their luggage in the room and tipping the bellman, Savannah went inside, sat at the desk, and flipped through the materials they'd been given during their orientation. She learned that in order to have a romantic dinner at their full-service French cuisine restaurant, she needed to make reservations. She also read about hidden Jacuzzis on the garden side of the property. Although Savannah had read all about these attractions in the brochure, reviewing them again only added to her sense of excitement.

"Okay, hot and sexy. He's gone. Now, where were we?" Franklin was ready to get started. He plopped down on the bed, fully expecting an afternoon filled with hot lovemaking.

"We're about to take a walk around the property," said Savannah.

"What?" Franklin said with disappointment.

"Don't worry, Franklin. We have an entire week to be down here making love. Now come on. Let's take a walk around and see what it's like."

"Can't we wait to do that?" Franklin began pouting.

"Baby, I want to see everything this all-inclusive resort has to offer. Come on now. Make Momma happy and take a romantic stroll with her."

"All right." Franklin surrendered to Savannah's wishes.

Savannah and Franklin ambled around the property, admiring its beauty. They inspected the romantic outdoor Jacuzzis that were camouflaged by the lush gardens. They found the fitness center, the pool, the restaurants, and the bar. Nestled near the swimming pool was the buffet area. Franklin and Savannah were both hungry, so they decided to eat. After eating dinner, Savannah wanted something sweet.

"I'm going to get some dessert," Savannah informed Franklin. "Do you want anything?"

"No, baby, I'm good," responded Franklin.

Savannah returned with a slice of cake for dessert.

"Oh, my god, Franklin. This pineapple cake is out of this world," Savannah said as she nibbled on her large slice. "You know that I've said the hell with my diet this week, don't you?" Savannah savored the flavor of her cake. Icing from the cake was coated on her fingers. Savannah fixed her tongue to lick her fingers but stopped when she caught Franklin staring at her.

"Franklin," Savannah snapped him out of his lustful daze. "Why are you looking at me like that? What's that look for?"

Franklin leaned across the table and whispered in her ear, "You know damn well what that look was for. You know how freaky my mind is." Franklin took one of her icing-coated fingers, put it in his mouth, and swirled his tongue around it. Franklin's words ignited Savannah in a way she didn't anticipate. That was one of the things about Franklin that had her so hooked. She was discovering so many new things about herself sexually with him.

"I have never in my life met a man who is as sexual as you are," Savannah whispered as she wiggled her wet finger around in his mouth. She now realized that she'd been making love all wrong. It had never been as much fun with anyone she'd ever been with as it was with Franklin. There was so much untamed eroticism between them. Their passion for each other was like some unbridled beast dashing about wild and free. Savannah had never felt this way with any man. She was always a good girl, and sex with any partner was always scheduled. Her love life was void of creativity, passion, and energy. Now that she had these elements, it opened doors that she didn't know existed. Savannah feared and welcomed everything that Franklin was helping her to discover.

"Stop it. You're turning my ass out and you know it."

Franklin noticed her breathing had quickened as she removed her wet finger from his mouth.

"Come on. Let's go back to the room," Franklin said. "I can finish turning you out in there."

Oh how Savannah loved the way Franklin spoke to her. She put her napkin down and they both sped away to their suite.

The next morning, Savannah and Franklin went to the breakfast buffet. Franklin secured a table while Savannah went to grab a plate and stand in line. She stood behind the woman who had given her the friendly sister-girlfriend stare on the shuttle bus yesterday.

"Are you eating alone?" Savannah asked the woman casually, because she didn't see the older gentleman she was with.

"I've done it before," replied the woman. Savannah knew right away she'd unintentionally struck a sensitive nerve with the woman. "I'm sorry, I didn't mean to snap at you. I'm pissed off this morning, that's all." Before Savannah could say she was sorry to hear that and move on, the woman completely vented. "Can you believe that my guy has come all the way down here to paradise to sit in the damn room? He doesn't want to do a thing except order room service and watch television," the woman grumbled. "That's okay, though, because I am not about to sit in the damn room for seven days. I'm going to enjoy myself. He can behave like a fool if he wants to."

"I'm positive he'll come around." Savannah tried to offer the woman some sort of comfort, even though at that point she could have cared less. She was looking forward to the full day that she and Franklin had planned together.

"You're lucky, girl. To have a man as fine as the one you have." The woman glanced over at Franklin, studied his muscular physique, and undressed him with her eyes. Savannah closed her eyes to slits at the woman's bold and unwanted inspection of her man. *Women!* Savannah thought to herself. *You can never trust them.*

"What's his name?" the woman asked before she caught the evil glare in Savannah's eyes. "I'm sorry," she apologized. "I shouldn't have said or asked that. Excuse me, have a good day," she said, and whisked away with her plate of food.

Savannah returned to the table with food for both her and Franklin. When she sat down, she began whispering to Franklin.

"That woman over there"—Savannah tilted her head in the direction of the woman—"has some major issues."

"Why do you say that?" Franklin asked as he picked up a slice of honey-cured bacon. The salty and sweet taste of it made Franklin close his eyes and hum.

"First of all, she and her boyfriend have had a spat and now she's dining alone. Secondly, she boldly asked me what your name was while she undressed you with her eyes. Old stank bitch," Savannah voiced her sudden dislike of the woman.

"Damn," Franklin said. "I've never heard the black woman in you come out like that. She must have really pissed you off." Franklin supported Savannah's feelings.

"She had no right to fucking stare at you like that." Savannah was becoming increasingly irritated the more she thought about it.

"Baby, come here. Lean forward toward me."

Savannah rested her elbows on the table and did as Franklin asked. Franklin placed the palms of his hands on both her cheeks and kissed her. Again, his kiss made Savannah tingle all over.

"Now, get your mind off of her and focus it on all of the fun we're going to have. We're not going to allow her relationship issues to interfere with our happiness, understand?"

"Yes," Savannah agreed, then dropped the conversation completely.

*   *   *

It was nine o' clock in the evening when Franklin and Savannah returned to their room. They'd spent their day scuba diving, and the early part of the evening was spent horseback riding.

"I can't wait to get some food," Savannah said as she flipped the light switch on in the bathroom. Franklin heard her turn the knob on the shower as he opened up the patio doors to inhale the island air and feel the evening breeze giving his skin goose bumps. The air was blustery, which was just the way Franklin loved it. The last sliver of daylight was fading away, and Franklin watched as the resort boat brought everyone who was on the nude island back to shore. He watched as the other vacationers walked down the pier toward the beach where another resort employee was stacking the rental canoes in an orderly fashion.

"I'm going to sleep so well tonight," he whispered to himself. Franklin focused his gaze toward the pool because he could hear loud merriment from other resort guests and the sound of reggae music wafting through the air. It was then that he remembered that the resort was having a grand pool party for its guests and that Savannah wanted to go to it. He suddenly found new energy as the thought of a party consumed him.

Savannah stood behind Franklin and cleared her throat. "Tell me how I look in this two-piece bathing suit." Savannah struck a pose, modeling her chocolate-brown bathing suit. "This is a Brazilian-cut bikini bottom," she offered more details about the suit. "Is my stomach too puffy?" Savannah asked, trying not to suck in her tummy. Before Franklin could give her an answer, she offered up another criticism of herself. "What about my butt? It doesn't look all sloppy does it? And this"—Savannah pinched her side—"I don't look bad, do I?" she awaited his answer.

"Shit, your ass looks fine to me." Franklin tried to palm her perfectly shaped behind.

"Stop it. I'm serious, now. I don't want to go down to the pool party looking crazy. Now honestly, look at my ass and tell me what you think." Savannah turned her back and glanced over her shoulder at him.

"I think you have the most succulent ass I've ever seen."

Savannah noticed the devilish glint in his eyes.

"You're no help," Savannah huffed, and then paused in thought, considering whether not to even go to the party at all.

"Baby, you look spectacular," Franklin complimented her. "You look sexy. We're going to have a great time at the pool party."

"Spectacular may not be good enough." Savannah's insecurities were getting the best of her. "That bitch may be lurking around. I wouldn't be surprised if she came butt naked," Savannah hissed.

"Baby, let it go," Franklin said.

"Okay, I will. What suit are you going to wear?"

"Hmm, I haven't given it much thought," Franklin admitted. "But since you're wearing such a hot swimming suit, I'll wear my Speedo swimsuit." Franklin noticed the coy smile forming on Savannah's face.

"You are so bad," Franklin teased her.

"I don't know if I want you out there with all my goodies exposed." Savannah stepped into his social space and rubbed her hand up and down his dick.

"Savannah," Franklin whispered, and he felt his pride growing stronger.

"Yes, baby," Savannah whispered her words as the thought of his pride inside of her made her weak. She kissed him before he could speak.

"Now, if we get out there and discover we're the only two people dressed in next to nothing, we're coming back, understood?"

Savannah looked Franklin directly in the eyes and winked at him.

"Understood," she said.

When Savannah and Franklin arrived at the pool party, the first thing they did was stop at the all-you-can-drink bar.

"I'll have an apple martini," Savannah said.

"And I'll have a strawberry daiquiri," Franklin followed up with his order. The bartender began preparing their drinks as they sat on the bar stool and watched people gyrate with wild abandon to the music of Sean Paul's "Gimme the Light."

"Here you go." The bartender sat their drinks on the bar behind them. Savannah and Franklin each took their drink. After two more drinks, they were feeling frisky.

"Come on, baby, let's show them how it's done," Savannah said, pulling Franklin off of the stool and towing him out to the dance area. They found some space to dance, and Savannah turned her back to Franklin and moved her hips sensually as if she were a Jamaican goddess entertaining her man. Franklin placed his hands on her hips and focused his gaze downward on her ass.

"Damn, shake that motherfucker," said Franklin, wanting to spank her naughty ass. Savannah was getting lost in the sensual rhythm of the reggae music. Franklin pulled her close to him so that he could grind against her.

"Damn, what do you have in there, baby, a baseball bat?" Savannah turned and faced him. She pressed against his warm chocolate body and focused on his eyes, which were the windows to his soul.

Franklin loved the emotional connection his heart felt as he studied the sensual expression on her face. Her readiness was unmistakable. It was everywhere—in her eyes, in her lips, and in her movements.

"I want you," said Franklin.

"I want you too," Savannah said as she lowered her eyes and kissed his bottom lip. Franklin could taste traces of her apple martini.

"You're so fucking sexy," Franklin said as he held her tightly. "Let's go back to the room."

Savannah had purchased some sexy lingerie and was eager to model what she had for Franklin. She came out of the bathroom wearing harem lingerie she'd purchased from Fredrick's of Hollywood. It was by far the most daring lingerie she'd ever purchased. It was a black four-piece set with a foam-shaped bra that had coin trim, sheer pants, sequined panties, and a veil.

"Do you like?" Savannah asked, hoping that Franklin would appreciate her attempt at being more adventurous.

"Oh, hell yeah!" Franklin howled.

"I thought I'd dress as if I was a woman in your harem," Savannah said, crawling into the bed and posing sensuously.

"We're about to have some fun tonight," Franklin said. "I have a surprise for you too."

"Is that so," asked Savannah, sensing the untamed energy between them swirling like the eye of a hurricane.

"Wait right here," Franklin said, and took a mysterious bag into the bathroom. When he came out, Franklin had transformed himself into a gladiator.

"Oh, my god!" Savannah screamed with unrestricted excitement. "Where on earth did you get that costume?" She couldn't believe that he'd purchased a costume.

"Do you like it?" Franklin asked.

"Oh, shit yeah," Savannah said as she studied his black leather skirt with studs, his leather wristbands, lace-up sandals, and warrior helmet. "Hell, all you need is a damn sword," said Savannah.

"It's at home. I couldn't bring it on the plane."

"Damn!" was all Savannah could say. She couldn't believe that Franklin had gone through this much trouble to excite her.

"Are you ready for an erotic adventure?" asked Franklin, who had determined that he was going to unload his sexual arsenal on her that evening.

"Yes, I think so." Savannah was tingling all over. "What do you have in mind?"

"Don't worry about what I have in mind. All you have to do is allow me to take you over the edge," Franklin said. "Here, put on this robe." Franklin tossed her one of the hotel robes. Savannah did what he'd asked. "Now follow me."

"Franklin." Savannah paused when Franklin grabbed the room key and opened the door. "Where are we going?"

"You'll see," he said. Savannah was at a crossroads. She had to trust Franklin and go along with whatever freaky exotic adventure he had in mind. She wanted to just stay in the room where they could play safely. Savannah swallowed hard because she feared this new territory they were about to enter, but yet she had to admit that the mystery of what Franklin had in mind was alluring.

"This had better be good, Franklin," Savannah said as she slipped on her sandals and walked out of the room with him.

"Relax, you're going to have the most exciting time of your life." Franklin and Savannah walked down to the beach under the cover of the night. When they got to the beach, Savannah took off her sandals and stepped onto the warm sand.

"Look at how bright the moonlight is tonight, Franklin," said Savannah, who believed she'd figured out what Franklin wanted.

"You want to make love on the beach, don't you?" asked Savannah.

Franklin laughed. "Nope, that's too typical."

"What?" Savannah became paranoid.

"Shhh!" Franklin said. He went over to the stack of canoes and freed one. He coiled the rope at the stern around his hand and dragged the canoe across the sand to the shoreline.

"Come on, get in," he whispered, but Savannah stood frozen.

"Franklin, is that thing safe?" Savannah's nerves were buzzing out of control.

"It will be fine, trust me," Franklin said. Savannah willed her feet to move. She sat down in the canoe and got situated. Franklin shoved the canoe off into the ocean and then leaped aboard. Once he was on, he grabbed an oar and began to paddle toward the deserted nude island.

Savannah watched Franklin's muscular arms plunge into the water like powerful pistons. He stroked on the left side for a while and then the right in order to keep the canoe moving forward and in a straight line. As they moved away from the shoreline, the soothing melody of the oar splitting the water was the only sound that could be heard. Savannah began to relax and allowed her fingers to drag across the surface of the ocean. She studied Franklin and the entire situation felt as if she'd been transported back in time. A trapdoor to an erotic chamber in her mind had been unlocked. For the first time, Savannah was able to see lovemaking through the imaginative mind of a lovestruck young woman. Franklin was teaching her that lovemaking didn't have to be routine or stale. Franklin was teaching her that with a little bit of courage and an unlimited imagination, lovemaking could be taken to an entirely new plane.

"We're almost at the island," said Franklin as Savannah watched his sexy arms and broad chest glow under the illumination of moonlight. Franklin was her renegade, her rouge, her untamed warrior who went against tradition for the sake of her pleasure.

"Oh," Savannah cried out as the moment consumed her. "This is so liberating," she declared, feeling energized and sedated all at the same time. "I have to give you a name," Savannah said, twitching with passion.

"I already have one," Franklin informed her.

"Okay, who are you supposed to be dressed in that warriors costume?"

"I am Thor, the thunder god," Franklin said, laughing. "I've just come back from the Trojan War, and now I'm whisking you away to Mount Olympus."

"Oooh, shit, Franklin." Savannah's pussy was buzzing like a vibrator. "I like that. I love Greek mythology. If you're Thor, then I'll be Aphrodite, the love goddess."

"Then, during our stay at Mount Olympus, that's who you shall be."

"I can work with that," Savannah smiled and began to feel freakishly wicked.

"Okay, we're here," Thor announced as he guided the canoe close to the pier. "There is the ladder, climb up it," Thor directed. Aphrodite followed his instruction and waited as he secured the canoe and joined her.

Thor and Aphrodite explored their fictitious Mount Olympus, which was a small man-made island about the circumference of a two-hundred meter track. The side of the island facing the ocean was cluttered with lawn chairs for sunbathing. The side that Thor and Aphrodite were on housed a swimming pool where other gods and goddesses could swim up to the bar and order a drink.

Aphrodite went behind the bar and discovered it was still fully stocked. Thor came over to where she was. "Thor, look," Aphrodite said. "Would you like for me to mix one of my special love potions?"

Thor smiled wickedly. "Prepare me a blue martini, shaken, not stirred."

"One blue martini coming right up." Aphrodite prepared Thor's drink for him.

"We have all of Mount Olympus to ourselves," she declared, feeling as if she were in some magical place where lovers lost themselves in felicity. Time seemed to stop just for them. Aphrodite gave Thor his drink, which he gulped down like a barbarian.

"Now it's time to play." Thor was ready to enjoy Aphrodite in every way that a man and woman could. Aphrodite playfully backed away from Thor, giggling as she swallowed the last of her drink.

"Now, wait a minute. I want to show you something I learned from Beyonce, the goddess of the booty bounce." She stopped and took off her coin-laced skirt and the rest of costume. She turned her ass to him, looked over her shoulder, and bounced her ass for him.

"Damn. Your ass has attitude," noted Thor as he watched her bare-naked ass bounce and slap together like hands clapping.

"Do you want to discipline my ass's attitude?" Aphrodite teased.

"Yeah." Thor licked his lips, the thought of brushing his tongue over her rump excited him.

"First you've got to catch me," Aphrodite announced before she took off running.

"Come back here, woman." Thor took off after her. Aphrodite squealed as she dodged his grasp several times, ran back toward the swim-up bar, leaped into the pool, and swam away from him.

"Woooo." Thor's hammer became solid at the sight of Aphrodite swimming nude in the water. Thor noticed how the moonlight shimmered off of her body underneath the pool water. Thor rushed to the other side of the pool and caught Aphrodite as she was climbing the ladder to get out.

"I got you." Thor grabbed her arm. Aphrodite continued to play their game of cat and mouse by attempting to free herself from his clutch. But Thor, using his colossal strength, hoisted her up on his shoulder and carried her toward the lawn chairs.

"Bad Aphrodite!" Thor growled like a ruffian; he smacked her bare ass, then rubbed away the sting of the slap.

"Put me down," Aphrodite demanded. "But spank me again before you do." Thor complied and spanked her ass again.

"Ooh," Aphrodite cooed. "You're making my pussy juicy."

Thor gently placed her down on a lawn chair. Aphrodite got situated and stared up at Thor, who was towering over her.

"Damn you look so . . ." Aphrodite couldn't retrieve the right words she was searching for. She could only stare at him in awe. It was the way the moonlight glistened off of his chocolate skin. The way his chest heaved as if he were about to devour her at any moment. She felt helpless, powerless, and as hot as the sun all at the same time. She reached up and raked her fingernails down the six-pack that he worked constantly to maintain. His thunderous thighs looked mighty underneath his leather skirt.

"Get out of that skirt." Aphrodite didn't recognize the voice that came dashing out of her mouth. She had allowed some new person within herself to escape. She helped Thor unfasten the snaps and expose his pride, which was long, cinnamon brown, and hooked. Aphrodite gasped. The sight of his chocolate dick hanging down and freed from its confines made Aphrodite's pussy quake. Her sexual history never included giving a lover oral sex because it was viewed as taboo. However, after Thor taught her how wonderful pleasuring him in that fashion was, Aphrodite became obsessed with sucking his large hammer.

"Do you have any idea of how delicious you look?" Aphrodite asked. Thor straddled the lawn chair, rubbed his stomach, and stroked his pride. Thor began to grow solid, and Aphrodite became fascinated with watching his dick come to life.

"You want some of this?" He teased Aphrodite with the way he was stroking himself.

"Oh, please let me do that." His chocolate hammer hypnotized Aphrodite. She stroked him and rubbed her thumb across the mushroom-shaped head the way he'd taught her.

"You're wet at the tip," she said. "I love it when I get to taste you. Come closer," she said, and placed him inside her mouth.

Thor enjoyed being inside of Aphrodite's mouth; it was so warm and soft. Her strokes were soft, long, and loving.

"No hands," Thor directed her. "Don't act as if you don't know my hammer. You don't need to shake his damn hand. Put your hands on my ass. Yeah, that's what I like. Wet it up, make it sloppy."

Aphrodite complied with his request.

"Oh, damn." Thor sighed. "Rake your fingernails across my ass," Thor directed her once again. "Yes," he howled. "Leave your claw marks on me. Mark your territory, baby!"

Aphrodite could feel his ass muscles contracting. *Oh god*, she thought to herself, and spanked his tight ass. He felt so impenetrable. She took him out of her mouth, lifted his pride up against his stomach, ran her tongue along its length, and flicked her tongue around his jewels. She adored the fact that Thor kept his dick completely shaven. It made pleasing him in this manner more enjoyable and made his skin feel silky. It was fascinating to her that he could be so tightly packed and yet have a very soft and sensitive area that she could stimulate and make her warrior god buckle down.

"Lie down on the lawn chair," said Thor. "Now it's your turn." One thing Aphrodite had to admit, the way Thor gave her head was mind-blowing.

"Yes, Thor, reacquaint yourself with my pussy. Let her know who the fuck you are." Aphrodite was tangled up in the rapture of the moment. She lay flat on her back. Thor grabbed her legs at the ankles and pushed them toward her chest. The soles of Aphrodite's feet were pointing toward the stars. As she glanced up, she felt as if she could curl her toes and pluck a star from the sky.

"I'm going to make you see stars," Thor said.

"Ooh, baby." Aphrodite sighed as Thor began kissing the back of her legs. He ran his tongue from her ankle to the back of her knee and back up again. Aphrodite shuddered when he did that. Thor used his thumb and index finger to gently spread her vagina's lips. He placed soft kisses on her pussy before he pulled a bit wider and exposed her love button. He licked the length of her pussy paradise, devouring sweet nectar.

"Damn, Thor." Aphrodite shuddered as she cupped her breasts and pinched her nipples.

"Are you ready to see some stars, baby?"

"God, yes," Aphrodite cooed.

Pushing up lightly, Thor inserted two fingers inside of her, just to the first finger joints. He curled his fingers so that his fingertips touched the back of her clitoris. He began pressing his fingers one at time until he found her most sensitive spot. He then placed the tip of his tongue on her clit and began making small circles with it. He alternated between stimulating her clit from the inside with his fingers and then the outside with his tongue.

Aphrodite couldn't help herself. The sensations she was experiencing caused her entire body to shake, shudder, and quiver with earthquake-force tremors. Her back bowed and she cradled the back of his head with her hands, holding him to her hot spot.

"Oh, Thor!" Her words were loud. He began making larger circles around her clit with his tongue. Thor could feel Aphrodite's legs shaking uncontrollably, rewarding him with confirmation that he was pleasuring her. Aphrodite was going out of her mind. Thor had her pussy buzzing. She felt as if he'd taken his hammer and gonged a giant tower bell, and the vibrations from his blows were too much for her body to handle.

Thor listened as her breathing became more rapid and uncontrolled.

"Oh, God, Thor!" Aphrodite cried out his name as she slapped the top of his head. Thor flicked his tongue from left to right while alternating finger presses in perfect rhythm. This sensation pushed her over the edge. Aphrodite's body detonated with such exquisite force, her eyes shot open, her body froze, and she gasped for breath as if she'd been beneath water. At the exact moment of her rapture, Aphrodite saw a shooting star flame across the Jamaican sky.

"Oh, God," Aphrodite cried out. "How in the fuck did you do that?" She had tears in her eyes. "Make love to me, please,"

Aphrodite begged. Thor removed a condom from a small pocket of his outfit. He removed it from the wrapper and slid it on. Thor then positioned himself on top of her and invaded her love tunnel.

"Damn, baby. You're so wet," Thor said, enjoying his pussy bath.

"Get it, baby," Aphrodite encouraged him. "Hit it. I want you to get all up in it." Thor used his brute strength and pumped Aphrodite. Her pussy grabbed and squeezed his cock sporadically at various locations. The head of his pride, the shaft itself, and then the base. Her orgasms were arriving at a blistering pace. They were arriving so quickly that Aphrodite felt as if she'd black out if she kept climaxing at this pace.

"You can have this pussy, baby," she cried. "I'll be whatever you want me to be. I promise, I'm all yours."

The greatest gift Aphrodite gave Thor was her appreciation of his efforts to please her.

"I want you to think about this dick all the time," Thor said. "As long as you have breath in your body, I don't want you to even think about being with another man. I'm all the man you need. Do you hear me? I'm all the damn man you need."

"Yes!" Aphrodite looked into his eyes and into his soul. Something happened to the both of them at that moment. They'd reached a level of pleasure they'd never reached before. Time stopped for them both as a strange type of electrical current flowed through them. Thor could see her soul, too. He united with Aphrodite emotionally. He felt his heart and emotions become one with hers. At that moment, he lost control and surrendered to the passion that was swallowing them up like a giant hole in time. Thor's orgasm separated from him; he was no longer in control of it. His body was being commanded by a divine connection he'd made with Aphrodite. Suddenly, he, too, gasped for air as if he'd been under water.

Aphrodite felt his manhood expanding wider inside of her. She focused on his eyes and the life within them as his essence poured into her body.

Later that week, Franklin and Savannah took a bus into town to do some shopping. They entered a large gift shop, and each of them milled around, searching for the perfect item that would remind them of the exquisite adventure they had in Jamaica. Franklin was toying around with the different varieties of hats that were available while Savannah stood in the checkout line to purchase a sundress.

"I'm sorry, miss," said the cashier, "your card has been declined." Savannah laughed.

"That's impossible. Try it again," Savannah said, confident that the machine hadn't read the card. A few moments went by before Savannah's card was once again declined.

"Sorry, miss," the cashier said politely.

"Hang on." Savannah had suddenly become irritated. "Franklin," she called.

"Hey, baby, what's up?" Franklin appeared, wearing a silly baseball cap that had phony shoulder-length dreadlocks.

"I'm having a problem with my credit card. It's not going through. I don't know why. First thing Monday morning, I'm going to call the credit card company to find out what's going on."

"Sometimes when you're on vacation thieves somehow get your credit card number and do bad things," said the cashier. When the cashier said that, Franklin's mind began racing.

"Sir, are you okay?" asked the cashier, noticing the instant change that had washed over Franklin.

"Franklin, what's that look for? Why do you have that expression on your face?" asked Savannah.

"Nothing." Franklin snapped out of his daze and reached into his pocket. "Here is a hundred dollars. Will that cover it?"

"Yes, that is more than enough," said Savannah, and paid the cashier.

Franklin moved away from Savannah and began contemplating. *I never gave Lois Savannah's credit card number,* he thought to himself. *I certainly hope her card is malfunctioning because of technical problems and not fraud.*

14

Franklin

On Monday evening, Franklin's health club was packed with fitness fanatics. Franklin was in his office talking to one of the young managers he'd hired. He was interrupted by a phone call from Savannah who'd had a difficult day because she discovered that somehow someone did actually swipe her card number.

"Baby, I'll be there in a few minutes. You will not believe what some asshole did."

Franklin felt like shit. Although he was confident that the culprit wasn't his mother, he was now on the opposite side of fraud, experiencing the effect it had on someone he loved. Twenty minutes later, Savannah was sitting in his office, sharing what her credit card company had told her.

"Some bitch purchased a ton of knockoff Gucci handbags and other knockoff designer shit on my credit card. They even ordered cases of fucking aspirin." Savannah was clearly irritated. Right then, Franklin knew who'd wronged Savannah. This realization knocked the wind out of him. He held his head down, not wanting to accept his share of blame.

"Baby, are you okay? You don't look so good."

"I'm just very upset that this has happened to you," Franklin uttered, feeling his heartache. *But how?* he pondered. *How did Lois do it?*

"Baby, don't feel bad. I had fraud protection. I'm not responsible for the charges. I'm just pissed off that it happened."

"So am I, Savannah." The more Franklin thought about it, the angrier he got—not only at himself but at Lois as well.

Thirty minutes later, Franklin was at the front guest counter greeting members when Lois and Latoya hustled in with two boxes. Lois and Latoya set the boxes on the countertop.

"Franklin," said Latoya, "I didn't tell her where this place was; she found it on her own and forced me to come down here with her."

"What the hell is all this?" Franklin tried to contain his dissatisfaction.

"Franklin, honey, I've figured out a way to make money using your health club," Lois said excitedly. "A vanity scam. People are always searching for a miracle pill that will help them lose weight, and I have a box of them right here." Lois slapped the box with her hand. "Just let me set up and I'll sell them right here," Lois said, glowing and confident that her con would go over well. Franklin needed confirmation before he lost his cool completely. He needed to know what type of pills she had in the box.

"What types of pills are in the box?" he asked.

"Don't worry, honey. I've labeled them fat-burning pills, but they're really just aspirin. Aspirin aren't going to hurt anyone."

"Woman!" Franklin roared like a madman.

"Oh, shit," said Latoya. "I'll wait out in the car. This is going to get too ugly for words," she said, and rushed off.

"You are the most—"

"Why are you shouting like that?" Savannah walked up to Franklin and hugged him.

"Oh, so this is the girl!" Lois wrinkled her nose as if she smelled a foul odor. Franklin could see Lois shooting ice picks at Savannah with her eyes. Franklin wasn't even about to put up with Lois's shit. He turned his back to his mother, something he'd never done before, and looked directly at Savannah.

"Baby"—Franklin paused—"I have something I need to take care of with Lois here. I need you to give me about ten minutes to straighten her out."

Savannah had never seen that look of intensity in Franklin's eyes before. She wanted to ask if the woman standing there was his mother, but didn't. She respected his wish.

"All right, Leatha and Emilio are working out together. I'll be with them. Come see me when you're finished," Savannah said, and kissed Franklin. "I hope everything works out, baby," she said before she walked away. Franklin waited until Savannah was a good distance away from him before he snapped off.

"Lois!" Franklin's tone was as sharp as a samurai's sword.

"I'm your mother. Why are you calling me by my first name like you're my daddy or something?"

"Get yourself into my office right now. Follow me!" Franklin's voice was unmistakably vicious. Never in all her life had Lois seen Franklin behave in the way he was now. Her heart was racing with nervous energy. She followed him to his office, and he slammed the door shut so hard the walls in the office rattled.

"Sit down," Franklin barked.

"Don't talk to me like that. I'm your mother. You need to show me some respect."

"Lois, sit the fuck down before I do something I'll regret. Mother or not, I'm so pissed off at you I can barely restrain myself!"

Lois studied the evil in Franklin's eyes and knew that he wasn't toying with her.

"It's a motherfucking shame that I have to get this ugly with you for you to understand that I'm a grown man. At some point, a boy grows into a man and leaves his mother's bosom to make a life for himself. Your problem is that you don't want me to leave. You're choking me, Lois. You're too much dead weight to carry around. I've let you manipulate me for the last damn time. So listen up, Lois, and listen well. That beautiful lady you were about to tear down is my woman. She is Savannah Styles! Does the name ring a fucking bell to you?"

Lois was speechless for a moment. Her mouth was agape but no sound came out.

"Oh, Jesus. Franklin, I . . . I . . . I . . ." Lois couldn't find her words quickly enough. She felt exposed. Franklin had finally opened his eyes and saw who she truly was.

"How in the hell did you get her credit card number?" Franklin wanted to know.

"I was at your house. I found it and thought that you forgot to give it to me." For the first time in her life, Lois felt terrible for what she'd done.

"Give me my damn house keys," Franklin roared.

"Frankie." Lois's heart shattered because she knew that a deep trust had been violated. She pulled out her keys, removed his keys, and gave them to him.

"Walking into my home and stealing from me on any level is unforgivable, Lois." Franklin's chest was bursting at the seams with contempt. "I'll admit that I'm not an angel, and I've done some shit that I'm not proud of, but I have a good heart! I have a caring heart. And never would I have ever abused the trust between us the way you have." Franklin paused, and for the first time he understood how violated Cassandra, his ex-girlfriend, felt when he stole one thousand dollars of her money. He understood pain of broken trust.

"Frankie, baby, I'm sorry." Lois began tearing up. She could see the hurt in his eyes. His pain was connected directly to her heart.

"I don't want to see you for a long while," Franklin said. "I don't like you right now, and what's even more painful is that I don't like myself for what I did. It was wrong, and I knew it." Franklin paused in thought. "Don't call me, don't come by here, and don't even think about me."

Lois saw Franklin's eyes turning red with rage and pain.

"Go," Franklin whispered. "Leave, and don't look back."

Lois felt weak. She somehow managed to get to her feet and walk away, holding on to her tears until she reached the car where Latoya was waiting to take her home.

Franklin sat in his chair thinking. "There is truly no honor among thieves," he whispered.

He needed to be truthful with Savannah. He began searching for the right words to explain how regretful he was about his dishonorable behavior. He prayed that she'd be forgiving.

A Man and a Half

Phillip Thomas Duck

Prologue

"I wish I'd died instead of you," a grieving son whispered.

The words fluttered with the breeze to wherever foolish and rash thoughts go to rest in peace. Wesley Matthews stood by his father's fresh grave absentmindedly digging the toe of his Bacco Bucci loafer into the mound of soil underfoot.

"I hope you aren't upset about the funeral, Pop. I know you would have wanted Wilson Pickett, Solomon Burke, or one of them to sing you home. But you know Mom. She insisted on 'Precious Lord' and 'Blessed Assurance.' "

Wesley choked the words out. His father loved those old soul singers. *Loved.* It would be hard for him to think of his father in the past tense. He didn't think he could.

Wesley thought of his father's old-fashioned record player. The last 45 he'd heard blasting from his father's sanctuary in the basement. James Carr's "A Man Needs a Woman." A woman needs a man, too, Wesley knew.

"Mom is holding up well," he spoke to the fresh grave, yet without a headstone. "She might do some traveling now that you're gone. That's what she says. I don't know what I'm going to do yet. I've never been without you before, you know?"

A laugh of hurt escaped from Wesley's lips. He sighed and looked heavenward. The glare of a full orange sun beat down on him. He crinkled his forehead and squinted his eyes. If asked, he'd have said he did this because of the sun's bright stare. He'd have taken off his glasses and wiped the lenses to solidify the point. Truthfully, though, he narrowed his eyes and frowned because of the grief. It left a huge void in his gut.

"How do I deal with this, Pop?"

"Day by day," came a response in a soft voice.

A familiar and feminine scent immediately caught Wesley's nose. Sweet, alluring, laying truth to the claims written in gold-embossed letters on the perfume's shapely bottle.

He looked over his shoulder. The sight of Sheila, his one and only love, brought a smile to his face.

Sheila moved to Wesley, stylish sunglasses hiding her eyes, which were strained from heavy crying. She'd loved Wesley's father, taken him as a surrogate, used his goodness and love to replace all the mess that was her own family.

"How much longer you plan on staying out here, Wes?" she asked. "We really should get over to your mother's place."

"As long as it takes, Sheila," Wesley replied.

"Takes for what?"

He frowned, shook his head, but said nothing.

As long as it took to move through this cloud, Sheila realized he meant. She tried to think of something comforting to say. Came up with, "The service was nice, don't you think?"

"As funerals go, yes, I suppose," Wesley replied through an even deeper frown.

Sheila silently chastised herself for the stupid question. She wasn't helping the situation. She wasn't serving as the anchor she desperately wanted to be.

Wesley balled the funeral program in his hand, careful he didn't catch eyeshot of his father's photo on the front. He couldn't look at that picture now. He might never be able.

"After what happened to Pop, I never want to see another person puffing on a cigarette ever again," he told Sheila. "I swear. Nicotine is a death sentence. A freaking skinny white coffin nail."

"What are you talking about?" Sheila asked, perplexed. "Your father died in a car accident."

"Woman that hit him took her eyes off the road to light a Virginia Slim. It was all in the police report." Wesley smiled, even though his heart ached.

Sheila touched his shirtsleeve and held it as if it were his hand. "Don't do that, Wes. You don't have to make light of this hurt. Let it be. That's the only way to move on from it."

"You want a strong man," Wesley said, shaking his head. He looked at the fresh grave to avoid her eyes. Avoiding her eyes by way of the grave didn't help him any. Summoning his courage, he shifted his gaze to Sheila again. "Told me yourself the other day I needed to 'man up.' " Her words were still eating at him, even with the grief of his father's loss occupying his heart. *Man up.*

Sheila had said horrible things to Wesley the other day. Intentionally, too, so she could have an excuse to run off. Do her dirt.

Before she could offer a lukewarm apology, Wesley started swallowing large gulps of air, expelling each gulp much too quickly. Hyperventilating.

Sheila thought to do a thousand things—touch Wesley's face, kiss his cheek, hug him, pat his back, tell him to breathe slowly— but she did none of them. She felt guilty offering her comfort, knowing that she'd done him so wrong lately.

After a moment, Wesley regained his normal pace of breathing. Without Sheila's aid. He apologized right away.

"Sorry?" Sheila said. "You're hurting, Wes. You have nothing to be sorry about. You just loss your father."

"Sure I do," Wesley bitterly replied. "Today's Pop's Homegoing Celebration Day." That's how the minister had described the occasion during his poetic eulogy. It sounded nice on the ears but didn't register in Wesley's heart no matter how hard he willed his soul to accept it.

"We should go, Wes."

Sheila tugged at the sleeve of Wesley's shirt again. He didn't budge.

"Over thirty years," he said somberly.

"What?"

"My parent's marriage," he answered.

"That's something to cherish," Sheila said. "Your mom and dad were blessed." Sheila thought of the parade of men that marched through her own mother's bedroom. Her father, married several times but never to her mother. Her parents were the blame for her own issues, she decided. They taught her where to find a woman's worth. In the soft give of a mattress, the backseat of a car, or some run-down motel off the strip where respectable folk never found themselves.

"I think we can have something like that," Wesley went on.

"What?" She'd been lost in her thoughts, but this announcement set Sheila back on course, quick.

"Pop's death has me thinking," Wesley said. "I want to be the man he was. He'd done a lot of catting around, especially during his time in the service. But then my mother came along and stole his heart."

"A wonderful love story," Sheila said, hoping those words would move Wesley from talking about her and his relationship.

It didn't work.

"He'd be happy to see us thriving together," Wesley added. "He never wanted to see me lost as he was. You know . . . looking for a quantity of women instead of one quality woman."

Sheila remained silent. Thoughts swam through her mind, though. *Don't do this, Wes. We're not what you think we are, Wes baby. I'm not who you think I am.*

Wesley gripped the sides of Sheila's face and turned her head up. "I love you, Sheila."

Please, God, stop him.

"You've made me appreciate monogamy," he continued. "My boys, Omega and Tyndall, don't get it. They think our friendship will suffer because I love you, because I don't want to run the streets any longer. They didn't want me to put away all my old phone numbers, but I did. I haven't regretted it one second, either."

You shouldn't have, Wes. I never asked that of you.

"I want what my parents had. And I want it with you, Sheila."

Oh, Wes, don't say what I think you're going to say. Stop him, Lord. Make it thunder, drop rain on our heads, do something.

Wesley wiped his tears away with the back of his hand and straightened his posture. "Sheila, I want you to be my wife. I know this is an awkward place to do this." He bent to his knee. "I don't have a ring yet, but I have sincerity. My father's watching. And I know he's smiling. Will you marry me, baby?"

He'd said it.

Sheila looked at him, those doe eyes, magnified behind his eyeglass lenses and begging her for the right answer. She looked down at the fresh grave. Then quickly looked away from it.

"You're pausing," Wesley said. He attempted a smile. "I hope that isn't a bad thing."

Sheila licked her dry lips and took a deep breath. Her insides churned and doubt plagued her mind. "Yes, I'll marry you," she said. Surprisingly, her voice didn't catch and her legs felt steady.

Maybe, just maybe, this could work after all. She hoped so. Prayed for it.

Have to be different from my mother, expect and get a lover much better than my father.

Wesley took Sheila in his arms and whispered words of love to her. The two lovers stood a foot from the fresh grave. For the time being, grief put aside.

It would only be a matter of time before grief returned.

A Side

1

His muscles glistened with sweat. The cuts in his body were the work of a master chiseler. Tight gray shorts hugged his crotch. Sweat stains covered the front of the shorts. The shirt he'd been wearing earlier lay in a crumple in the corner of his loft, similar sweat stains covering its front and armpits. He moved closer to the woman standing in the center of his large room and wrapped his arms around her waist. She tightened up for a moment, and then gave in to the comfort of his touch.

"You're tense today," he said to her.

She smiled and shook her head. The both of them knew her denial was a lie. She marked it as such by replying with a gesture instead of a spoken reply. She never was at a loss for words. She was a talker.

"Wedding jitters?" he asked as he tightened his hold around her waist.

She moaned as he stretched her lower back farther than she thought it capable of moving. When she caught her breath, she shook her head again. No wedding jitters.

"Can't picture you married," he said. "You're too vibrant, too boisterous for one dude."

She licked her lips and fingered her bangs away from her eyes. She wished he would stop talking about marriage. Wished he would just continue taking her body to the heights.

"You want me to shut up about the marriage, don't you?" he asked, reading her mind it seemed.

She shook her head again, batting her eyes and smiling. She hated that he made her bat her eyes like a teenager. She hated his strength, his muscles, and his arrogance. She hated how much he made her think, how much he made her question the decision she'd already thought through and settled. She hated that, after all this time, she'd called him on the night before her wedding. She should have gone out with her girlfriends as planned. But no, her mother's hoodoo brought her here. *Not an excuse, a fact*, she told the part of her conscience that considered blaming her mother for her problems, a cop out. *My mother gave me my foundation, shoddy and crumbling as it may be.*

Her thoughts broke as he touched her thigh and then pulled her leg over his shoulder. She gritted her teeth and tried not to concentrate on the warmth of his sweat on the back side of her leg. She throbbed through the middle. He was right. She was too vibrant, too boisterous for one man. She glanced at the clock. In less than twenty-four hours, it wouldn't matter. She'd belong to one man . . . forever. She pushed away from him. He eased her leg down, dropped his hands away.

"That's enough," she said.

"Was a good workout, no?" he asked.

"I'll be sore tomorrow," she replied.

The devil's image was in his smile. "Yes, you will. You'll have a lot of aches and pains, starting tomorrow. Wedding day for Miss Sheila."

Sheila didn't appreciate the double meaning of his words. "I was built for marriage," she defended. *Unlike my mother*, she was thinking. "You hear me, A.J.?"

A.J. looked her up and down, pursed his lips as his eyes scanned the contours of her body. "Built for something," he agreed, "just not sure it's marriage."

"All I want from you is a good workout," Sheila replied. "I don't need any pop psychology from my *former* trainer." She emphasized the word *former*.

A.J. nodded. "Fair enough, Sheila. And did I, your *former* trainer, give you a good workout?"

"Yes."

A.J. moved to the corner, collected his sweaty shirt, and hung it over his shoulder. Sheila couldn't help looking at his broad shoulders, his thick neck. That thick neck brought to mind that other thick part of him.

Seeing Sheila staring so hard, A.J. smirked, decided he better dress, and snaked his muscled upper body into the tight T-shirt.

"Okay, Sheila," A.J. said. "You know where to find me. Should you want any future workouts, you know?"

"I do," Sheila answered. She wondered why she was lingering because that should have been it. She tried to will her legs to move. She considered her answer, "I do," wondering if she'd be able to say it tomorrow. Wedding day for Miss Sheila.

A.J. looked around his loft, studied the high ceiling and the open space. Then he turned his gaze back to Sheila. "Since you'll be a married woman after tomorrow, I think you should come to the gym for any future workouts, though, rather than here. No?"

Sheila touched her naked wedding finger. Her platinum and diamond engagement ring was downstairs in her car, hidden under some bills in her glove box. "That sounds reasonable to me. That way we avoid any problems."

A.J. smiled, forming deep dimples in his cheeks. "Right, we wouldn't want any problems."

Sheila was still lingering. "I can't be having problems," she said, her tone absent of any conviction.

"Okay, Sheila, I wish you the best." A.J. moved to Sheila and extended his hand for a shake. She took it. He held on to hers. She let him. They stared into each other's eyes for a few seconds before A.J. broke the silence. "I'm gonna go jump under the water. Make sure you lock up behind you. And again, congratulations. I'm sure you'll be a beautiful bride."

They were still holding hands when Sheila nodded. She still wasn't moving. A.J.'s crooked smile hypnotized her. She knew she was staring, but she couldn't take her eyes off him.

Looking at the want in Sheila's eyes, A.J. said, "Problems, Sheila. Remember you didn't want any?"

She bit into her lip.

He didn't say another word, simply guided her down the hall, her fingers loose in his hands.

When they reached his bathroom, he asked her, "You like the water really hot, if I remember correctly, right?"

"Yes."

He noticed the hitch in her voice. "One final-final," he assured her as he slid a shower cap over his dreads.

"That's a must," Sheila said. "Tomorrow I'm marrying."

He pulled the shower curtain back and turned the water on. Turned to her and started peeling her skintight clothes off, piece by piece.

"Don't feel guilty, Sheila. It's been a while since I've seen you naked. You've been a good girl."

"Over a year," she said.

"Since the day your Wes proposed," A.J. observed. He loosened the strap of Sheila's bra. Her fruit spilled out. "Ahh," A.J. said, smiling at the artistry of the nipple ring on her left breast.

A.J.'s appreciative smile made Sheila nervous. "I've been faithful to him, too. I love him," she said.

"It's not uncommon to look up an old love before the leap," A.J. told her.

"He's probably doing the same," she said, knowing that wasn't a possibility with Wes. She closed her eyes then, ashamed, but determined to press on. She needed this one last bit of vibrancy, this one last boisterous act.

A.J. stripped naked, revealing a caramel Adonis. Sheila *really* needed this last bit of vibrancy, this last boisterous act.

A.J. took her by the hand and tenderly escorted her under the water. "How's the temperature?"

"Perfect," she answered.

He lathered his hands with soap and cleaned her back, from neck to heel. Then, he cleansed her front, spending extra time at her breasts and pubis. He finished by washing her hair with shampoo scented like strawberries. A pang of jealousy struck Sheila as she wondered how many other women's hair A.J. had shampooed since the last time she shared a shower with him. She tossed aside the jealousy when he softly rubbed in the cocoa butter conditioner.

Sheila tried to wash A.J. in turn, but he gently objected. She could feel something move inside herself when he took his log-thick penis in hand and scrubbed from the mushroom top to the base. His inches were a shiny black gun, and she wanted desperately for him to pump a couple shots in her.

A.J. toweled her off, placed her panties back on. They moved from the bathroom to the loft where they'd worked out earlier. Sheila immediately offered A.J. her right breast. He took it with pleasure, flicking his tongue across her nipple. Then he gently sat her on her back, put on a condom, and took his place atop of her.

He hooked a finger in her panties, pushed them to the side, and gave her every one of his inches. She moaned and tears spilled from her eyes. She growled, said, "God" and "shit" in the same sentence. This sex would be her EZ Pass to hell.

Afterward, they showered again, and A.J. kissed Sheila's forehead and walked her to her car. She looked at her glove box for a moment but didn't open it. Didn't take out her platinum and diamond engagement ring. Instead, she started the car. As she drove off, she watched A.J. turn to a dot in her rearview mirror.

She would be sore tomorrow for sure. Wedding day for Miss Sheila.

2

A feminine voice had answered the apartment's intercom, imploring Wesley, Omega, and Tyndall to come on up. She had something special in store, she said.

Wesley had turned to Omega Barksdale. "O, what's up with this?"

Omega shrugged.

"Ten?" Wesley asked his other friend, Tyndall Williams.

"You insisted we didn't go to a strip club. Said if you even *saw* a woman on the streets wearing clear heels and clutching a dollar you'd get out and walk back home. So here we are. This is definitely not a strip club. You can tell Sheila you didn't do the strip club thing the night before your wedding. She'll like that, even though God knows where she is."

"Out with friends," Wesley quickly said.

"Cool, then," Omega interjected. "You're out with friends, too."

Omega and Tyndall each took one of Wesley's arms, and they ushered him toward the elevator.

Three beautiful women greeted them at the door on the fourth floor. Within minutes of being inside, Omega drifted off into a bedroom with one of the women. The second woman ran a bath and came out into the living room to retrieve Tyndall. She'd worn only a thick terry cloth robe. She didn't bother to tie it, leaving her breasts and pubic area available for all to see. Wesley could hear the woman and Tyndall in there now, splashing water and giggling loudly. He could only imagine what was happening behind the closed bedroom door with Omega and the other woman. The third woman, as beautiful as the other two, sat on the couch across from Wesley, quietly watching him.

"I make you nervous," she said after a while.

"I'm getting married tomorrow," Wesley said to her. He tried not to look into her eyes, for they were the color of maple syrup, large, sexy. Her hair braids were microscopic twists. She wore a T-shirt, tied and knotted below her small breasts. Her velour sweatpants hung low enough on her hips that Wesley knew she had on thong underwear. He'd known that from the door, actually. Standing in her hall earlier, wishing he was home with Sheila, he'd seen the silk outline of her panties. They peeked from above her pant waist. The things that ran through his mind at that moment now shamed him.

She crossed her arms. "I guess all you want to do is talk, then? Maybe play Scrabble."

Wesley moved to the edge of his chair. "Sure, we can talk."

"Pillow talk?" she asked.

Wesley edged back in his chair again.

"I'll settle for Bill Clinton if going all out bothers you," she offered. "But I must admit I'm craving much more."

"Bill Clinton?"

She made an O with her mouth, balled her hand in a fist, and moved it to her luscious lips as if sucking a flavorful ice pop. Then she opened her thighs, pointed a slender finger at her middle, and then took that finger and pointed it at Wesley. I suck you. You lick me.

Wesley didn't reply.

"What do you say, Wesley? Sixty-nine might turn out to be our lucky number. Are you down for oral satisfaction?"

"You know my name," he said, "but I don't know yours."

She patted a spot next to her on the couch. "Sit next to me."

Tyndall growled down the hall, the splashing and laughing replaced by splashing and lots of grunting and moaning. The closed bedroom door kept any similar sounds from Omega and his woman from leaking into the living room. Wesley thought about Sheila's intense desire to spend the night away from him. He rose and found the offered spot on the couch.

"So what's your name?" Wesley tried again.

"You're stalling, Wesley."

"You ready to roll, like that, don't even know me?"

"I'm not a prostitute, if that's what you think," she told him. "My girl has known Tyndall for a long time. My other girl has hung out with Omega a few times in the past. I've been celibate myself for five years. Tyndall and Omega went on about your situation with the both of my girls for so long, they asked me to step in and set you straight."

"What situation?" Wesley asked, confused.

The woman acted as if she didn't hear Wesley. "I decided I wanted to feel again," she said, "that I needed the heat of a man against my skin again. I chose you to get back on the horse with."

Wesley asked, "Why?" despite his better judgment.

"Your situation intrigued me," the woman said. "Plus, Omega e-mailed me your picture. I thought you were kinda cute."

"What situation?" Wesley's voice had risen a notch. His back held the tension that his voice carried.

The woman touched his face, rubbed his clean-shaven jaw line. "You have soft skin. And your eyeglasses really bring out the golden brown of your eyes."

Wesley couldn't deny that her scent was alluring, her body unbelievable, and her touch heaven-sent, but still he couldn't go there. "I'm getting married tomorrow," he told her.

She leaned forward. "We can give each other something the other desperately needs."

Wesley smirked. "I'll give you . . . ?"

"Wood," she said, looking down at his crotch and licking her lips. "I've denied myself long enough."

He looked at her eyes. They now looked dark, brooding, molasses instead of maple syrup. "And you'll give me?" he dared to ask.

"A dose of reality," she said.

He all out laughed now. "What reality?"

"Reality about your situation," she quickly answered.

He stood but didn't move.

"You'd much rather be with your wifey tonight, wouldn't you?" she asked. "But you aren't. I bet that's not of your doing."

Wesley was quiet. He wondered what Omega and Tyndall had been telling these women.

She continued, "Us hooking up would be a good thing for your spirit, Wesley. At some point, you'll realize that. That is your reality."

"I don't think so," Wesley said.

"Why, Wesley? Because"—she put a finger to her chin, feigning deep thought—"let me guess, Sheila is so faithful to you. Surely you know better than that?"

Wesley frowned. He hated her that instant, sudden as a flash rain that comes from a sunny sky to pound the earth. Anger bubbled inside him. She tried to apologize, to touch him, but he shrugged away her attempts. He marched down the hall and banged on the bedroom door and then the bathroom door. "Wrap it up, O," he hollered to one door. "Enough with the splish-splash, Ten. Let's be out," he yelled to the other door.

The bedroom door opened, and Omega came into the doorway wearing only boxers. The bathroom door opened, and Tyndall stepped out with a towel wrapped around his waist. Their women came behind them, held each man's shoulders as if they were a significant part of their lives and not booty calls.

Wesley looked at his two friends. Tyndall with his hair in cornrows, excessively large diamond studs in each ear. Omega, Tyndall's physical polar opposite. Dark skin, goatee, bald head, and an onyx ring his only jewelry. Tyndall was most comfortable in those wifebeater T-shirts and a pair of baggy jeans. Omega's comfort zone was a Giorgio Armani wool suit, a Canali silk tie, a Tiffany & Co. timepiece on his wrist. Wesley? He was most comfortable in Sheila's arms.

"I don't know what you two have been thinking, sharing details of my life with these women," Wesley chastised his friends, "but I don't appreciate it. Tomorrow I'm getting married. Get that through your thick heads, okay? I have a good woman, and tomorrow I'm marrying that good woman. I have no desire to run the streets, poking around in any old body with two legs and a hole-in between."

Omega tried to say something, but Wesley cut him off. "Just take me home, O. Aiight?"

Omega leaned against the doorjamb and frowned. Wesley turned to the woman who was to have been his. "My situation is under control, aiight, sweetheart?"

She nodded.

3

"You're positively GQed down," Tyndall told Wesley.

Omega, moving from a far corner of the room, seconded the opinion. "Yes, I have to admit, I'm jealous. Almost makes me wish I was the one getting married so I could get my GQ on like that."

Tyndall arched an eyebrow. "Wish you were getting married, O?"

Omega smiled. "I said 'almost.'"

Wesley sat quietly through their banter. He was still seething from last night. But Wesley had to admit the tuxedo did fit perfectly. He turned to his left to get a profile of himself in the mirror. He liked what he saw. You could barely notice the extra weight in his midsection. He couldn't wait to get Sheila's reaction. She was bound to be impressed.

Wesley moved from the mirror and took a seat behind the minister's big oak desk. They were in the back of Bethlehem Baptist Church. The hues of burgundy that decorated the office and the pews outside were the same color as the dresses worn by Sheila's bridesmaids. Wesley settled himself into the leather recliner chair and swiveled it to face the door. He craned his neck, nodded toward the door. "Is the church filling up?"

"I'll go check," Omega volunteered. He disappeared out into the hall.

Wesley turned the chair so his back was to the door. He sat quietly, thinking to himself. Tyndall fumbled with his hands for a few moments. The silence between them was deafening.

"Hey, yo," Tyndall began. Wesley turned to listen. Tyndall fumbled with his hands some more. "Look, Wes, I'm sorry about last night. We should have respected that you wouldn't want to get down like that."

"That woman was under the impression that I'm in a bad situation with Sheila," Wesley said.

Tyndall's gaze dropped. He stood quiet.

"That what you and O think?"

Tyndall didn't look up, couldn't. "What *you* think is all that really matters at this point, Wes."

"Don't be a politician, Ten. Answer the question. And look me in the face when you do."

Tyndall met Wesley's eyes. "You're more wrapped up in Sheila than she is with you. That's all."

"You say this based on what?" Wesley asked.

Tyndall frowned. "I don't want to get up in all this today, son. Don't matter at this point."

"Matters to me," Wesley informed him. "You and O are my closest, oldest friends." He'd used "are," but in his mind, "were" was probably more suitable. He still couldn't believe they'd been telling those women that his happy life was anything but.

The door of the office opened. Omega breezed through. "Church is filling, Wes."

Wesley hadn't taken his eyes off Tyndall even as Omega spoke. Waiting patiently for an answer to his earlier question. How was his love for Sheila exponentially more than her love for him?

Omega looked from Tyndall to Wesley. The room felt devoid of air, hot and sticky. He knew immediately what was up. He had hoped they could avoid this.

Tyndall turned to Omega. "I was apologizing to Wes about last night. He won't take it and settle. He wants to know what we really think about his relationship with ol' girl."

Omega clucked his tongue inside his mouth and shook his head.

Wesley's eyes widened. "Man, O, all this time I've been thinking you guys had my back. You're telling me it's that bad?"

Tyndall went and found a seat in a corner of the room. Omega settled into the chair directly facing the minister's big oak desk. Omega leaned back in the chair, eyed Wesley.

Wesley waved his hands. "Come with it. We might as well get this all out before I run down that aisle." In his mind, he figured this would be the last heart-to-heart with Omega and Tyndall. Soon he'd replace them with his bride—gladly.

"You love her more than she loves you," Omega said flatly.

"You and Ten have been comparing notes," Wesley noted.

"What has she sacrificed for you, Wes?" Omega asked.

"Nothing," Tyndall piped in. "You making all the sacrifices, Wes. Wednesday's . . . basketball. Tried those stupid contacts and got an eye infection. It takes an act of God to get you to come hang with us for a night, but ol' girl be up in the clubs with her girls any chance she get."

"See, that's where you guys have it twisted," Wesley said. "Sheila never pressured me to do any of that stuff. I did it all willingly. And, for the record, she asks me all the time to go to the club with her. That's not where my head is at."

"Hers is, though," Omega said. "Sounds like you two aren't a match."

Before Wesley could respond to that dig, a knock came at the door. Tyndall, the closest to the door, called out, "Come in."

Teresa, one of Sheila's bridesmaids, stuck her head inside. She looked from Omega to Tyndall. "Wassup, you two?"

Omega just looked at her.

"You're working that dress, Reesy," Tyndall told her. Neither of them would cop to it, but they'd shared a passionate night together months before. Teresa still didn't know why she and Tyndall hadn't gotten together again. 'Cause Tyndall didn't do seconds, not a part of her understanding.

Teresa's light brown cheeks blushed. She lost her focus as Tyndall eyed her without pretense from head to toe. Okay, maybe occasionally a second roll was in order, he thought.

Wesley broke through the silence of lustful thoughts. "You wanted something, Teresa?"

Teresa shot her glance at Wesley. Cursed him in her head for messing up her flow. "Yeah," she huffed. "You talked to Sheila today?"

Wesley furrowed his brow. "No. Why?"

"She isn't here yet, and we haven't been able to reach her at your place. Her old apartment is already rented to somebody else, so we don't know where she is."

"What do you mean she isn't here?"

"She isn't here."

"She wouldn't be at my place," Wesley said. "She said she'd spend the night with one of you."

Teresa's frame slid back from the doorway.

"Teresa," Wesley barked, freezing her in place, "didn't you hang out with Sheila last night?"

Teresa shook her head, dropped her gaze. Omega shook his head as well. Tyndall smirked, sucked his teeth.

Wesley waved Teresa aside. "Okay, I'll handle it."

Teresa disappeared from the doorway, looking back only briefly to catch another glimpse of Tyndall.

Omega and Tyndall looked at each other without uttering a word or making any facial gestures. Still, the alliance of their minds was as present as the growing drama of the day.

Wesley leapt from his seat and went to retrieve his cell phone from his leather bag.

"Few people have her cell phone number," he announced. "She doesn't like giving it out to everyone. I don't think any of the bridesmaids have it. Her friend Janet does. And me, of course."

Wesley rifled through his bag, found the cell phone, quickly dialed Sheila's number. It rang three times before the voice mail message picked up. "It's me . . . Wesley," he started. "We've got a church full of people, a groom, but no bride." He laughed it off. "You have me nervous here. Call me when you get this message. Love you."

He closed the phone and stuffed it in his pocket. When he turned, Omega and Tyndall were staring at him. He looked away from them.

4

Sheila listened to Wesley's message one final time. Took a deep breath and dialed him back. It barely rang once before his frenzied voice came on line.

He sounded in need of a mentholated throat lozenge. "Sheila, baby, are you all right?"

Sheila's eyes watered. Wesley was concerned about her. She'd be livid, cursing him out if the circumstances flip-flopped, if she was at the church in her wedding dress wondering where the groom was. "Wes, honey . . ." Her voice broke.

"We're behind schedule, baby. Is everything okay? Are you on your way?"

"Can't go through with it," she heard herself say into the phone. Silence met her from the other line. She did hear Wesley's soft breathing, though, his chest was probably heaving. "I'm sorry, Wes," she added. Before he could respond, try to change her mind, she hung up, turned her phone off, and closed the flip. The tears came harder. She hugged and rocked herself for a few minutes. Got it all out. She should have seen this moment coming. Should have known, as she stood by Wes's father's grave, that she wouldn't make it to the altar. But her mother's sins had clouded her vision; her desire to avoid those same sins had informed her actions, had caused her to say yes to Wes's proposal.

She'd wanted the white dress, a long train trailing behind her, Wes's warm fingers removing the garter belt from her thigh.

Caught up in the fantasy of it all, fooling herself the entire time.

Sheila picked up the house phone and quickly dialed. A.J. picked up the other line after a few rings. "I called," Sheila said into the receiver. "The wedding's off. What time can I come by for that work-out tonight?"

"Around eight is cool," A.J. said. "You did a good—"

Sheila cut him off, slammed the phone back in its cradle. She flopped against her pillow, cursed her mother and father, asked Wes's father for forgiveness.

5

The day after and the hurt and pain still clung to Wesley, a fresh cut in need of salve and bandage. He'd managed to get a few hours of rest, falling asleep in his living room chair, the television station broadcasting a show of colorful bars on the screen. Now, as he sat in the same chair trying to put together the puzzle of his life, he thought back on yesterday. Sheila's phone call was the first misshapen piece. She'd hung up before he could respond to her insanity, leaving the room swirling around him. Omega and Tyndall had been kind enough to inform the guests of the wedding's postponement. Wesley could imagine the murmur that must have ringed through the church. His mother had rushed to the back office and had attempted to console him. But she was off to the airport, headed for another tropical vacation before he'd stopped trembling and sobbing. Omega and Tyndall, the friends he was ready to replace, saw him home, got him settled, made sure his cabinet was free of pills, his kitchen drawers of knives. Then, he was alone. He drifted off to sleep, hoping that Sheila's key turning in the lock would wake him late in the morning. But she hadn't come home, and he hadn't heard from her.

Wesley shook aside the hurtful memories, stood from his chair, and moved to his kitchen island. He pulled his phone from the cradle and dialed the number for *Stunt* magazine. Desiree, the receptionist, picked up.

"Weitz/Gleemer Publications," Desiree said. "How may I direct your call?"

Wesley tried not to sound desperate. "Sheila Fuller, please."

"Ms. Fuller is currently on vacation. She'll be returning in one month. I can patch your call to her editorial assistant if you'd like. She's handling all of Ms. Fuller's messages in the interim."

Wesley shook his head as if Desiree could see him over the line. "No, thank you. I'll call back in a month." As he said it, he couldn't imagine what his state would be if he was unable to track Sheila down before a month.

"That's fine. Anything else I can do for you?" Desiree asked.

"No."

"Please look out for the June issue of *Stunt*, on newsstands now," Desiree cheerily replied. "This month's cover features Vivica—"

Wesley hung up.

He tried Sheila's cell phone again and got the same response he'd gotten calling her job at the magazine—zilch. Frustrated, he went into the bathroom and ran water over his face. It was there, looking at his pitiful reflection in the medicine cabinet's mirror, that Wesley remembered the phone number he'd found in Sheila's pocketbook months ago. Guy named A.J. She'd explained it to Wesley and they'd moved on. Wesley grabbed his keys and dashed out the door, headed for the gym in midtown where he and Sheila first met, that paper in her pocketbook the only thing on his mind. A.J., Sheila had said, was just a friend. Wesley would see.

He arrived at the gym before he'd clearly decided how to play the situation. He parked his car and reminded himself he had to keep his cool, no matter what happened. He took a few deep breaths and exited his car. It was a humid beginning to the day, the sun already glowing hot. The day would be perfect for a lover's stroll down a beach boardwalk, a romantic picnic in the sand, sexy clutching and grabbing under the shield of waves. If Wesley's thoughts were on a movie screen, an arrangement with lots of violins would be playing as part of the score.

Inside the gym, one of the first people Wesley saw was Tyndall, on a bench jerking a bar with several plates attached to it above his head. Wesley headed in that direction.

Tyndall looked up to see Wesley standing over him. He put the weight down on the bar stand and sat up, wiped his brow. "What's up, player? Standing tall?"

"Yeah," Wesley said. He nodded to the weights. "How much are you pressing now?"

Tyndall smirked. "Damn near two of you, son."

Wesley turned to look around the vast interior of the gym.

Tyndall stood, put a hand on one of Wesley's shoulders. "You want to talk. I can cut my lifting short and we can go grab some java and build."

Wesley shook his head. "Actually, I'm looking for someone. You know a guy named A.J. that works here?"

"That pimp." Tyndall laughed. "Yeah, I know him. He was here when you used to come. You don't remember him?"

"No."

"He's a personal trainer; that who you looking for?"

"Yeah, is he in now?"

"I saw him back by the treadmills earlier. What's up?"

Wesley put his hands in his pockets. "Sheila used to date him . . . back before we were an item. I want to ask him something."

Tyndall cocked his head to the side. "He's crazy cut. Dreadlocks," Tyndall said as he pointed to a far-off section of the gym.

Wesley didn't look at Tyndall as he thanked him and headed for the treadmills.

A.J. wasn't on the treadmills. Instead, he was doing stomach crunches on the mats. His abs was so carved they looked like a pan of brown 'n' serve rolls. Wesley sucked in his own gut as he moved to speak with A.J.

"A.J.," Wesley said.

The trainer grunted, pulled his body up, breathed out of his mouth. He frowned as he asked, "Do I know you?"

"I don't think you do." Wesley hesitated. "You know my lady, though."

A.J. completed another rep. Sweat dripped down his forehead. "Who's your lady?"

"Sheila Fuller."

A.J. grunted again, pulled his body up, breathed out of his mouth. He didn't say a word.

"You know of her, right?" Wesley asked.

A.J. turned over and started doing push-ups.

Wesley moved around, positioned himself so he could see A.J. and A.J. could see him. "We were supposed to get married yester-day but she called it off. I was wondering if you've heard from her recently. I know she was—" Wesley stopped, regrouped. "She has your phone number in her pocketbook still. She's told me that you two were close, that if she kept male friends, you'd be one of them." She'd actually snatched the slip of paper with A.J.'s number on it from out of Wesley's hand the day he came upon it. That memory stuck with Wesley. The anger in her eyes, the way her nostrils had flared. Too much. Where there was smoke there had to be fire.

A.J. finished his push-ups, quickly popped up to a standing position. He towered over Wesley's frame. He looked to be about six-four or five to Wesley's six foot even. His dreads a stark contrast to Wesley's closely cropped hair, his chiseled jaw line seeming to mock Wesley's soft curve of a jaw line. A.J. moved over to the treadmill, adjusted the settings, and stepped onto the machine.

Wesley came over, stood on the dormant treadmill that neighbored the one A.J. worked out on. "Have you heard from her?"

A.J. moved at a nice leisurely pace beside Wesley. His breathing was rhythmic, controlled. He didn't meet Wesley's glance. Instead, he looked off in the distance as if he were hiking toward a majestic mountain.

"Have you?" Wesley pressed.

A.J. wiped a bead of sweat from his forehead with the back of his hand.

"I'm not going to start any trouble if you have," Wesley told him. "I'd like to know where her head is at. I'm trying to track her down and talk this out with her. If you've seen her, I'd—"

"Last two nights," A.J. cut in.

Wesley eyed him. His heart raced; he could feel his pulse clogging his throat as if he'd swallowed an apple. He didn't know what to say. He hadn't expected this answer, had truly hoped for something different.

"I don't know where she is now," A.J. added. "She was pretty upset last night. Confused, hurt, unsure of what she was doing with her life. She left early in the morning without waking me to say good-bye. I don't think I'll be seeing her again anytime soon to tell you the truth."

"Okay," Wesley said, his voice cracking over the two syllables.

"I'm sorry about your wedding, man," A.J. offered. "I'm sorry about Sheila, too."

Wesley pulled a business card from his breast pocket, handed it to A.J. The trainer took the card, bent down, and stuck it behind his gym sock. He raised himself to full height again and looked across at Wesley. "I'll call you if I hear from her. My word is bond."

Wesley walked off. He was by the gym's front door when a hand touched his shoulder. He turned, startled, his eyes going blurry on him.

"Everything okay?" Tyndall asked.

"Yes," Wesley answered.

Tyndall hesitated before saying, "Was he able to help you out?"

Wesley looked his friend in the eyes. "Yes, he was able to help me out. I'd hoped he wouldn't have been able to, but he was." At that, he turned and started walking for the exit again.

"Holla at me later," Tyndall called out for him.

Wesley waved his hand and moved through the door. Outside, the sun's summer rays did nothing to quiet the chill in his bones. He sat in his vehicle for a while, trying to figure his next move. He turned on his cell phone to call Sheila again. A voice message waited for him. He quickly dialed to retrieve it. Could it be Sheila? His shoulders sagged, though, as he listened. It was Sheila's friend Janet offering a few words of support. He erased the message before it reached the end. He didn't need anybody's comfort. He needed his life back. The life he'd envisioned since proposing to Sheila. A wife and two-point-five kids was how he imagined it. A nice brownstone with wrought-iron fences around it. Forget the picket fence.

A thought hit him as he tapped his hands against the steering wheel. Sheila would have spoken with Janet. It made perfect sense. Janet was so quiet, so unassuming, and so loyal to Sheila. Sheila wouldn't worry about Janet dropping the dime on her. But Janet was also caring and kind. Her voice message proved it. She'd always shown Wesley concern. She wouldn't be able to stand him hurting, with the key to unlocking his pain in her hand. She'd tell him where Sheila was.

Wesley started his engine and peeled away from the curb without checking his blind spot for oncoming traffic. He ran the red light at the corner, made a wild turn down the next street. He could practically feel Sheila's soft skin under his fingertips. He'd find her and make everything right again.

6

Janet was moving down the steps of her brownstone when Wesley pulled up to the curb. She had her hair tied in a brown scarf and wore a dress with more colors patched together than could be found in a bag of Skittles. A dark purple Jansport backpack hung over one of her shoulders. Her skin was the color of her scarf, and the flip-flops on her feet clanged so loudly against the concrete a blind man would have figured her for a loud, tall, meaty woman, not the petite little wallflower she was.

Wesley moved from his car as Janet paused at the bottom of her steps and hefted the backpack.

"Janet," he said as he neared her.

She looked up with her eyes squinted. It was hard to tell if the gesture was to keep the sun at bay or was out of pity. "Wesley?"

Wesley stepped up on the sidewalk. "Are you headed out? I'm glad I caught you."

Janet looked up the block. "Actually, I'm in kind of a rush. I don't have the time to talk right now."

"I won't take but a minute," Wesley promised.

"If it's about Sheila, forget it. I don't want to get in the middle."

"You put yourself in the middle when you left me that message this morning."

"What?" Janet couldn't believe Wesley's assessment of the situation. "I wanted to offer you support," she told him. "I know it must be a difficult time for you. That's the extent of my involvement, a quick call."

"You've spoken with her since the wedding," Wesley said. He

caught himself and corrected his statement. "Since what was supposed to be our wedding day."

"I might have," Janet acknowledged.

"You did."

"Look," she said, "I need to get going. I have a busy day ahead, and I need my walk and relaxation in the park first."

Wesley looked up the street. "I can walk with you. And I haven't been to a park in years."

Janet gripped her backpack straps. "Suit yourself then." She started walking, Wesley in tow.

Farther up the block, they came upon a man who smelled strongly of urine. His clothes hung off his thin frame. He had a thick piece of rope tied to hold up his pants. His sneakers were several sizes too large. One was a Reebok, the other a Nike. He stood over a garbage can with a metal trap lid, banging the lid as if it were a steel drum. His voice was soft and melodic, but he sang an off-key tune. Janet moved to him and tapped his shoulder. The man turned, his last note hanging on his tongue.

"You have a beautiful voice," Janet told him.

He smiled, not the least bit embarrassed by his missing teeth.

"If I gave you five dollars for that song you sang, you wouldn't spend it on alcohol, would you?" Janet asked.

"No, ma'am," he said.

"What would you spend it on?"

"Get me some grub," the man replied.

Janet pointed to the Chinese food restaurant across the way. "You like Chinese?"

"Do Diana Ross got weave? Do Al Green hate grits? Do—?"

"Come on." Janet motioned to the man, and they moved to cross the street. She turned back to Wesley before crossing and tossed him her backpack. "I'll be right back; hang tight." Wesley caught the backpack and watched her cross. Watched her tell the man to sit tight while she went inside the restaurant.

In a few minutes, she emerged from inside, handed the man a plastic bag that appeared loaded with white food cartons, and slowly walked across the street.

"He's a pork-fried-rice guy," she said to Wesley as she reached for her backpack. She took a pen and notebook from the backpack and scribbled something down in the notebook. Then she started walking again, pressing it to her chest like a child's security blanket.

"What's that all about?" Wesley asked.

"He looked like he was hungry."

Wesley pointed to her notebook. "I'm talking about that."

Janet tapped it. "This? Oh. Nothing. Thoughts. My journal. Poetry."

> *What brought me here?*
> *What keeps me strong?*
> *Why aren't you near?*
> *Why is this all wrong?*

"Thoughts about the bum?" Wesley asked.

"Yes," Janet lied, adding, "vagrant. Sounds nicer."

"Tell me where Sheila is," Wesley said, back on track.

Janet didn't answer. She looked away, and remained silent until they reached the park. Found a seat there on one of the benches.

"See that man playing Frisbee with the little girl wearing those baby blue shorts?" Janet asked after a while.

"I see him clocking her in the head with the Frisbee," Wesley said.

"My father was like that," Janet observed. "He always had me outdoors doing something active. I never did go through the make-up and dresses phase."

Wesley looked at Janet. "I was surprised Sheila didn't have you as one of her bridesmaids. She said you weren't the girly girl type."

Janet half smiled. "I would have proudly worn a weave down to my butt to watch you guys get married. I know Sheila wanted the Cinderella wedding. Unfortunately, I didn't fit the profile. Still, I believe strongly in black love." She forced a laugh. "Oh, well. Not only am I not the bride, I'm not even the proverbial 'always the bridesmaid.'" She looked off into the distance.

Wesley only heard what he wanted to hear. "Black love?" he asked, a smile dawning on his face. "So you acknowledge that Sheila loves me?"

"About as much as Sheila is capable. I really thought you two had a shot. I prayed for you."

"Tell me where she is, Janet."

Janet took a deep breath, thought about the best way to say what needed saying, settling on, "You two are what I call 'disharmonious.' You don't align correctly."

Wesley grumbled, "If I ever want my palm read, I'll look for you. In the meantime, please tell me where she is."

"You're better served going on with your life, Wesley. There's a woman out there who would be perfect for you. You have to look harder, more carefully." She dropped her gaze to the ground.

"I have no life without her, Janet," Wesley whined.

Janet looked up. "Don't say that." Her face contorted. "*My God*, watch what you say, Wesley. You have your health, a good job; if I didn't know you and I saw you behind those glasses, I might even think you were smart. You're a good-looking man—"

"Tell me where she is."

"She's away, working on rebuilding her soul."

"Dammit, Janet. Where is she?"

"You're out of balance, Wesley. That's never a good thing."

Wesley took Janet's hand in his and tenderly rubbed her fingers. "Please, Janet. I want to talk to her, figure this mess out. Don't you think I deserve that closure?"

Janet swallowed as Wesley's fingers brushed against her hand. She could feel goose pimples sprouting on her arms and back. The gesture confused her. She didn't know whether she should or shouldn't divulge Sheila's whereabouts.

"Please," Wesley said again. His voice was like a smooth R & B song in Janet's ear. Earth, Wind, and Fire. She hated to see him hurting so badly, to see him pleading with so much fervor. Tell him where Sheila is, Janet decided finally, and he'll see how wrong they are for each other. Then he'll be free. Free to move on to someone better suited for him.

"She's house-sitting for her father's third wife, Claudette. She'll be over there the rest of the month, I believe," Janet told him. She didn't feel any remorse at betraying Sheila's confidence.

Wesley rubbed Janet's fingers in appreciation. Janet gave him Claudette's address. Wesley hugged her and stood to leave. Janet's heart raced inside her chest; she could feel sweat on her forehead. Her mouth was dry. It felt as if Wesley's arms still encompassed her, though the hug had been broken.

"Thanks again, Janet. You're the best."

She nodded, unable to speak. Wesley took off at a trot. Janet watched from the bench as he moved away from her. When his image had disappeared from her view, she leaned back against the bench and closed her eyes, picturing his arms around her again.

7

"Hello. Who is it?"

Wesley's stomach did somersaults. Hearing Sheila's voice over the apartment intercom system brought to mind the exotic drinks, clear blue ocean, and toe-curling sex they should be experiencing on their Cancún honeymoon. He needed her back in his corner, badly.

"Sheila, it's me. . . . May I come up?"

Dead air met him with the force of a powerful fist. He buzzed again, then again. He'd spent all day steeling himself for this moment. The sun was starting to recede from the sky, the heat of the day leaving with it. Wesley would wait here until the sun returned tomorrow if need be.

An older woman stepped through the locked door. Wesley quietly slid in behind her, a thief looking to pick the lock to Sheila's love. On the elevator ride up, he thought about his approach with Sheila. He still hadn't come up with a good one when the doors opened at the third level. He decided to let his heart guide him. He stepped off the elevator, the heart that would guide him pounding hard in his chest. His hands were clammy, his mouth dry, his footsteps heavy, as if encased in mud-caked boots.

Claudette's door was the seventh one he came to. He paused, thankful that Janet had the decency to tell him where Sheila hid out. God was on his side, he decided, populating the world with kind souls like Janet. He quickly prayed that Sheila's kind side would reappear as well.

He knocked, then knocked again.

The door opened as far as the latch would allow, then closed and reopened, this time with the latch released.

Wesley's tongue left him as he eyed Sheila, standing before him with hands on hips.

Sheila's mouth contorted. "I knew I shouldn't have told Janet bo diddly." She walked off, leaving the door swinging behind her.

Wesley moved inside, closed the door, and followed Sheila.

"Apartment's nice," Wesley said once he'd caught up with Sheila in the kitchen. "Claudette really landed on her feet after the divorce from your father."

Sheila took a glass from the cupboard, poured herself apple juice, and sat on the counter. Wesley stood by the table that centered the kitchen, his hand propped on a chair for balance.

"Where's Claudette, on vacation or something?"

Sheila watched him but didn't respond.

"Have you spoken with any of your family?"

Sheila looked at Wesley, incredulous. Now, he knew she didn't speak with her evil witch mother, her little fat-assed sister, or her skirt-chasing father. Wesley could be so dim for a smart man. She decided not to answer his question, make him continue grasping for something to talk about.

"Probably not," Wesley acknowledged. He pulled the chair from the table, took a seat.

Sheila sipped at her apple juice.

Wesley folded his hands on the table in front of him. "I called the magazine. You weren't there."

Sheila smirked and jumped off the counter to put her glass in the dishwasher. She moved into the living room without inviting Wesley to join her. He sat at the kitchen table, frustrated that he couldn't get himself together. Sheila reappeared in the kitchen's doorway. "Are you coming?"

"Me?" Wesley asked, with his voice pitched high, a finger pointed at his chest.

"Lord, Jesus." Sheila rolled her eyes and left the doorway.

This time Wesley followed her. In the living room, Sheila sat on the couch, television remote in hand but the set off. Wesley wanted to sit next to her, but he stood instead.

"Claudette sure does like her lavender," he observed, looking around at the various fixtures and miscellaneous items in that hue.

"Cut to the chase, Wes, this dancing-around crap is wearing my nerves. You're like the ghost of freaking Gregory Hines up in here."

Wesley met her eyes. He hurt so much inside his chest felt sore.

"Why did you do this to us? We were happy, had our future planned."

"*You* were happy," Sheila corrected.

"You make me happy, Sheila. I did my best to make you happy."

Sheila tossed the remote on the coffee table. "What, by hanging up under me all the time we weren't at work? Or by cutting out your Wednesday night basketball games? Running your guilt trips on me whenever I wanted to step out of the house without you?"

"You're the one who complained that I worked too hard and that I might as well be dating O and Ten, much as I hung with them. I made changes, for you. The basketball was one of them."

"Careful what you ask for," Sheila said, really to herself. She looked at Wesley. "I didn't know you were going to take it to the level you did. I didn't realize your life would become work and me, that's it. I thought you'd keep some of your other interests. I didn't realize that one little night of basketball was keeping your stomach from getting all . . ." Sheila plopped back against the couch cushions, sighed.

Wesley frowned. "Finish your thought, Sheila."

She waved her hand. "Forget it."

"No, let's not forget it," Wesley objected. He sat on the corner of the coffee table. "What's the problem with my stomach, Sheila?"

She eyed him for a beat. He wasn't letting this go. She pointed at his stomach, her nose crinkled as she noticed it hang slightly over his belt. "It's gotten flabby. There, you happy?"

Anger rose up in Wesley, but he kept himself remarkably calm. "You don't have that problem with your boy A.J., though, do you?"

Sheila tried to hide her surprise. "Why would A.J.'s name even come up?"

Wesley looked crossways at her. "I want to think of you with respect, Sheila. But screwing around with that dude on the night you were supposed to be marrying me, I don't know."

Sheila jumped up, went to leave, but turned back. "Screwing around? What, have you been talking to A.J.? I reached out to him because he was a male *friend* who might help me understand you. I didn't do anything with him but talk." The lie eased off her tongue. Wesley bought it.

"Understand me?" he asked.

"You don't excite me any longer, Wes. When I first met you—at the gym, too"—she laughed at the irony of it all—"you were strong and confident. Every woman there wanted Omega, Tyndall, or you. You especially, because you didn't look like a player like those two. Some of the women wanted all three of you, at the same time even."

Wesley remained silent. The playboy way hadn't served him well, or anyone he knew for that matter. He'd bedded many women during that period and couldn't remember any of their names today. He doubted any of them remembered his name either. Omega and Tyndall, as much as they pretended, weren't happy. Wesley hadn't been happy until Sheila stole his heart, made him realize dating games never produced a winner.

"We got together and you changed," Sheila went on. "You were all about pleasing me. You lost yourself in the process. I lost myself, too. I want to dance, cut loose, and have my fun. You make me feel guilty about that, because you're so, so, so, not in that vibe. Damn, Wes, you're thirty. I'm three years older and yet I feel like I'm with somebody's father."

"Good guys always finish last," Wesley said, shaking his head.

"No," Sheila corrected. "The henpecked guys with no back-bones finish last."

"Loving your woman makes you henpecked nowadays? That's sad."

"Spontaneity, excitement, toughness, that's what I need, Wes." Her voice was soft, pleading, a cry for help.

Wesley ignored it. "I bet if I cheated on you and hit you upside your big-ass forehead you'd be happy," he said.

Sheila touched her head. "I do not have a big-ass forehead."

Wesley couldn't help but smile. "Girl, you got a nine head. I could read your mind without my glasses."

Sheila punched him in the shoulder. It felt good to Wesley, the mood in the room less serious, playful. They weren't a couple with shredded seams; they were a couple that needed a quick sewing job.

Sheila wanted spontaneity, excitement, and toughness. Okay. Wesley grabbed her.

She struggled to break his embrace. "What the fu—"

He kissed her forcefully, swallowing the balance of her words. At first she resisted, but eventually her lips gave in to the familiarity. He moved to her neck. A soft moan escaped her mouth. He pulled back the collar of her T-shirt, nibbled at her shoulders. She gripped his head and pulled him lower, to her breasts. He lost himself in her cleavage.

"We shouldn't do this," she said. "A lot is unresolved."

"I'll stop," Wesley offered.

"Don't you dare, Wes," she blurted. "I swear."

He picked her up and moved her down the hall, searching for the bedroom. She pointed to the last door on the right. He moved her through, a knight carrying his princess.

He placed her down on the bed and paused.

"What now, Wes?" she asked. Her breathing was a bit ragged.

"Should we be making love on someone else's bed?"

She pulled him by the waist of his pants, brought his weight down on her body.

They made the best love they'd ever made, falling asleep in each other's arms. She dreamed of her mother. He dreamed of his father.

8

The light of morning peeked through the venetian blinds in Claudette's bedroom. Sheila turned away from the pursuing sunlight. She stretched and yawned. The scent of bacon caught her nose. She turned back again. The place beside her in bed was wrinkled, warm but empty. She gripped her head in her hand. A smile crept to her face as she remembered the sex. She'd awakened an animal in Wesley—a wild, roaring, hungry animal. Sheila's thighs tingled from the thought. The bacon caught her nose again. Curious, she rose from bed, threw on a T-shirt that hung to her knees, and made her way to the kitchen.

Wesley stood about five feet from the oven, spatula in hand, the flame turned way up with a frying pan resting atop it. He was rocking on the balls of his feet as if preparing to jump into a double-Dutch rope.

"What are you doing?" Sheila asked, moving to turn down the flame.

"Trying to cook breakfast," Wesley replied. "But that oil got to popping and I couldn't get close to the oven."

Sheila elbowed Wesley aside, took away the spatula. "Give me that before you burn Claudette's place to the ground."

Wesley gladly took a seat at the table. "You slept late. I knocked your butt out, huh?"

Sheila touched her middle. "You did a little something-something."

"A little," Wesley scoffed. "That was you in there saying, 'Oh my God, my nine head is about to burst, baby. You got my blood pressure up. My nine head is about to burst,' wasn't it?"

"Funny."

Wesley smiled. "I aim to please."

"You did last night. I'll admit it."

"I want to please you every night for the rest of your life, Sheila."

Sheila's shoulders tightened. She was quiet, standing over the stove with her back to Wesley.

"You heard me, Sheila?"

She turned to him. "Quick lube, Wes."

"Excuse me?"

"Last night. My body needed maintenance. You serviced me, wonderfully I might add."

Wesley's mouth dropped open.

"Don't do this, Wes. Don't look at me like that."

"Are you telling me that last night wasn't the start of a new beginning for us?"

"No, it wasn't."

Wesley stared at her. Close-cropped brown hair. Light brown eyes. Thin, curvy build. She was the woman of his dreams. The only woman he'd ever desire with an intensity bordering on insanity. "What, Sheila, you don't love me anymore?"

"Of course I love you, Wes."

"But you don't want to press on as a couple?"

"No."

Wesley sat there for a moment. He squinted a few times. Sheila didn't want to see his soft side, couldn't take that. She turned back to the oven, removed the burnt bacon strips from the pan, and dropped fresh strips in the oil. These strips she wouldn't allow to burn.

9

The dim lighting, good food, excellent service, and beautiful people at Trends made the bar/restaurant one of the city's hottest recreation spots. But for Wesley, sitting in one of the exclusive booths with Omega and Tyndall, he might as well have been in any run-of-the-mill fast-food joint. The ambience and beautiful people were lost on him. His mind focused on the encounter with Sheila yesterday.

"Cynthia Covington is one of the most alluring women in the world," Omega was saying. "And her latest movie will end up breaking box office records, but that gives her no right to treat her people like trash. I've seen her personal assistant reduced to tears. If her people don't meet her every expectation, she cuts them off at the head."

"Not you, though," Tyndall said.

"Hell no, not me," Omega scoffed. "I grew up in a house with four sisters and a single mother. I know how to deal with overbearing women."

Tyndall crinkled his brow. "Thought you said you have three sisters. How come the number always changes?"

"Semantics," Omega said. "Anyway, CC is driving me nuts with her latest demand."

Tyndall leaned inward. "Ol' girl is throwing her stuff in this new flick, though. I've been to see it twice. Both times I managed to keep my jimmy out of my hand until that last sex scene. I'm proud of that."

"The screen doesn't do her justice," Omega replied. "She's thick with a capital *T*. Still, though, her attitude is doo-doo on a stick."

"Speaking of sticks," Tyndall said, "just pass her the baton, calm her ass down maybe."

Omega shook his head. "Never get involved with my clients like that, man. I'll handle her publicity, but I can't handle her."

"Seems like an open and shut situation, then," Tyndall remarked. "You don't need my advice on this one."

Omega whined, "But she wants me to handle her, man. She wants it bad."

"So do it."

"I'm trying to be professional, adhere to the Publicist's Creed."

"Get your nut. You're not hurting anyone. You're helping your client, keeping her happy."

"You think so?" Omega's eyes crested.

"I wouldn't lie to you."

They raised glasses, clinked them together.

"So what's up with you and Ana?" Omega asked Tyndall.

Tyndall frowned. "She puts Tyana in the middle all the time. I keep telling her that ain't healthy for a child, but Ana's a chickenhead."

"That's an eighteen-year-chickenhead commitment," Omega added. "Do they get better with time, like a fine wine?"

Tyndall sat back. "If Tyana wasn't such a special child, I'd be pissed."

"So what's Ana's beef now?"

"Money," Tyndall said. "What else? She watched the Soul Train Awards, saw all the industry cats in the audience with their bling bling, and she thinks I'm holding out on her. Thinks I'm not really trying to produce a hit record."

"Doesn't she know it's a struggle to get to that level?"

"Chickenhead logic," Tyndall said.

Omega and Tyndall both looked to Wesley. He was quietly sipping at a ginger ale, not the least bit cognizant of their conversations. He looked as if he was looking at the people milling around and mingling, but he was really looking through them. Omega tapped Tyndall and nodded toward Wesley. Tyndall shrugged.

A woman walked by and took Omega and Tyndall's attention away from Wesley. She wore a miniskirt, had legs for days. Her breasts stood perky beneath her sheer blouse. She had a nice tan, and though she was Caucasian she could pass for a Latina.

"Thirty-five-twenty-four-thirty-five," Omega said, eying the woman. "Victoria."

Tyndall ran his finger across his chin, studying her hard. "I don't think her breasts are that big, and I'm thinking an Ericka. Friends call her Ricky and shit."

"Look again at the breasts, Tyndall. They're deceptively large."

Tyndall watched as she moved to one of the bar stools, sat, turned with legs crossed. "You might be right about the breasts."

"I am."

"No way she's a Victoria, though."

"No way she's an Ericka," Omega shot back.

"I spent the night with Sheila," Wesley called out. His proclamation immediately ended Omega and Tyndall's customary game of guess-the-woman's-measurements-and-pick-a-name-that-suits-her. They both turned to Wesley. Omega was slack jawed. Tyndall took a sip of his drink to wet his suddenly dry mouth.

"We had the most mind-blowing sex ever," Wesley added.

Omega scrunched his eyes. Tyndall took another sip of his drink.

"I woke up early and tried to cook her breakfast in bed."

Neither Omega nor Tyndall responded to that.

"I thought we were in the process of rebuilding what we had," Wesley said. "She ended up telling me that the sex was just a quick lube, the maintenance her body needed."

"Damn," Tyndall said.

"Typical Sheila," Omega added.

"That hurt like hell, her saying that," Wesley admitted. "I was supposed to marry that woman."

Omega leaned forward, his arms propped on the table. "Sheila has been manipulating you from the beginning, Wes. You're better off without her. I never wanted to tell you because she had your nose so wide open, but she was always pestering me to connect her with my celebrity clients."

"She writes a fashion and gossip column, O," Wesley defended. "That's the business."

"Always my male clients," Omega added.

Wesley looked pained but said nothing.

Tyndall jumped in. "Omega's right, Wes. You don't need her bringing you down. Look at how much you've changed since you started dating Sheila. You're a different person. That ain't cool, can't be good."

"I disagree. I'm a much better man today. I wasn't meant for this single life, not like you guys."

"I know it seems like a decade ago," Tyndall said, "but before Sheila came along you didn't have any problem sticking your hand in the cookie jar. You ate a lot of chocolate chip, pecan sandies, whatever."

"Glad I didn't get HIV," Wesley said. "I'm not too keen on the dating scene. It's not me."

"We could debate that for the rest of the evening," Omega said. "But I want you to admit it's time you moved on from thinking about Sheila. She pretty much laid it out for you anyway. If you want to find your soul mate, I can't fault you. Realize Sheila wasn't and isn't it."

Wesley dropped his gaze.

"I got to second that," Tyndall said. "You ready to let her be?"

Wesley sat silent, head down.

"Wes?" Omega and Tyndall called in unison.

Wesley looked up, faked a smile. "As usual, you guys are on point. Sheila's just another part of my history."

Omega nodded toward a passerby. Wesley turned to see the woman from before walk by. Omega's Victoria, Tyndall's Ericka. She smiled in Wesley's direction as she breezed past, looked back over her shoulder to see if he was still looking. "You see her checking you out, Wes? That could be your future," Omega said.

Wesley eyed the woman. She *was* beautiful. She didn't look a thing like Sheila, though. That was the problem.

10

He knew he shouldn't have come here. But he had.

Wesley pressed the buzzer for Claudette's apartment. To his surprise, the lobby door opened. He moved inside and quickly found his way up the elevator. Salsa music played loudly, leaking out into the hall from the door down from Claudette's apartment. Wesley rang the bell, prepared to dance slowly, sensually, and in step with Sheila for the rest of his life if she'd have him.

Sheila opened the door, wearing a smile that faded when she saw Wesley. She looked over his shoulder, her forehead lined with frustration.

Wesley moved to enter.

Sheila put her hand out. "Actually, Wes, I'm expecting someone."

Wesley scanned her. She wore a tight-fitted blouse, a long patchwork skirt, and the expensive leather boots that he'd bought her. "You look nice," he said.

"I'm going out when my company arrives."

Her words were a knife, stuck deep in Wesley's flesh, then twisted for good measure. "Is A.J. going to give you more counseling?" Wesley bitterly asked. "Lay you on his couch and *poke* and *prod* at your inner conscience."

"Graham and Calvin, actually," Sheila confided. Two of her dearest friends, a gay couple she hung with for laughs, and, interestingly enough, sisterhood. "They're celebrating their fifth anniversary." She spit the words out as if they were those burnt strips of bacon from the other morning. Anniversaries were something she and Wes would never share in the future.

Wesley leaned against the doorjamb. "I'm sorry, Sheila. This is all new for me. I'm being stupid."

Sheila's voice dropped. "You shouldn't be here, Wes. This makes it harder."

Wesley ignored her. "Graham and Calvin are still together, huh? How are they?"

"Black, gay, in love, happy . . ." Sheila sighed, exhaled long and hard. She reached forward and touched Wesley's cheek.

"What's on your mind?" Wesley asked.

"The good times," Sheila said.

"We had them?"

Sheila smiled. The smile looked uneasy on her face, teetering, ready to leap off to its death at a moment's notice. The buzzer sounded in the apartment. Sheila jumped. She turned and looked at the intercom system as if it might explode and reduce the building to rubble. She turned back to Wesley, her eyes drinking him up. The buzzer sounded again. Sheila ignored it. She continued to look at Wesley, the both of them eyeing each other but saying nothing.

"I better let you get going," Wesley said.

"They're waiting," Sheila agreed. "You know Graham hasn't got any patience. Calvin is probably rubbing his back, trying to calm him down."

Wesley reached forward and touched Sheila's wrist. He left quickly and went to the elevator. Before he got on, he turned back to see Sheila in the hall, watching him. No matter what anyone said, he could feel the possibility of a second chance.

11

The next morning, a Saturday, Wesley was back at Claudette's apartment. Sitting in his car outside, sipping a cup of Starbuck's blend. Watching the front of the building as if on a love stakeout.

Sheila emerged after Wesley had arrived. She wore running shoes and a Lycra outfit. She bent over and stretched her legs against the stoop. Wesley took in the curvature of her ass. He could feel his rock coming to life in his shorts. He swallowed the last of his coffee, crumpled the cup, and placed it in the Starbuck's bag on the seat beside him. Sheila moved into another stretching position, her muscles womanly but defined. Wesley moved from the car in her direction.

"Hey," he said, once he'd come upon her.

She turned and looked at him. Her gaze dropped to his feet.

"I was hoping you still did your early morning jog," Wesley said.

Sheila took in his tank top, shorts, and the fresh out-of-the-box sneakers. "You're not thinking of running with me?" she asked him.

Wesley rocked on his heels. "Sure, why not?"

Sheila pointed at his feet. "Finally decided to try out the Nikes I bought you. About seven months too late, though."

Wesley tapped the sneakers against the ground and held his head down. "I should have run with you all those times you asked. I grant you that. But that was the only thing I didn't jump and do because you asked. Can't you give me that? I want to run with you now. Talk more."

"You're out of shape. You haven't stretched or warmed up, and I'm not waiting for you to. And you'll need a bathroom break before I come close to wanting to stop. That coffee you were drinking is a diuretic, you know?"

Wesley looked up, crinkled his brow. "You saw me in the car?"

"Yep, as soon as I stepped outside," Sheila admitted. "I'm a city girl. You have to be aware of your surroundings."

"So all that twisting and bending was a show for me?"

"I'm done talking, Wes. I've got to get running before the sun comes all the way out." She took off. Wesley moved tread, too, and caught up with her.

They kept a nice leisurely pace. They didn't speak because even at the slowed pace, Wesley was breathing hard through his mouth. They came to the park, a long runner's trail before them. Sheila pulled away. Wesley tried his best to catch her. After a while, his focus changed to simply keeping her in eye range. She was smoking him like a Cuban cigar.

She made the wide turn around a bend in the trail. When Wesley made the same turn, Sheila was nowhere in sight. He pressed on anyhow. His legs ached and his lungs burned. His heels would need serious soak time in the tub later.

A few minutes later, his bladder felt as if it would explode at any second. He prayed to God that he'd find a bathroom soon. A few other runners passed him by. A couple walking their dog stopped and cut through a grove of bushes to avoid him. Wesley jogged on, half bent over, holding his stomach.

Eventually, he found Sheila sitting on a bench. A smile caught her face when she noticed Wesley headed in her direction. She was in hysterics as he quickly passed her and went inside the bathroom unit that neighbored the bench.

Wesley found a seat next to Sheila when he came from the bathroom.

"Would you like more coffee?" she asked between laughs.

"Ha-ha."

"I'm sorry, Wes. You looked so cute, hunched over like that, unable to let go and run but too desperate for a bathroom to walk. Moving like a penguin."

"You remember this day, Sheila Fuller." He stopped, pained by her last name, her maiden name. She was destined to be Sheila Matthews. Didn't she realize that?

"I'm sorry, Wes," Sheila said.

"What are you sorry about?"

"You know . . . I'm sorry that I'm still a Fuller."

Wesley sighed. "I'm that obvious?"

"Yup," she said.

"How was it with Graham and Calvin? Are they still treating the Bible like it's *Vibe* magazine? Light reading and not a blueprint on how to live life. You know, Adam and Eve, not Adam and Steve?" Wesley wasn't ready to talk about his pain yet. It was easier to break down another's relationship.

Sheila smirked. "And you're one to throw stones. Handcuffing women to your bed and pleasuring yourself in every hole in her body. And I mean *every* hole."

"That's a real nice way to talk, Sheila."

"Where's that," she continued, ignoring him, "in the Gospel According to Wesley? Chapter twelve, verse nine. Thou shalt handcuff thy mistress to thy bed. Thou shalt use her for accordingly good."

"Look," Wesley said. "I'm not proud of things I did in the past. That was one incident. I wouldn't go back to those days for anything."

Sheila wasn't convinced. "What was her name again?"

"Samantha," Wesley admitted.

"I'd never spread my business around like she did," Sheila said. "Everybody at the gym knew about it. But it did get me interested in you. I saw the glasses, thought about what you were like. Handcuffing women to your bed wasn't one of my thoughts. I was excited by that."

Wesley shrugged. "Samantha got it put on her. She couldn't keep news like that to herself. But how did we get on this? I was talking about your boys, Graham and Calvin." He rolled his eyes.

"I envy them, if the truth be told," Sheila said. "They're enduring in a world that frowns on their love. That's special."

"Enduring, why can't that be us?" Wesley asked.

"Janet says we're disharmonious," Sheila said. "I think I agree with her on that."

"My parents would still be together today if my father hadn't died," Wesley said. "And they were night and day. I don't know that I'd say they were in harmony. They loved each other, respected each other, and wanted to see each other happy."

"You think your mother was happy, Wes?" Sheila shook her head. "No, *now* she's happy. Traveling the globe. I don't want to start living when my husband dies, Wes. I want to live every minute of my life to the fullest."

Wesley disliked her, even as he loved her, for trampling on the thirty-plus years of his parent's marriage.

"You're so against marriage, Sheila. Why didn't you realize that before we rented the hall, before we sent out the invitations? Before the church filled up with people?"

Sheila sat back against the hard bench. "I wanted to make you happy, Wes. I wanted us to have this dream you sold me. A fantasy wedding. Twenty-foot train. White lace everywhere. I lied to myself about it until the end."

"I don't buy that."

"I've always had an aversion to marriage, Wes. I think it speaks to something in my subconscious that I'm close to my father's ex-wives but to no one else in my family."

"I don't think you gave us a fair chance, Sheila."

"My heart wasn't one hundred percent in it. What could I say to your proposal? Your father had died. You needed me. I wanted to be needed."

Wesley moved to a philosophical place. "One hundred percent invested isn't always necessary. Look at it as you look at your finances. If you put one hundred percent of your investments in Company X, and Company X falters, you're crapped out."

"You're relating that to marriage?" Sheila asked.

"I don't think you have to be one hundred percent believing in marriage for it to work, Sheila. Too many marriages fail for people to go in acting as if they don't know the possibility of failure exists. I think you and I were reasonable enough adults to realize that loving each other gave us a shot, but it didn't mean it would work."

"You're telling me you were willing to give it a shot, knowing the pain that would come later if it failed?"

"I'm not going to say I thought without a doubt we'd be married forever," Wesley offered. "I hoped we would. I loved—love—you enough to take my best shot at forever."

Sheila sighed, leaned her head on Wesley's chest. "You make it all so much smaller than it is. You make it seem doable."

"It is if you have love," Wesley said.

"Love, huh?"

"Yes, Sheila, love." He rubbed her head. She closed her eyes and enjoyed his caress. "Do you love me, Sheila?"

In many ways she did. Not the right way, though.

"I know you do. So let us try again," Wesley said. "We'll move slower this time."

"Oh, Wes," Sheila said. She thought of her mother and the different men who moved through Susan Fuller's bedroom. Could Wesley save Sheila from recycling her mother's ways? Sheila hoped so. She wanted the voices in her head silenced.

Wesley touched Sheila's cheeks, touched her lips with his warm fingers. She lay against his chest, breathing softly.

Second chances were a blessing.

12

"Mandarin oranges and an oats n' honey granola bar." Sheila placed the items before Wesley on his desk.

He looked up and smiled. "I missed your cooking while you were gone. And now that you're back . . . I still miss your cooking."

She bent and kissed his forehead. "Whoever said the way to a man's heart was through his stomach didn't know bo diddly."

Wesley took her around the waist, brought her down on his lap. "I'm glad we're getting our life back to normal."

Sheila rubbed his face. Her eyes glowed as she watched him. After some time of this, she nodded at the lit computer screen in front of him. "How's your work going?"

Wesley sighed. "I've been running numbers to see if the project will pass the ROI threshold. Even when I inflate them it doesn't."

Sheila frowned. "You lost me after 'I've been running numbers.' I was expecting a simple good or bad as an answer."

"Bad, then," Wesley replied.

Sheila pinched his cheek, cooed, "Poor baby." Then she leaned down and whispered in his ear, "I do find it extremely sexy, though, when you talk all businessy with me."

"Do you?" Wesley asked.

She flicked her tongue at his sensitive earlobe as an answer.

Wesley moaned, said, "EBITDA is off for one of the new up-and-running projects."

Sheila kissed behind his ear. "Oh, sweetie, that's terrible."

"And the ROI threshold I was talking about before," Wesley added, "corporate doesn't recognize that the number is too high, above industry standards for sure. I don't have twenty-twenty vision and I can see it. Why can't they?"

Sheila removed his glasses and kissed each eyelid.

Wesley held up his hand. "I hurt my pinkie finger, stretching it to reach the shift key when I was writing my acquisition recommendations."

Sheila took his finger and softly caressed it. "Battlefield wound, honey?"

He nodded the affirmative. "And—"

Sheila put a finger to his lips. "Save some war stories for tomorrow night. I'm going shopping at Victoria's Secret in the morning. I'm focusing on something frilly that accentuates my best features."

Wesley's eyes widened. "Oh."

Sheila glanced at the digital clock on his desk, patted Wesley's shoulder, and rose from his lap. "I think I'll go by Claudette's now and relax for a bit, check that everything is in order, let you get your work done with no interruptions."

"Dang, do you have to?" Wesley said. "I've gotten used to you sleeping beside me in bed again. I'm on vacation." He moved past thoughts of the honeymoon he was supposed to be on with her. Sheila was here again; no need to zone in on the past. Focus on the future. He tapped his desk as a gesture to move forward. "This is work I'm doing on my own to make sure I'm not inundated when I return. It's all about you and me right now."

Baldwin, Wesley's German shepherd, came bolting into the room. Jumping for Wesley, knocking Sheila aside in the process.

"See that," Wesley said. "Baldwin doesn't want you to go either."

Sheila regained her footing. "What's wrong with this dog, Wes? Why's he acting so rambunctious?"

"He wants a walk." Wesley pet Baldwin's stomach and the animal calmed. "You know, the first time around, you and Baldwin didn't click. This time I think we need to work on making you two friends."

Sheila crinkled her nose. "He's big and obnoxious. I don't think so."

Wesley covered Baldwin's ears. "He can hear you, Sheila. Be nice."

Sheila glanced at the digital clock on Wesley's desk again. It was past ten o'clock at night. She looked at Wesley, then Baldwin. "Okay. Come on, Baldwin. Let's go for your walk."

Baldwin immediately moved from Wesley's lap and went to Sheila, sniffing at her feet. Even canine males were fickle when it came to beautiful women.

Wesley turned to his computer. "Let me save this file. We can all go."

"We're cool. Just me and Baldwin, okay?"

Wesley raised an eyebrow. "What?"

"A bonding moment for us, like you said."

"You can handle him alone?"

"I believe so."

Wesley sat back in his chair. "Now I'm getting jealous. Baldwin is stealing my lady."

Sheila smiled halfheartedly and moved to go retrieve Baldwin's leash.

"You know the way I take him, right?"

"Three blocks to the east and back," Sheila droned as she kept walking.

"Be careful out there," Wesley called after her.

She waved and disappeared from his sight.

After twenty minutes, unable to concentrate, Wesley clicked the button on the front of his computer monitor. The screen went to black. He glanced at the digital clock on his desk. It was foolish and selfish of him to let Sheila take Baldwin for a walk all by herself. At nighttime in this crazy city. Damn. He quickly grabbed his keychain and left the apartment. He'd catch up with Sheila and Baldwin and they could all go to the ice cream store around the corner. Sheila could get her favorite—banana split—and he'd get himself a scoop of butter pecan. So Baldwin wouldn't feel cast aside, he'd get him a waffle cone to paw and crunch on.

Outside, Wesley walked down the sidewalk path to the street and turned to walk east. The block was quiet and still except for a late-model Mercedes Benz parked along the curb at the end of the street with exhaust coming from its tailpipe. Walter Faye's Benz; belonging to the tenant who lived above Wesley. He considered his dislike for the man as he crunched the gravel underfoot and moved up the street in the direction of the Mercedes. Faye and Wesley rarely encountered each other in the building, but when they did, the tension between them was palpable. Wesley was one of only two African American tenants. That was two too many for Faye, Wesley was sure.

Up ahead, a heavy layer of fog covered the Mercedes' windows. The frame of the automobile faintly swayed.

Wesley wasn't one for gossip and innuendo, but he'd caught wind of one of the rumors in the building. Supposedly, Faye stepped out on his devoted wife with an alarming regularity. In the parking lot behind the building, used rubbers often dotted the ground. Whispers attributed the condoms to Faye's illicit dealings with prostitutes. Under the veil of night's darkness, down in the lot breaking his wedding vows. While his wife, a deep sleeper, sprawled in their bed upstairs none the wiser.

Men like Walter Faye made Wesley's blood boil. His heart ached for poor Mrs. Faye.

Wesley moved near the idling Mercedes. The body of the car was rocking. Faye's inside with a whore, Wesley found himself thinking. The thought of it angered him. Without considering the consequences, he decided that he'd knock on the window, rouse Faye and his paid-for lover. He'd apologize and ask if they'd seen Sheila walking Baldwin. Wesley busting him might make Faye think twice about his behavior in the future. Wesley would be doing Mrs. Faye a service.

Wesley reached the car and rapped his knuckles on the side window. The faint rocking stopped. Wesley tapped the window again. A circle opening appeared in the glass, a large spot wiped clear from inside the Mercedes. Wesley bent and peered in. To his surprise, Walter Faye wasn't inside. It wasn't Faye's Mercedes after all. An angry black man's face came into view. The man had a diamond stud in his nose, cuts in his eyebrows, old-school hip. His naked upper torso was thin but toned with muscle.

Wesley stepped back a foot, then made a move to apologize. He held his tongue, though, when he noticed the nude form of a woman on the man's lap. An unwanted erection sprouted in Wesley's pants as he took in the roundness of the woman's breasts and the sweat-covered glimmer of her skin. Her nipples dark like plums, the left one pierced and housing an unmistakable black barbell. Wesley gritted his teeth and leaned down closer to look through the window's wiped-clean opening. His erection grew so hard it throbbed. So did his heart.

Sheila was inside with the man.

Sheila's eyes widened and she sat frozen on the man's lap. Wesley banged furiously on the side window.

The door opened finally and the man emerged, zipped his pants, and pumped his fists at Wesley. Sheila jumped out, her dress hanging down around her waist, and grabbed her lover by the arm. "Calm down, Herschel," she said to him. "This is my boyfriend."

Herschel looked to Wesley and started to say something, but he remained quiet. Boyfriend, damn. Sheila hadn't said anything to him about a boyfriend. It was all, "Let's get naked, Herschel. Let's do it. Hump me, baby." Nympho, Herschel could accept. Somebody's girlfriend, that was too deep.

Wesley's gaze drifted to Sheila. She covered her nipples with her crossed arms. Wesley's mouth salted over as he looked at his woman, his love, trying desperately to shield her naked self from his eyes. He could feel the vomit working its way up through his intestines.

"Why, Sheila?" Wesley asked.

"I'm sorry." All she could offer.

"I don't give a shit about your sorry. Why?"

Sheila dropped her gaze and her voice. "I warned you something like this would happen, but you insisted we get back together."

Wesley balled his hand in a fist.

She met his gaze again. "You must have known we wouldn't make it, Wes."

Herschel reached in the car, pulled out his shirt, and placed it over his head, simply a spectator to the emotional roller-coaster ride happening in front of him.

Wesley struggled to get his breath. He looked around to see if anyone was walking the street. "I don't believe this shit."

"I'm looking for something I can't have with you, Wes. I can't see myself baking cookies and wiping off kitchen countertops. I tried to warn you a long time ago, before you asked me to marry you. Did you know I was with A.J. the day your father died? I started that argument with you so I could go be with him."

Wesley held a hand to his chest. What were the signs of a heart attack? "Where's Baldwin?"

"Wes, please."

"Where's my dog?"

Sheila pointed to the dark alley behind them. "He's okay. I tied him to a pipe."

"Oh, Sheila," Wesley cried.

Herschel opened the Mercedes and sat on the passenger side with his feet hanging out, the door cracked. He looked impatiently at Sheila as if he wanted her to hurry this situation with her boyfriend along so they could resume their tango in the backseat.

"I better get going," Sheila said, taking the hint.

"You blew us out of the water, just like that?" Wesley asked.

Sheila turned to Herschel without answering Wesley and nodded her head. Herschel got up and moved around the front of the car to the driver's side. Sheila sat in the front. She finally pulled her dress up to offer cover. She closed the door without looking in Wesley's direction.

The car pulled from the curb, Wesley rooted in place. He watched as it turned at the corner.

In the distance, a dog barked and whimpered. Wesley recognized Baldwin's cry. He turned and headed toward the alley, stumbling over a large inefficiency in the pavement. A pipe on the side of the building had Baldwin's leash tightly wrapped around it, little slack to allow the dog room to move. Wesley loosened the leash and bent to hug the German shepherd.

His warm, wet tears fell on the dog's coat.

13

Wesley walked the quiet corridor to his office. He passed a few coworkers, hastily replying with one-word answers to their queries of how he was doing. Several of his coworkers had been at the wedding-that-wasn't; he was glad that he hadn't encountered any of them yet today. He could imagine how their words would lodge in their throats and their eyes would focus everywhere but on him. His situation was a sad one. He thought about the Mercedes from last night, the windows fogged, the car rocking faintly. He thought about Sheila, covering her breasts. Baldwin strapped to a pipe in an alley.

Maybe, just maybe, coming back to work a month early would bog down his brain with enough material that his vision of the Mercedes, the fogged windows, and Baldwin in the alley wouldn't come into focus.

He reached his office door. He could feel his throat tighten as he looked at the small rectangular window of the door. It placed his mind on the last looking glass he'd peered through and the horrors he'd seen on the other side. An angry black man's face came into his view, and then those small, exquisite breasts with the dark nipples. The left breast nipple pierced.

Wesley squeezed his eyes shut and took a deep breath. Relaxed, he opened his office door and went inside. He placed his leather portfolio bag on his desk and settled into his chair. His desk was neat, with everything, from his stapler to his reports, in their own spot.

Too bad his life wasn't as orderly.

Wesley removed his office phone from its cradle and quickly dialed to check for voice messages.

A soft voice echoed in his ear.

"Mr. Matthews, this is Kidada Campbell."

Wesley swallowed. Kidada's voice placed him in mind of *her*. Backseat of the Mercedes *her*. The woman he loved and was to marry. He couldn't even think her name; *her* would have to do. Well, Kidada's tone was a mirror image of *hers*. Feminine, obviously ethnic, and softer than any fabric he could think of.

"I don't know if you remember me. I introduced myself to you when I first came to Real Estate Acquisitions from Sales and Marketing," Kidada went on in the message.

Of course he remembered her. Her complexion nut brown, a shade darker than a complexion with which he'd already fallen in love. Her eyes, too, were darker than the hypnotic light brown eyes of *her*. Kidada had graduated from Texas State instead of Hunter College, had a degree in business instead of journalism, worked for an oil company instead of a glossy magazine. That day he'd spoken with Kidada, she wore a loose-fitted sweater and a long skirt, instead of a short skirt and tight-fitted blouse that exposed the impression of a nipple piercing. Her build was thick. Kidada's bosom a cup size or two bigger than *hers*.

He was doing it again. Comparing Kidada to *her*. He blinked and refocused on the playing message.

"I was wondering—if you have any free time when you return to work—if you'd be so kind as to meet with me," Kidada continued. "I'd like a veteran's eye view of what to expect in Real Estate. I still haven't gotten myself acclimated to the different responsibilities from Sales and Marketing."

She ended abruptly. "Thanks in advance."

Wesley saved the voice mail and moved to the next. Kidada again, sounding embarrassed.

"Kidada Campbell, extension one-two-zero-nine. I neglected to leave my extension in the previous message. Thanks again."

Her voice noticeably dropped.

"Look forward to hearing from you." Her last words.

No more messages, Wesley replaced his phone in its cradle. An attractive, young, and as far as he could tell, single, black woman wanted to meet with him. A few years ago, he'd have been accessing the possibility of getting her to discuss work over wine and filet mignon. Now, all he could think about was the last time he and Sheila had gone out to dinner and how good the lovemaking had been afterward. She'd raked her long fingernails across his back and told him after her climax that she loved him. She'd drifted to sleep and he'd lain beside her, feathering his fingers over her nude body.

As that Boys II Men song proclaimed, it was so hard to say good-bye to yesterday.

He picked up his phone anyhow and dialed Kidada's extension, his best attempt at telling yesterday sayonara.

14

The restaurant swam in soft lights that brought out the richness of its wine-red and beige color scheme. Kidada had spent the better part of the short walk here with Wesley, two blocks over from their office, doing all the talking. She'd noticed during their walk that his arms and legs were stiff, that he kept looking over his shoulder, and that he made sure several feet separated them. She'd move close to him; he'd immediately move away. Okay, her sweet perfume, her shapely body, her almond-shaped eyes, and the basketful of abuse he'd taken from that sorry sista he was supposed to have married hadn't loosened him up any. His eyes shut tight to the possibilities that lay right before him. Kidada decided during the walk that she'd have to try harder.

Now, sitting at a table covered in linen, she resumed talking.

"I was planning on sneaking in a few chapters of this new Marcus Major," Kidada was saying as she raised the hardcover book for Wesley to see. "But work before play, right?"

Kidada and Wesley's wrap sandwiches arrived then, saving Wesley from having to respond to a question he hadn't actually heard. His mind, as usual of late, was elsewhere. He did remember to close his eyes and say a quick blessing. Then he reopened them, took his sandwich, and nibbled at the turkey wrap.

"Rare I see that," Kidada said.

Wesley looked up from his sandwich. "What's that?"

"A public profession of faith," she responded. Her eyes sparkled as she observed Wesley. Her own sandwich lay before her, un-touched. She had her book in her lap and her pocketbook draped across her chair by its straps. A smile made her prominent cheek-bones stand out more. Her lips looked ready for a kiss.

Wesley dropped his head, couldn't look at her. Her soft femininity made him ache as he thought about what men did with women of a soft femininity. They bounced them on their laps in the back of Mercedeses.

"I say a prayer, too," Kidada added, "but I don't close my eyes and call attention to myself. I'm of the reluctant faithful, I guess. Not good, I know." She said it with conviction, as if, starting today, she'd correct this apparent flaw. Knowing how seriously Kidada took everything, she would, too.

Wesley looked at her for a brief moment. "When you get swept off your feet," he softly responded, "land on your knees." He immediately dropped his gaze after he'd said it. Where had that come from?

Kidada rested her arms on the table. The three bangles on her wrist clanged together. She leaned in, not enough to scare him off, and practically sang the question, "You've been swept off your feet, Wesley?"

Wesley remained completely still, his eyes diverted. Hating how his name rolled off her tongue. How sexy she was. How sexy women were. How men responded to sexy women. How sex ruled with such an iron fist that it easily trumped decency, morals, and judgment. How the woman he'd committed to, in a forever kind of way, could shatter his life so thoughtlessly. Had he been swept off his feet? He looked up and smiled at Kidada despite the hurt on his soul. "Swept off my feet? I'd say so."

"The wedding fiasco?" she asked. She touched her mouth. That had slipped out before she could catch herself.

Wesley frowned. "You know about that?"

She smiled as an answer and shrugged her shoulders.

Wesley sighed and dropped his head again. "I bet my wedding fiasco is office legend by now, huh?"

"I wasn't here," Kidada replied. "But do you remember a former administrative assistant coming out of the former regional manager's office with her hair disheveled and suspicious white stuff on her jacket?"

Wesley winced. "Oh yeah, they both ended up leaving their spouses. They married, and then divorced within a year. Those two were the definition of hot and horny. They had sex in every corner of the building."

"Outside, too, I'm told," Kidada said.

Wesley smiled, the first time today. "That's right . . ."

"In the recycle shed," they said in unison. It brought a titter of laughter from them both. Kidada was more than overjoyed to see Wesley relaxing. Maybe now he'd notice the curve of her hips, her manicured fingers, and that her complexion was so divinely blemish-free.

After their shared laughter died down, Wesley said to Kidada, "Don't tell me my little situation is in the running with those two?"

"One-two on the office legend's chart, I'm told," she admitted.

"Wonderful," Wesley said.

Kidada reached across the small table, touched his hand. Her three bangles rubbed his skin. He didn't flinch, didn't go running for his personal space. "It'll die down. Give it a few weeks," she told Wesley.

"For my coworkers," Wesley said. "I don't know how long it'll live on for me; if it'll ever die down."

Kidada reached across the table again, this time with her other hand, now touching Wesley in a way that lovers do. Both of their hands clasped together. "What happened?"

"I don't know," he admitted.

Kidada's voice softened. "Handsome guy like you, with a thriving career to boot, what is she, crazy?"

"She must be, right?"

"I'd take her spot in a second," Kidada told him.

Wesley looked at Kidada. She didn't break the eye contact. She was serious. He could feel himself coming alive at the possibility. Imagine the shock on Sheila's face if she were to see him, on his feet, surviving, the lovely Kidada on his arm. Sheila would want him back in an instant. That's how women were. They cried about all the games men ran, but they were just as adept on the playing field.

"You haven't responded, Wesley," Kidada said, still holding his hand. "I'm a bit hurt by that because I'm seriously in flirt mode."

"I'm flattered, Kidada. I mean, you're beautiful—"

"Smart, enterprising, ambitious, too," she cut in.

"All of that and then some."

"So?"

"I don't know," Wesley said.

"Nothing beats a failure but a try, Wesley. I'd like to get to know you. Will you allow me to?"

Wesley didn't know how to respond. So he didn't.

"From the first time I met you, my antennae went up," Kidada told him. "I fell back, out of respect when I found out you had a fiancée. But now . . . you're fair game; you know that, right? And, Wesley, I am very, very attracted to you."

Wesley pulled his hands back, loosened the collar of his shirt, sat back in his seat, and smiled self-consciously. "You say that as if you just have to snap your fingers and I'll come running."

Kidada looked at him, deep. "I believe you would."

Wesley's eyes crested. "Oh, do you now?" Kidada was arousing him. He hadn't touched his sandwich since the first bite. She hadn't taken the first bite of hers.

Kidada smiled mischievously. She made a big play of snapping her fingers as if to say, Just like that, you'd come running. Wesley smiled.

"What's on your mind?" Kidada asked.

"Your lips, they look so kissable."

"So kiss them."

"You wouldn't mind?"

"I'd mind if you crashed my car speeding away from some woman's house you had no business in because her husband came home early. Then told me you crashed it avoiding a squirrel. I'd mind if you rifled through my trash for old bills so you could steal my identity and run up a bunch of credit cards in my name." Sadly, Kidada was speaking from experience. Dante had crashed the car. Ashton had bought a bunch of tools from Sears, lingerie from Macy's, and CDs from Sam Goody. Never again. Kidada was prepared to go tit for tat with anyone who didn't have her best interests at heart.

Kidada took a deep breath. "A kiss," she finished, "I wouldn't mind."

"I like you, Kidada."

"I'm waiting on that kiss."

Wesley leaned forward and they touched lips.

He wished Sheila was in the restaurant so she could have seen it.

15

Wesley truly hated himself.

For coming home, renewed after his lunch date with Kidada, only to compose, and send, a heartfelt e-mail message to SheDiva@aol.com. The account belonged to Sheila.

Wesley fell asleep after sending the e-mail, laptop, as the name suggests, resting on his lap. Fell asleep, hating himself.

He dreamt that he was a professional basketball player at the top of his game. His team, which had signed him to a long-term contract at the beginning of the previous season, had traded him unexpectedly. He found himself in his bedroom. A naked woman with small perky breasts, the left one pierced, stood massaging his shoulders and whispering him encouragement. He couldn't see her face but her touch was magnetic, her voice as soothing as the sound of ocean waves. She laid him down and eased herself on top of him. He could feel his rock stiffening. She took it in her soft hands and rubbed it a few times before plunging it in her wetness.

"It's just a game," she whispered to Wesley as her hips gyrated above him. She shrugged her shoulders. "So they traded you. Not the end of the world."

He could feel himself closing in on an explosion as her hips gyrated more furiously.

Then a knocking sound interrupted his flow. He turned, noticing that they were now in the backseat of a Mercedes. He pressed a button that rolled the power window down. Kidada stood outside the car, smiling.

"You've been traded," Kidada said.

"I know," he replied.

"You've got to get on a plane to Phoenix. You've got a game there tonight."

"When's my flight?" His voice was thick with frustration. The naked and faceless woman on his lap sat back, waiting for his conversation to end so she could regain her rhythm of movement atop of him.

Kidada examined her watch. "Oh, snap. You missed it already."

"Can you book me another?"

"You got it," she said before vanishing.

Wesley turned back to the woman on his lap, the naked woman with the small perky breasts, left one pierced. "Sorry about that. Now, where were we?"

The woman commenced to gyrating her hips again. Warmness moved up through Wesley's groin as her breasts slapped against his face. He tried to stop the release but couldn't. He closed his eyes and growled in ecstasy. The woman was gone when he reopened his eyes. He was standing by the curb, looking in the Mercedes.

He fought back tears, a complete and utter emptiness taking hold.

Wesley had several more dreams follow. They, too, made no sense.

Now awake, he yawned, stretched, and moved his laptop to the nearby coffee table. He blinked his eyes a few times, the room coming back into focus. Remembering the e-mail he'd sent, he retrieved his laptop to see if a reply waited for him.

One message was in his inbox. A reply to an e-mail sent with the subject "A Man and a Half."

Wesley quickly clicked on the e-mail and opened it.

In a message dated 6/15/2004 9:53:43 PM Eastern Standard Time, SheDiva@aol.com writes:
A Man and a Half. _. I remember you playing me that song. Your father would be so proud that his love of Otis Redding rubbed off on you. Anywho. Yes. I know you love me. And you did make me happy. True. The problem doesn't lie with you. It's my issues. Enough said. I need to come by and get my things. I'm missing my Helmut Lang dress something terrible. I'll come by tomorrow night around eight. I'll try to explain why things are the way they are between us then.
Best,
Sheila

Wesley saved the e-mail and shut his laptop. *Wilson Pickett, Sheila, not Otis Redding.*

Sheila would be coming by tomorrow night. That realization brought about a plan.

When Sheila arrived at his doorstep, Kidada would be lounging on his sofa, a drink nearby, her eyes drunk with lust. Wilson Pickett, O.V. Wright, Solomon Burke, one of the old-school singers would be playing softly in the background. Wesley would have his tie loosened. He'd have a candle burning, maybe two, one on the dining table and one on his coffee table. His lips would be moist from kisses, a smudge of Kidada's mahogany lipstick on his cheek. No! Wait a minute. On his neck, that's better.

Wesley smiled now, thinking about it. He couldn't wait to see the shock on Sheila's face. Maybe then he could stop hating himself for still loving the woman who'd done him so terribly wrong. Maybe then she'd understand his pain. Maybe then, she'd recognize the error of her ways. Come back to the love she'd so carelessly tossed away.

Wesley picked up his phone and hurriedly dialed.

"Ms. Campbell, what's up?" he said into the receiver when the line picked up.

"Who's this?" Kidada asked.

"You wound me," Wesley told her. "I treated you to lunch and everything."

"Trevor?"

"Say what?"

Kidada smiled through the phone. "I'm joking, Wesley. To what do I owe the pleasure of this call?"

Wesley leaned back in his chair, molded to its comfort. "I'd love to have you over for dinner tomorrow, finish what we started with lunch."

"I'd love to finish, too," Kidada said.

"Then it's a date, Kidada. Around seven."

Get Kidada in place, early, for the fireworks. Sheila wouldn't know what hit her.

16

Solomon Burke's soulful timber filled Wesley's apartment. "Tonight's the Night," one of Wesley's father's favorites. "Don't answer the phone, the door, or have any friends around," the crooner sang, "because tonight you belong to me."

Tonight, Kidada belonged to Wesley. And soon, if his plan worked correctly, Sheila might again, too. Wesley had spent all day visualizing the shock on Sheila's face when she arrived to gather her things and found Kidada lounging on his sofa. He could actually hear Sheila's crestfallen voice in his ear as she begged for a chance at reconciliation.

Tonight's the night, indeed.

Kidada sat on the edge of Wesley's sofa, one of the spaghetti straps from her dress falling off her shoulder. A half bottle of Bacardi O stood at attention on the coffee table. Kidada's lips were moist from her last sip. Her eyes fluttered to the rhythms caressing her ears in surround sound. She swayed her head from side to side, soaking in the music.

Wesley stood behind the island in his kitchen, a Bic lighter in hand, sparking flame to a scented candle. Kidada licked her lips as she watched him, as the song lyrics heightened her erotic senses, as she thought through the different ways she could mend the broken heart of her coworker. She imagined Wesley enslaved by the heat her sultry body could bring. She imagined him kissing her soft lips, massaging her shoulders, moving slow in and out of her. She also imagined herself conducting a meeting from the head of a long conference room table, Wesley tossing her sexy glances as she moved through a PowerPoint presentation. She dreamed of a fabulous life of both business and pleasure.

Wesley stepped around his kitchen island, his hands shielding the candle's flame from blowing out as he moved to sexy Kidada on the sofa.

"Music, candles," Kidada said as he neared her. "I'm beginning to not care about dinner." She bit into her lip and drew Wesley's gaze to her. "I'm thinking we should skip right to dessert. What do you think?"

Wesley sat the candle atop his coffee table. He took his seat next to Kidada on the sofa, as close as physics would allow. "I'm thinking we should take our meal *slow*. I wouldn't want you to get a stomach ache."

Kidada ran her hand over his head, her breasts pressed against his shoulder. "Would you rub my tummy if I did?"

Wesley eyed her flat stomach. "You know I would."

Kidada sat back, fanned herself. "Slow," she said, "nice and slow. Okay. I'm gonna have to remember that."

"You like the music?"

"Love it. Who is this?"

"Solomon Burke."

"I never heard of him."

"Old soul singer," Wesley told her. "This is one of my father's favorites."

Kidada spider-walked her fingers across Wesley's shoulder. "Are you and your father close?"

Wesley frowned. "He passed away over a year ago."

Kidada's fingers stopped. "I'm so sorry. I didn't know."

"It's okay."

Kidada hesitated. "Is your mother still alive?"

Wesley looked at his watch. "She should be landing in Brazil within the hour." He cleared something from his throat. "She's taken to traveling since my pop passed."

"That's good she's continuing on with her life. I know how difficult it can be after your loved one passes on. My father had a heart attack and died my freshman year of high school."

For the first time tonight, Wesley forgot about Sheila coming through his front door and finding a beautiful woman on his sofa. He really focused his attention on Kidada. The grief they had in common. "That must have been tough, losing your father so early in your life."

Kidada held up her wrist. "Went out and bought these three bangles the day after his funeral." She touched the bracelets, one by one. "A bangle for me, another for my mother, and then this last one is for my little sister. We had to be one another's glue during that time. Hold one another together."

Wesley looked at Kidada as he'd once looked at Sheila, with a collector's appreciation of a fine piece of art. "I wondered about those bracelets. I think that's wonderful."

"You do what you must to face difficulty in life," she mused. "I believe in symbolism, and it seemed like something that would help me."

Wesley smirked. "I got engaged."

"Excuse me?"

"After my pop died," Wesley said. "I asked Sheila to marry me the day of his burial, right by the grave site."

"Deep," was all Kidada could say.

"Very much so," Wesley agreed.

"She was of help, though? You know, dealing with your father's death?"

Wesley nodded. "She wrote me a poem shortly after he died. Used the song titles from a bunch of my father's favorite old soul songs and had the poem stitched into a pillow. I keep it at the head of my bed. I kneel on it and pray every night before I go to sleep. I guess in a way that pillow is my three bracelets."

"Nice," Kidada said. Stories like that always warmed her heart.

Wesley tossed aside reflections of the past. "So tell me, Kidada. What do you want out of life?"

Kidada paused for a beat as if she had to think it through. In actuality, she'd been mapping out a plan of course for her life since her daddy clutched his chest, right after dinner, and said his last word, "tight." She sat back against Wesley's sofa and threw her gaze across the room, fixated on one of his walls. "A bunch of kids, some my own, some I'd adopt," she began.

"A regular old Josephine Baker," Wesley said. "You think you can do a naked dance for me someday with bananas, uh, strategically placed over your, uh, other fruit?"

Kidada tapped his shoulder and moved to her next thought.

"Maybe one day I can stop reading all these novels and actually write one. I'd like that."

"Everybody thinks they have a book in them."

Kidada gripped his arm, feeling very comfortable. "One of my girlfriends in Texas is working on a manuscript. She has me read over every new chapter she writes."

"Is she any good?"

"I call her Zane E. Lynn Dickey because she doesn't have her own style. Just a mixture of who's popular."

"Zane E. Lynn Dickey? I don't follow," Wesley admitted.

"You read?" Kidada asked him.

Wesley frowned. "Do Excel spreadsheets count?"

"I'm afraid not," Kidada told him. "But speaking of that, what are you working on at work right now?"

"Nothing," Wesley said. "But De Matteo has something big coming down the pike, I've heard." David P. De Matteo, regional manager for the oil company where Wesley and Kidada worked.

Kidada released her hold on Wesley and fell back against the sofa's cushions. "De Matteo's a jerk. Makes me wish I'd gone to work for ExxonMobil or Shell instead."

"Wow, you don't like him?"

"If I could bleach my skin, get rid of my boobs, and grow a dick—excuse my French—and the company gave me his job, I'd show you what a real regional manager is. I've gone to him with a few concerns, and each time he's disregarded me. He won't again, though, I assure you."

"Damn! *Dick* is French?" Wesley asked, straight-faced.

Kidada laughed and something compelled her to touch the side of Wesley's face. "You're so cute."

"Uh-oh," Wesley said as his cheeks drew the warmth of Kidada's fingers. "Cute guys get taken advantage of, *used*."

Before Kidada could reply, Wesley's doorbell buzzed. Wesley jumped. He'd forgotten about Sheila because Kidada had been such good company. He looked at the bracelets on Kidada's wrist and his stomach dropped. Using Kidada to get back at Sheila no longer seemed a good idea.

"Are you expecting someone, Wesley?"

"Me, no," he lied.

The doorbell rang out again. "Are you going to answer that?" Kidada asked.

"I better," Wesley said. He rose from the couch and moved slowly to the front door.

He opened the door, his mouth gone dry all of a sudden.

"Janet?" The surprise clung to his voice.

"In the flesh," she responded cheerily. Then stopped, craned her neck. "Hmm, that's Solomon Burke playing, isn't it?"

Wesley ignored her question. "What are you doing here?"

"I was—" Janet's voice halted as she noticed the beautiful nut-brown woman with three clanging bangles on her wrist coming up behind Wesley. Janet cleared her throat, tried to focus her eyes on Wesley and not on the woman a few feet behind him. "Sheila asked me to stop by and get her things."

Now Wesley's voice cracked. "I thought she was coming to get them herself?"

"Nope, me," Janet responded. She eyed the woman in Wesley's apartment, who turned on her heels and moved back into his space, grabbed her pocketbook, slipped her feet in her shoes, and headed back toward the front door. Wesley stood silent, unaware of the rustling behind him.

Kidada reached Wesley's back and tried to brush him aside. He turned, surprised to find her near. "What's going on, Kidada?" Then noticing her keys in hand, "You aren't leaving, are you?"

Kidada smirked. "The candles, the music, the drinks—it was all a setup."

"What do you mean?"

"Don't play dumb, Wesley. I heard you. You were expecting your ex to show up and find you and me together."

Wesley didn't deny the accusation. Now, though, after having spent some time bonding with Kidada, his thwarted plan made him feel as badly as he did on what was to have been his wedding day. Kidada deserved better, as he had.

"I guess I must be cute, too, huh?" Kidada barked.

Wesley frowned. "What?"

"Remember you said cute guys get used. Cute girls, too, I suppose. You took advantage of me, Wesley. I believed in you, liked you, and you *used* me."

Wesley dropped his head. Kidada moved past, gave Janet an evil eye, and drifted down the hall.

Wesley looked at Janet. She shook her head and moved past him, inside. Baldwin, who'd lain in the corner, uninterested, while

Kidada was in the apartment, ran to Janet and she rubbed his side.

Janet looked up from petting Baldwin. "Where are Sheila's things?" she asked Wesley.

Shell-shocked, Wesley pointed to his bedroom. "A couple boxes in the walk-in closet in my bedroom. I need to help you find it. The closet's a mess."

"I bet it is," Janet replied. "I bet it is."

17

The crystal tumbler Kidada had sipped from sat lonely on Wesley's coffee table. Dim light, coming from a standing gooseneck lamp in the corner, illuminated the living room. The Solomon Burke album from earlier had run its course. Wesley didn't have the strength to place Wilson Pickett, Otis Redding, or Sam and Dave under the needle of his father's old record player to replace it. Instead, he picked up the crystal tumbler and traced his fingers over the mahogany-colored lipstick marks Kidada had left behind. He thought of her three bracelets and shook his head at the blown opportunity of becoming the inspiration for a fourth. Sheila had damaged him when they were together, and now, separated, her voodoo still cast a pall over his life.

He sprang forward suddenly. Picked up his cordless phone and dialed. It was time, he considered as the phone rang, for him to stop playing the victim. It was time he reconstructed his life.

"Hello," a soft and sleepy voice said in his ear.

He shifted on the couch, got comfortable. "Janet, this is Wesley. Sorry I'm bothering you so late. I really needed to reach you, though."

The sleep that had seemed so urgent a moment ago became a passing thought to Janet. Hearing Wesley's voice on the other end of her phone made her pulse race. "Wes? What's wrong? Did you find something else of Sheila's?" She quickly prayed for another opportunity to visit Wesley's apartment, lose herself in his scent of Just Cavalli Him, and passing his kitchen, visualize herself in there chopping onions. She hoped he found a pair of Sheila's jeans or one of her blouses tucked under that mess in his closet.

"No, no, I gave you all of Sheila's things." His voice lost its direction. "Did you drop her things off to her yet?"

"Tomorrow I will."

"Good, I'm glad I caught you then," Wesley said. "Would you do me a favor?"

I'd do anything you ask, Janet wanted to say. *Even though my best friend is your ex, and you had that woman in your apartment tonight, and you never even notice me, and I know that my palms shouldn't sweat when I'm around you, and you make me angry chasing behind all these women that are so wrong for you, and you're so blind.* Instead, she said, "Depends on the favor."

Wesley cleared his throat. "I, um, need you to rip up that letter I asked you to give Sheila."

Janet huffed, though she was glad the letter would meet its death.

"The letter you made me sit and wait for for an hour while you composed it?" she asked.

Wesley had sat at his kitchen table, Janet on the couch in the living room, his face serious as he wrote. Though no words had passed between them, it had been the best hour of Janet's week. She'd spent it in Wesley's presence.

"Yes," Wesley said, "that letter."

"The letter I had to sit by myself watching an episode of *Friends* I'd already seen?"

"Sorry I put you through that. Did Joey at least take off his shirt or something for you?"

Janet ignored him. "The letter you made me take an oath on a stack of Bibles that I wouldn't read and that I'd deliver to Sheila safely and in the same condition as when it left your apartment?"

"Yes, Janet, that's the letter."

"Okay," she said. "Consider it ripped."

"Okay? Just like that. After all you just put me through?"

"You know I like to have fun with you, Wes," Janet said. She thought of the dreams she'd started having about Wesley. She wished the fun of those dreams that awakened her, sweaty and out of breath, was the variety of fun she shared with Wesley in real life.

"Everyone likes to have fun at old Wesley's expense."

"I'll get rid of the letter," Janet said, serious.

"Thanks." Wesley's posture straightened once he realized that letter would exist only in his memory. Now, it seemed so juvenile and foolish to have written it. At the time he composed it, he'd considered it the poetry of his feelings that needed airing.

After an awkward bit of silence, Janet asked, "So what happened to make you decide this all-important letter isn't so all important after all? Is it the woman who was at your place?" She hoped it wasn't the woman at his place.

"In a way," Wesley acknowledged.

Janet sat silent.

"Kidada's a beautiful woman," Wesley continued. "I'm coming to the conclusion—thickheaded as I am—that Sheila isn't right for me and that I need to direct my energies elsewhere. I need to move on somehow. Sending Sheila that letter isn't moving on. It's humiliating for me, actually." He wondered if Janet knew about the episode in the back of the Mercedes. He started to question her but didn't.

"This Kidada," Janet asked, "and you are getting close?"

Wesley sighed. "We could have. But I think I blew that one. You saw how angry she was. I don't think that plane will take off."

Thank God for that, Janet thought. "I'm sorry to hear that," she lied.

"Clichéd as it might be, there are other fish in the sea. I believe there is a good woman out there for me," Wesley told her.

"There sure is," Janet said. And she's right on the phone with you as we speak.

"I'll find her, too."

"She's probably right up under your nose."

"What?"

"In your building or something," Janet quickly responded.

"Maybe," Wesley said.

Despite her inner objections, Janet offered a bit of advice. "Figure out where the good women are, and make sure that you're there as well."

"You're a woman," Wesley noted. Janet rolled her eyes at the way he said it, as if it was a revelation that had just come to him.

"Yes, I am, Wesley, since 1976," she replied. "Mood swings. PMS. No Adam's apple. I'm legit."

Wesley didn't notice the sarcasm in Janet's tone. "Where are the women? The good women, I mean."

Janet looked around her small apartment. She ate alone on the sofa most nights, so she didn't have a dining table. On her bookshelf stood a photo of her parents and another of a cousin she was especially close to. Minutes ago, when the phone rang, she was sure it was Sheila. Sheila would call any time of the night because she knew she wasn't "interrupting anything" by calling Janet. Hardly anyone else called. The few boyfriends Janet had been with, she'd been faithful to and had made sure their needs were satisfied. Not one of them thought that enough when a woman with a bigger chest and less to discuss came along; especially her last boyfriend, Parrish. Thinking his name made her shudder. She quickly cast it aside, knowing that she'd been worse than Wesley was now after Parrish moved on without her.

Where are the women?

"You don't want to divulge the secrets, Janet?"

"I'm sorry, Wes," she apologized. "I don't know. Everywhere. You have to look deeper than bra size and hair length if you truly want a good woman."

"I've never been superficial, if that's what you're implying," Wesley defended.

"No, Wes," Janet said, "you're one of the good guys. Any woman who has your love has something powerful and special."

"Thanks," Wesley said.

"Anytime," Janet replied. There was so much more she wanted to say.

"Well, I'll let you go," Wesley said.

"Take care, Wes." Tonight wouldn't be the night she told him all the emotions bubbling inside of her.

Wesley said his good-bye and hung up. Janet held the phone a moment, and then hung up herself.

In his apartment, Wesley smiled, lying back and looking at the roof as if it were a sky of stars, his spirit renewed. Janet always had a way of picking him up. That time he worked late and forgot he had a dinner appointment with Sheila. That time Sheila was upset because he'd come upon her journal, though he hadn't read any of its entries. All those times Sheila was angry enough to think about breaking things off with him, Janet picked up the pieces. Janet made everything okay. Janet comforted him.

Meanwhile, in her apartment, Janet frowned, rose, and went to draw a bath, having to settle for a powerful and special soak instead of the love she desired.

18

During the night, Wesley dreamed again. He dreamed of the number three. Sheila's three strikes: the wedding-day snub, the backseat of the Mercedes, and sending Janet to get her belongings. He also dreamed of the three gold bangles on Kidada's arm. They jingled as she danced to one of his father's old soul records. They brushed against his back as he and her made love. Upon awaking in the morning, Wesley decided that apologizing to Kidada was his top priority of the day.

Now, standing outside her office door, knocking softly, his chance would soon come.

"Come in," Kidada called out after his first few knocks, "it's open."

Wesley cracked her door and stuck his head inside. The smile she'd had on her face quickly faded. A scowl replaced it. Determined, Wesley didn't let her disposition reverse his course. "Hey," he said, "do you have a minute? I'd like to talk to you."

Kidada huffed and dropped her eyes. She searched her neat desk for something, settling on a lined yellow notepad. She snatched a black ballpoint pen from her organizer and began to write absent-mindedly on the pad. She scribbled in hard sweeping strokes, the three bangles on her wrist clacking together from the exaggerated movements. She rocked in her leather chair, the springs wailing, screaming for relief.

Wesley waited for her to acknowledge his presence. She wouldn't.

He stepped inside and shut the door behind him. "Yes, you'd love for me to come in? Great." The dream flashed through his mind again, Kidada's three bangles brushing across his naked shoulder. Sheila had stolen enough from him. He wanted to move on. He wanted to move on with Kidada. He was determined to warm Kidada's chill and parlay a second chance with her.

As it was his first time in Kidada's office, he looked around, gathering a sense of her. The wall beside her desk displayed her college diploma. It was a bone-colored document with a raised seal and attractive cursive lettering. Wesley imagined Kidada on campus, all the frat boys concocting schemes to get her to study with them. Eye candy, Omega would say of her. Measurements 34-24-34, Tyndall would add. Angelica; friends call her Ange and shit. Kidada was eye candy, for sure. With a level of beauty capable of blurring away all the women of a man's past. Even, Wesley decided, women with a fondness for a Mercedes backseat.

Wesley moved to directly in front of Kidada's desk. He leaned down to try to gather her eyes. She refused to look up. He refused to let this deter him. "I know you're upset, Kidada. I can't say that I blame you. I was hoping you'd at least let me explain."

Kidada muttered something under her breath. Wesley didn't hear what she said, but he figured it was something you wouldn't repeat in the presence of a reverend or a two-year-old. He shook it aside and settled into the seat facing her. She looked up briefly before turning back to stab at her notepad with the black ballpoint pen.

Wesley scooted the chair as close to her desk at it would go, leaned forward, and touched Kidada's hand. She looked up at him, her eyes on fire. She turned her gaze to his hand covering hers. Her eyes told the story of a mad woman contemplating ways to cut a hand off at the wrist. Wesley noticed. He quickly removed his hand. "I want you to relax with the pad and hear me out, Kidada. Please. Okay?"

She put down her pen and gave Wesley her attention. Now that he had it, words escaped him. He paused, trying to come up with something prudent to say, and then decided to take the easiest route. "I want to apologize for my behavior last night, Kidada. I know I was wrong. I hated to see you leave." He sighed. "I thought about you all night. I had a dream about you." The memory brought a smile to his face. "Hopefully, one day we can do the things I dreamed about. I'll have to buy silk sheets to make it happen, but that's cool."

No, this fool wasn't getting sexual, Kidada thought. She leaned back in her seat and formed a pyramid with her hands. Wesley watched her. She looked every bit the CEO of a Fortune 500 company. He'd never seen a woman pose in such a manner. Never seen a man this way either, except in mobster movies. It was a position of power. It fit Kidada.

"Will you accept my apology, Kidada?" he asked.

She looked at him, hard, her eyes still on fire, burning through him. He blinked several times. She didn't blink once.

"Will you, Kidada?"

Her first words were not what he wanted to hear. "No, I won't," she told him.

"I made a mistake," he defended.

"That you did."

"How can I make it up to you?"

"You can't."

"Come on, Kidada. We have to move past this. You do realize we have to work together."

Kidada smiled. A smile so full of evil it would make the devil himself cross to the other side of the street if he saw Kidada headed his way. "One day I'll be your boss," Kidada told Wesley. Her shoulders squared and her chest poked out a bit as she said this. "You better pray that day doesn't come soon. Because when it does, your ass is grass and I'll be the bitch grinding my three inch Manolo heels in your back."

"A *Sex in the City* fan," Wesley said, and then shut up. He'd long learned that when a woman was angry it was best to sit silent; let the angry tide ease on its own.

Kidada wasn't finished with him. She pointed a finger at his chest. Her voice pitched higher as she said, "You tried to play me. I don't like being a pawn. I'm not about games." She stopped to take a breath. Her jaw muscles tensed up. "What did you think would come of your ex stopping by to pick up her things and finding me on the couch? Be truthful."

Wesley shifted in his seat. He realized Kidada would never allow him to plead the fifth, so instead he focused on perjury. "I hadn't thought about it."

"Cow dung," Kidada said.

"Okay," Wesley said. "I wanted Sheila to see that I moved on, that I'd upgraded." He made no mention of wanting to make Sheila so jealous she'd come crawling back to him. Now it seemed foolish to him that he'd ever thought that possible. Foolish, with Kidada looking so lovely before him, that he'd wanted it. Kidada was an upgrade from Sheila. As his father would say, Ray Charles could see that.

Kidada's eyes crested. "Upgraded?" She picked up her pen again and commenced to scribble on her yellow pad.

Wesley smirked. Kidada seemed to buy his line, though she was scribbling on that pad as if her life depended on it. The angry tide was close to subsiding. It was empowering to move a woman from hate to love. He was determined to move Kidada. He carefully thought through his words, placed himself in Omega or Tyndall's shoes. "Yeah, baby, an upgrade. Sheila's a Lexus, I'll grant her that, but you're a Maserati Quattroporte."

Kidada crooked her head to the side. "Oh, I'm a Maserati, huh? What are you, R. Kelly now? I remind you of a jeep?"

"Not a jeep, Kidada, a luxury Maserati. A fine, sleek body, for sure." He basked in the poetry flowing so smoothly.

"A fine, sleek body," Kidada said. Her face held no expression, but Wesley was sure she was feeling him.

"High performance, too, I bet." He leaned forward, deepened his voice. "The dream I had about you got me to thinking. If Janet hadn't come by, I bet I would have found out how high performance you are, wouldn't I have?"

Kidada studied him for a moment. She straightened herself in her chair. Her cheeks had turned a shade of strawberry.

He had her. From hate to love, just like that.

"Wouldn't I have?" Wesley repeated in a singsong cadence. He imagined himself Ruben Studdard or Luther, a superstar yearning for another dance with his father. His father, sadly, wasn't coming back. However, Wesley would be content cutting the rug with beautiful, three-bracelet-wearing Kidada.

"We were headed to a nice place, I thought," Kidada admitted.

"So let's get back on track, baby." He'd never used the word *baby* so much. It liberated him to hear it, sounding so smooth, coming from his mouth. Sheila would be shocked to see him kicking game with such ease and flair instead of lying in a corner, balled up, and missing her like crazy.

Kidada picked up her yellow notepad and tapped it against her desk. "You're something, Wesley."

"You don't know the half. So can we move forward?"

"You'll hear from me," Kidada told him. "How is that?"

"Lunch time?" Wesley wanted specifics. He couldn't let another woman get away from him with no fight.

Kidada could see the seriousness in his face. "Possibly," she allowed.

"Cool." Wesley smiled. He knew he had her, but she needed to play a little tough to save face and not set herself up to be his doormat.

He left her office with a song on his lips and thoughts of her three bracelets brushing against his naked shoulder.

He had no thoughts of Sheila.

19

Twelve o'clock noon was the time, Wesley noticed as he glanced at his watch. Where had the hours gone? He hadn't gotten much work done. He spent most of his morning after leaving Kidada's office thinking about the possibilities that existed between them. His mind kept returning to the same place. Kept falling on a visual of Kidada's three bracelets brushing against his naked shoulder.

He picked up his phone and dialed Kidada's extension. Her voice mail kicked in. He replaced the receiver in the cradle without leaving a message. He pushed back from his desk and stood. Kidada had already established a reputation for being a workaholic. Most likely she was still in her office, hunkered down over a project, ignoring all phone calls. Wesley decided to try to get her to cut away with a promise of Thai food. They'd ladle out spoonfuls of steaming tom yum soup, a hot-and-spicy dish to match hot-and-spicy Kidada. Wesley grabbed his car keys and prepared to go knock at Kidada's office door for a second time today.

Wesley backed from his office, keys jingling. He bumped someone. "Excuse me," he said; then noticing it was the regional manager, said, "Oh, David. I'm sorry. Rushing, not looking where I'm going."

"And where are you off to in such a rush?" De Matteo's cap of perfectly coifed silver hair framed a face reddened by something. Was it anger? His deep-set blue eyes narrowed. The frown of his countenance caused more wrinkles than normal to sprout from the corners of his eyes. Black pants and a suit jacket covered a dark gray turtleneck, the ensemble tailored especially for his physique. Wesley wondered if De Matteo had mob connections.

"To lunch," Wesley stuttered. "I thought I'd see if any of the new consultants wanted to grab a bite to eat." The only new consultant he cared about, Kidada.

"Kidada Campbell?" David asked, reading Wesley's mind.

Wesley smiled weakly. He wondered what the employee manual said about office romances. He remained silent.

De Matteo studied Wesley for a moment, and then shifted weight from one foot to the other. He already knew the answer to his question. He didn't appear happy about it.

Silence sat heavy between them for what felt to Wesley like minutes.

De Matteo looked around, checking for eavesdroppers. Satisfied the few employees still at their desks were consumed with work only, he turned back to face Wesley. "Might I have a word with you? You can extend your lunch hour after we've had our say, if need be."

"Sure." Wesley's voice cracked a bit, as he wasn't certain of where this was headed.

De Matteo pointed behind Wesley. "In your office, if you don't mind."

"Sure." Wesley turned awkwardly and bumped into the door. He shrugged aside the pain and fumbled to twist the doorknob. He frowned, away from De Matteo's sight. He wasn't handling this little unexpected meeting well. And didn't he have any word in his vocabulary besides *sure?*

Somehow, Wesley got the door to open and they both stepped inside. De Matteo closed the door behind him. It slammed shut, the sound a horrible noise to Wesley's ears.

"Have a seat, Wesley," De Matteo said. "I'm not going to beat around the bush."

Wesley shakily moved to his desk, fumbled with his chair, found his seating. His heart continued to roar inside his chest. This couldn't possibly be good.

De Matteo found a seat in front of Wesley's desk. "Something disturbing has come to my attention, Wesley."

Wesley tried to keep his posture straight. A lump formed in his throat. His mouth and lips were dry. "Something disturbing," he said. "Regarding me?"

De Matteo nodded. "Yes, unfortunately, regarding you."

Wesley didn't say anything, afraid of how his voice would sound.

"I promised not to lollygag," De Matteo said. "Kidada Campbell has filed a complaint against you, Wesley."

Wesley felt his hard-beating heart slow. "I don't understand," he managed. "What kind of complaint?"

De Matteo frowned. He generally didn't care how many black cats his employees killed, as long as they didn't dump their stiff carcasses on his porch. "Sexual harassment," he answered. He made a face, as if his throat was sore and it stung to say the words.

Wesley dropped back in his seat. He knew he should have a response, but he didn't.

"Very serious charge, Wesley," De Matteo said. "What do you say to it?"

"It isn't true," Wesley said in a soft voice. He didn't look De Matteo in the eye. De Matteo made a note of the fact.

"She had detailed information, Wesley."

Now, defiance shot up through Wesley. He wasn't letting another female tear down his house. "Like what. What could she possibly have? It isn't true."

De Matteo reached inside his jacket, pulled out his eyeglasses and a sheet of lined yellow paper. He carefully placed the eyeglasses on, yet still narrowed his eyes to look over the paper slip. "Did you stop by her office, uninvited, this morning?"

"Yes, I did. I stopped by Jeremy Daniels's office, too, today. They're coworkers. It's natural to have dialogue with your coworkers I would think."

"Not natural to touch your coworkers without their permission, though, is it, Wesley?"

This was really starting to burn Wesley up. "No, it isn't. And I never have."

De Matteo adjusted his eyeglasses. He took his gaze off the paper and looked at Wesley. "You didn't touch Kidada's hand?"

Wesley thought back. He had in fact touched her hand. "Yes, but—"

De Matteo shook his head, halting Wesley, and returned his eyes to the paper slip of evidence. "Did you tell her about a dream you had involving her? Did you insinuate that the dream was of a sexual nature?"

Wesley's forehead flashed hot. He pulled down the collar of his shirt, immediately regretting it. Nothing spelled guilt as distinctly as that gesture. "This is all a misunderstanding."

"Did you compare her to an automobile?" De Matteo continued. He looked up from the paper. "A Maserati Quatro-something,
with a fine, sleek body?"

The walls closed in on Wesley. He was angry with everyone now.
De Matteo knew the information on that piece of paper by heart,
Wesley supposed. The regional manager kept glancing at it to un-
nerve Wesley. Wesley knew all about it, realizing now that it was
the paper Kidada had scribbled on, making notes to bury Wesley
instead of doodling as Wesley had thought.

De Matteo wouldn't let up. "Did you tell her you bet she was
'high performance' in the bedroom?"

Wesley's voice had no fight. "This is all blown out of proportion.
She was at my apartment last night. Did she tell you that?"

De Matteo nodded. "She did. She said her hope was that you
would mentor her. Obviously, you had different thoughts about
what mentoring truly is."

Wesley rocked back in his chair. "This is crazy. Everything mis-
construed."

"That's why I'm here, Wesley. To clear away the muck and find
the truth."

Wesley leaned forward and looked De Matteo in the eyes. "And
what do you believe? I've been a valuable asset to this company for
five years. I haven't had a single complaint from anyone before.
What do you believe?"

De Matteo returned Wesley's gaze. "I believe without a doubt
that one thing Kidada told me is unequivocally true."

Wesley harrumphed. "This should be real interesting. What?"

De Matteo shook his head, saddened by the unfolding events.
"The horrible situation with your former fiancée has made you into
someone different," he told Wesley.

"That has nothing to do with these false accusations," Wesley
said. "And for the record, I haven't changed one bit. I'm still the
same guy who has given this company my blood, sweat, and tears
ever since I graduated college."

Cliché, but it applied.

"You have been an exceptional employee, Wesley."

"But," Wesley said, knowing a "but" was coming. He braced
himself for it.

"But," De Matteo said, "there is a certain protocol that must be
followed. Ignoring a hot-button claim, such as sexual harassment,

isn't a prudent thing for any regional manager to do." De Matteo smiled again. "Any regional manager, that is, who expects to remain employed. Six more years, Wesley, and I can sail my boat to my heart's content."

"No beating around the bush, remember?" Wesley said.

De Matteo folded his hands together and sat back in the chair. "Kidada's not likely to drop this. She's already intimated that she'll take this as far as it needs to go. We've already suffered enough embarrassing missteps as a company. The media is ready to pounce on "big oil" any chance they get."

"Beating around the bush," Wesley said again.

De Matteo cleared his throat. "It's not just this, Wesley. For whatever reason you haven't been as sharp as I'd come to expect from you." De Matteo sighed. "I'll have legal draw up a reasonably fair severance offer for you, Wesley. I do hope you sign it."

Wesley's mouth dropped open. Another woman had gotten him.

20

"I'm having a tough time with women," Wesley admitted to Omega and Tyndall. He sat back after his proclamation and took in the dinner crowd at Trends, the bar/restaurant they used as a meeting place. The events of the day, especially losing his job, still hadn't settled itself in his mind.

"You just got Sheila's foot out your ass," Tyndall said, "and now this Kidada chick comes and has you tasting her slingbacks. You ask me, you need a new philosophy in dealing with these women. I'd change, it were me."

Omega picked up a chicken strip, but held it in his hand. "I have to admit Tyndall is on to something, Wesley. You're stood up at the altar and lose your job, both at the hands of two different women, in the same year." He paused. "It's time to reevaluate the good-guy role. You need less Will Smith and more DMX. These women cross you, growl at them." His advice dispensed, Omega took a bite of his chicken strip.

Wesley was about to respond, but Tyndall shooed him off. "You can start," Tyndall said, "with shorty headed our way."

Wesley and Omega turned. With all eyes on her, the woman put extra sway in her hips as she approached. She wore a snug-fitting honey-colored dress that ended several inches above her knees. Her body was one big curve. She had a nice dark brown complexion and wild, curly hair that brought out the exotic aspects of her nature.

"Damn," Omega said. "Honey's about thirty-six-twenty-four-thirty-six. My nose is telling me Stacey."

"Then you need Nyquil 'cause your nose is stuffed," Tyndall cut in. "Ol' girl's a Veronica. Friends call her Ronnie and shit."

Wesley was impressed. "I can see myself losing my life behind her," he added. "That would be the natural progression of things, right? Stood up at the altar, lose your job, die."

Tyndall looked at Wesley. "You are one corny dude, you know that?"

"DMX," Omega said. "You have to go DMX on this one."

"She's eyeing you hard, Wes," Tyndall said. "You better get her math. And once you get it, wait at least three days before you dial those numbers. Make her sick waiting on you to holla at her."

"Oh, boy," was all Wesley could say. He took a deep breath.

The woman reached the table and pointed at Wesley. She said simply, "You."

She looked too tall, especially with her mountainous heels on, for the backseat of a Mercedes. Wesley shot his gaze to her arm. She didn't have any bracelets on her wrist. Okay, she was fair game. Wesley licked his lips and made sure his posture was strong.

"Me?" he asked.

"But of course." She directed his attention to a table at the other side of the restaurant. Two attractive women waved and giggled toward Wesley.

Through gritted teeth, Tyndall said, "Handle this, man. Your boys are counting on you."

The woman shot Tyndall a quick glance, and then turned her attention back to Wesley.

"My girlfriends and I are Cosmopolitan women. Buy us drinks," she demanded.

Wesley's shoulders sagged. Did he have a sign that read USE ME FREELY on his forehead? He smirked, shook his head, and fell back against the booth's cushions. Tyndall muttered something under his breath and took a sip of his drink. Omega undressed the woman with an appreciative stare.

Ms. Cosmopolitan put her hands on her hips and cocked her head. She held her eyes on Wesley. "Well?"

Wesley could smell the vodka and cranberry juice on her breath. He hadn't caught the scent until Ms. Cosmopolitan demanded he buy drinks for her and her friends. "I think you've had enough already," he told her. He nodded at Omega and Tyndall. "We were having an important conversation; could you excuse us?"

"Oh, you're one of them," the woman said. She held her position.

"What does that mean?" Wesley asked her. Tyndall shook the ice cubes in his glass and took one last swallow. Omega cocked his head so he could gather a rear view of the woman.

"Bet you got a Cindy in your life," Ms. Cosmopolitan said.

Wesley frowned. "What are you talking about?"

Ms. Cosmopolitan narrowed her eyes and shook her head. "You can't handle a beautiful, voluptuous, African American sister like me, so you go get yourself a Cindy."

"A Cindy?" Wesley shook his head. "I'm not following you."

Ms. Cosmopolitan huffed. "A white girl, fool."

Wesley sat up in his seat. He'd loved a backseat-of-a-Mercedes woman and had his heart broken. He'd lusted after a three-bracelet-wearing woman and lost his job behind her lies. He'd eventually find another woman to wreak havoc on his life. She, as all the others were, would be black. He loved the sisters, even if they didn't love him back. He always would, too. "You couldn't be further from the truth," he said to Ms. Cosmopolitan. "I adore black women."

Ms. Cosmopolitan smiled. "Then, chop-chop and order those cosmos."

Wesley frowned. "You don't have to talk to me like that."

"You adore black women. Show and prove. Buy those drinks."

Wesley smirked and looked to his two friends. "You believe this woman?"

"DMX," Omega said. Tyndall nodded in agreement.

"I'm waiting on those drinks," Ms. Cosmopolitan said.

"You're going to be waiting a long time, girlfriend," Wesley answered. He picked up his glass of ginger ale, took a long swallow, dragged out an "Ah," and then placed the glass back on the table. He looked at Omega and Tyndall and smiled. They smiled back.

"Is that a diss?" Ms. Cosmopolitan asked.

"I'm done talking to you," Wesley told her. "Now you, chop-chop back on over to your table."

Ms. Cosmopolitan quickly grabbed Wesley's glass. Before he could move, she'd splashed the remaining ginger ale all over his Kenneth Cole shirt. Wesley popped up out of his seat, dabbed at his shirt with a napkin, and gave Ms. Cosmopolitan the meanest face he could muster.

"Learn how to treat a lady," she said. She walked off, sashaying hard.

Wesley's nostrils flared as he watched Ms. Cosmopolitan rejoin her friends. Several patrons looked at him. Wesley turned and looked at Omega and Tyndall. His jaw muscles bulged. "You guys are right. These women want a bad boy. They don't respect a good man who treats them well. Okay, cool. I'm going to give them their bad boy."

B Side

21

Wesley's fingers trembled with excitement as he pressed in the numbers on his cordless phone. He hunkered over the island in his kitchen, his address/phone book opened in front of him. As rings cycled in his ear, he thought about a night, years ago, that he'd shared with the woman he was now calling. It had been incredible. He especially remembered her seriously studying the dimensions of his bed.

"What's up?" he'd asked her.

"Seeing if I have room to do this position," she'd replied.

Wesley was so happy at night's end that his bed had been bigger than a twin size.

A forgotten part of Wesley's past. A freaky and exciting past he hoped to revisit.

The line picked up. A female voice answered.

Wesley sat up straight, moved his eyes from his phone book. He smiled to ease himself. "Anita?"

"Yes," Anita hesitantly replied.

"Wesley Matthews. How've you been?"

"Blessed," she said enthusiastically. "And you?"

"I've been better, but that's why I thought to call you. I ran across my old phone book. I looked through it and there was your name, on the first page. I got to thinking about all the good times we shared. I could use a good time right now. I thought we might reconnect."

"Reconnect?"

"Yes. You know, hook up."

"I don't think I can do any 'hook up,' " Anita told him.

The smile that had graced Wesley's face faded. "Well that's too bad, Anita. Are you involved with someone?"

"You can say that, yes."

"Serious?"

"Yes."

"You don't ever get the urge to step out on him?" It didn't faze Wesley to ask this of her. He didn't feel any guilt. Some man had done the same to him, after all. Had gotten Wesley's "serious" other in the backseat of a Mercedes.

"Sometimes," Anita admitted. "Temptation is a powerful beast."

"I won't tell if you won't tell," Wesley sang.

Anita smirk-laughed and moved the phone to her other ear.

She didn't reply, so Wesley said, "Are you nervous about stepping out on him?"

"He'll know," Anita said. "He won't be pleased, either, to find that I've partaken of Satan's pie."

Wesley cocked his head. Anita was sounding as if she were a few songs short of an album. "Come again?"

"My love of Jesus Christ, most blessed savior, is real, Wesley Matthews. I will not step out on him, ever. I'm ashamed of the numerous fornications I committed with you and others. I have repented those dirty ways. My love, sweet Jesus, has washed away the grime that clung to my wretched soul." Wesley could hear the sound of pages turning from Anita's end. "If you have your Bible nearby," she continued, "I'd like you to turn to—"

Wesley hung up and took a deep breath. He looked at the phone as if it were his greatest enemy. "Strike one," he said aloud. He flipped through his phone book and settled on another number. "Please don't be born-again, Danielle," he said before quickly dialing her digits.

"Hello?"

"Danielle?"

"Yes, speaking. Who's calling?"

Wesley cleared his throat. "Wesley Matthews, remember me?"

"Sure I do!" she gushed. "You helped awaken my latent sexual desires. I think of you often."

Wesley's eyes widened. Now this was more like it. "That's good to hear. How've you been?" The grin that formed on his face threatened to crack the corner of his lips.

"My clitoris is pierced," Danielle said. "And I'm no longer confused."

Wesley frowned. "Pardon me?"

"Samantha. You remember her?" Danielle asked.

"Sure," Wesley said. She was the woman he'd handcuffed to his bed. He'd done the do with Samantha, and then with her best friend, Danielle.

"We had a commitment ceremony a few months ago," Danielle gushed. "I'm pregnant, isn't that wonderful? I'm having Samantha's baby."

Wesley slammed the phone in its cradle and sat back in his chair. Now he was sure the phone was his greatest enemy. Still, he picked it up again after a brief pause and dialed another number.

When the line picked up, Wesley said, "Okay, I give. Hook me up with one of your freaks, Ten."

Tyndall smiled on the other end. "Two are better than one. First one, DeDe. And when you see her chest, you'll know why her name is DeDe. Double Ds. She's guaranteed play, Wes. The other, quite different type of girl—Norah. You'll probably dig her more. She's the type a man could catch feelings for."

Wesley procured a pen. "Yeah, yeah, and their numbers are?"

22

On the way to answer his door, Wesley stopped and surveyed him-self in the hallway mirror. Happy with what he saw, he nodded ap-proval to his reflection. Soon he'd have a woman's soft hands rubbing across his shoulders. The short-sleeve yellow polo by Ralph Lauren would find itself draped across the back of the chair in his bedroom. The cream-colored GF Ferre wind pants would lie across the arm of that same chair. His boxers would sit in the chair's lap. Hell, he might do the do in the chair itself. He shrugged away his carnal thoughts and offered the mirror one last smile be-fore moving to answer the door.

When he opened the door, Percy Sledge's voice leaked out from behind him and into the hall. Through song, Percy preached the merits of taking time to know your woman. "It's not an overnight fling," Percy sang. But the words were lost on Wesley. He wanted this to be an overnight affair and nothing more.

Wesley offered the woman standing before him a smile. Despite his best effort not to leer, his eyes drifted to her chest and stayed there longer than appropriate. She wore a tight white T-shirt with MADE YA LOOK airbrushed on the front. The words were done up nicely inside an artsy cloud. Her jeans clung to her like a second skin, displaying the thickness of her thighs, the bottom half of her hourglass. Instinctively, Wesley licked his lips. He left no doubt about his intentions. He smiled. She smiled in return.

"DeDe?" he asked.

DeDe's smile faded. She cocked her head to the side and put her hands on her hips. Her posture showed a promise of mucho attitude. Her mantra: Let these niggas know from the gate they ain't playing you. Her eyes honed in on Wesley. She stopped chewing her gum, which for her was a big effort. "Yup, I'm DeDe." She paused, let that sink in, and then added, "Why, you were expecting some other fly female to be at your door? 'Cause if you were, I can bounce. Bunk that."

"Not at all, DeDe, I was surprised to see *such a* fly female at my door. I figured you must have got your floors crossed or something. There's a casting director who lives above me."

DeDe scrunched her face.

Wesley realized his compliment was lost on her. "Casting directors decide which actors and actresses will be in a movie," he told her. Her eyes remained vacant. He tried again to make them flash with understanding, to make her smile in appreciation. "You look like you belong in movies. That's what I was thinking when I opened my door."

"Oh, okay. I feel ya."

Wesley extended his arm, indicating she should step inside. She moved into the apartment. A strong scent of perfume caught his nose as she passed. He disregarded the perfume and stole a glimpse of her ass. It was rounded to perfection, a bubble wrapped tightly in her denim jeans. The Apple Bottoms insignia graced one of her back pockets. Wesley smirked, imagining himself biting into that apple, getting DeDe's juice on his fingers and lips. He closed the door behind him and locked up. DeDe paused inside, waiting for Wesley.

"Can I get you something to drink, DeDe?"

She scanned the apartment. "I doubt you got what it takes to warm my belly. Tyndall told me you were high class and stuff. Me, I drink that straight gutter stuff."

"Try me," Wesley said. "I might surprise you. And if I don't have what you want, I'll make a quick run to the bodega."

DeDe liked the effort Wesley put forth. Other than a few needless pounds around his stomach, nothing a few crunches couldn't solve, and him acting like he was expecting some other female to knock at his door the same time she said she would, he was kinda fly, too. Dem glasses he wore made her think of Superman.

"Are you going to just stare at me, DeDe? Or are you going to let me warm your belly? Tell me what you want."

"Coqui 90," she said. "You got some of that?"

Wesley's face lapsed into a sheepish smile. "You weren't lying about drinking gutter liquor, were you?"

DeDe's cheeks went hot with embarrassment.

"Tell you what," Wesley said, noticing her discomfort. "You find yourself a soft spot on my sofa. I'll run out to the store."

DeDe popped a bubble with her gum. "I can't have you doing that. What do you have here?"

Wesley looked toward his kitchen. "How would you like a glass of Bacardi O?"

"That's cool. I can get neck deep in that."

DeDe moved into the living room as Wesley went to the kitchen. She stopped by the stereo and turned down the volume a few notches. "You got any good music we can chill out to?"

"That's Percy Sledge," Wesley called out from the kitchen.

"You got any good music?" DeDe repeated.

Wesley stopped, Bacardi bottle in hand, empty glasses on the counter before him. He frowned. "That's good music, DeDe. A classic."

DeDe looked over her shoulder. Wesley looked as if she'd kicked him in the nuts. She realized, again, that she was messing up this good opportunity. "You're right," she yelled to him. "I can't front on the classics."

She stood and moved toward the kitchen, softly singing about liking it raw—Ol' Dirty Bastard her real idea of classic—as her pointy-toed boots dug into Wesley's thick carpet.

When she reached the kitchen, Wesley passed her a crystal tumbler. She took a quick gulp and handed the empty glass back to him. His eyebrows arched, but he refilled it without comment and passed the glass back. This time, having noticed Wesley's subtle show of displeasure, DeDe took a quiet little sip.

"So you work for the gas company?" she asked. "What you do? Read meters?"

Wesley hesitated. "Not that kind of a gas company. More like Texaco. I acquire land and property for the company to build stations. I also broker deals to bring in cobrands. Dunkin' Donuts, businesses like that. I'm not sure I'm staying with them, though." He didn't offer any more details about his employment situation. Didn't tell her he'd gotten the proverbial pink slip. DeDe didn't need to know. She wasn't going to be around for the long haul.

DeDe took a seat on the bar stool next to Wesley. "That's cool. Gun Smoke would be into all that type of stuff. She's got a better business head than me."

"Who's Gun Smoke?" Wesley asked. He had his glass in midair, unable to take his sip until he found out.

"Mmmm . . ." DeDe held up a finger as she rushed a sip of her Bacardi. She sat the empty glass on the counter and swallowed the alcohol. "Gun Smoke's my aunt. Her government name is Gwen Saunders. Niggas around the way took the letters of her name, *G* and *S,* and came up with Gun Smoke as her nickname."

"That's a wild nickname."

DeDe smirked. "Gun Smoke's a wild lady. Nobody messes with Gun Smoke because they know she goes all out."

"Does she like the name?"

DeDe shrugged her shoulders. "I don't know. I'm not sure. She sometimes says that people expect she's walking around with a biscuit in her pocketbook."

Wesley frowned. He had no idea what DeDe was talking about. A Russian mail-order bride with limited English would have served him as well, or better.

DeDe touched Wesley's hand. The gesture surprised him. He didn't particularly like it. It was too personal. He moved the hand away and wrapped his arm around DeDe's waist. She scooted her bar stool over and laid her head on Wesley's shoulder.

"You've got strong shoulders," she said. "And you're smart, too. Know all that different stuff."

"Thanks." Wesley's gaze moved around his apartment. What had he gotten himself into with this woman?

"No problemo," DeDe said.

"So, DeDe," Wesley ventured. "You said something before I didn't understand. What's a biscuit? I assume you weren't talking about bread."

DeDe raised her head from his shoulder and looked at him. Her expression was one of disbelief. "You know, ratchet, burner, heat, and biscuit. All names for a gun. Street slang. Why, you ain't up on all that?"

"I guess I'm not," Wesley admitted. "I never heard those names before."

"I didn't mean to get all deep on you," DeDe said. "Throwing my vocabulary at you and stuff."

Stay focused, Wesley told himself. It didn't matter if she wasn't a great thinker. He didn't want to play chess with her. He wanted to play with her chest. That was a big difference.

Wesley was about to suggest they move to his bedroom but a chirping sound stopped him. DeDe sprang up.

"I gotta get that," she said. "My celly's ringing."

Wesley waved his hand. "Do your thing."

DeDe pulled her cell phone from the clip at her waistline and looked at the screen. A smile spread across her face. She pressed a button to receive the call. "Tammy, what's up, girl?"

Wesley gathered their empty glasses and moved to the sink.

"Naw, you're lying?" DeDe yelled into her phone a second later.

Wesley opened his dishwasher, placed the glasses on the rack, and closed the door.

DeDe swung her arms wildly as she moved to Wesley's living room. "Damn, Tammy, I told you don't be poking holes in no nigga's condom. That isn't the way to go, girl. You have to let him get to know you. Let him know you got goals and stuff. Did you tell him you wanted to open a cookie store at the mall? That dope name you got for it, Cookie Store at the Mall. Like that restaurant we had seen them talking about on the news the night we watched to see if they caught them fools shot Jerome. What was it . . . Tavern by the Blue, I think?"

Wesley sighed and moved to the living room with DeDe.

Later, with DeDe still on the phone, Wesley's doorbell sounded. He wondered who it could be. Sheila? He padded across the floor, looked through the peephole, and then opened the door with a smile. "Janet, hey, what are you doing here?"

"You, um," she sputtered out. She didn't go beyond those few words.

"Yes?"

She ran her fingers over the straps of her backpack. "When I picked up Sheila's things that night you said you were interested in doing work with my foundation. I have brochures and other literature for you."

Wesley remembered. It had been a casual response on his part. He really didn't intend to volunteer when he said it. It was small talk, to keep his brain from exploding as Janet stood by the door with Sheila's belongings in a box. Now, though, with his employment situation all muddled, he had plenty of free time. He heard

DeDe chattering behind him. He smiled. Doing DeDe was one thing to do, but a man only had so much juice. "You could have mailed it, Janet, saved yourself a trip."

Janet didn't reply. She silently cussed herself out. *Dummy, why'd you come to this man's house?*

Wesley looked back at DeDe. She paced the room, oblivious to his eyes following her, spouting ghetto wisdom to Tammy, who, from what Wesley could gather, was a condom's worst nightmare. He turned back to Janet. "I've got company, but come on in."

Janet peered over his shoulder, expecting to see Kidada. What she did see made her feel even more foolish for being here. A different woman paced Wesley's floor. She turned her gaze back to Wesley. "I can drop this literature with you and we can talk about it some other time."

Wesley reached and took hold of her wrist. "No time like the present." Janet reluctantly shuffled inside.

"You have to be smart, you want to keep a nigga," Janet heard the woman in Wesley's apartment say. Janet turned to Wesley and arched her eyebrows.

"Not only is she beautiful, she's also a relationship expert," Wesley cracked. "Dr. Phil better watch his heels, I'm telling you."

Janet could feel her stomach drop. Her mouth salted over. She took a couple deep breaths. "This isn't your Kidada."

Wesley sighed. "That died a painful death. I'll have to tell you about it sometime."

Janet nodded toward DeDe. "This one can't be too far behind. I can smell it rotting as we speak."

"DeDe's cool."

Janet eyed Wesley. Her stare made him shift his balance.

"She's cool," he repeated.

"You can do better," Janet said.

Wesley blew out a laugh. "What? Have you looked at her chest? And homegirl's ass in those jeans? Those two things alone put her on the you-can't-do-better-than-this list."

"Why are you doing this to yourself?" Janet asked.

Before he could answer, DeDe ended her call, turned, and realized they had more company. "Sorry about that," she said to Wesley. "I had to set my girl straight on some stuff." She looked at Janet and moved toward her. "How you doing? You Wesley's sister or something?"

"Friend," Janet said. It hurt her ears to say it; she'd much prefer a two-syllable-word response. Like, oh, girlfriend, lover, or wifey, for instance.

Janet waited for DeDe to kick off her Reeboks and challenge her to a fight for Wesley's affection.

"Those jeans are kind of slamming, girl," DeDe said instead. "Where'd you get 'em?"

Janet's lips creased into a sad smile. DeDe wasn't the least bit intimidated by her. And why should she be? Janet wasn't any competition. "Thrift shop," Janet answered.

DeDe hunched down to look closer at the jeans. "I'm gonna have to try a thrift shop, then. I've never seen jeans like those in the stores." She raised her head and smiled warmly. "One of my goals is to have the biggest collection of jeans. I love jeans, girl."

Janet flashed a condescending smile. "One of your biggest goals is it?"

DeDe popped another gum bubble. "Hell yeah, girl, you gotta have goals."

Wesley moved in-between them. "Janet was dropping off material for me to read over."

"You a Witness?" DeDe asked her. "'Cause I've been trying to get right wit him." She said "him" in a whisper and pointed to the ceiling.

"No," Wesley answered for Janet. "Janet heads up a foundation that preaches literacy to underprivileged youth."

Janet noticed the blank look on DeDe's face. "Literacy is the ability to read, and comprehend what you're reading," she told DeDe.

"Oh, okay. Well Wesley could help you out. We were breaking ice before and I realized how smart he is."

Janet frowned. "Breaking ice?"

"Yeah, you know. Talking and stuff. Getting to know each other. He was telling me all about his work with the gas company. I thought he read meters or something, but he schooled me."

"Did he?" Janet said.

"Yup," DeDe replied. "And I was telling him how Gun Smoke— that's my aunt's nickname—would like him, 'cause she has a good head for business."

"You should get your aunt Gun Smoke and Wesley to compare notes," Janet offered. "Maybe they could come up with an entre-

preneurial venture." She looked at DeDe's expression. "An entrepreneurial venture is another name for a business," she clarified.

"Oh, okay. That's an idea," DeDe admitted. "I have to see what
Gun Smoke says."

Janet smiled and looked at Wesley. He swallowed and looked away.

"So what is it you do, DeDe? For a job, I mean."

"I did Nelly, R. Kelly, a bunch of others."

"Excuse me?"

DeDe smiled. Now it was her turn to educate Janet. "I dance in
videos. I've done mostly hip hop, but R & B, too."

"That's nice," Janet said. She bent to retrieve the literature from
her backpack, handed some to Wesley, some to DeDe. "You guys
check this out. I'd better go so you two can continue your lovely
evening. Nice meeting you, DeDe."

"You, too," DeDe said as she squinted and looked over the material Janet had handed her.

Janet turned to Wesley. "I'll talk to you."

DeDe looked up from her brochure. "Hey, we should get together sometime and double date. You could bring your man and
me and Wesley could hook up with y'all."

Janet swallowed. "I'm single at the moment." She looked at
Wesley. He returned the look, frowning. It then dawned on him,
Janet *was* single, had been for as long as he'd known her.

"What!" DeDe shouted. Her voice broke Janet and Wesley from
looking at each other. "A pretty female like you that knows how to
find cool-ass jeans and stuff ain't got a man. We gotta do something
about that, girl."

Janet's cheeks pinked. DeDe was the first person in recent memory to describe her as pretty. It felt good to hear. She flashed DeDe
a smile, this one sincere. "Yeah, we do." She looked at Wesley. "A
good man is hard to find, though."

"Don't I know it," DeDe said. Then she took Wesley's arms and
wrapped them around her waist.

Janet moved to leave, but turned back. "That's Percy Sledge,
isn't it, Wes?"

"A classic," DeDe answered for him.

Something appeared in Wesley's eyes as he watched Janet, appreciation the best way to describe it.

Janet wanted so very badly for Wesley to toss this DeDe out and
invite her inside instead. "Where's Baldwin?" she asked, lingering.

"Bathroom, locked up," Wesley answered.

"Pat him for me," Janet said, and then left.

Wesley moved to the doorway and looked out after her.

"You got somebody bald locked in your bathroom?" DeDe asked behind him. She seemed excited by the possibility.

"Yeah," Wesley answered. It was easier than explaining.

DeDe popped a bubble. "Dang, that's kinda crazy."

Crazy, he thought, his mind already on his upcoming date with girl number two, Norah. Something else clouded his thoughts, too. Strange. He couldn't figure why. Janet. His thoughts were also on Janet.

23

A pair of jeans, soft shoes or sneakers, and a T-shirt or sweatshirt had been Janet's daily uniform for as long as she remembered. Comfort over fashion, her modus operandi. Backpack instead of a pocketbook. She'd never worn a pair of pumps. Maybe that was why Wesley never noticed her, even when the only other woman in the room had an aunt named Gun Smoke and an ambition to establish the world's largest collection of hip-hugging jeans.

On the other hand, Janet's girl Sheila didn't, couldn't, and wouldn't fathom leaving her house without her MAC frost eye shadow and Revlon Super Lustrous lipgloss. She wouldn't go to retrieve her mail unless she wore a head-turning ensemble that barely covered her many curves.

Today, as usual, Sheila was overdressed. In her defense, the silver blazer was a nice touch. Her Gary Graham skirt was fashionable. But she could have done without the leather gloves, the knee-length boots, and ditto for the teardrop earrings that hung down to kiss her shoulders.

Sheila had dressed with a purpose, softly shuffling from her closet to the full-length mirror in her bedroom, trying different looks. However, during those seconds she wasn't in front of the mirror, she thought of Janet's message from earlier while she walked back and forth across her carpet.

"Let's try something different today, Sheila. Meet me at the mall outside the Lord & Taylor's. I'd like to go clothes shopping."

Sheila still wasn't sure she'd heard that correctly. What about the thrift shop around the corner from Janet's block? DO OVER, the wording across the awning read. Sheila noticed the sign every time she passed by. Not once had the expertly crafted lettering on the sign, or the window displays out front, made her want to venture inside.

"So what got into you?" Sheila asked now as she came upon Janet at their agreed-upon meeting place in the mall. "You've never, ever been interested in shopping before. I had to check my message twice to make sure that was you. I sat down and I swear to you my body trembled as I wondered what could make my dear friend of so many odd years brush aside our usual Tuesday lunch for a day of . . . gasp . . . shopping." Sheila put her hand to her chest and closed her eyes.

"Hello to you, too," Janet replied. She held on to the straps of her backpack as if she were about to climb a jagged mountain rather than find clothes that would make Wesley want to climb her.

Sheila tilted her head and focused her gaze on Janet. Her look demanded an answer.

"The foundation is having a banquet," Janet finally replied. "I need your help in picking out something nice to wear."

"Whew!" Sheila rubbed a hand across her forehead. Ms. Drama Queen. She took Janet by the arm and began walking. "For a minute there I thought this was about some man, Janet."

Thoughts of Wesley crept into Janet's head and she tried to chase them away, because she knew those thoughts would show up as a blush on her cheeks.

"Wait a minute." Sheila stopped moving. Janet kept on a few steps farther, then stopped and turned back. Sheila narrowed her eyes and pointed an accusing finger in Janet's direction. "This *is* about some man. Who is he?"

Janet frowned. "No man. My foundation's banquet. Say it with me, Sheila—foun-day-shun bank-wet."

"And who is escorting you to the foun-day-shun bank-wet?" Sheila wanted to know.

Janet shrugged. "Richard Gerard, the foundation's largest bene-factor."

"Sexy name," Sheila replied. "Have you let him hit it yet?"

"He's seventy-three and uses Bengay as a cologne and Fixodent as a breath mint. If he hit anything, he'd end up on a surgeon's table. Not exactly my type."

Sheila cocked her head. "Since your little mishap with Parrish a few years ago, I was thinking you switched over, a carpet muncher on

the low. But nah, my girl got a type. Ain't that nothing-something?"
She broke into a smile and pointed that hateful finger again. "You,
you, you," was all she could manage.

"You're crazy," was Janet's reply.

"Crazy is putting your love life on hold for some foundation. I'd
be damned."

"I care about the work of the foundation. I've sacrificed things
in my life to support a worthy cause. So shoot me." Janet shook her
head in disgust and walked on.

Sheila moved after her. "You're tired of all the sacrifices," she
observed. "Whoever this man is he's got my girl wanting out of
those dingy jeans and into something slinky."

Janet picked up her pace, refusing to slow or look in Sheila's direction. "DeDe thinks I have great taste in jeans."

"And who the fudge is DeDe?" Sheila asked, frowning.

Janet moved her hands to grip the straps of her backpack as she
turned a corner.

"Who's this DeDe?" Sheila repeated. "I need to slap the taste out
of her mouth for making you think you don't belong on *Ambush
Makeover*."

Janet stopped suddenly and wheeled. Sheila barely escaped crash-
ing into her. "DeDe's a friend of Wesley's, okay?" Janet hollered,
and then dropped her head.

Sheila crinkled her nose. "Wesley. I never heard Wesley talk of
any DeDe."

"She's this girl he's involved with. First there was Kidada, now
this DeDe and I don't know how many others. He's out their trick-
ing off because of you, Sheila."

"Good for him," Sheila said, waving her hand.

Janet looked up and burned her gaze into Sheila's eyes. "How
could you say that? It isn't healthy for him."

"Why are you so concerned with Wesley, anyhow?" Sheila
asked.

"No reason."

Sheila stopped and looked at Janet. "Why are you so concerned
with Wesley, Janet?"

Janet held tighter to her backpack straps. "I care about Wesley,
that's all."

"I can't believe you, Janet."

"Believe me, what?"

"You're making a play on the man I was going to marry."

"You weren't going to marry Wesley," Janet said. "Don't kid yourself."

"And you're not going to marry anybody, Janet. At least not anybody with twenty-twenty vision," Sheila shot back.

Janet gasped.

"That's right, girlfriend," Sheila continued, "no man wants his woman looking like his mama. Put a rainbow flag in front of your apartment and you might be on to something. I'm sure there are many lesbians in the city who would find you a whole lot more appealing than some woman with a crew cut. You're not too tight with your style, or lack thereof, but you aren't butch, either. That's your one plus."

"You're being very hurtful," Janet managed.

"Forget about Wesley," Sheila replied. "If it didn't work for me, no way will it work for you."

"I suddenly don't feel like shopping anymore," Janet softly said. She shifted her backpack and walked off without another word.

Tears came to Sheila's eyes. Hurting the people she cared about was becoming a common occurrence in her life. Sad, but others hurting meant one thing. Meant she wasn't alone.

24

The black Lexus ES was a blur on the highway. Wesley shot a glance at the speedometer. A frown formed on his face as he felt for the seatbelt strapped across his waist. He tugged it to make sure the fit was snug. He could feel perspiration pooling in his armpits, then snaking down his side. He prayed the scent of Just Cavalli Him on his neck and wrists would mask the must he knew would soon come if DeDe didn't ease her foot off the gas pedal. His head hurt as Notorious B.I.G's husky voice crackled in his eardrums. How could DeDe concentrate on her driving with the music playing so loudly? He looked at her. She had her lead foot bearing down on the gas pedal and didn't notice Wesley's discomfort. She was silent except for an occasional call to kick in somebody's door waving something, which she sung in unison with the slain rapper.

Wesley spotted an opening as the song cycled to its end. "Turn this down?" he asked DeDe. His hand hovered by the volume dial of the stereo.

But Snoop Dogg's "Beautiful" followed the Biggie cut. DeDe's mouth opened into a large O and her eyes came to life. She leaned forward, swatted Wesley's hand aside, and turned the volume knob farther to the right. "This is my joint," she yelled to Wesley. "I ain't heard it in a minute."

Wesley sat back in his seat. Why was he here? He should have gone out on another date with Norah instead. But Norah had been somewhat clingy. Attractive, intelligent, her clock ticking loudly for marriage. Too much for Wesley. But again, why was he here? With DeDe? Then, out of the corner of his eye, he noticed DeDe's bouncing breasts, her oversized nipples stressing the fabric of the T-shirt that was so tight she had to suck in a deep breath to remove it. That's why, he thought to himself.

He searched for something to say. "Gun Smoke has herself a nice ride," he hollered.

DeDe popped a bubble. She knew Wesley had spoken to her, but the song on the radio drowned out whatever he'd said. She continued to sing without missing a beat, something about Cuban women with long hair.

Wesley eyed the speedometer again. The needle lunged forward. He swallowed and turned his gaze to DeDe. He forced himself to smile. Leaned over close, and with his hands cupped over his mouth, screamed, "Your aunt doesn't mind you driving her nice ride like you're in the Indy 500?"

"Uh-uh," DeDe managed.

Still yelling in DeDe's ear, "Me, I'd want you to baby my ride all the way. I'd give you specific instructions not to push her pass fifty-five, sixty tops."

DeDe was really into her song now, fully absorbed in the catchy hook. She closed her eyes and swayed as she sang the words. "Beautiful . . ."

"The tint is nice," Wesley hollered. He hoped his voice would compel her to keep her eyes open and on the road.

"Six percent limo tint," DeDe quickly responded. Then it was back to the music. "Beautiful . . ."

DeDe sped by a grove of trees that dotted the side of the highway. Wesley spotted a dash of white within the brush. His pulse quickened as he turned back to corroborate his suspicion. Sure enough, his stomach sank as he saw a flash of red trailing them. A police cruiser gave chase.

He turned face forward, tapped DeDe, and pointed over his shoulder. "Five-oh is on you, DeDe." He would have said "police" if he weren't with DeDe.

DeDe glanced in her rearview mirror. "Dang," she muttered. Her gaze honed in on Wesley. "Get that shoebox off the backseat and put it under your seat. Don't shout out what you doing, do it sly. Do it slowlike."

"Why?"

"Shoebox's got a gang of weed in it."

Wesley closed his eyes and palmed his head. What had he done to deserve all this drama in his life? Why wasn't his father looking down and guiding him down the correct path with his invisible hands of love?

"Come on," DeDe said, breaking Wesley's thoughts. "Get rid of that shoebox while I pull over."

Wesley looked back and saw the cruiser closing in on them. He quickly reached into the backseat, scooped up the shoebox, and turned to tuck it under his seat. His armpits were dank with sweat. He could feel it beading on his forehead, too. All he could think about was the embarrassment of having his name in the police blotter.

DeDe looked down to examine Wesley's placement of the box. "Aiight, cool," she told him.

DeDe slowed the Lexus, turned down the stereo, and pulled to the side of the road. Her tires kicked up gravel.

"I don't believe this," Wesley said as the police cruiser pulled behind them.

"Keep cool," DeDe said. She touched his hand. The sight of her extra-long nails, done up in exuberant colors, made Wesley sigh. "If I mess up," DeDe instructed him, "pull out that smooth talk and stuff you got up your shirt."

Not up my shirt, up my sleeve, you chickenhead, Wesley wanted to yell out. But he didn't. Instead, he put a vicelike grip on the door handle. Thinking, a woman enamored with the backseat of Mercedeses or adorned with three bracelets was more appealing than DeDe. Wesley no longer cared if he unraveled all the mysteries of DeDe's body.

DeDe powered her window down. The scent of freshly cut grass and burning wood wafted into the car. A state trooper shined a flashlight inside the car. The brightness of the light blinded Wesley. He blinked and shielded his eyes with his hand. This had to be a dream. The thin air must have dropped the officer by the Lexus because Wesley hadn't seen him exit the cruiser. A dream, that's what this was, yeah, a dream.

DeDe leaned across Wesley, popped open the glove compartment, and pulled out a packet of papers. She sifted through the packet and came upon the required documents. She handed them to the trooper, making sure her hand brushed against his as he took the paperwork.

"You Gwen Saunders?" the officer asked. He squinted his eyes and flipped the registration card over in his fingers. He'd asked the question, though the name on the license DeDe had handed him made it clear she wasn't.

"Nah, that's my aunt," DeDe answered. "I'm DeDe Turner."

"Is your aunt aware you are in possession of her vehicle, Mrs. Turner?"

"Ms. Turner," DeDe corrected. "And yes she is. She gave me the keys."

The officer looked past DeDe to Wesley. Wesley slunk down in the passenger seat. The trooper turned his gaze back to DeDe. "Where were you headed, Ms. Turner, in such a hurry?"

"Club Fluorescent." DeDe turned her torso to face the officer. When she noticed his gaze tiptoeing across her breasts, she added, "Have you ever been?"

"No, can't say that I have."

"Oh," DeDe cooed, "you gotta get over there. I'm there all the time."

The officer nodded toward Wesley. "What's your passenger's story?"

"Along for the ride," DeDe told him.

Wesley bit into his lip.

The officer handed DeDe her paperwork. "Take it slow out here, okay? Next time I won't be so lenient."

"Next time?" DeDe asked, batting her eyes.

"Hypothetically," the officer said.

"Oh, okay." She'd have to ask Wesley the definition of "hypo-whatever" later.

The officer scanned her body one last time, made a grunting sound, and then backed away from the vehicle.

DeDe fell back against her seat. "My heart is bumping a mile a minute."

Is it *beating* a mile a minute, too? Wesley wanted to ask. Instead, he said, "Why? You handled yourself well. I'm glad I didn't have to say anything."

"I was worried the whole time he'd see the box and want to look inside."

"You said a gang of marijuana," Wesley said. "How much is that?"

DeDe smirked and waved her hand in a dismissive manner. "I ain't worried about the weed. It was the gun that had my heart bumping."

Wesley frowned. "Gun?"

"Yeah, man."

"In the shoebox?" Wesley gulped.

"Yup. Serial's scraped off and it has hollow points in it. Definite no-no's."

"Gun Smoke's?"

DeDe smiled. "They don't call her Gun Smoke for nothing."

"Thought you said she didn't carry a biscuit," Wesley said.

DeDe touched his arm. "Not in her pocketbook. No." She leaned on Wesley's shoulder. "I ain't mean to stress you out. I'll make it up to you later. For sho."

Wesley rubbed a hand across DeDe's cheek. She purred like a kitten. He considered all of the night's drama. He'd earned a nut. He'd get one, and then kick DeDe to the curb.

25

After the club, Wesley and DeDe stopped under a streetlight on their way to his apartment and started foreplay. The lamp provided them with atmosphere and lit their path, a flickering candle for their romantic stroll. Wesley could taste rum and coconut on DeDe's tongue. She rubbed his erection with her hand while he cupped her ass with his. A moan escaped her mouth and he swallowed it whole. His mind raced toward his bedroom. He broke their kiss, rubbed his fingers across his lips, and let out a grunt of pleasure.

"You're tasty, DeDe. Did you know that?"

"You gonna eat me," she replied. Lust was in her eyes, her voice tinged with sexy double meaning. She had the keys to Gun Smoke's Lexus in one hand. She hoped she wouldn't need them until long after the sun stretched its morning muscles.

"What are we going to do when we get upstairs?" Wesley teasingly asked.

"You're gonna mash it up, nuh, brudder man?" Her breathing was ragged and her panties damp. The dance-hall music from Fluorescent had truly infused her soul. She laughed at her fake Jamaican patois.

"I'll try, mon," was Wesley's response. His Jamaican was worse than DeDe's.

DeDe's eyes narrowed to the shape of bananas. The alcohol she'd consumed at Fluorescent swirled in her system. Piña coladas. "But before you mash it up," she told Wesley, "I gotta go wee-wee." She laughed and stumbled clumsily. Wesley caught her by the arm.

"Come," he said as he took her hand and led her down the path toward the front entrance of his building.

"Mash it up. Mash it up," DeDe cooed. She giggled. She would have broken into a skip if her legs weren't so rubbery.

Wesley stopped. He could hear soft footsteps coming from the shadows behind them. He turned to look.

"No stopping," DeDe warned him. "I'm on *fiya* for you. You can't let this flame burn out."

"Hold up." Wesley held a finger up. "Did you hear that?"

"That what?" DeDe replied. She touched his arms and smiled. "The only thing I want to hear is you mashing it up."

Wesley frowned. Her little Jamaican vibe was beginning to work his nerves. He moved on. DeDe stumbled along beside him, her arms draped around his waist.

DeDe kissed his arm. "Mash it up, Wesley. You gonna mash it up."

"Chill, DeDe."

DeDe tugged at his arm. "You want me to chill? Come put me on ice then, baby."

"Put you on ice," a voice called out in disgust. A woman moved from the shadows. Wesley and DeDe turned. The sight of the woman made Wesley's mouth fall open. He didn't, couldn't, say anything.

"Who is this, Wesley?" the shadow woman asked as she examined DeDe. She had her mouth twisted to the side. She looked as if she could vomit just from the sight of DeDe. "And why is she hanging all over you and talking that nonsense, sounding like a knockoff Miss Cleo?"

DeDe loosened her grasp on Wesley. She stepped forward, hands on hips, seconds away from pulling her blade. "Who is you to be dissing me?"

"I'm the woman who'll put her foot in your ass if you don't step away from Wesley."

"Ladies, please." Wesley tried to part them. They moved around his feeble attempt.

"Foot in my ass," DeDe said. "I don't hardly think so."

"Oh no?" the shadow woman asked.

"Nope," DeDe replied.

"Whatever, you dirty tramp. I'm not worried about you." The

shadow woman bore her gaze into DeDe. A satisfied smirk came to her face. "You look like a simple-minded blow-job ho. That's all. Got lips like Jay-Z or somebody."

Wesley frowned. He liked DeDe's luscious lips.

DeDe was speechless.

"That's cool, tramp. Keep swallowing his babies," the shadow woman added.

Wesley made a face as if he'd pulled a muscle. He had a new-found respect for Norah. She was no joke. He noticed the growing scowl on DeDe's face. Norah's hands balled into fists by her side. Blows were in order.

DeDe, on cue, moved toward Norah, swinging wildly. Before Wesley could step in, Norah had thrown a single punch that landed smack dab on DeDe's chin. The blow staggered her. DeDe touched her face, her eyes wide with surprise. She made another wild move forward, again flailing her arms with no rhyme or reason. As she'd done before, Norah caught DeDe with one single shot that staggered her again. DeDe's eyes welled with water. She wrapped her arms around herself and took off toward her car.

"DeDe," Wesley called for her. Norah turned to him. He saw the Lorena Bobbitt in Norah's demeanor and said no more.

"What kind of game are you playing, Wesley?" Norah asked after DeDe's tires squealed and the Lexus moved up the street.

Wesley shrugged. "Dating, Norah. You didn't expect me to be exclusive with you this soon, did you?"

Norah frowned. "You implied as much."

He had been a bit mushy-cushy-gushy during their first date. Catching feelings, but smart enough to pull back after the fact.

"Never that," Wesley said as he vehemently shook his head. "After all I've been through with you women, never that." Far from the truth.

Norah sighed. "I'm so stupid for falling for your pack of lies."

Wesley took her hands in his. She let her hands fall slack, but Wesley still caressed them tenderly. "Listen, I'm sorry if I've misled you, Norah. Come upstairs. I'll make it up to you. You just showed some serious spunk. Very courageous considering DeDe had a gun in her car."

"I wish I'd known," Norah said. "I would have asked to borrow it so I could teach you a lesson about walking right."

Wesley ignored her. Kissed her hands. "Come upstairs with me."

Norah snatched her hands away. "What kind of fool do you think I am?"

Wesley swiveled his head around the perimeter of the building. He made a play of glancing at his watch. He smiled. "This time of night, you're out hiding in the bushes of my building. I'd say you're a fool in love, Norah. I can relate. There's nothing wrong with that."

"Love?" Norah laughed. "You must be crazy, neegrow. I got a feeling you were playing me. There's too much junk out here for me to risk myself with a man I can't trust to be faithful to me. I decided to do I Spy and see what was up with you. I knew you were too good to be true. All your words, some act. Those damn glasses fool a sista, have her thinking you're the genuine article."

"Come on up with me, Norah."

"Never that," she replied. Touché.

Wesley held his hands out to the side. "Give me a chance, Norah. Come upstairs with me. We can talk and work this out. Communication is the key to any relationship."

"And then what? You'll tell me lies about loving me so you can get me parallel to your mattress."

Wesley shrugged. "We have to start somewhere. It might as well be parallel to my mattress."

Norah made a move to leave. Wesley grabbed her shoulders and turned her to face him. "I was joking, Norah, trying to lighten the mood a bit." He sighed and made his saddest face. "Look, I've been through tough times in the romance department. You know about my ex dogging me out. I've been dating different women, true. I was looking for a good match. I think you could be that match, to be honest with you. You're the one going with me to the banquet my friend's foundation is throwing."

Norah thought that through. He was right. Of all his choices, and apparently there were a few, he'd chosen her. That had to stand for something.

"Come upstairs with me," Wesley begged. "We didn't start the night together but we can end it together. What do you say?"

Norah eyed him suspiciously, trying to find a crack in his façade, an outward show of deception. She couldn't find anything of the sort. She listened to her heart and made a move toward the lobby.

Wesley fell in step behind her, a huge smile on his face. The voice inside his head imbued him with a feeling of pride he hadn't felt since the day Sheila accepted his proposal. "Player, player," the voice said. "Your mack game gets better with each passing day."

Wesley stepped inside the lobby of his building, feeling powerful and in control.

26

"Didn't want to see you happy while I was so miserable," had been Sheila's words when Janet opened her door.

"Why are you miserable?" Janet had asked back.

"Because Wesley's a good man and I messed that up," Sheila said.

"Why did you?"

"If I knew that answer I wouldn't have," Sheila mused.

"Well you don't have to worry about me," Janet said. "You had a right to be angry with me. I had no business thinking of Wesley the way I was. You two were so close to being married."

Sheila shook her head. "We weren't. You were right about that. I hope you can forgive me for the things I said."

Janet hugged her.

"Now," Sheila had said, once the hug elapsed, "we've got to get you a makeover so you can knock Wesley's socks off at that banquet."

Janet shook her head. "I'm done thinking about Wesley."

"No, you're not, girl. You two deserve each other. I'm going to help you get him."

"Really?"

That earlier conversation was on Janet's mind now as she looked around Eye of the Beholder beauty salon. There were women in every corner of the place, all of them looking to beautify themselves. For some man's affections probably.

"This is insane, Sheila. Why did I let you talk me into this?" Janet whined.

"Relax," Sheila calmly replied.

She reached for Janet's shoulder and squeezed it in a sign of support. She'd done the same thing when Janet tried on dresses at the mall, complaining the entire time. "I didn't go to my high school prom, much to do about a dress, uh-uh," Janet had droned, to Sheila's dismay, like a damn broken record.

She'd also squeezed Janet's shoulder when Janet paused at the cash register, with the perfect dress in one hand and her other hand holding her credit card, not wanting to part with it; as if it were the Bible and Jesus himself had signed it.

Janet looked around the salon again. Women took up space in every inch of its real estate. Some were under dryers, others at the shampoo station, and still others, laughing and talking with unread copies of *Jet* and *Essence* in their hands. To Janet, none of the women looked as if this was their first time inside a salon. It was for her, though. She dropped her gaze to her lap and shook her head. "I can't relax, Sheila. What can they possibly do for me here? I've never worn make-up a day of my life, and I've always had my hair in a natural."

"I wouldn't be bragging about that."

"I'm not bragging. Stating the actual factual."

"My girl Renee is going to hook you up, Janet. Trust me."

Janet shook her head. "This is ridiculous. I don't have to be all girly to feel good about myself. I'm okay as I am. I don't need a makeover."

Sheila ran her gaze up and down Janet's body. She shook her head when she came to Janet's face. Janet had nice eyes and beautiful lashes that had no business being naked of mascara. Her hair was long, but unruly in its natural state. Curly and off on its own. "Trust me," Sheila said. "You do need a makeover. Girl, you need a makeover like James Brown needs Just for Men hair dye."

"Thanks a lot," Janet replied. She sat back in her seat and dropped the bag with her dress to the floor. It thudded to the ground, much the same as her big talk about her unwavering self-esteem. A makeover was calling her . . . Janet, Janet.

"You're a plain wood bookcase in desperate need of a coat of paint," Sheila told her.

"Thanks, I got you." Janet reached for a *Jet* and flipped through to the wedding announcements. She held it up in clear view of Sheila. Look at what your life could have been, woman in a glass house, Janet's gesture said.

Sheila gently took the magazine from Janet's hands and tossed it in the pile with the others. "Stay focused."

"I—"

Sheila held up her hand to silence Janet. "Don't try to sell me anything because my credit is shot. You looked like I licked the red off your lollipop when I told you I couldn't have you as a bridesmaid. I didn't tell you why, but you knew. It hurt me to make that decision. But I had to. Your style got lost in some time warp. We need to get you updated."

Janet waved her hand dismissively and reached for another magazine. "Whatever."

"You were happy not going to your prom?"

Janet stopped, an *Essence* in hand. She put on her most serious face and looked at Sheila. "Yes. As a matter of fact, I was."

"Wow, with no foundation to pin it on?" Sheila swayed and softened her voice to a whisper. "Oh, my foundation is so much more important than a dumb old prom," she mocked.

"I had a boyfriend," Janet said. "He was a geek like me. We both decided we weren't in for the prom."

Sheila's eyes widened. "So you acknowledge you were a geek."

"Back then." Janet nodded. "Yes."

Sheila threw her head back before turning her eyes on Janet. A smirk covered her face. "You're not now, though? I mean, a grown woman carrying a backpack instead of a purse is cool, isn't that right? Combing your hair with your fingers, that's the way to do it, right?"

Sheila really knew how to hurt Janet. This was the conversation when Janet found out she wasn't to be a bridesmaid in Sheila's wedding all over again.

"Dial soap serving as your fragrance is enticing to men, correct?" Sheila added. "Screw Burberry, right?"

Janet threw her hands up. "All right, Sheila, I get the picture. I need the makeover."

"In the worst way," Sheila said.

"It doesn't matter," Janet said. "No matter how good a woman looks, a man will move to something better."

"You still studying Parrish and his mess?"

Janet looked away. "Left me a voice mail breaking it off; couldn't even do it in person. And this was the day after I relented and put on trashy lingerie for him. He wanted me looking like a whore, in the bedroom, outside, everywhere I went with him. I wasn't about that, never will be."

"No need to go to an extreme, Janet. But walking around looking like Larry Johnson in those old grandmama commercials isn't the remedy."

"Well, I'm here now. I'm letting them relax my hair. I'll go blow my next paycheck on a Coach bag and a bottle of Burberry. Are you happy?"

Sheila shook her head. "This isn't about my happiness, Janet. This is about yours. And when Wesley sees you looking like a woman should look . . ."

Sheila didn't have to say anymore. Janet sighed. Sheila was right. This was a moment of great significance, no point in downplaying this. She hadn't broken down and confessed all of her feelings about Wesley to the woman he was to have married for nothing. She hadn't taken this risk to pretend it was a normal day at the office.

Janet reached across and squeezed Sheila's shoulder.

Thanks for your help, the squeeze said.

Sheila smiled and nodded in return.

You're welcome, the smile and nod implied. Now forget Parrish's stupidity and go get Wesley.

27

Yellow light bathed the banquet hall. Fine linen covered each table, and colorful roses arranged in wooden angle pots served as a center-piece. White cloth draped the guest chairs, and a gold tassel hung down their backs. A pianist tapping a melody on a baby grand and the buzz of energetic voices created a cacophony of sound that made the room vibrate. A burgundy carpet ran the length of the dining area, straight down its center, separating the room into two sides. The left side of the room, which housed the service bar, happened to be the most congested area in the room's symmetry.

Norah sat beside Wesley at one of the tables. She was dressed in a lavender-colored metallic tube gown with two slits high up the thighs. Her make-up was flawless, lipstick to match the hue of her gown, eye shadow a seductive sparkle, and a hint of maple coloring in her foundation. Though her breasts weren't as bodacious as DeDe's, they still sat high and caused a stirring in Wesley that had him taking too many sips of his ginger ale. Norah had finally let Wesley's hand go once they took their seats, but oddly, he still could feel her touch on his palms. She sat so closely to him he couldn't move his elbows. He thought of her hiding in the bushes the other night, confronting DeDe, how she'd clung to him once he talked her upstairs. He scooted his seat over an inch. Norah did the same. Wesley sighed. He was now officially Norah's possession. Would he ever win at the dating game?

"Enjoying yourself, Norah?" Wesley stopped as he saw some-thing flash in Norah's eyes, her gaze stuck on something at his back. He turned. His breath caught and his heart changed rhythms as he noticed the woman entering the hall, a man Wesley hoped was the woman's father holding her arm.

"Gold digger," Norah scoffed.

"What?" Norah's voice broke Wesley's daydreaming. He turned back to Norah, pretending the vision of the woman he'd seen wasn't still dancing in his head.

"I said she's a gold digger," Norah explained. "Viagra couldn't help that guy she's with."

Wesley hoped Norah wouldn't notice the change in him upon seeing the woman. He was still undressing her with his imagination. Sliding the halter neck, teal-colored Lycra gown down, solving the mystery of her every curve, the secret the skintight gown had such a difficult time keeping to itself. The color of her dress brought with it hopes of the beach. Wesley could see her lying on a blanket, sand between her toes, his hands rubbing suntan lotion on her back. He took another sip of his ginger ale and chewed an ice cube. His mouth still felt dry, as if the ice cubes were cotton balls instead.

"Don't you think?" Norah asked him.

"Think what?"

"That she's a gold digger," Norah said as she nodded toward the woman, now navigating the aisles to find a seat with her date. Wesley couldn't help but sneak another glance. He quickly turned back to Norah. Otherwise, he'd stare at the woman until his eyeballs walked over to her table and sat with her.

"Wouldn't know," Wesley told Norah.

"Go roll up that guy's sleeve," Norah said. "I'd be shocked if you didn't find an AARP tattoo somewhere on him. Now tell me, what do you think she's doing with him? And what do you think he has to offer her besides his blank checkbook?"

"Conversation," Wesley tried.

Norah gave a hearty, "Yeah right," to that possibility.

"A sense of nostalgia then," Wesley offered. "She looks like she could be a history buff. I bet her television is always programmed to the Discovery Channel."

Norah shook her head.

"We are at a literacy event," Wesley said. "Maybe they read books together."

"Uh-huh," was Norah's not-buying-it response.

"Why are you so hard on the sister, Norah?"

"Women like her perpetuate this situation that has men dogging decent women. I hate it." She tossed her linen napkin on the table. "I'm going to the bathroom. Don't move, I'll be back."

Wesley stood and pulled Norah's seat, held to her elbow as she rose, and offered her a smile to think about as she hovered over the toilet in the bathroom, trying not to get the seat on her and herself on the seat.

Within a few moments of Norah's departure, a waiter came to the table. He sat a ginger ale at Wesley's place setting.

"Oh, I hadn't ordered another, but thanks," Wesley said.

"Compliments of the lovely lady," the waiter told him.

"Lady?"

The waiter nodded his chin to a point beyond Wesley. Wesley turned. The woman in the teal-colored dress raised her own drinking glass. Wesley quickly turned back to the table. He could feel his knees buckling, though he was sitting.

He turned again to see the woman heading out. He jumped up to follow, knowing Norah would pitch a fit if she came back and found his seat empty, but not caring just the same.

The mystery woman waited in the hall, with her back to Wesley. A large mirror was before her. Wesley could see in his reflection that he needed to slow his stroll. Desperation, and overexcitement, never served a man well in his approach to a woman. Despite knowing this, he was unable to slow.

The woman turned as Wesley came within a few feet. A smile painted her face.

Wesley stopped. His eyes widened. It was Janet. Looking like he'd never seen her look before. All he could do was look.

"Say something," she said. "You're making me worried staring."

"I don't know what to say."

"You look nice, Janet. Thanks for the ginger ale, Janet," she offered. She stopped and a titter of a nervous laugh leaked from her. "Let's blow this function, Janet, and go to your place so I can ravage you." Her gown, make-up, and styled hair had her feeling bolder than normal.

"You know I can't do that."

"Why?"

"I'm here with someone, for one. She's in the bathroom. You're here with someone. He's over at your table hoping they hurry up with the food so he can take all his pills." Wesley paused to get Janet's response.

"Ha-ha," she indulged him. "And for your information, he isn't a date-date. He's the foundation's largest benefactor, lost his wife earlier this year. I didn't want him to stay home, so I offered my arm."

"He would have probably preferred your hip," Wesley said in a deadpan.

Janet's face tightened. "Look, Wesley. I know that you start cracking jokes when you don't know how to deal with a situation. I'm gonna put this out there and let you decide how you want to handle this." She moved closer to him. "I like you. I have for as long as I've known you. I see you're trying to find your way. I'd like to be there to help you. I'd like you to be here to help me."

Wesley scanned her over. "You are absolutely beautiful. I never realized you were put together so, so, nicely."

"Thanks."

"We get along well," Wesley said.

"Yes, we do," Janet had to agree.

"You'd make someone a good girlfriend. An even better wife, I bet."

Janet reached forward and touched Wesley's elbows. A smile graced his face. Janet smiled in return. Her stomach no longer jumped and fell. "I've put myself out here, Wesley. I never thought I had the courage to do such a thing. Sheila helped me gather my wits."

"Sheila?" Wesley's expression changed. He pulled away.

Janet knew immediately that evoking Sheila's name had been a mistake. "Yes," she said. She smiled to try to blow out the fuse. "She's known for a long time, I guess, that I've had a thing for you."

"So Sheila's involved with this?"

"Involved? I don't know what you mean."

Wesley's jaw bulged. "She put you up to this. What's this, another way for her to get a laugh at my expense?"

"Sheila gave me her okay to pursue this," Janet said. "That was important to me. She told me to follow my heart. My feelings for you are pure."

"Well I'm following my head," Wesley fumed. "And my head is

saying do not settle for the second-string friend of the woman you loved with all your being."

Second string?

Janet's eyes welled up. She begged them not to, but they rebelled. Damn, was this Beat on Janet week or something? "Okay, Wesley," she sputtered. "Your point is well taken. I wouldn't want you settling."

Wesley calmed, noticing Janet's glistening eyes. "Look—"

Janet put her hand up. "Don't even," the last words she said before dragging herself toward the bathroom.

Wesley watched as she struggled up the hall. He could see the slump in her shoulders. He knew that slump all too well. He wanted to chase after her, let her know that he dreamed about Mercedeses and wrist bracelets on a nightly basis. That he awakened from those dreams with his forehead moist with sweat. He'd been hurt, and now he distanced himself from the possibility of any more hurt. He dated women who couldn't find their way to his heart with a map and compass. Entering into a relationship with possibilities was scary beyond imagination. He was gun-shy.

And you, Janet, looking so good, and after all that we've shared and how well we get along, best friend of the woman I was to have married, you scare me to death. "Damn!"

28

Wesley eyed the woman who'd come into the gym. He elbowed Tyndall in the ribs and cranked his head toward her. "Thirty-four-twenty-four-thirty-four," he said. "Christina. Friends call her Chris and shit." Wesley laughed at his impression of Tyndall.

But Tyndall didn't join in the laughter. "I think you need stronger lenses," he told Wesley. "She's a Sheila."

Wesley waved his arm and laughed louder. "Sheila, come on, no way is she a—" Wesley stopped as she made her way toward him.

Tyndall was correct. She was a Sheila.

"Wes," she said, then looking at Tyndall, "Ten, hey."

Tyndall nodded and slid to another part of the gym.

"Come to see A.J.?" Wesley asked. His face drew up in a scowl.

"You first," Sheila said. "Then I'll probably make my way over to A.J." She smiled at this. Wesley didn't.

"I don't have any time for this," Wesley vented. "I need to get into my workout."

"That's good you're working out."

"Sure."

"Look, Wes. I wanted to apologize to you for how things went down. I was wrong."

"It's too late for that, Sheila."

"Janet told me you were pretty upset with her at the banquet. Said mean things to her. I hope I haven't caused you to turn mean, Wes, because you aren't a vicious man. You're kind, compassionate, and decent."

"Too good for you," Wesley said.

"Right, you are. I won't argue you on that," Sheila said. She moved to him and touched his wrist. For some reason Wesley didn't pull away. She looked him in the eyes. "I wish I knew why I do what I do," Sheila continued. "I don't. I despise my mother, and yet I'm like her."

"You can save all this, Sheila."

"I wanted to say I'm sorry and you should give Janet a chance. She really cares for you."

Wesley shook his head. "I'll pass."

"Remember the gift I gave you after your father died, Wes?"

"Of course," he said. "You wrote that poem using the old song titles and had it stitched into a pillow."

"Actually," Sheila said, "Janet did it all. She wrote the poem. She had the pillow made. It was all her idea. She asked me to give it to you, so I did. I didn't think it was that much, but when you made such a big deal over it, I took credit."

Wesley was speechless.

"I knew then that I wasn't right for you," Sheila said. "But I wanted to be right for you. I wanted to be like Janet. I wanted to know what would make you happy. What would bring you comfort. I had to work at it, and I got sick of that. Janet wouldn't have to work at it. You should give her a chance, really."

"I hope I never see your face again," Wesley said.

"Take care, Wes," Sheila replied, and then she walked off.

Wesley plopped down on the mat. Tyndall came up to him.

"You okay, Wes?" he asked.

"I could have been." Wesley shook his head. "If I wasn't so stupid and blind, I could have been."

29

Giving in to the reality of her lonely life, Janet went out and bought a puppy. A Border collie, with dominant black fur, patches of white around the paws. The breeder she bought the puppy from told her the collie would be loyal, was one of the smartest breeds, but would require an inordinate amount of Janet's care and dedication. Care and dedication were two of her strong points, Janet noted, so Misty—the name she'd christened the dog—and she went home together.

She'd already taken the puppy to the vet once. Misty slumbered around Janet's apartment that day, howling in agony over something. Janet had checked her paws and found nothing. Combed through her coat and found no fleas. Concerned, she stuffed Misty into a cab and directed the driver to floor it.

"Does she take to chewing, eating your clothes?" the veterinarian had asked Janet an hour later.

Janet crinkled her eyes. "I don't believe so."

"We found fabric in her teeth. I think she ingested something, a piece of dress, or so it appears from the material." The veterinarian placed his glasses on his forehead. "Do you have a teal-colored dress? Or I should say from the look of things, had?"

Realization came to Janet. She nodded, embarrassed, wondering what the vet would have thought if he'd seen her tossing the banquet dress beside Misty's feeding dish. "I forgot she got a hold of my dress. That's what's bothering her?"

"Yes, I'm certain."

"Is she going to be okay?"

"She'll be okay." The doctor offered a smile. He bent down and rubbed Misty's stomach. "You scared your mommy, did you? Eating her dress like that. Quite a shame, because I bet Mommy looked wonderful in that dress. And I bet Daddy had on a nice suit, too. We must see that you get a Kong toy to chew, won't we?"

Janet felt tightness in her chest. It was tough being single, everyone assuming you weren't. The looks on their faces when they found out that you, young and relatively attractive, warmed your pillows alone. The next thing they wanted to know was what was wrong with you. Of course, they wouldn't ask. They'd do worse. They'd look at you so hard you felt invisible. After so many years of pretending it wasn't an issue and finally confronting the situation by exposing her true feelings for Wesley, to have that blow up in her face, Janet abhorred her singleness.

Misty, as much as Janet had come to love the puppy, was simply a Band-Aid for Janet's loneliness.

Now, Janet had Misty by the leash, taking the Border collie along for her morning stroll.

They came upon an old man, one leg amputated, trying to cross the busy intersection in his creaky wheelchair.

"Traffic is nonstop," Janet said to the man. "It's hard to get across. I step out at some point and put my hand up. Shame them into stopping for me."

The wheelchair-bound man turned, looked at the puppy first and then Janet. "True, what you speak."

"We can try to cross together if you'd like," Janet offered.

"Thanks, your offer," the man said.

"Okay." Janet took a tentative step off the curb. She wondered, as she looked for an opening on the busy thoroughfare, if the same thing that took the man's leg also took his ability to speak in any other way than the clipped way he droned. She put up a hand as a delivery truck lumbered toward them. Hope coursed through her. The truck stopped.

She turned to the man, a smile of accomplishment on her face. "Our opening, let's go."

Safe on the other side of the street, the man thanked Janet, offered Misty a pat on the head, and moved on up the block.

Janet tied Misty's leash to the light pole on the corner. She then pulled her notebook and a pen from her fanny pack. She'd long since given up on her backpack. The fanny pack was a step up. She wrote an entry in her notebook.

> *Misty*
> *My eyes*
> *Longing for you*
> *Misty*

Misty yelped and jumped. She tested the strength of the leash, pulling so hard.

"What's wrong, Misty?" Janet tried to calm the dog.

Then, another dog came hurtling toward them. Janet jumped back. The other dog licked Misty. Misty appeared to enjoy it.

Janet frowned in disgust. "Oh my God! Get a room." She sighed and shook her head. "Have your fun getting licked, Misty. But as soon as I see him try to turn you around, the fun stops. Do you understand? You're not having any fun if I can't."

"Why can't you?"

Janet turned to the voice. Her jaw dropped.

"You still look as lovely as the night of the banquet," Wesley said. "You've really got it together. What's that, Donna Karan? And your backpack is gone. Wow."

Janet didn't speak. Who knew what sounds might come out and whether her thoughts would be coherent.

Wesley nodded to Janet's dog. "I see Baldwin has found a new friend. What's her name?"

"Misty," Janet eked out. Like my eyes at night, she wanted to add, but didn't.

"I know about misty," Wesley said to Janet. Their gazes met. They recognized the feelings of misery and pain in each other's faces. Wesley held his gaze on Janet. She turned away.

Janet reached down and rubbed Baldwin's head. "How are you, fella?"

"Lonely, sad, smarting over all the mistakes he's made," Wesley said.

Janet looked up.

Wesley pointed a finger at the dog. "Oh, you meant Baldwin. I thought you were asking about me."

Janet stood to her full height. She looked Wesley in the eyes.

This time she wouldn't look away. "What are you doing here walking your dog? Your neighborhood is blocks away."

"It's a long story, but I'll try and shorten it."

"Please do."

"I started coming to this neighborhood a few weeks ago. I'd drive my car by here in the morning. I kept seeing this beautiful woman. Out walking, taking her time, enjoying the world. I wondered about her. I dreamed about her. She inspired me."

"So this woman got you to thinking?" Janet asked, playing along.

"She did. I'd see her scribbling in her journal and I wished she was writing about me."

"She might have been."

Wesley's eyes widened. "You think?"

"No, I don't think so. I wanted to add to the romanticism of your story. So go ahead."

"Anyway," Wesley began again. "One day, I saw her walking a dog all of sudden. And the next day and the next."

"You're sounding like a stalker, Wesley."

Wesley shrugged. "Maybe. Well, I decided I had to bring Baldwin out and introduce him to her dog. Baldwin wanted me to tell the woman that his eyes have finally opened and he'd like to spend time getting to know . . . ?"

"Misty," Janet answered.

"Misty, right," Wesley said.

"I know this woman you're talking about, and her dog. Misty's kind of particular in her mates," Janet said. "She only likes"—she cleared her throat—"dogs, that are sure they can give her the loyalty, respect, and love she deserves. She wants to be first in their life. Misty is nobody's second string. Can your Baldwin give her those things?"

Wesley grimaced. He'd said that to Janet, hadn't he—second string? "I've taught Baldwin well," Wesley said, sad he hadn't gleaned the knowledge for himself.

"Okay, I'll see if I can get Baldwin and Misty together."

Wesley reached forward and touched Janet's wrist. There weren't any bracelets on it. "Thanks. Baldwin is so happy to hear this news."

"Misty might seem composed, but inside she's doing cartwheels," Janet said.

Wesley reached around Janet, his hand brushing against her waist on its way to her fanny pack. "What are you doing?" she asked.

"Your journal," he told her. "I want to write down something. I won't peek at what you've already written, tempted though I may be. I promise."

"I'm the only one who writes in my journal. What do you want to write?"

Wesley touched a finger to his lips, thinking for a moment. Then he said, "Write, today at seven-thirty A.M. I saved a dog named Baldwin." He looked at Janet. "Baldwin was lonely, you know. I had to keep the seat on my toilet down to keep him from going into the bathroom and drowning himself."

Janet smirked. "Okay, I can write that."

"There's more," Wesley said.

Janet looked at Wesley. He was serious about this. "Okay," she huffed. "What else?"

"Write, today at seven-thirty A.M. I also saved a man named Wesley." He put his hands out to his sides. "At least, I hope you'll save him. You think you can let Baldwin get to know Misty, and at the same time, let this Wesley character get to know you?"

Janet studied him for a moment. Her mouth trembled. "I'm nobody's second string, either."

Wesley smiled. "No, you're not."

"What about your recent lifestyle? The woman you brought to the foundation banquet. How's she fit in your life?"

"Norah has been jettisoned," Wesley said. He'd had to change his phone number and threatened a visit to the police, but Norah was finally gone. "She's gone good-bye. Like your backpack, Janet. I'm ready for something substantial."

"Not superficial," Janet said. "But you weren't thinking about me until I got my hair done and updated my wardrobe."

"What can I say," Wesley responded, shrugging. "I'm a man."

"A man and a half," Janet noted. "When you act right, that is."

Wesley's mouth dropped open. "A man and a half. You read my e-mail?"

Janet frowned. "E-mail? I don't know anything about any e-mail. That's a Wilson Pickett song, boy. I thought you knew your soul classics."

Wesley shook his head. "You're incredible, Janet. I'm so sorry it took me so long to notice."

"Incredible? I mentioned an old song. What did I do?" Janet asked.

"Nothing," Wesley said. "And everything. I can't wait to get to know you better."

"You better not hurt me, Wesley."

"My woman and a half," Wesley said. "I wouldn't think of it."